© 2007 by Katie Vandyck

About the Author

Born in 1960, D. J. TAYLOR is a novelist, critic, and acclaimed biographer of William Thackeray and George Orwell. His *Orwell: The Life* won the Whitbread Biography of the Year in 2003. He is married with three children and lives in Norwich, England.

Kept

Kept

A NOVEL

D. J. Taylor

HARPER

NEW YORK • LONDON • TORONTO • SYDNEY

HARPER

Originally published in a different form in Great Britain in 2006 by Chatto & Windus.

A hardcover edition of this book was published in 2007 by HarperCollins Publishers.

FIRST HARPER PAPERBACK PUBLISHED 2008.

Designed by Leah Carlson-Stanisic

The Library of Congress has catalogued the hardcover edition as follows:

Taylor, D. J.

Kept: a Victorian mystery / D. J. Taylor.—1st ed.

p.   cm.

ISBN 978-0-06-114608-4

1. Great Britain. Metropolitan Police Office—Fiction. 2. Train robberies—Fiction. 3. Collectors and collecting—Fiction. 4. Mentally ill women—Fiction. 5.Poachers—Fiction. 6. Women domestics—Fiction. 7. Swindlers and swindling—Fiction. 8. Greed—Fiction. 9. City and town life—England—London—History—19th century—Fiction. I. Title.

PR6070.A9118 K47 2007

823'.914—dc22   2006052101

ISBN 978-0-06-114609-1 (pbk.)

08 09 10 11 12   ID/RRD   10 9 8 7 6 5 4 3 2 1

TO MY MOTHER

CONTENTS

Part One

Part Two

Part Three

Part Four

Please to remember that I am a Victorian, and that the Victorian tree cannot but be expected to bear Victorian fruit.

—M. R. JAMES

Beneath the signs there lay something of a different kind.

—MARCEL PROUST, *À la recherche du temps perdu*

Kept

MR. HENRY IRELAND

We regret to inform our readers of the death of a gentleman long known and respected in this locality. Mr. Henry Ireland, who had lately returned to his estate at Theberton after some years spent in the metropolis, was found stunned by the roadside in the vicinity of Wenhaston this Thursday last, the wound sustained to his head sufficient as to altogether forestall any hope of recovery. In the opinion of Sergeant Morgan of the Suffolk constabulary, who attended the case, Mr. Ireland was the victim of a tragic misadventure, his horse running away with him and precipitating him upon the hard surface of the road. The coroner's court, meeting at Woodbridge, confirmed this judgement. Mr. Ireland, who had recently passed his two-and-thirtieth year, will be remembered as an enlightened landlord, a fond husband and the charitable benefactor of his parish, fully deserving of the regard in which he was held by tenant and peer alike. In token of this esteem a large and genteel congregation assembled at St. Wedekind's, Theberton, to witness his passing, including the Lord High Sheriff, Sir Jeremy Teazle, His Honour Judge Beeves, currently presiding at Ipswich Court, and not a few gentlemen whose names are known beyond the county in which their work is done . . .

—WOODBRIDGE CHRONICLE AND INTELLIGENCER, *August 1863*

DREADFUL INCIDENT AT EASTON

Police from the Watton station attending at Easton Hall this Friday last were the witnesses to a most melancholy scene. Constables Lambert and Farrer had been summoned to the property, the seat of Mr. James Dixey, by Captain McTurk of the metropolitan force, who had called at the house on a private matter. The premises were at first supposed to be empty. A search of the grounds having been ordered, however, an awful discovery was made on land adjacent to the back parts of the house. Here, dreadful to remark, lay the body of an elderly man, his clothing very much disordered and his throat torn out with such savagery as to suggest the agency of a wild animal. The deceased was later identified as Mr. Dixey. Constable Lambert, who said that he had seen nothing like it, confirmed that the deceased was found in the lea of a high thorn hedge and that a quantity of animal tracks, doubtless those of the beast that brought about his terrible end, could be observed in the wet earth. Further piquancy was added to this unfortunate event by the discovery of a young woman, insensible but alive, in an upper room of the house. . . . As for an explanation of this deplorable crime, none is yet forthcoming, although Captain McTurk, in a confidential communication, has assured us that the best efforts of his officers are being directed to a speedy resolution.

—WEST NORFOLK GAZETTE, *December 1866*

Part One

EGGMEN

I will happily declare that there is no sight so harmonious to the eye or suggestive to the spirit as Highland scenery. A man who sits on the Metropolitan Railway to Marylebone may be comforted by what he sees, but I do not think he will be inspired. A ziggurat raised by some bold industrialist for the purposes of his manufacture is an edifying spectacle, no doubt, but a mountain is moral. Philosophy quails before it, science grows mutely respectful and literature is both exalted and cast down. The traveller who desires a sense of his own insignificance will discover it here on some descending slope, down in the shadow of some mighty summit, there beneath some rill that has run since the dawn of time. God walks in the mountains, but it is the mountains that will drive Him out, with their granite secrets and the truth that lies concealed in their stone, and mankind be reduced to an antlike insubstantiality beside them. Or so we are told.

It was late in the afternoon of an April day in the year of Our Lord 186–, on a steam engine moving slowly forward—impossibly slowly—along the Highland line through Inverness-shire, a line so lately instituted that everything about it had an air of novelty. The uniforms of the officials shone as if they had only that morning arrived in bandboxes from the seamstress, the engine appeared to have been polished overnight, and even the passengers—subdued Highland folk, for the most part, with their baggage piled at their feet—seemed to have donned their best clothes for the occasion. All this Dunbar observed from his seat in the corner of the third-class carriage, and though grateful for the mechanised wonder that drew him nearer his destination, he thought that he did not like it. Outside the window the sky was darkening, so that the distant peaks and the valley through which they ran turned red and purple, and for a moment he bent his eye on what lay beyond him rather than things nearer at hand. A herd of Highland cattle grazing the sloping moor; a woman and her child waiting patiently at a wayside crossing; a flock of birds—he knew about birds, for in a certain sense they were his profession—wheeling away to the north: all these Dunbar saw and brought together in his mind to feed his sense of dissatisfaction.

"Of course," he said at length, "it's not as if they're civilised folk in these parts."

The words brought Dewar, who lay sprawled next to him on the double seat of the compartment, one arm thrown over the square teak box they had brought from Edinburgh that morning, out of his half slumber.

"Ain't they, though?"

"Surely not! Why it's not more than a century since Cumberland smoked them out and made them pay. My grandfather's father fought at Culloden. Saw a man stick a babby with a bayonet. Said it would stay with him till his dying day."

Dewar drew himself up from his slouch and began to dust down his shirt-front with a spotted handkerchief that he took from the pocket of his coat.

"Why would a man stick a babby with a bayonet? It seems an uncommon devilish thing to do."

A fellow passenger, moving along the train's corridor, had that traveller peered in through the compartment window, would have seen an odd assortment of persons and their gear. Dunbar, a tall, gaunt man of perhaps fifty years of age, wore a green sporting jacket and a pair of corduroy trousers, which combination made him look not unlike a gamekeeper. Dewar, shorter and rather younger, was the more ill-favoured of the two, fat and somewhat unhealthy-looking, his costume completed by a shabby frock coat of which the braid was beginning to part company with the lapels. Rolled up in bundles on luggage racks, or strewn about on the floor, lay a variety of miscellaneous items, each of which posed some question as to the object of their journey: a pair of heavy walking boots, two cork life jackets, a woollen scarf and a coiled length of rope. Dewar's gaze, which had fallen for a moment or two on the square teak box, widened to take in this further cargo.

"We seem to have brought a deal of stuff with us. How are we to carry it all, I should like to know?"

Something in the set of Dunbar's eye perhaps disclosed that he did not regard his associate with complete confidence. "I can see you're new to this game, my boy. Green you are indeed. Why, when we get to the other end there'll be a gig to meet us. Take us right to where we want to go as well, I shouldn't wonder."

There was an unspoken question in this statement which the younger man either did not appreciate or chose not to answer. But his companion persisted.

"What line of trade was you in before Bob Grace pushed you my way?"

"Grocer."

Something in this spoke of ruinous mischance, of hope denied, tragedy even. Another man would have given up the pursuit, but Dunbar continued easily.

"General or green stuff?"

"General."

"Any reason for giving it up?"

Dewar stared before him at the cork life jackets draped over the opposing seat. "Wife took bad and I had to nurse her. It's hard on a fellow when that happens."

"Harder still when she dies. Very hard. Here, have a fill of this and you'll feel better."

They smoked Dunbar's tobacco companionably for a while, nodding at the people who wandered along the corridor and resting their feet on their bundles. It was now perhaps half past four in the afternoon, and the light was growing grey. Outside the land continued to rise, and there were shadows creeping down among the granite escarpments of the hills. The day was drawing in. Dunbar was not an imaginative man—a rock to him was a rock that might have to be scaled, a mountain stream the hazard of wet feet—but nonetheless something of the bleakness of the prospect communicated itself to him and he clasped his hands together against a cold that he could not yet feel but knew would come.

D. J. TAYLOR

"D——t! This ain't Piccadilly Circus, by George! Did you ever see such a place?"

Dewar, less impressionable even than his mentor, stared vaguely beyond the window. "They say Highland air's very bracing. I believe that's the case. Will it snow, do you reckon?"

"I shouldn't wonder. I took an eagle's nest in a blizzard once, twenty miles south of here at Loch Garten, and had three fingers bitten by the frost. No trains in those days. Nor a path for a pony either. Why, the fellow I was with, he and I had to haul our boat over the hills to reach the river."

The words seemed to waken in Dewar a curiosity that had previously been lacking in him. Rubbing his small eyes with the flat of one hand and knocking his pipe out on the iron casing of the carriage window with the other, he cleared his throat once or twice, looked as if he were about to speak and then thought better of it.

"You look as if you wanted to say something," Dunbar chided him. "Why don't you let it out?"

"You're a professional man. You'll only laugh at me like as not. But never mind, I will say it. Why would a man pay good money for you to bring him eggs?"

Dunbar beat his hand sharply on his knees. "Why, there are any number of queer trades. There are fellows in London who collect up slop pails and sell what's in them for fertiliser. You'll have seen them about their business. I knew a man that traded in dolls' eyes—blue, brown and green, only the green ones was a farthing a dozen dearer. Why shouldn't a man take ospreys' eggs, or eagles', if he's a mind?"

"He can't eat them."

"I daresay he can't. But he can look at them. Haven't you got anything that you sits and looks at?"

Dewar thought. "My wife had a fancy for china dogs once. As much as a shilling she'd pay for a china dog at Hoxton market. But there isn't no china dogs now."

"There you are. China dogs. Waterloo medals—look at the market there is for them. Why, I was at the sea once, Devon way, and there was a dozen folk out under the cliff looking for those rarey stones that are made so much of. Fossils, they call them. But what we're after, there's few enough of them to be had now. Take these ospreys, that the people here call eagle fishers. They don't come to Loch an Eilein crag no more. It's six years since I've taken from Loch Morlich. There may be nests at Loch Arkaig, I don't know. But think of it! These might be the last of them in all England. That's worth a ten-pound note if ever a thing was."

"And what if there aren't no more?" Dewar wondered.

"What about if there aren't? I had a gentleman come to me the other day—a clergyman he was, many of them's from the clergy—enquiring of auks' eggs. Now there hasn't been an auk seen in these parts for a century. On St. Kilda's perhaps, or Shetland, but not here. There are some that would have given him guillemot with a touch of dye, but I'm not one of that kind, which is perhaps a weakness in me."

He lapsed into silence, perhaps imagining that he had said too much. Dewar thought regretfully of the china dogs that had once processed over the mantelpiece in Hoxton and now, like certain other things, were gone from his life.

"We shall be there soon, I suppose," he ventured.

"Yes, we shall be there soon. You had better help me pick up these things."

Together, swaying a little against the rhythm of the engine, they began to reduce the mass of luggage to some kind of order. This task accomplished, Dunbar selected a thick greatcoat from the topmost sack and placed it over his shoulders. Beyond the window he saw that twilight was falling. A furious tawny sun hung low over the furthermost crags so that their sharply descending slopes seemed livid in its shadow. Skeins of birds flew north above their heads, following the train's course for a moment and then veering away into invisibility. Dewar looked up.

"What kind of birds is they?"

"Black-backed gulls. Curlew. Nothing there for us." He resumed his position at the window. "Put on your coat, man. There'll be an end to trains before too long."

Doing as he was bidden—his own coat was a threadbare affair from which the buttons hung by solitary threads—Dewar sensed that

D. J. TAYLOR

the train had begun to reduce its speed. A great black hedge shot up suddenly to the left of them, so near that he could have reached out from the window and plucked at the trees. In the distance there was a glimmer of water. Then, in what seemed only an instant of time, the darkness receded and the tawny light illumined their surroundings once more. They were travelling—rolling, gently descending—at ever-decreasing speed and with a great shudder of brakes through a country of flat fields and broken stones, at whose outer edge a spur of dark forest could be seen approaching from higher ground to the north.

"This is the place," Dunbar announced. "I recollect it." He saw Dewar's face, somehow mournful in the gloaming as he bent to retrieve his kit. "Come now. There are worse trades for a man to follow."

"It's not work that I'm used to," Dewar volunteered. For a moment Dunbar thought that he could see him in his grocery, obsequious behind the counter, hands dusty with flour, meal sticking in his sparse hair. Near stationary now, the train shook convulsively once or twice and then came to a halt. "But I hope I shall give satisfaction."

Dunbar did not answer but seized the first of their bags and began to heave it to the door. It was no more than a halt—a long, low platform with a granite slab for a seat, a single lantern, a pair of stone outhouses at the further end and a solitary attendant gaping at them from behind a muffler. Beyond the clump of buildings a narrow road descended through the fields. Here a pony and trap waited in the gathering dusk. Dunbar saw it and sniffed.

"I don't doubt Mackay to be the most punctual man in Strathspey. Here, see if the place runs to a handcart."

His voice was lost in the noise of the engine's wheels as they began once more to revolve. A cloud of steam, blown back on the wind, enveloped them both in dense white vapour. The station attendant said something in a broad Scots accent that Dewar could not interpret. There was no handcart. He began miserably to arrange the baggage in a kind of pyramid upon the granite seat, while Dunbar went to greet a tall figure, with a mastiff dog at his heels, who now loomed into view at the further end of the platform.

"Mackay," Dunbar said on their return. He seemed strangely

exhilarated, poking at a strip of his shirt collar levered up by the wind. "Invaluable factotum to the gentry. The laird's right-hand man, forbye. Whose own great-grandfather brought the Prince over from Skye in a rowboat, or so they say. Is that not right, Mackay?"

"I'll thank you to hold your tongue, Dunbar," said the laird's right-hand man. Dewar could not tell if he was amused or made angry by this familiarity. "That's a deal of clutter ye've brought with ye."

"But you'll carry it for us, Mackay. Is that not right?"

"There's snow coming, I have no doubt. I can take you to the boat-house. And maybe return in the morning. But no further, mind."

"Suit yourself, old party." Again Dewar caught the lilt in his companion's voice. "Suit yourself."

Silently, they began to load their belongings onto the cart. It was quite noiseless now, except for the rumble of the train as it descended into the valley beyond them, altogether dark save for the sparks flying up along the track which danced for a moment in the air above the engine stack and then fell back into nothingness. Dunbar stopped loading to watch its progress, murmured something unintelligible under his breath and then resumed his labours. Presently, illumined by the pale light of Mackay's lantern, the cart bore them away down the hill, past thickets of pine trees, a mass of undergrowth in which something unseen moved briefly for a second and then was gone out of the lantern's range.

"There's no wolves, are there, in these parts?" Dewar wondered cravenly.

Dunbar laughed. "No, no wolves. Not for a hundred years and more. That was a fox, most like. Or a marten. But no wolves."

It was by now quite dark, and with an absence of moon that, Dunbar calculated, boded ill for the night's activity. Something of the place's immensity communicated itself to him—a silence that, he acknowledged, proceeded from the entire absence of man—and he fell quiet, recalling similar excursions: walking twenty miles from Grantown once in the middle of a snowstorm; a journey into the upper reaches of Norway, where in the few hours of daylight the sun seemed to hang on the rim of the horizon like the yolk of an egg. At the same time his eye began to accustom itself to the terrain and its distinctive

D. J. TAYLOR

character: the cracked stone on the path that glittered in the lantern light; dense banks of fir heralding the innermost parts of the glen; what his memory told him was the smell of water borne back over the treetops. The mastiff dog, huddled up at his master's feet, caught some second scent and moved its muzzle restlessly. They were nearing their destination.

"Stop the cart!" Dewar cried suddenly. His face, caught in the lantern glare, was unnaturally white: submerged, Dunbar thought, like the underside of a fish thrown breathless upon the riverbank. "Stop the cart, sir, I beg you."

Mackay jerked on the reins. "Why, what ails you?"

Dewar took in a gulp of air. A fish, Dunbar thought again: the belly of a trout turned up from the Wensum or the Yare. "I must . . . that is . . . a man has to relieve himself occasionally," he protested. "I've had no opportunity since Edinburgh."

"A nervous creature, that," Mackay remarked, as a series of violent detonations marked Dewar's progress into the undergrowth.

"He'll do," Dunbar said. "It's little enough he's getting. And at least he'll stay dry."

"He may not, for all that."

Shamefacedly, Dewar returned to the cart. The warm aroma of excrement trailed behind him. So woebegone did he appear that Dunbar, conscious of the hours that stretched before them, determined to lighten the younger man's spirits.

"Come, Dewar, this will never do. We must take you out of yourself, indeed we must. Look, this is where our journey takes us. Did you ever see such a spot?"

The sight towards which he now extended his hand, as the cart came suddenly out of the forest's edge and onto the fresh turf, was certainly a magnificent one, whether seen by day or night. Illumined now by faint streaks of moonlight, the loch stretched for perhaps a mile beyond them, falling away at its uttermost extremity into impenetrable borders of trees grown right up to the water's edge. Cold and depthless the water seemed, black in the moonlight, its surface ruffled here and there by the tremor of the wind but otherwise undisturbed. In the very midst of it, so centrally placed that it seemed to accord to

Kept

some geometrical plan, lay a small island topped by a cairn of rock. This, closer inspection revealed to be a ruin some twelve or fifteen feet high, the topmost ramparts altogether crumbled and fallen away. As they watched, a dark shape moved off the surface of the water a quarter of a mile distant, soared briefly into the night sky beyond the tree wall and then was gone.

"There's our tenant," Dunbar remarked. "What will he say when he finds the bailiffs have called? I wonder."

A little way along the loch's surround, at a point where an inlet dipped into the forest, they found a boathouse, very blear and empty in the darkness, with a couple of canoes hung on hooks from the wall and a nest of field mice that scurried away at the approach of Mackay's lantern. Dunbar stood by the glassless window, clapping his hands together against the cold, as between them Dewar and Mackay unloaded the baggage. In his mind he was calculating shrewdly, but the nature of the calculation was lost on the other men, both of whom now regarded him expectantly as the great mastiff dog loped around the hut poking its nose into the empty nest and worrying out an abandoned straw hat from beneath the table.

"You'd best be off, Mackay," Dunbar said. "You have business to attend to, no doubt. Back after the dawn, mind. You can leave the lamp." The Scotsman gave a nod and moved off into the darkness, the dog following at his heels. "Now," he went on, "we've work to do. Attend to me, if you please." As Dewar watched uncertainly, he slipped out of his greatcoat and began to tug open the buttons of his green jacket.

"What's that you're doing?"

"What does it look like that I'm doing? However else do you suppose a man could reach the rock?"

"I thought we might . . ." Dewar gestured at the two canoes.

"Both in need of caulking and not a paddle in sight. No, I'll not drown in an upturned coracle. Not while I can swim. Here, take this."

Standing in his underthings, as he strapped the cork life jacket around his chest, Dunbar indicated a bundle of rope that he had taken from a sack. "Now, tie the end to this loop here. A good strong knot."

D. J. TAYLOR

Wondering, Dewar did as he was bid. "This is our means of contact, d'you see?" Dunbar went on. "A single tug and you're to draw me in. Two pulls and there's danger."

"What am I to do then?"

"Do? Why, pull on the other jacket and swim out to find me! Come, let's be off."

They moved out once again into the silence of the loch, two tiny figures swallowed up in space and silence. Dewar felt something light yet piercing strike against his forehead. It was a snowflake. He clutched at it and felt it melt between his fingers.

"It's cold enough," he muttered.

"And you haven't even to swim. Take the rope!" They were at the water's edge now. Dewar felt his feet sink into mud. Without turning, Dunbar slid into the water, like an otter, immersing himself limb by limb until only his head and shoulders remained above the surface. "Here's luck!" he called back. Then with a powerful overarm stroke he launched himself out into the moving blackness.

Alone on the bank, Dewar tried at first to keep his eye fixed on his companion's bobbing head. Within fifty yards, however, it had vanished altogether. After that he bent his mind on the noise of Dunbar splashing, but after a moment or two even this passed out of earshot. He looked vainly at the rope, which lay coiled in his hand, and wondered what he would do if there came two tugs on it. It was certainly very cold. Narrowing the range of his vision, he strained to glimpse the outcrop to which his friend was headed, but found only shadow, vague shapes of nothing in the dark air. He was quite alone, he realised, altogether thrown upon his own resources. A sudden thrill of terror struck through his body. Was that a twitch on the rope? No, he assured himself, it was merely the coil playing out as Dunbar swam on. A moment or two passed: Dewar had no means of knowing how long. Then, from far off, from some place he could not see, high over the lake, there came a shriek of something—human or animal, he could not determine—which sent him into a paroxysm of fear. The rope, he observed, had ceased to play out. Despairing, he pulled on it himself, but there was no response. It hung slack in the water, disappearing from sight only a yard or two from his feet.

What was to be done? There was a box of sulphur matches in his pocket, and remembering them he pulled one forth and struck it on the heel of his boot, but the wind caught it and extinguished it almost from the moment of its striking. What was to be done? he asked himself again. He resolved to fetch the lantern from the boathouse and then told himself that this would be the action of a fool. There was more snow falling now, gently descending on his scalp, on his shoulders, on the coil of rope that still lay in his hand, and he watched it with a kind of benevolent detachment. Surely it was too cold for a man to swim out there in the frozen lake? What should he do if his companion failed to return? He was conscious that, apart from believing that he had been set down in Inverness-shire, he barely knew where he was, that he possessed no return railway ticket—this was in Dunbar's care—nor the means of purchasing one. All these thoughts tumbled about his head and oppressed him in a way that was immeasurably increased by the solitariness of the place and the lateness of the hour. A man could die out here, he thought, could perish under a rowan bush or out on the open moor and not be found. What if he were to be that man? He had a sudden vision of himself dancing helplessly through driven snow, falling to his knees as the drifts piled up above his head.

Almost without apprehending that the thing was upon him, he became aware of a disturbance to his left, out in what seemed to be the darkest part of the lake: a shout—undoubtedly a human voice—and a splashing of water. The rope jerked so violently in his hand that for a second it fell from his grasp into the mud. Seizing it, he began to pull with what seemed to him superhuman industry, staring all the while into the blackness before him. "Dunbar," he called into the raw air. "Where are you? Answer me." But there was no more shouting, only the slow, steady noise of someone beating a path through the water towards him and a black lump that, through some mysterious agency of the light, suddenly declared itself to be a human figure swimming on its back.

"Gracious heavens, Dunbar, is that you?"

Teeth chattering, water cascading from the extremities of his body, Dunbar made his way through the shallows. He seemed in excellent spirits.

D. J. TAYLOR

"Who the devil did you think it was? And why didn't you pull the first time I tugged on the rope, eh? But never mind, it's all well that ends well—look here!" He extended his hands, palms upwards, and Dewar saw that in each lay a small ruddy-brown egg. "Quick, man, to the boathouse, and the whisky, or I shall perish of cold."

Later Dewar would remember the strangeness of the scene: the snow continuing to fall over the silent lake; himself on his knees in the doorway of the hut attempting to light a fire out of brushwood and old paper; an owl calling out in the trees and contending with Dunbar's voice as, towelling himself with a piece of rough cloth, he recounted his exploits.

"I got over quite safe—it was a distance of a quarter mile, perhaps, no further—and tied the rope to a stone. The cock bird flew off before I reached the island. After I had climbed up to the top of the ruin and was just on the nest I put out my hand to catch the hen, but when she felt me she gave a scream and shied away also. Anyway, I took two eggs and was thankful for them. The question was: how to carry them, for in my haste I had forgotten my cap. I tried putting one egg in my mouth but I could not breathe with it. There was nothing to do, I decided, but to swim ashore on my back with an egg in each hand. Which is how you found me. Still, I have had worse journeys. Now, be a good fellow. Step outside and fetch me a reed from the shore."

"A reed, did you say?"

"Naturally. How else am I to blow the eggs?"

"Blow them, you say?"

Dewar went shivering out into the night and stumbled to the shore. The reed fetched, Dunbar trimmed it with his knife until he had fashioned a tiny straw three or four inches in length and pointed at one end. Then, craning towards the lamplight with the first egg in his palm, he made a tiny mark in the shell with the tip of his knife. This done, he inserted the straw and placed the blunt end between his lips. "You suck away, see, and then discharge the yolk"—he spat suddenly and a gob of white, viscous slime spattered onto the floor—"thus. There is no art to it. Then rinse the inside with a little of this whisky, line your travelling case with some moss, and we are done."

And so they laboured on for half an hour or so, as the fire burned down to its embers and the snowflakes fell hissing onto the hot coals, so that a passerby chancing to peer through the boathouse window might have thought Dunbar's gaunt, bony face that of an old wizard instructing his protégé in the magical arts and the eggs some rare treasure sprung from their devisings.

Dunbar whistled as he worked, or sang snatches of the "Skye Boat Song." He seemed in the highest spirits still, his manner ever more confidential and mysterious.

"You see, we are getting on famously," he remarked at one point. "You must come and look me up in London, indeed you must. Eighteen Watling Street, above the chandler's, will find me when I'm not at my business."

Then something else struck him, and he said, "That was a bad business in Suffolk, to be sure."

"What business was that?" Dewar wondered.

"You don't know? Or perhaps you are a cleverer fellow than I take you to be and pretend not to know?"

"I know nothing."

"At any rate, it was a secret that should have been kept and has not been. But let us say no more about it."

And so the lamplight flickered, the snow fell desultorily over the loch, the mice came scurrying back beneath the boathouse door and nothing more was said about it.

D. J. TAYLOR

II

MR. HENRY IRELAND
AND HIS LEAVINGS

At the time when our story commences, Mr. Henry Ireland of
Theberton in the county of Suffolk had been dead a year. It
is perhaps necessary to say of this gentleman only that he was subject to the gravest misfortune. Black care had waylaid him and flung
him from his horse, and though he had struggled to regain his seat
and continued on his way, it was to find his assailant ever grinning
from the saddle behind him. And yet there was a singularity about Mr.
Ireland's tribulations sufficient to imbue them with a terrible pathos.
Who does not know the man who is ruined in an instant, so to speak,
who breakfasts very heartily with his wife and children, only to arrive
at his countinghouse to find the blinds still drawn, the funds fallen and
the clerks whispering among themselves? Such men, if they possess
fortitude and friends, can generally salvage something from the wreck.
Rothschild was a bankrupt once, they say, and Lord Palmerston's
stamped paper the delight of the bill-discounters.

On the contrary, Mr. Ireland's misfortunes had crept up on him by
stealth, so gradually in fact that he barely glimpsed their approach. At
the age of twenty-five, on the death of his father, he had come into his
property. The enthusiasm with which the young man set up as squire
would have touched the heart of the stoniest philosopher. He proposed to make a study of agriculture, to import breeding cattle from
the continent, to build model cottages, even, for his tenants. There
was nothing, in fact, that might not have been done, could the payment have been received in good intentions rather than ready money.
But then it was discovered that Mr. Ireland Senior had encumbered
the estate with debt and that there was, in addition, an entail that
no man, and certainly no lawyer, could break. After this, Mr. Ireland

Junior gave up his schemes of marsh drainage and tenants' cottages and retired to London to live off his rents.

All this, however, would have counted as nothing to the young man—would have mattered to him as little as the fine Suffolk rain —had he succeeded in his chief ambition. This, it may be flatly stated, was the gaining of a wife whose hand would be worth the winning, whom he could love and be loved by in return, and whose affection would be the lasting glory of his days. Such paragons are not easily found, and yet Mr. Ireland, in the weeks before his marriage, had dared to hope that he had secured one. He was at this time a man of thirty: soft-voiced and even-tempered, well-disposed towards his fellow men, conscious of the failure of his agricultural schemes, but resolved that, as a husband and a father, he would conquer the world anew. Many men have made such resolves, and many have wished that they could make them. Alas, it was here—here in the hour of his nuptial triumph, as the very orange blossoms descended on his hymeneal carriage—that Mr. Ireland's troubles began.

At the time of his marriage, which took place at St. George's, Hanover Square, and was reported in the fashionable newspapers (for Mr. Ireland wanted the world to know of the grand prize he had brought down), Miss Isabel Brotherton was a young woman of three- or four-and-twenty: of medium height, graceful in her carriage and with abundant auburn hair of which it was said that Titian might have painted it. Her father, now dead, had been a literary man, it is true, but of an altogether superior kind. Dickens had called at his house, and duchesses pressed him to attend their parties. Mr. Thackeray himself had stood pallbearer at his funeral, and a royal prince subscribed five guineas to his memorial edition. And so Mr. Ireland felt that in the matter of station, though he might have done worse, he could not have done better.

Of all the things in the world, perhaps, a marriage is the most per-plexing to write of. Who can tell whether Mr. Brief, of Her Majesty's Northern Circuit, the proud father of three bouncing girls and the proud owner of an elegant stucco house in Kensington Square, is a happy man, and whether his Drusilla, formerly Miss Bates of Cheam, is all to him that she should be? By the same token, who knows whether, on

D. J. TAYLOR

the days when her lord and master quits her for the Northern Circuit, Mrs. Brief does not creep away into her bedroom and weep bitter tears for the hardness of her life? At any rate, Mr. Ireland, seeing his wife as she stood before him, felt that he was a happy man and the friends to whom he opened his doors said that he was a lucky fellow and that Mrs. Ireland was a woman of spirit. For myself, I am inclined to agree with them. There are, heaven knows, some women to whom the duty of hospitality is merely that, who bid you to their table with the same air that they rattle florins in the church collection plate, but Mrs. Ireland was not among their number. Though she spoke little herself, she had a way of listening to those who did that mingled the highest seriousness and the richest mirth, and the gentlemen who snuffed up her husband's beefsteaks and sampled his claret went away convinced that they had eaten a very agreeable dinner. As to their wives, well, I am not certain that Mrs. Ireland was altogether a great favourite among ladies. She had a habit, in a soft, feminine way, of poking fun, of saying sharp little words that were remembered long after her smiles and her solicitations were forgotten.

"As to having nobility in the house, I am sure I should make some dreadful blunder," she once exclaimed to Mrs. Desmond de Lacey, "serve up peas out of season or forget which was a Liberal and which was a Conservative." Mrs. Desmond de Lacey, whose husband was the younger son of a cousin of the Marquis of Lothian, laughed, but I do not think she liked it. Happily, there were enough people who did like it to make an invitation to Mrs. Ireland's drawing room worth the having for a while, and Mr. Ireland, as I have said, watching his wife among the teacups, or telling Lord Fawkes that he was the wickedest old man alive, thought that he was happy. There was a child, and the child died, but though Mr. Ireland mourned sincerely he did not allow this mischance to prey upon his mind. There would be other children, nurseries full of them, the gardens of Eccleston Square would ring with their voices. And yet it seemed to him in the months after the infant's death that a change had come over his wife. She grew melancholy, no longer smiled at her dinner guests or told Lord Fawkes, to his lordship's great delight, that he was the naughtiest old sinner in Christendom. Her sharp words grew sharper, her gaze less placid. A judge's wife went away in tears from the house in Eccleston Square and her friends said that Mrs. Ireland was deranged with grief.

All this Mr. Ireland observed with the most painful unease. It seemed to him that it behoved him to speak to his wife, without having the least idea of what he ought to say, that soft words were needed, but of a subtlety that was altogether beyond his power to frame. Finally, one afternoon in February when the square lay invisible in the fog, having spent the morning brooding over his dilemma, he approached a drawing room on an upper floor of the house in which it was his wife's custom to spend her leisure hours. She was seated in a small armchair with her hands clasped in her lap, and though her eyes were open it seemed to him that she scarcely saw him and that his very presence in the room was painful to her. But he was a courageous man in his fashion and he determined to speak the sentences he had come to say.

"My dear," he said, "it seems to me that you are very unhappy."

"You are right," she said, not looking up from her chair. "I am very unhappy. And yet if I am it is my responsibility, and mine to bear."

There was something so dreadful in these words that he was quite nonplussed. It seemed to him that, in these circumstances, nothing he could say would have any effect. And yet, however savage might be his reception, he knew that he had a tougher skin than the judge's lady and that to say nothing were simple cowardice.

"My dear," he began again. "Isabel. You are labouring under a great grief."

Again she did not look up but continued to stare fixedly at her lap. "That is so. It is a great grief. I had hoped it was a shared one. If that were so, it would be easier to bear."

He understood that this was a reproach, and the words were torture to him. But he could think of nothing to say, was merely conscious of a faint terror of things unseen, things altogether beyond him but capable of reaching out to strike him a mortal blow. Standing thus in this irresolute state, not knowing whether to stay or go, he found his attention drawn to his wife's hands, which were turning ceaselessly, as it seemed to him, over a twist of some pale material held in her lap. This motion of her fingers, though disagreeable to him, was somehow

D. J. TAYLOR

fascinating, and he studied it for a full half minute before enquiring, "Isabel. What is it that you have there?"

She looked up at him, but blindly, so that even now he fancied that she did not see him. "It is a lock of the child's hair, cut from his head on the morning that he died. Surely you must remember that?"

He did remember it—remembered it as if it had happened but a moment ago—but there was something in her attitude, some secret steeliness, that he feared to provoke. Her face, seen in the shadow of the room, seemed very white. Outside the lamps were being lit, one by one, in the square.

At length he said, "I would not give you further pain for all the world. There are people coming tonight. It cannot be helped. Shall I have them turned away? You have only to speak, and it shall be done."

"No, do not send them away." She rose suddenly to her feet, and the twist of hair fell fluttering to the Turkey carpet. "I have been weak. But I shall be strong. You had better go now, Henry, if you would be so kind."

That evening she dashed a wineglass over the tablecloth, shrieked that her husband meant to murder her and was led away in hysterics. After this people ceased to say that Mrs. Ireland was a woman of spirit and she retired altogether from polite society.

What was to be done? Mr. Ireland, in his distracted state, was of the opinion that doctors were needed. Let doctors be summoned! Let the house in Eccleston Square be turned into a sanatorium if it would stop his wife from swearing that he meant to kill her and crooning over a twist of a child's hair in her lap! The doctors who examined her were cautious. There was no sign of organic disease, they assured Mr. Ireland, but perhaps his wife might benefit from a change of air. A sea voyage, a tour around the Swiss lakes, a month or two at the continental spas sampling the waters—all these were proposed by the deferential gentlemen who stood in Mr. Ireland's drawing room as a cure for his wife's lowness of spirits. And meanwhile perhaps it might be best to keep Mrs. Ireland from company, late nights and associations that might be distressing to her.

Mr. Ireland received this advice with the gravest misgivings. And yet, he assured himself, all was not lost. His wife was estranged from him, but it might be possible, if care were exercised, to win her back. To this end, and mindful of certain ancient connections of his family, he arranged a journey to the country with which he shared his name. Even in the pit of his anxieties, the thought was pleasant to him. An inn or a castle or hilltop where he and his wife could be to each other as they had been in the early days of their marriage—all this, surely, would supply a balm beyond the realm of medicine. And so a passage was booked on the *Bristol* to Cork ferry for the last day of April, and, in a closed carriage, accompanied by a single servant, the Irelands set off. It was a fortnight since Easter, and the flowers were out in the Wiltshire lanes as they rolled by. What occurred during the three weeks they were away I am not at liberty to say—Mr. Ireland would not speak of it even to his closest friends—but there were no inns, or castles, or hilltops. And from the day of their return there was no more talk of lowness of spirits. The deferential gentlemen who had advised sea voyages and Swiss lakes and the pump room at Baden-Baden were all thrown over, and the celebrated Dr. John Conolly, of whom the world knows, was summoned to give an opinion. Like those he had supplanted, Dr. Conolly was a prudent man. He would not say that his patient was . . . mad. But perhaps it might be better if Mrs. Ireland were to be removed from Eccleston Square and to a place where care might be taken that she should not injure herself. Throughout these proceedings Mrs. Ireland was confined to her room, and the door of the room was locked with an iron bolt.

Not the least of our misfortunes is their mockery of bygone hopes. A month after his return to England, Mr. Ireland discovered a parcel thrown amongst the discarded trifles of his dressing room. It contained a copy of Mr. Thackeray's *Irish Sketchbook*, which Mr. Ireland had thought it well to carry with him while he surveyed the castles and the hilltops, and a nosegay of flowers presented to his wife on a bright morning in Cork before certain dreadful events of which he could not bring himself to speak. And it seemed to Mr. Ireland, examining these items as he stood in his dressing room with the sun streaming in through the casement window, that his life was ruined and that the

D. J. TAYLOR

book and the flowers were far more a testimony to his wretchedness than the woman in the next room. Failure lay all around him. He had inherited a property, and the property had crumbled to ashes in his hands. He had married a wife, and Dr. Conolly would say only that extreme caution and tender ministrations might yet produce a favourable result. At any rate, Mr. Ireland assured himself, there should be no more pretence, whether as regarded himself or the world at large. The house in Eccleston Square was shut and the servants were paid off, the gardens where he had been wont to walk on summer afternoons given up to nursemaids and their charges, and Mr. and Mrs. Ireland departed to Suffolk and fell altogether out of the life they had known.

It may be wondered whether there is anything more instructive than the person who disappears in this way. A man pursues his professional calling in a certain street, let us say, for twenty years, eats his dinner in a certain chophouse, talks with certain cronies and then, mysteriously, is gone. Who notices his passing or remembers him? The agent's board is up above his chambers for a fortnight until a new tenant engages them, the waiter at the chophouse regrets his patron for a day or so—that is all. So it was with the Irelands. Such of their friends as wrote letters received courteous but unforthcoming replies. A pertinacious gentleman who proposed a visit was told roundly that the state of Mrs. Ireland's health would not permit it. And thus the Irelands slipped altogether out of view, so that they might have died or followed the emigrant trail to Oregon for all that anyone knew. For there are some mysteries that are always hidden, and some secrets that are forever kept.

* * *

FROM GEORGE ELIOT'S JOURNAL

22 March 1862
A bright day of radiant sunshine, not the least inclemency. George engrossed in literary tasks, articles for the Cornhill, *writing to Mr. Martin anent his translations &c. I, having no other occupation, spent the afternoon in reverie, reading Mr. Hutton in the* Spectator—*at*

least I supposed it were Mr. Hutton—on Arnold's last words on translating Homer. Thence to dine with the Irelands at their house in Eccleston Square. This I was interested to see: a pleasant, commodious residence, the rooms all crammed with dull, old furniture, scarlet draperies. A profusion of mirrors, many portraits of old gentlemen in periwigs. A dozen of us sat down: a sucking barrister from Lincoln's Inn, Mr. Masson who writes for the magazines and a silent wife, a literary man whom George recalled from some endeavour lost in time. With Mr. Ireland I was, of course, familiar. A conventional kind of a man, I should suppose: tall, ruddy-faced, soft-spoken, talking a little of his property in Suffolk (it is embarrassed, George says, and a source of shame to him) and equestrian pleasures, solicitous of his wife. I acknowledge freely that it was she to whom my eye turned the more often: a slight, sorrowful woman with exquisite (there is no other word) red hair—I would have run my hands through it, negotiated to buy it at six shillings the yard like some Russian huckster—in whom deep reservoirs of feeling contended with the topics of the day. In short, a decidedly unusual representative of the female species, and yet some deep unhappiness so manifest in her that it pained the heart to see. Thus, on my asking would she and her husband go away this season, she replied with great emphasis, Go away? Why, I have been drifting rudderless for too long. This seemed such a singular expression that I enquired, what did she mean by it? She replied with perfect politeness and yet, it seemed to me, great private misgivings that there were times when she felt like a boat rowing on the ebb tide and could not for the life of her steer herself to safety. Mr. Ireland, I saw, was watching her closely and here interjected, "My wife has peculiar fancies, Miss Evans." Although there was suavity in the words, I fancy they were troublesome to pronounce.

Meanwhile the dinner was proceeding around us—soup, cutlets, a beefsteak, none of which was sufficient to distract the eye from the curious intelligence at my side. As the meal continued, Mrs. Ireland's behaviour became more singular still. While the servants were clearing the savoury from the table I observed her carefully decant the contents of a saltcellar upon the tablecloth. This task accomplished, she availed herself of a half-empty glass that lay nearby and, with infinite care

D. J. TAYLOR

and solicitude, began to drip claret wine upon the salt. All this with a look of such stealth—cunning, rapt introspection—as to suggest an animal bent on evading capture. Fascinated, and somehow liking her for this absorption, I enquired again, what was she doing? To be sure, *she replied*, was it not well known that salt was a sovereign remedy for spilled wine? And would not the servants thank her for it in the morning?

I had hoped for further converse but, on retiring with the other ladies, I noticed that she was gone. Indeed we had not been a moment over our negus before Mr. Ireland appeared to announce that his wife was indisposed and had been conducted to bed by her maid &c. I will confess that I missed her presence in that little room—talk all of the Queen, the Duchess of A——'s ball—would have liked her there, if only to drip claret onto the tablecloth, and that the rest of the evening had no pleasure for me. Reflecting on these incidents, I felt that I had observed a rare and generous spirit, yet struggling to convey some great distress of which it was perhaps only partly aware: the effect disturbing to the mind, a life wreathed in shadow breaking out now and again in hard, bitter laughter. George, to whom I explained something of this, unhappy, *said that Mrs. Ireland's afflictions were well known, her husband near beside himself with anxiety. All this, I found, worked on me very curiously—the silent woman in her house of dull old furniture and serried mirrors—to the point where, the following day, I determined to call, neglected an article I had promised to Mr. Chapman and took an omnibus to the further end of the Buckingham Palace Road. Alas, it was a fool's errand. The house seemed quiet, the blinds drawn down, with only a little servant girl in a creased mob cap to tell me that "Master and Missus" had gone away that morning to the country, although the number of coats, hats, etc., upon the hallway hooks suggested that, if this were the case, they had taken very little of their clothing with them. And so I took my leave and walked for a while in the Square's gardens, past the nursery maids and their carriages and the small boys with their hoops, musing on the peculiar circumstances to which I had been witness, casting an occasional glance at the house, from whose upper window, I am tolerably certain at one point, a woman's face stared balefully down.*

Kept

* * *

Jas. Dixey, Esq.
Easton Hall
Near Watton
Norfolk

My dear Dixey,
Although our acquaintance is not so very intimate, yet you are
the man that my father always said that he respected most and
have ever been a friend to me. Be assured, then, that I should
not have cared to burden you with this letter were it not for the
extremity in which I have been plunged. In truth I have been so
sorely tested this last month and more that I have not known
which way to turn. You will perhaps more fully comprehend
the pain of these afflictions if I say at the outset that not one
particle of what follows is exaggerated, coloured or in any way
distorted in the telling.

You will have heard—who has not?—of our troubles. It was
ever the case that when a man stands well before the world, the
world is silent, yet, should adversity strike, the air is filled with
clamorous voices. Thinking that sea and country air might be
beneficial, I proposed a tour of the southern counties of Ireland.
(We had property there once, in Roscommon, though, alas,
the estate is fallen into ruin.) To this, in a lucid moment, Isabel
heartily assented. Indeed, prior to our departure she seemed
better, almost—less languid, more sensible of her condition,
sorrowful even, that her state was so.

Alas, that the hopes I had entertained of her recovery should
be so cruelly dashed! We had set out on our journey by carriage,
stopping at London and Devizes, were a day out from Bristol
in the packet, seated on deck in the morning sun, when Brodie
our servant came to me from below in a state of much anxiety
to say that her mistress could not be found. Needless to relate, I
straightaway instituted a thorough search of the ship but could
discover nothing. Our cabin was empty, the keepsake at which I

D. J. TAYLOR

had left her reading discarded on the bed. Near out of my mind at what this might portend, I rushed hither and thither about the deck peering beneath the canvases of the rowboats, even turning up the very coils of rope in an effort to find some clue. On the instant a gentleman who had been amusing himself by looking out across the stern of the vessel came rushing up to declare that he had seen a large object floating in the waves, resembling, as he put it, a giant water beetle resting on its back. At my urgent solicitation the ship's boat put out and in half an hour retrieved my darling from the sea. It appears now that she concealed herself in a water closet to the rear of the ship and by this means flung herself from its window, would have drowned had not the air become trapped in her skirts. When found, she was paddling in a feeble way and was pulled out quite demented . . .

Of the hours that followed—we were then two days' journey from Cork—I can scarcely bring myself to speak. So fearful was I that she would once more seek to destroy herself that in the night I lay beside her chained at the waist by a piece of ribbon, so that I should know if she stirred. Happily, the ship's cabinet contained a supply of laudanum and this, freely administered, was sufficient to pacify her until such time as we put into harbour. What was to be done? Knowing too well what would be the likely outcome, I could not immediately propose that we return to England. There was no one to whom I might apply. In the end I secured rooms for us in the city, representing my wife as excessively fatigued by the voyage, &c. . . .

We were a fortnight at Cork. You cannot conceive the horror of it. The dull, *hopeless* look on her face, as if she knew full well the secret of her malady but could not bring herself to gainsay it. Of Irish doctors I think nothing. One prescribed brandy and milk, another walks by the shore—this when the poor creature could scarcely stir from her bed!—a third hot baths and chafing. Finally there came a little man—a Mr. Fitzpatrick—who did, I think, do her some good: ordered that she should not be disturbed, but her mind kept occupied, &c.

Kept

She remarked once that her head "ran away with her like a carriage that would not stop," which both he and I thought significant. And yet even here, when given rest and occupation, it was clear that her intellect was forcing her back upon a particular course, viz., when read to out of one of Mr. Smith's novels, in fact a humorous piece about a tipsy labourer and his family, she burst out in a passion, talking of the poor children, and how should they have clean shirts, and what could be done, as if these were real infants living in some shanty a furlong distant.

Come the end of the first week she was, if not recovered, then a dozen times better than she had been. Indeed she read to me, as we sat in our lodgings, a comical piece from *Punch* about a servant girl who mislaid her mistress's things, and swore it was the cat, and was found drinking porter with the boots over a pair of pawn tickets, over which we both laughed much. I remember it above all, a Sunday morning with the bells ringing and the folk hurrying to service in the street below our window. (There is no Protestant church else we should have joined them.) She ate a good dinner, drank a glass of "clar't" that Dr. Fitzgerald had prescribed for her—he is a Sligo man with the most uncouth brogue you ever heard—and seemed content, but for certain remarks that betrayed to me the febrile tenor of her mind. Thus, at one juncture, picking up a newspaper—this was after the *Punch* reading—she observed that the print *swam* before her, made it impossible for her to contemplate, that there were shapes she saw between the adjacent columns as clear as day to her tho' perhaps not discernible to all . . .

Still, the afternoon waxing fine and there being no other occupation available to us, I determined to take her walking upon the sands. Indeed, she seemed to relish it, took off her stockings even—they are very free and easy here, the gentlemen march about the shore in their shirtsleeves—and paddled in the rock pools in such a droll way that I could not forbear to laugh. There was a little black-haired tinker girl playing nearby—I could see the family's wagon drawn up on the shale and an old

D. J. TAYLOR

father smoking a pipe on its seat—and Isabel befriended her, searched with her among the rocks for crabs, walked with her to the sea's edge and looked for ships, &c. All this was very poignant to me, a circumstance that I would have prolonged to its utmost limit, were it not that suddenly there came a terrible shriek from the water. Looking up from this reverie, I saw to my horror—you will scarcely credit it, but it is true nonetheless—that she had picked the child up in both arms, as one might seize a bolster, and dashed her into the waves. What was to be done? In an instant a crowd had gathered around us—the old father hastened across the sands yelling "Murther!"—and it was all I could do, having ascertained that the child was unhurt, to spirit Isabel away. The people looked at us very strangely as I half pushed, half pulled her along the street. Yet once taken to our lodgings, she grew tractable, did as I bade her, but sat in a chair by the window wearing the most desolate expression I have ever seen on a human countenance and pray that I shall not see again. Dr. Fitzgerald, who presently arrived in answer to my summons, looked very grave and vowed that he could do nothing, in fact insisted on our immediate return . . .

Since that time it has gone very hard with us. There is no pattern to her madness, which manifests itself first as a fury of self-reproach, then as stark dolorousness, then again as a curious silent melancholy. On our return I of course consulted Mr. Procter, formerly Her Majesty's Commissioner—you will perhaps know him by his other name, Cornwall. Procter's opinion was that an institution might suit, and to this end he conducted me around what he termed his "favourite place." This, I freely confess, I feel quite sick to think of even now—a great grim house out in the wilds of Herefordshire, with bars on every window and wild-eyed women roaming the gardens. Procter shook his head about other places . . .

Lately she has been at Camberwell with Mrs. Baxter, a most respectable person, with experience of these cases, &c. Here she is humoured, has a parlour to herself, is kept clean and seems well enough. And yet I am filled with the gravest foreboding.

Kept

Visiting her this Whit Monday past, thinking to take her to Peckham Fair or on some other jaunt, I found, to my disquiet, that she did not know me, merely stared up interestedly from beneath her bonnet, enquired of her keeper who was that man, why had he come, & so forth. On my asking her at one point if she would take a turn in the garden, she replied only, "Alas, sir, I had better not," following this with some rigmarole about the Queen, the Houses of Parliament, like fragments of the morning's *Times*, almost, picked up from the floor. The sadness is that in all other respects she is unchanged, the gracefulness of her form and gesture just as I remember. Half a dozen times indeed I found myself regarding her in the absolute confidence that her next utterance would make perfect sense, that the events of the past months had been no more than a ghastly nightmare. Alas, this was a delusion as grave as that which has afflicted her . . .

This has been an infernally long preface, my dear Dixey, to what is a simple request, but there was much that you should know and much to tell about our life since last you saw us. Rest assured that if you can find it in your heart to accommodate that which I now propose, I shall be eternally grateful, as indeed would Isabel, could she but grasp the nature of what I ask . . .

* * *

And then, quite unexpectedly, Mr. Ireland died. According to the *Gentleman's Magazine*, which furnished a synopsis of the affair, he fell from his horse out riding in the Suffolk back lanes, was brought home with half his skull stove in and never spoke again. It was said also, though not in the *Gentleman's Magazine*, that his wife, when the news was brought to her by the village clergyman, gave a solitary shriek of laughter and then resumed her embroidery. It was said, lastly, that at his funeral, during the singing of the final hymn, when the coffin was about to be removed to its accustomed resting place, a woman dressed all in black with a veil over her face appeared as from nowhere in the church porch only to vanish before anyone could address her, and that this woman was Mrs. Ireland.

D. J. TAYLOR

The will was read and proved. Are not wills always proved? It is only in novels that mysterious strangers arrive to frighten the lawyers and codicils are discovered under the deceased's bedstead. The property, being entailed, passed to a cousin of Mr. Ireland's, the Fellow of an Oxford college, who, arriving to inspect his inheritance, pronounced it inconveniently rural and returned to his lecture rooms having left his benefactor's two dozen fields and water meadows in the hands of a bailiff. Mr. Ireland's money, such as it was, was reserved for the upkeep of his wife, the capital sum to be placed in a fund administered by certain trustees and released at so much per annum. All this was reported, and embellished, in that highly respectable Suffolk journal, the *Woodbridge Chronicle and Intelligencer*. Beyond that, however, lay much that those who took an interest in Mr. Ireland's leavings professed to be unsatisfactory. There was talk, for example, of another sum of money, a substantial sum, the quidnuncs maintained, bequeathed to Mrs. Ireland by her late father. There was yet further talk, as there could hardly fail to be, of Mrs. Ireland herself. Where was the beneficiary of this testament, of whom nothing had been seen since the day of her husband's death? Certainly not at the late Mr. Ireland's house, which was shut up and administered by an old housekeeper. But if not there, then where? Why, answered the lawyers to whom this question was put, Mrs. Ireland had been placed in the care of a relative, expressly selected by her husband in the event of his early decease. Beyond this, Messrs. Crabbe & Enderby of Lincoln's Inn did not care to elaborate. There were rumours about the lady's situation, about an earlier bequest, about her condition—only rumours, to be sure, but there is many an established fact that begins life as a rumour.

All this, in fact, had the makings of a singular mystery. An evening newspaper that had once employed old Mr. Brotherton produced a very severe lead article baldly enquiring what had become of his daughter. A celebrated literary gentleman wrote a satirical essay in *All the Year Round*, "Lost, Stolen or Strayed: On a Vanished Young Lady,"[*] in which not a little fun was had at the expense of Messrs. Crabbe & Enderby and mention was made of the duties of the Lunacy

---

* *See Appendix I, page 448.*

Commissioners. And in this manner Mrs. Ireland's whereabouts became, in a small way, a matter of public remark. She was supposed to have been seen variously at Brighton and at Edinburgh, in a hotel at Paris and on a steamer cruising the Rhine. A gentleman who had known her husband swore that he had glimpsed her on the platform of a metropolitan railway station in the company of a group of nuns, and for a week a rumour went round London that Mrs. Ireland was the victim of a popish abduction. To all these representations, Messrs. Crabbe & Enderby replied in their blandest manner. They had followed their late client's instructions; they were answerable only to his trustees. Of Mrs. Ireland's lodgement, health, condition of mind and so forth, nothing could be said without prejudice to that high degree of confidentiality on which her late husband had insisted. So, at any rate, said Mr. Crabbe of Crabbe & Enderby when the matter was put to him.

Now Mr. Crabbe was the most persuasive old lawyer who ever presented his petition at the King's Bench, but it was thought that in the business of Mr. Henry Ireland's will he was not lying—for no lawyer ever lies—but not saying as much as he might have said. It was at this time, furthermore, that mention began to be made—nobody knew where the tales came from, but ever so many people believed them—of a certain Mr. James Dixey, of whom it was said that he knew everything about the case that was to be known. As to his connection with the Irelands, no one was exactly sure, but those people who made it their business to be cognisant of their fellow men, soon discovered that they knew all about Mr. Dixey: that he was an elderly man, somewhere between sixty and seventy, who lived in great seclusion at Watton in the county of Norfolk, occupying his time in correspondence with learned societies, and that he had once presented a pair of stuffed lions—acquired nobody quite knew where—to the Norwich museum. This was Mr. Dixey, of whom it came to be asserted that he was Mr. Ireland's second cousin on his mother's side, and the person to whom the care of his wife had been assigned.

When these facts became known—or rather when these speculations became prevalent—a body of opinion grew up whose aim was

D. J. TAYLOR

direct action. Let Mr. Dixey be addressed, this body proposed, let representations be made to him concerning Mrs. Ireland's well-being, either by letter or in person, and then the mystery—and practically everyone had now assured themselves that there *was* a mystery—could be solved. But Mr. Dixey lived in West Norfolk, from which fastness he could rarely be enticed: letters sent to him came back unopened, for there is, alas, no law requiring a gentleman to answer his correspondence. At this, certain elements of the Ireland party waxed wrathful. Hot-tempered old ladies demanded that deputations should be sent to Watton, that raiding parties, even, should be encouraged to break down Mr. Dixey's door for the purposes of confronting him. Needless to relate, no such steps were ever taken. Norfolk, to be sure, is a long way distant. Gentlemen, too, have their business to attend to. Further, it was felt that however uncertain the legal provisions surrounding his ward, when it came to outright trespass on his property Mr. Dixey might be supposed to have the law on his side.

* * *

Upon my word, John, I think something ought to be done!"

"Done! I don't doubt that something should be done. The question is: who is to do it?"

The participants in this exchange were a mother and her son, the former a stout, grey-haired lady of perhaps sixty years, the latter a tall, bearded gentleman, clad in the latest metropolitan fashion, of about half that age. The scene of their conversation was a small back parlour in a house in the vicinity of Marylebone High Street and the time about ten of the clock on a bright morning in early March.

"Really, John! I sometimes think you are the worst person in the world for putting yourself forward. There is that young man from Oxford that is to have the property who never set eyes on poor Henry Ireland but once in his life."

"Mother, the estate was entailed, as you very well know. I could no sooner have inherited it than could Lord John or the bench of bishops."

"And then poor Isabel disappearing off the face of the earth and being forced to live with a dreadful old man in the country. And you that used to be so fond of her."

"As to that, Mother, it's all gammon. I don't suppose I ever saw her since she was twelve years old. And though I never did care for Ireland I think we can take it that he knew what he was about when he made a will."

"Even so, John."

Mrs. Carstairs, as she stood regarding her son, was conscious that their conversation was not proceeding in quite the way that she had intended. She was aware, too, that much of what she had said was, to a degree, disingenuous. No doubt the property that Mr. Ireland had bequeathed to his distant cousin from Oxford was entailed. No doubt, too, a young gentleman of thirty can scarcely be induced to intervene on grounds of sentiment in the affairs of a young lady whom he last met when she was in short frocks. Nonetheless, despite this admission Mrs. Carstairs imagined herself to be rightfully aggrieved.

The connection between the Carstairs and the Brothertons—Mrs. Carstairs was a widow, John her eldest son—was this: that the late Mr. Carstairs had been the cousin of Isabel Brotherton's father: not a very close cousin, it is true, but of sufficient proximity for there to have been dealings between the two families. These, for reasons that nobody could now remember, had ceased some fifteen years before. Yet Mrs. Carstairs, as she now poured out a third cup of tea for the young lord sitting before her, knew that she was driven by something more than considerations of mere loyalty. It occurred to her, for she was a shrewd and purposeful woman, that something was amiss about the entire undertaking—she could not at this point say what it was, but something nonetheless—and that justice, let alone the memory of the infant Miss Brotherton in her pinafore, required it to be investigated.

Shrewd and purposeful as she was, Mrs. Carstairs was not so sanguine as to suppose that she would secure the ready assistance of her son. For Mr. John Carstairs—this his mother had known for some years—was a weak man: a gentleman, a kindly man according to his lights, but a weak one. Three years previously the electors of a parliamentary borough in the Midlands had petitioned him to stand

D. J. TAYLOR

against the sitting member—for Mr. Carstairs was a political young man—but he had havered, vacillated, begged time to consult with his friends, &c., and when the election came the sitting member had been returned unopposed. Then again, a year since there had been talk of a young woman, the daughter of an East India merchant living in Russell Square with ever so many thousands a year, whose hand in marriage Mr. Carstairs might have commanded, it was said, by a single snap of his fingers. But somehow that snap had never been administered, the merchant's daughter had gone off to be consoled by an earl's grandson and Mr. Carstairs remained in a state of bachelorhood. All this Mrs. Carstairs had observed, and from it drawn certain conclusions. Knowing the nature of the man with whom she dealt, she now replaced upon its spigot the teapot that she held, gathered her hands before her, smiled fondly upon her son, who continued to drink his tea, and resumed her discourse in a rather more comfortable tone.

"I declare, John, it's uncommonly pleasant to have you for company at breakfast."

"Well, I suppose it is—uncommonly pleasant."

"And let me see, at what hour are you expected at the office?" Mr. John Carstairs was employed in an undersecretary's chamber at the Board of Trade, where it was not thought that he fatigued himself very greatly.

"Eleven o'clock. That is, perhaps half past."

"Well, I wish you would oblige me—you know, you are the head of the family now, and such words must come from you—by calling at Mr. Crabbe's chambers and enquiring"—here Mrs. Carstairs faltered just a little— "enquiring of the matter of which we spoke. It will take no more than a moment, and I should count it a great kindness, indeed I should."

"D——t, Mother! I beg your pardon"—John Carstairs corrected himself hastily, seeing the expression on his parent's face—"but I cannot see that it would do any good. I know old Crabbe. I meet him at the club and . . . and at other places. He is the civillest old file in Christendom, but I don't doubt that he'd think it a piece of interference. In fact I should swear he would. There—I do not mean to be severe! I shall call at his chambers as you wish, but I'll lay even money it's a fool's errand."

And with that he picked up his hat, saluted his mother affection-ately on the cheek, as was his custom, and quitted the house before further words could be exchanged, leaving Mrs. Carstairs to superin-tend the disposal of the breakfast things and reflect on the excellence of her understanding of human nature.

For myself I am inclined to believe that Mrs. Carstairs had not arrived at a true estimate of her son's character. He was a weak man, but not perhaps as weak as his mother supposed him. In his heart he believed that there was something amiss in the matter of Miss Brotherton—Mrs. Ireland—and that it behoved persons such as him-self to take an interest in her well-being. And yet his experience of the world told him that information about Mrs. Ireland would be difficult to come by. "After all," he said to himself as he raised his hand for a cab on the pavement of Marylebone High Street, "old Crabbe has been the family lawyer for nigh-on half a century and will know what he is about." Nonetheless, he had given his word to his mother, and so, not without all private misgivings, he directed the cab to Lincoln's Inn Fields, sent in his card, was smiled upon by Mr. Crabbe's clerk and conducted to Mr. Crabbe's chamber to await that gentleman's arrival.

It was here, however, that his courage began to fail him. I do not know that Mr. Crabbe's office was any more forbidding than other legal chambers in which John Carstairs had at one time or another sat, but there was something about its arrangement, its faded damask hangings and its shelves of dusty law reports, that seemed to impress upon him the futility of his task. Five minutes passed, then ten, not one of which did anything to raise John Carstairs's spirits. After a while he sprang from his chair and walked restlessly around the room with his hat in his hand, stood irresolutely before the great long window look-ing out over the square, peered into one of Mr. Crabbe's black-backed law books with a kind of horror and examined the row of invitations on the mantelpiece, which told him nothing more than that Mr. Crabbe dined out perhaps three nights in the week. It was in this attitude that Mr. Crabbe discovered him as he came into the room, gliding in so silently and with so slight a disturbance to the door handle that John Carstairs gave a start, rather as if he were a burglar who proposed to make off with one of Mr. Crabbe's deed boxes.

"I must . . . must beg your pardon . . . that is, I am very pleased to see you, Mr. Crabbe."

Mr. Crabbe was a hale old gentleman of seventy-five, white-haired and demure, of whom it was said that he knew many secrets worth the knowing. Forty years ago he had written books and exerted himself in the legal reviews, but those days were long behind him. There were young men, doubtless, who appeared in court and presented petitions in Mr. Crabbe's name, but Mr. Crabbe, here in the twilight of his years, contented himself with offering opinions. Again, I do not know whether Mr. Crabbe's judgements were particularly scintillating, or whether it was merely the gravity of the demeanour with which he offered them, but it was felt that these opinions were worth the having. At any rate, Mr. Crabbe was a circumspect old man, and it was apparent to him—apparent from the moment he entered the room—that John Carstairs's visit was something out of the ordinary, and that whatever the nature of his business he was doubtful of his ability to prosecute it.

"Delighted to see you, Mr. Carstairs. I hope I find you well?"

John Carstairs's health, which was excellent, having been disposed of, Mr. Crabbe pressed on.

"And is there some way in which I may be of service?"

"As to that, Mr. Crabbe, I—well, in fact, I have come about my cousin, Miss Brotherton."

"Miss Brotherton?"

"That is—Mrs. Ireland."

"Indeed? Mrs. Ireland." Mr. Crabbe's face as he said this was quite without expression, so that Mr. Carstairs, who had assured himself when the conversation began that at any rate the old gentleman could not eat him, now feared that he might be devoured on the spot. "What is it that you wish to know about Mrs. Ireland?"

And here John Carstairs felt that he was placed in a quandary. He too believed that there was some mystery surrounding his cousin's whereabouts, and yet this belief was not something that he could exactly put into words. Indeed he scarcely knew what he did believe, or suspect, about Mrs. Ireland's apparent disappearance, other than it was a subject of popular remark and had excited the general curiosity. So he contented himself by saying rather lamely, "My mother and I—my father is dead, you know—would be very glad to hear the terms of Mr. Ireland's will."

"Mr. Ireland's will?" Mr. Crabbe, who had hitherto been standing, now seated himself in a chair on the further side of a large deal table littered with documents and pieces of paper bound up with coloured tapes, hooked one black-clothed leg over the other and stared at his visitor as if the question of Mr. Henry Ireland's will was quite the gravest matter to have come before him in fifty years of legal practice.

"Well, as probate has been granted, I think I may say something of Mr. Ireland's will. But in which particular?"

"Well—in the provisions made for his wife, let us say."

Mr. Crabbe—wholly disingenuously, it may be said, for he remembered the terms of Henry Ireland's will almost as well as he remembered the names of his children—took a file from the shelf that ran behind him and made a pretence of examining it.

"Mr. Carstairs. Do not think me impertinent"—John Carstairs shook his head, as if he could not for the life of him imagine Mr. Crabbe guilty of impertinence—"but are you at all acquainted with Mrs. Ireland's state of health?"

"We had heard that she was not well."

"Not well! That is one way of putting it. I regret to say that the last doctor who examined her pronounced her . . . mad."

"Mad, you say?"

"At the time of her husband's death and for some months previously, I am reliably informed, she had lost her reason to the extent of being unable to recognise him when he entered a room. Naturally this state of affairs was foremost in her husband's mind when he made his will."

"Naturally."

"At present she is residing with her husband's kinsman, Mr. Dixey, who is responsible for her care. You will appreciate that she is not at all able to appear in society."

"I feared it was so."

There was a silence in the room so profound that each of the other sounds that had formerly run in counterpoint to Mr. Crabbe's voice—a

D. J. TAYLOR

church clock striking the hour in the distance, the old clerk scuttling up the stair—seemed magnified and made unreal by it.

"And really, Mr. Carstairs, that is all I am prepared to say about Henry Ireland's will. But perhaps you have some other question?"

John Carstairs shook his head; he had no other question. He was aware that what the old lawyer had said had been perfectly reasonable, and yet he was conscious, too, that in some way he could not perfectly fathom Mr. Crabbe had had the better of him, that he had failed to extract certain pieces of information that, through skill and persistence, another man might have been able to acquire. All this irked him, for he felt himself placed at a disadvantage—feared, too, that all the business with Mr. Crabbe's files was a sham. But he was a man who was disposed to accept what was told to him, especially when the teller was so lofty an authority as Mr. Crabbe.

At the same time, he was now definitely oppressed by the atmosphere of the room—Mr. Crabbe's dusty papers, his damask hangings, his dinner invitations, the framed testimonies to Mr. Crabbe's juvenile accomplishments dating from ever so many years ago—and determined that he would take his leave. Consequently, he picked up his hat, shook hands with his host, escaped down Mr. Crabbe's staircase through the gate of Lincoln's Inn and had himself driven away to the Board of Trade.

And Mr. Crabbe, having watched him go across the square, stalked around his chamber pulling first one book from his shelves and then another but always failing to discover whatever it was that he wanted from them, then summoned his old clerk and informed him that he would see no callers, sat in apparent abstraction for half an hour and finally slipped away down the staircase to his club, as demure and confidential a shadow as ever passed beneath the portals of Lincoln's Inn Fields and out into the City beyond.

III

SOME CORRESPONDENCE

MR. DIXEY
Easton Hall

Dear Sir,
This is a line as requested to notify you that the young woman as was spoken of has been put into my care.

She may be collected from this house at any time convenient.

The sum of four guineas in respect of her board and lodging would be gratefully received.

Your respectful servant,

SARAH FARTHING

*   *   *

JAS. DIXEY, ESQ.
Easton Hall
Nr. Watton
Norfolk

Dear Sir,
I am commanded to inform you that a bill bearing your signature in favour of Mr. Jabez Zangwill of Leadenhall Street, to the value of five hundred pounds, due on the 17th ult., is in our possession, and that we should be glad of either a prompt settlement or any terms that you may care to propose.

Most faithfully yours,

R. GRACE
Clerk to Mr. Pardew

* * *

JAS. DIXEY, ESQ.
Easton Hall
Nr. Watton
Norfolk

Dear Sir,
I am commanded by Mr. Pardew to inform you that he is in
receipt of your letter of the 14th inst., and will communicate
with you at his earliest convenience.
   Most faithfully yours,

R. GRACE
Clerk to Mr. Pardew

* * *

JAS. DIXEY, ESQ.
Easton Hall
Nr. Watton
Norfolk

Dear Dixey,
I have your cheque for two hundred pounds. Come now, it
won't do! The bill was picked up from Zangwill in our usual
way, as you well know. And here is some more paper with your
name on it for three hundred pounds drawn on our mutual
friend Mr. Ruen! Look here—I must have specie: another two
hundred pounds and your promise to pay at six weeks. That's
about the strength of it.
Yours, &c.,

R. PARDEW

* * *

Kept

Jas. Dixey, Esq.
Easton Hall
Nr. Watton
Norfolk

Dear Sir,
We regret to have to inform you that as you decline to communicate with us in regard to settlement of the two bills bearing your signature in our possession, the total value of which plus interest now stands at £660, we are reluctantly compelled to place the matter in the hands of our legal representatives.

Most faithfully yours,

PARDEW & CO.
Bill brokers, Carter Lane, EC

* * *

Jas. Dixey, Esq.

My dear Sir,
In accordance with your instructions, received by letter and stated verbally on the occasion that we met, I have taken the opportunity of observing the patient in the manner that you suggested. This period of observation, I may say, occupied the greater part of a forenoon, during which time I was able to satisfy myself, I believe, of the lady's innate condition, as opposed to any vagary of expression caused by the novelty of my presence before her.

A prolonged maniacal attack is not infrequently characterised by continual activity and a most ingenious disposition to mischief. In the case of Mrs. Ireland I think it may safely be said that the majority of these symptoms have passed, notwithstanding a constant restlessness, eagerness to move about the room & so forth. From the strict medical point of view, the lady is somewhat emaciated and suffering from disorder of the stomach and bowels. I believe these afflictions to be consequent upon her mental state and not the result of any organic disease.

D. J. TAYLOR

Her articulation is, I suspect, much impaired by her malady. She will begin a sentence and then break off at some quite arbitrary point. Her conversation, additionally, is disconnected— almost rambling: the Queen, her late father, the names of persons unknown to me, memories of her girlhood, &c. She seems conscious of this failing yet unable to correct it. She is reliably informed—could name several of Mr. Dickens's novels, the Archbishop and his predecessor —but could do nothing with the information. Her recreations, while confined, have been of the most primitive cast. Thus I heard (from her attendant) that she will from time to time sing, not unmelodiously, to herself, or attempt to fashion small drawings on the sheets of paper that are provided for her. Examples of the latter, which I have seen, are incomprehensible. On one occasion, I believe, she asked to sit at a pianoforte, and, there being one available, looked longingly at the keys as if they stirred some recollection within her on which she could not quite bring herself to act.

I append a list of her responses to such questions as I put:

Q: What is your name?
A: *Mrs. Ireland.*
Q: Your age?
A: *I have passed my twenty-seventh year. (In fact, as I am led to believe, she is twenty-eight.)*
Q: Who came before the present monarch?
A: *The Hanoverian Elector.*
Q: What is the bird that sits in the tree beyond the window?
A: *A sparrow. (In fact it was a magpie.)*
Q: Have you living relatives?
A: *I have a husband.*
Q: Where is he?
A: *He is dead.*

In the course of my examination I placed a number of objects before the patient with the aim of gauging her reaction. In a book—a volume of children's tales—she took no interest,

Kept

yet the fastening of a horse's bridle, which I happened to have in my pocket, she shrank from, saying that it awakened in her the darkest fears and apprehensions. A handkerchief she received with the gravest solemnity, balancing it on the palm of her hand and inspecting it as if it were some rare token whose significance she appreciated without comprehending its function. A very sorrowful look came upon her as she did this.

As to whether this derangement betokens an outright imbecility, I am not yet in possession of sufficient facts to judge. I can see no reason for the use of the strait waistcoat, the muff, the leg locks and handcuffs, the restraining chair—or indeed any other form of material restraint. The arrangements that you propose for her seem to be admirable in every respect. The routines that I should additionally suggest are those of seclusion, quiet, repetitive yet undemanding work which may give the brain an opportunity to function without undue distress. A suitable sedative may perhaps be administered in the patient's food.

If I can be of any further professional assistance, or if a future consultation is thought to be advisable, then by all means apply to my secretary.

I am, my dear sir, yours most cordially,

JOHN CONOLLY, M.D.
Late resident physician to the Hanwell Asylum

* * *

JAS. DIXEY, ESQ.
Easton Hall
Nr. Watton
Norfolk

Dear Dixey,
Come now, there is a way out of this unpleasantness! Let me have that letter you spoke of (none shall know how I came by

D. J. TAYLOR

it, that I promise), and all shall be well. Why, you may have another one hundred pounds for all I care, and buy as many gulls' eggs as you choose!

Yrs., &c.,

R. PARDEW

IV

THE GOODS ARE DELIVERED

Early afternoon in Tite Street, and already the twilight is seeping up through the area steps and out into the grey pavements beyond. A bitter February day here in Tite Street ("that most respectable locality," as the house agents' particulars so truly represent it) with a raw fog hanging in the air since dawn, and little flicks of wind agitating the washing hung out in the smoky courts and byways—there is always washing in Tite Street, it will be there when all else has perished—like an unseen hand. Tite Street. King's Cross Station half a mile away and Somers Town hard by. "Tite Street!" the cabman echoes his passenger, as if to say, "You wouldn't go *there* if you knew about it."

Tite Street. Forty stucco houses in varying states of dilapidation, a profusion of polished brass plates (apothecaries, insurance agents, water bailiffs—Tite Street has them all), so many cards offering furnished apartments, pianoforte lessons and the like that to gather them up and deal them out would be to commence an all but interminable game of whist. Tite Street. At the nearer end an undertaker's parlour, with a couple of great horses, their plumes dyed nearly purple, stamping on the kerb. At the further, the Tite Arms and Refreshment Emporium, Jno Phelps, prop., the dreariest public house you ever saw, with a couple of smeary windows through which the melancholy figure of a man in a nankeen jacket and side-whiskers, possibly even Mr. Phelps himself, can be seen polishing a row of pewter pots. A shooting gallery, a tobacconist-cum-newspaper-seller and a faded French milliner's whose door no customer has been seen to enter in the three years of the shop's existence complete the scope of Tite Street's amenities. Tite Street. Forty brass doorknobs, forty dark casement windows, for all the world like forty dim aquariums were it not that no fish swim inside them, on a grim, grey day in February and no one at home.

Or not quite no one. For old Mrs. Farthing, seated at present in her back kitchen with the lamps turned low and the shadows crawling consequently up the pale wall like so many phantoms, is always at home. One might as well expect the Sphinx to pick up its skirts and go hobbling across the desert as to conceive of Mrs. Farthing quitting her roost in Tite Street, where she has squatted these past twenty years and become so much a fixture that were she to depart on a little excursion to Camden Town or Marylebone market, Tite Street would feel itself robbed of an essential part of its character and get up a petition for her swift return.

Who is Mrs. Farthing? To be sure, a queer old woman of seventy-five, with a queer old face whose nose and chin threaten to meet in midair like a pair of nutcrackers, peeping up out of shiny widow's weeds of black bombazine. There is no Mr. Farthing, has not been for thirty years, and nobody—least of all his relict—has anything to say of him. Perhaps he was a half-pay officer, or a commission agent, or took in lodgers—all occupations with which Tite Street is passingly familiar. Perhaps his is the face, having a pair of muttonchop whiskers and a sprightly blue eye, that gazes from the further wall of the back kitchen, but Tite Street neither knows nor cares.

Had this putative Mr. Farthing the ability to look down on his relict's back kitchen, what would he see? Well, a monstrous old black-leaded range looking as if half a ton of coals at least were needed to keep it hot, a dreary old mahogany sideboard covered over with cups and plates and what-not, a quantity of copper saucepans, warming pans and chafing dishes piled in a heap, an old white-whiskered cat looking as if she were placed on this earth at approximately the same time as her owner. Everything old, ugly and inconvenient, and sitting amidst them perhaps the oldest, ugliest and most inconvenient article of all, namely Mrs. Farthing, hunched up in a tall rocking chair above a smoky fire, with her face all shiny from the heat and the remains of some genteel refection (Tite Street inclines to pork chops and sweetbreads) lying on the rickety table beside her.

The capital's actor managers, did they know of this Tite Street faery's existence, would probably subscribe a respectable sum to induce her onto the London stage, so professed is her ability to reproduce the symptoms of inward agitation. There is no one in the room save the cat, but curiously Mrs. Farthing's attitude suggests that she believes there to be a burglar, say, concealed under the fender, or a bailiff with an eye on the mahogany sideboard sat at the breakfast table before her. Twice in the course of ten minutes Mrs. Farthing starts up in her chair and reaches forward, with who knows what constriction of her old bones, to stir the fire irons and administer a wholly unnecessary prod to the slumbering fire with the poker. Twice, again, she rises to her feet, makes a halfhearted sally in the direction of the parlour door, thinks better of it and retires. A man delivering circulars comes and pushes one through the letter box, and Mrs. Farthing pops her old head into the passage, catches sight of the white paper fitfully descending and mutters something scornful and unintelligible under her breath. Another glance at the parlour door, another rattle of the fire irons, and Mrs. Farthing resumes her seat.

Fast approaching four o'clock in Tite Street and the twilight is no longer a hint or a plausible speculation but an irrevocable fact. A few children, home early from the variety of select establishments in which the neighbourhood abounds, venture out to play at ninepins on the area steps or make cockshies in the corners of gloomy courtyards and are swiftly routed out and brought back by their nursemaids. A muffin man marches up Tite Street clanging his bell, to depart a few moments later with ever so few pence for his trouble. A mad old lady with a rolling eye and a ragged umbrella lingers before the door of the French milliner's, thereby awakening all kinds of unreasonable hopes in the breast of its proprietress, before skipping girlishly away in the direction of Somers Town.

Within the walls of the back kitchen, now practically drowning in a sea of inky shadows, Mrs. Farthing, who has spent the past ten minutes staring very vigilantly into the fire, as if it formed an additional door to the premises, rises once more to her feet and begins to shake out her skirts in a way that suggests thoroughgoing ill-humour, one ear cocked like a bad-tempered old fox hearing the huntsman's horn borne up on the wind. What is it that Mrs. Farthing hears? A footstep creaking this way and that on an uncarpeted floor? A voice—a female voice, by the sound of it—murmuring ever so softly somewhere? Whatever it is, Mrs. Farthing doesn't mean to put up with it. Taking a last angry

D. J. TAYLOR

glance at the clock face, in whose powers she has long since ceased to believe, Mrs. Farthing steams off in the direction of the parlour door like a fearful old battleship, pushes it half open and stands balefully under the lintel.

"No good will come of it, ma'am."

The noise, which might be that of a person—a female person—walking up and down, ceases abruptly. Surer now of her ground, Mrs. Farthing, in what she imagines—heaven knows why—to be a kindlier tone, extemporises further: "No good at all, ma'am, in taking on so. There is nothing to be done." The silence is by now so absolute that the ticking of the grandfather clock a dozen feet distant, very tall and ominous in the dark, seems to run away like some mechanical demon capering off in pursuit of an inventor's prize plate.

"Nothing to be done, ma'am," Mrs. Farthing remarks, darting sharp little glances at the room's interior, at the shadows wreathed around the principal armchair, and the solitary hand—very pale and delicate and tremulous—tapping restlessly away on its edge. "Will you take anything? A glass of sherry or a biscuit?"

The hand taps a little less feverishly, but there is no reply. Thoroughly disgusted, Mrs. Farthing bustles back into her kitchen, chivvies away the cat, which impetuous and foolhardy creature has taken possession of her rocking chair, seizes a taper and lights a pair of tall wax candles that very soon begin to gutter and fizz, and settles down to brood. There is a letter lying on the kitchen table with a scarlet seal on its reverse side, and Mrs. Farthing takes it up and reads for the thirtieth time the assurances of a certain legal gentleman that this day evening Mrs. F.'s services—for which his friend Mr. D. is very grateful—will be at an end. But what if Mr. D. don't come? Mrs. Farthing wonders. What if nobody comes? These are disagreeable thoughts, and Mrs. Farthing doesn't care to entertain them.

Outside in Tite Street the evening draws on. Lights go on in upstairs windows; smoke rises from the ancient chimneys to mingle with the darkening air. The faint melodious clatter of a pianoforte can be heard somewhere, as if to say "Why, d——, despite it all we *can* still be comfortable." Cats begin to appear around the area steps and athwart the chimney pots, their eyes full of nocturnal purpose.

Meek papas, thither conveyed from clerking offices in High Holborn and Fleet Street, are met at their front doors, relieved of their gloves and clerkly appurtenances, regaled with mutton chops brought in hot and hot and given babies to dandle while their supper beer is fetching. Such is the press of servant girls and stout matrons around the door of the Tite Arms and Refreshment Emporium that Little Sills, the celebrated comic tenor, engaged that evening to delight the company with the ballad "Villikins and His Dinah," and arriving early in a tall hat and a sateen waistcoat, grows suddenly sanguine of his prospects and imagines a roseate future in which he is summoned to Windsor, appears before the Lord Mayor's banquet and can introduce Mrs. Sills (at present with the children in Hoxton) to, as he puts it, "the kind of society that a woman of her refinement, sir, demands."

It turns colder, and a flake or two of snow—grey snow, soiled by the reek of a thousand chimneys, but snow nonetheless—drifts down over the street, where it is seen from out of the window of the Tite Arms and Refreshment Emporium by Mr. Phelps as he descends to the kitchen to relay orders for beefsteaks and whisky-punch, and by the ancient proprietress of the milliner's shop, now retired to a comfortable back bedroom with her hair done up in curl papers and a copy of the *St. James's Chronicle* in her ancient hand, and by Mrs. Farthing, who, knowing that it means wet underfoot, and pattens and footbaths, and all manner of inconveniences which Mrs. Farthing isn't prepared to countenance, drats it with all her heart.

The person concealed in Mrs. Farthing's parlour sees it and twists her shawl more tightly around her shoulders and thinks—but who knows what she thinks?—of certain former passages in her life, in which predominate the figure of a pleasant-faced old gentleman wielding a quill pen above a sheet of paper quite as if he means to stab it through and through, until her thoughts altogether sail away with her, go running up the wallpaper of Mrs. Farthing's parlour—which is all coy shepherdesses and their bucolic swains—to take sanctuary on the curtain pole.

It is at a late hour, unconscionably late for Tite Street—the meek papas, arrayed now in nightshirts and slippers, are yawning crossly for the candles while their wives wonder how it is that the winter nights *do* go on so; Little Sills, his engagement concluded and the landlord's half sovereign clinking against the farthings in his breast pocket, is riding home to Hoxton on the top of a twopenny omnibus (it is a triumphal carriage in Little Sills's imagination, with a phantom crowd huzzaing at the street corner)—when a cab comes briskly into view at that thoroughfare's nearer end. So muted is its passage through the receding slush—the snow has vanished now, gone to fall on Clerkenwell and Whitechapel and Wapping Old Stairs—that no one in Tite Street hears it except Mrs. Farthing, who, like an old bloodhound taking the scent, sees it from her front door and steps out into the road almost before the vehicle pulls up and an oldish gentleman in a wide hat and an ulster begins to descend laboriously onto the pavement.

"D——d cold for the time of the year, I should say," the gentleman remarks, and Mrs. Farthing bridles, as if to say, "This is not language I would use, but the sentiment is, at any rate, sound." A casual observer, overhearing them, would perhaps deduce that the gentleman and Mrs. Farthing were formerly acquainted. Certainly, Mrs. Farthing gives a little bob, hinting at great things in the curtseying line were further encouragement to be offered, while the gentleman gives her a glance that might be interpreted to mean "I would not dream of being so impolite as to suggest that I never met you before." This impression is reinforced in Mrs. Farthing's hallway, an immensely gloomy passage lit by a single lantern. Here the gentleman, having declined Mrs. Farthing's offer of refreshment, fixes her with a look and presumes that the patient—the young lady—has passed a pretty comfortable day.

"Pretty comfortable, sir," Mrs. Farthing assures him. "Leastways, nothing *I* would complain of."

"She has been quiet, has she?" the gentleman continues.

"Quite quiet, sir. Except that she took on once or twice, sir, which I never could abide, sir, and told her plainly that I would not."

"Took on, has she?" The gentleman's voice is very low now, very low and confidential.

"Crying, sir! Walking about the room! Not answering when spoken to!" Mrs. Farthing particularises these failings as if each of them should be dealt with at Snow Hill by Mr. Ketch in front of a baying crowd.

"Indeed? Well, I am obliged to you, Mrs. . . ."

"Farthing, sir," says Mrs. Farthing eagerly, as if to say that she knows this game exactly. "And now, sir, perhaps you would care to come inside?"

The gentleman duly comes. The parlour door shuts behind him. Mrs. Farthing lingers hesitantly before it for a moment, like a duenna uncertain what the young people are up to, before stumping off to the kitchen with the thought that it is no business of hers, which indeed it is not. Presently the parlour door creaks open, the gentleman and his companion—her shawl drawn up very tight over her face—are borne away (it is very late now, and the lights in the surrounding houses are all but extinguished) and Mrs. Farthing slips out of our story and back into the cramped and melancholy annals of Tite Street.

*　*　*

"You'll find Mr. Dixey an uncommonly peculiar gentleman," Dunbar said, drawing the collar of his ulster close against the drizzle.

"Pecooliar?" Dewar rolled the word around his mouth and made a tentative step on the path before him. "In what way pecooliar?"

"Well, I don't exactly know how to put it. Nothing out of the ordinary to look at, perhaps, but uncommon strange all the same."

"Ten guineas is ten guineas," Dewar suggested hopefully. "Pecooliar or not."

They were standing on the verge of a small country back road, poorly surfaced, against which wound an ancient brick wall, very worn about its extremities, which rose to a point almost level with their heads. Above them, and to the right, tall trees—firs and spruces—hunched into near-impenetrable thickets, with only a glimpse or two of pathways running on into the wood. To the left the land sloped down through fields and pasture to a low-lying plain, apparently devoid of human habitation, on which the weak late-afternoon sun shone faintly. Save for the drip of rainwater from the trees and the receding jingle

D. J. TAYLOR

of the cart that had brought them from Watton—now on the point of vanishing beyond the bend in the road—all was silent.

"Will he be expecting us?" Dewar went on. His eyes were red and inflamed from want of sleep. "This Mr. Dixey."

"There was a wire sent saying the goods shall be delivered," Dunbar told him. "Just that. Rather neat, don't you think? But, see, we must be getting on. There is a gate here, to my recollection. And have a care for that d——d casket."

They passed on along the road under the high trees, to a point where a five-barred gate, secured to its stanchion with a piece of rope, broke the wall's uneven course. Behind it a track, no more than a few feet wide, led away through the wood. Dewar would have climbed the gate, but Dunbar, gesturing at the burden he held under his arm, jerked at the rope and opened it to let him pass.

"I saw a man drop a sea eagle's egg," he explained, "on the doorstep of the clergyman that was booked to buy it."

"This Mr. Dixey," Dewar went on, whose curiosity had been pricked. "What does he do?"

"What does he do?" Dunbar stood for a moment with his hand on the topmost bar of the gate while he looped the rope-end around its post. "Why, he is a squire. Owns the land around here. That village where we put up our traps too, I shouldn't wonder. What does any gentleman do? Why, he has his occupations like any other man. Mr. Dixey here is great in the dog-breeding line. Keeps a whole pack of them chained up in a barn—you shall hear the noise of them presently. Why, when I was here last a great mastiff jumped a four-foot hurdle and made fair to tear out my throat."

"What did you do?" Dewar wondered nervously.

"Do? Why, I dealt it a blow on the nose that had it howling for a week, I shouldn't wonder. I never could abide a venturesome dog. But see, we are getting well on into Dixey's estate."

Following the cast of his arm, his companion saw that the tall avenue of trees was thinning out into a more random assemblage of grass and outbuildings. In the distance, perhaps a half mile distant, the outlines of a substantial residence could be dimly glimpsed. To Dewar everything that he saw was possessed of great novelty, and yet he was conscious that there was something lacking in the vista that lay spread out before him. Great piles of green-coated timber lay on either side of the path, looking very much as if they wanted a woodman to come and take them away, and there was rank, knee-high grass in the paddock. Presently they passed a long, low barn, sheltered on three sides by banks of fir trees, from which, as Dunbar had promised, a cacophony of barking ascended to the pale sky.

"Grim kind of a place, ain't it, though?" Dunbar remarked, as if following his thoughts. "But there is no one lives here, you know. Just a servant or so and a man to open the hedge gates to carriages. Not that there's many of them. The gardeners have been sent away, I believe, for Dixey don't care about the height of his grass. As for what he owes in London, why your guess is as good as mine."

"And yet he'll pay five guineas for an egg?"

"More than that sometimes. And not just eggs. Why, I brought him a pine marten last year, which I took in a wood in Carmarthenshire, that he paid twenty pounds for. There's no accounting for the rarey things he delights in."

"But he don't keep up his estate, and the gardeners is all gone?" Dewar's sense of propriety was offended.

"A solitary old gentleman he is. Why"—Dunbar's eye searched for some point of comparison— "like one of those rooks up there on the fence. You shall see. Here, we are almost in sight. That is the servants' hall, behind the long window. Dixey's butler is a decent old fellow, but the housekeeper is a regular tartar, so no chaff, you know."

They came now to a rectangle of bare, flattened earth, hedged around by currant bushes, that abutted the back parts of the house. Here some faint signs of human activity declared themselves. A man in a shabby suit of green, who might have been a gamekeeper, one foot braced against a tree stump, was sharpening the points of a trap with a little whetstone, while a maid with short yellow hair was taking in washing that had been spread to dry over the bushes. Dewar, staring about him, thought the scene a very dreary one—there were old harnesses piled up by the porch that seemed as if they had been there ever so many years, and what looked like a fox's pelt nailed up on the barn door—but he approved of the servant girl, who nodded unblushingly to Dunbar as he went by.

"That's a nice-looking girl," Dunbar observed as they passed out of earshot. "And here is old Randall. How are you, Mr. Randall? Tolerably well, I take it?"

Dewar, still registering the first impressions of a dozen other things that he saw, could not separate the butler's face from his surroundings. A row of pewter pots on the long sideboard behind him; a line of prints on the further wall, over which the soft rays of firelight played, a sheet of newspaper pale in the murk of an armchair—all these seemed to him elements of Mr. Randall's being and his worn old face. An elderly woman with shiny black hair looked up from a chair by the fire, where she sat stitching a cushion cover, and Dewar, thinking that some gesture was expected from him, touched his hat. The woman turned her head away, whether pleased or offended he could not tell.

"Quite an adventure," Dunbar was saying to Mr. Randall, as they proceeded into a wide, panelled hallway where portraits hung in dirty gilt frames. "But there is not much sport left in these isles. Why, Mr. Cumming says he thinks of taking his guns to Africa." A tall footman carrying a tray before him came hurrying down the staircase, bobbed his head to Mr. Randall as he passed and disappeared into the silence they had left behind them, and Dewar thought of the grocer's shop in Hoxton, with the great blinds drawn low over the window and the drift of white dust upon the lids of the flour barrels, and the two assistants all attentive behind the counter, and the pleasure it had been to command them.

A staircase of twenty-seven steps, a serpentine corridor whose lamps had not been lit, a man's face, hard and accusing, staring out at him from a picture frame, a closed door from whose lintel soft light gleamed—all this Dewar saw, and did not see, for his mind was lost in the airiest speculations over what lay around him: the footman with his tray, the casket in his hand, the murmur of a voice, whether above or beneath him he could not tell, elsewhere in the house. The door from behind which the soft light glowed having been wrested open for him by Mr. Randall, he tumbled into the room over a ridge in the carpet, regained his footing, assured himself that the casket was secure in his grasp and then looked around him.

Dunbar, in whom the strangeness of their surroundings produced no obvious disquiet, was already on his way towards the wide desk that lay at an angle to the fireplace. Dewar followed dutifully behind him. In the course of his commercial career he had attended upon many gentlemen in their studies—he had brought in his little bill, defended it, conceded alterations to it and negotiated its settlement—but he was conscious that he had attended upon no such person as Mr. Dixey and in no such surroundings. The gentlemen of Hoxton had sat, for the most part, in small, ill-favoured rooms with cash boxes on their desks, whose windows afforded a view of mean little gardens and stunted trees. Mr. Dixey, alternatively, sat in a great wide room before a high window affording glimpses of a receding gravel drive and an ornamental pool, around which the wind whistled and careened, and on his desk there lay not a cash box but what appeared to be a human skull. He was—and this could be inferred even from his seated position—a tall man, elderly but apparently vigorous, in a suit of black with a white stock tied around his throat and bony hands that, resting curiously on the desk before him, looked as if they might have concerns of their own and be about to go scuttling off across the veneer in defiance of their owner's wishes. There was a little tuft of grey hair on the point of his chin, which, whether left there by chance or design, enhanced this singularity, and Dewar became instantly fascinated by it, watched it as its owner rose to his feet (he did this cautiously but in a manner that suggested much steadfastness of purpose) and marked it as it moved up and down in response to the opening and closing of his lips.

"You are very punctual, Dunbar," Mr. Dixey said. "It is not a week since I received your letter."

"When goods are procurable, why, they should be delivered," Dunbar remarked. "That is a principle for the retail trade, I take it."

Pressing closer to the desk, Dewar gazed wonderingly at the paraphernalia that surrounded it. The bear he had anticipated and regarded only cursorily, but the great cabinets—some displaying pieces of stone, others with stuffed birds and animals set up in what seemed to him the

D. J. TAYLOR

most lifelike attitudes—captured his attention and he began to inspect them out of the corner of his eye. The movement drew Mr. Dixey's gaze upon him for the first time.

"This gentleman is not your brother, Dunbar? I don't believe I ever saw him before."

"No indeed, sir. Why, William is laid up at Twickenham with a hacking cough. This is Mr. Dewar, as came recommended to me by an attorney with whom I have dealings, and has given great satisfaction."

There was a small grey object on the desk, nestled in the delta formed by a pair of randomly cast books, which, as Dewar watched, came to life and, now revealed as a mouse, ran off towards Mr. Dixey's bony hand, was scooped up by it and deposited in his pocket. Dewar was conscious that something in the room—he could not tell what—oppressed him, and to counter this feeling, perhaps even to distance himself from the transaction on which they were engaged, he found himself placing the casket squarely down on the lip of the desk. Picking up a pair of spectacles that lay atop a third book and settling them on his nose, Mr. Dixey bent forward to examine it. There was an eagerness about him, Dewar saw, that contrasted very markedly with the diffidence of his greeting.

Rolling the eggs from side to side in their bed of moss, he balanced one finally on the palm of his hand and balanced his forefinger upon it: "There are only two?"

"Two is difficult enough, sir," Dunbar observed. "It is indeed. Why, there were two fellows, to my knowledge, that spent a week in Easter Ross not long back and came away with nothing. Besides, the folk there have turned cunning. They know the value of the things. The help's not gratis, if you take my meaning."

Looking at the old man as he peered over the desk, the spectacles balanced on the bridge of his nose, the egg in his hand, the light in his eyes, Dewar was aware that what oppressed him was Mr. Dixey. He looked out of the window, where a faint greyness had begun to fall over the late-afternoon sky and a wind had got up above the tops of the trees, and then back at the tuft on Mr. Dixey's chin. There was a pat-pattering of footsteps above them and a noise that might or might not have been laughter.

"These will do very well," Mr. Dixey said. "I am obliged to you, Dunbar."

"When goods are delivered, they should be settled for," Dunbar rejoined, in a tone that suggested there might previously have been some slight oversight in this department.

"And so they shall. See, the note is here in my hand. But there is another commission I should have you execute, if you are agreeable."

"Oh, I am always agreeable. What is it?"

"Did you ever see a wildcat in these islands?"

"I saw one took in Lincolnshire twenty years ago. A great thing that fell out of a tree and set the keeper's dog yammering into the bushes. The keeper himself, who was a man six feet tall, said he would not have cared to get in the way of it. And when we laid it out, it measured thirty inches from nose to tail. There are none of your farmyard tabbies that size, I'll guess. But there are no wildcats left in Lincolnshire, nor anywhere else that I heard of."

"But they could be looked for? In the Scots forests, say?"

"Oh, they could be looked for. Like the wolves. Looked for and not found. There was a gentleman shot a bustard the other day in Suffolk, and everyone said it was the last to be seen."

Mr. Dixey nodded. If he was displeased by this impediment, he did not say so, but contented himself with removing his spectacles and polishing their lenses with a handkerchief. The tall footman that Dewar had seen on the stairs came beckoning at the door.

"You must excuse me. There is an urgent matter to which I must attend."

Dewar found that the feeling of oppression had left him, that he stood not in the premises of some sinister theatrical showman but in a spare, angular chamber tenanted by an old man in black with a grey head who wheezed as he passed on his way to the door. Mr. Dixey and the tall footman disappeared immediately into the upper parts of the house. Dewar had a last glimpse of a pair of oddly truncated legs vanishing into shadow. Dunbar whistled crossly to himself as they negotiated the lower staircase and came again into the great hall.

"He'll find no great cats in Lincolnshire. Not if he drew every wood from the Wash to the Humber, for they are all gone." Thinking that some explanation was required for this access of temperament, he remarked, "A man gets tired of this work. I have been too long about it, I daresay."

There was no one in the servants' hall. The maid who had been bringing in the washing was still outside, with her laundry basket. In the distance the noise of the dogs came borne on the wind towards them. Dewar saw that twilight was stealing up through the tall trees.

"Cheerful kind of place, ain't it?" Dunbar remarked again. He hunched his shoulders more tightly into his greatcoat. "Ugh, but this Norfolk air chills the bones. I could not stay a week here. Let us be away."

Dewar stared back over his shoulder. Something in the appearance of the dismal house, its outlines now settling into the darker space beyond, caught his eye, and he rested his gaze on the row of windows, some lighted now against the encroaching dusk, others gathered up in shadow. The place, he now saw, was not quite devoid of activity, for a woman's face—at this distance he imagined it to be the housekeeper's—could be seen at one of the upper windows. It looked out for a moment or two and was then withdrawn. The noise of the dogs came up again on the wind. Dunbar pressed his arm, and they set off hastily through the trees.

* * *

She stood in the gathering twilight, on the wet grass. Behind her the men's voices receded into the shadow of the wood, dark now and silent but for the cries of the dogs. Through the lighted window before her she could see William, his jacket half pulled onto his shoulders, moving through the house to answer a summons from some distant room. The sight cheered her, and she bent to retrieve the wicker clothes basket: heavy and unwieldy, but no trouble to her for she was a strongly built girl and relished the work that was put before her.

The voices had altogether disappeared, and she lingered for a moment with the basket balanced on her hip, watching the last streaks of daylight diminishing over the far-off plain. Some arrangement of the drifting clouds, some gleam of the fading sun briefly issuing out of the dusk, awakened in her the memory of a time when Easton Hall had not been her home, its secrets not hers to speculate on, when all that she now saw with the eye of half a year's experience was novel to her, quite fresh and full of wonder. She brooded on these phantoms for some time, as the streaks of light faded almost to nothing, leaving only a vast diffusion of variegated shade.

Then the sounds from the house—sounds of tea things jangling, low voices and slammed doors—woke her from her reverie and, clutching the basket in her outstretched arms, she went inside.

D. J. TAYLOR

V

ESTHER'S STORY

(1)

She stood on the station platform, watching the receding train. The white steam curled above the few bushes that hid the curve of the line, evaporating in the pale evening air. A moment more and the last carriage would pass out of sight, the white gates at the crossing swinging slowly forward to let through the impatient passengers.

There were but few of these. A labourer with a pair of kids, one lodged under each of his elbows, their startled faces peering uncertainly out into the light, attested to the agricultural character of the place. A young clergyman, bespectacled and high-foreheaded, with a superfluous umbrella dragging at his feet, directed the passerby's attention to a church—round-towered and built of miscellaneous stone—poking up above a file of distant elm trees. Behind them came a girl of perhaps twenty, stumbling over an oblong box, rust-coloured and bound with twine. This she was attempting to propel before her, rather in the way that a brewer's man drives a barrel. She wore a faded brown dress and a calico jacket too warm for the day, and her burden, together with a faint nervousness about her face and in the movements of her hands, suggested a servant bidden to her new situation. It was a plump face, rather pinched at the nose and with wary eyes, a trifle sullen when in repose yet capable of a warm expressiveness when brought to laughter. She was laughing now, the porter having asked if she wished to leave the bundle she carried strapped around her shoulders with her box. Both, he ventured, could travel in the donkey cart that came down from the Hall each evening to fetch parcels.

"Is it far?" she asked. "Only I should rather walk than wait for the cart."

The young man regarded her favourably out of pale, watery eyes.

"Not what you would call far. That is, if you are used to walking and don't mind keeping off the roads."

"I am used to walking," the girl replied, with an odd solemnity not perhaps demanded by the question.

"Two or three miles, then, if you keep your wits about you."

He would have spoken further, but the stationmaster, who stood taking tickets along the platform, had his eye upon him, so he contented himself with a vague little gesture of his hands in the direction of the church. "There's a gate beyond the trees."

She thanked the man and strolled along the platform, gazing across the low-lying fields and the strew of houses from the nearby town, still deliberating whether she should leave her bundle with the box. The last of the passengers had by now departed—she could see the figure of the clergyman hastening along the upland path towards the trees—and the stationmaster, his duty all done, stood almost forlornly by the platform's edge, his eye fixed on the horizon of pale sky and far-off hedgerows. Unfamiliar with her surroundings, her sensibilities yet more aroused by the novelty of her position, she was struck by the silence of the place, the low, brooding hills before her and the faint oppressiveness of the early evening heat. There was dust in the air, borne from the chalk road that flanked the station approach, and she stopped for a moment feeling the motes rise against her skirts. Only the church clock, striking the hour across the empty fields, stirred her from her reverie. Seven o'clock! And the letter bidding her to arrive by eight! She must make haste. Abruptly, she swung the bundle down from her shoulders and, settling it in her arms—these were muscular and spoke of much early labour—set off in the direction recommended by her guide.

She was twenty years old and coming to Easton Hall. Of these facts she was sure, the one through frequent study of the dates inscribed on the flyleaf of her mother's Bible, the other through Lady Bamber. Of Easton Hall she knew nothing, as this was not a subject Lady Bamber had wished to pursue. For a moment Lady Bamber's face—aquiline and with infinitely wrinkled skin—drifted into her imagination, only to be gathered up and lost in the dust motes that beat against her skirt and the flat horizon. She was beyond the level-crossing now and approaching the incline over which the clergyman had hastened five

D. J. TAYLOR

minutes before. To her right lay a row of houses, newly built, with uniform gardens and gates looking out onto the unmade road. These finally conquered her confusion of spirit, banished all thoughts of Lady Bamber and the three hours' journey she had just accomplished, and brought her mind back to earth. She knew these villa houses, for she had worked in others like them. They were the kind of houses in which only one servant is kept, to whom, consequently, all the duties of the establishment are devolved. Unsummoned, the voices of half a dozen of her former mistresses rose to clamour in her head. "Esther! Have you nothing better to do that you should sit there in idleness?" "Esther! There is Mr. John calling for his shaving water, surely?" "Esther! Be quick and take this letter to the post." Esther had not resented these intrusions on her time, for she knew that they were occasioned by necessity and that the women drove her hard because they were driven hard in their turn. Nonetheless, she was glad to be rid of them.

But Easton Hall! Easton Hall would be different. And its vast remove from any situation she had yet occupied awakened in her both an unwonted confidence and an instinctive dread. There would be a butler, she supposed, and a cook, and a parlourmaid who dressed in the zenith of fashion, walked with the footman to church and looked with scorn on a kitchenmaid with twelve pounds a year. And yet twelve pounds a year was a fabulous sum of money to one who had worked for seven and been grateful for eight, and again, unbidden, the image of a dress rose before her, to be bought with the surplus of her first quarter's wages, once the greater part had been remitted home.

Comforted by these thoughts, Esther wandered on through a sombre, tree-lined avenue that skirted the back of the church. The bundle, which contained two or three books given to her by her mother, a pair of pattens and her second-best dress, had already become irksome to her, and she put it down at her feet and rested for a while, casting her gaze through the trees to the fields and hummocks of land beyond. A black, ugly bird, whose true name she did not know but called a cadder, flew out of a hedge, and she followed the line of its flight with her eye. She had come, she saw, to a point in the path at right angles to the churchyard, and some instinct prompted her to step inside the wicker gate and examine the stones.

There was not, indeed, a great deal to see—a fresh grave newly dug by the sexton, in the shadow of the tower, with the digging tools still laid out on the grass, and a few bunches of parched flowers—but the place had an attraction to the girl and she roamed here and there for a moment or two, remarking such peculiarities in the names of the deceased as took her fancy. Seeing that the hands of the church clock had now reached a quarter past the hour, she seized her bundle once more and marched back fiercely to the avenue, where the path veered round to the right and a tall young man lounged by the fence palings smoking a pipe.

"Please, sir, is this the way to Easton Hall?"

"Certainly it is. Through the stables over there, and beyond the trees." Glancing down, his eye took in her perspiring face, the shabby dress and the squat bundle clasped in her arms. "But see here! I'm going that way myself. You must let me carry your things."

Esther gratefully surrendered her load, which the young man swung over his shoulder with no apparent effort. In doing so he rose up to his full height, which, she saw, was even greater than she had first thought.

"Gracious, but you're a tall one."

The young man smiled at the compliment. "Six feet two in my stockings. But then footmen's always tall, ain't they?"

"Are you one of the footmen at the Hall?"

He smiled again, but less humorously. "*The* footman. There's only one. Though old Randall, the butler, will wait at table sometimes when there's company. But it's a poor thing to be in a house where only one footman is kept. I shall be off presently, I daresay, to London or some-where. Mr. Dixey knows my feelings and says he won't stand in my way, which is decent of him, I must say, for there's some masters you know as will move heaven and earth to keep a footman in his place."

Awed by this display of vigour and, it seemed to her, sophistica-tion, Esther said nothing. The footman—his name was William, he allowed—she judged to be a year or so older than herself. Looking at him now, she saw a sallow, bony face, a shade too small for the broad shoulders on which it sat, with a pair of dark eyes whose glint sug-gested that you would do very well if their owner were friendly but less

D. J. TAYLOR

so if he had cause to distrust you. They were walking now across a long, low hillside path, where amidst gaps in the trees the flat Norfolk plain ran on in the distance, the air growing cooler and with a faint intimation of approaching dusk. As they went, William pointed out various sites of interest to those who worked at the Hall: a certain meadow in which a servants' picnic had taken place the previous summer, a stream from which capital perch could be taken, a particular field in which Sarah the parlourmaid had fallen into peril with a bull. "It was a sight to see," William explained, laughing. "Her running off over the grass with her skirts pulled near unto her ears!" Not quite liking this exultation in another's misfortune, but perceiving that he meant only to be friendly, Esther smiled gravely back.

"They said at the station that the cart would bring up my box later on."

"The cart isn't going to the station tonight—that is, I don't believe so. But Sarah will help you make do. She's a good sort, is Sarah. But what brings you to Easton, eh?"

His interest was of such a frank and ingenuous kind that her natural reserve was swiftly conquered.

"It was Lady Bamber that got me my place."

"Lady Bamber! I knows that name. An eye that you could take out and hammer on an anvil if so that you had a mind. Comes to stay in the winter and makes no end of trouble. Tips bad, too." He bent down to prise out a stick from the hedgerow and balanced it thoughtfully on his palm. "Can you read, Esther?"

"Certainly I can." The thought that he might be making fun of her caused her to knit her brows in anger. "Why should I not?"

"I meant no offence. Truly now." He flung the stick high in an arc above his head and watched it fall. "Sarah can't read. She can't, though. She sits and looks at the stories in *Bow Bells*, but it's all shamming, really it is. She can't read no better than one of Mr. Dixey's dogs. Sarah and me are great friends," he went on, in answer to Esther's speculative glance. "Friends, that is—and no more. But if you can read you will be starting on the right foot, for Mrs. Wates, the cook, is always wanting the maids to read to her."

This glut of information—Sarah the parlourmaid, Mrs. Wates the cook, Lady Bamber's visits—served to depress Esther's spirits, for the protocols of which they spoke seemed altogether beyond her understanding. Yet they awakened in her a curiosity about her new situation which she was anxious to satisfy.

"Who is Mr. Dixey?"

"Mr. Dixey? Why . . . Mr. Dixey is the squire. Owns all the land hereabouts." He swept his arm over the plain visible beyond the hedge. "But you mustn't fear about him. Regular recluse he is. Shuts himself up in his room for weeks on end. Or wanders about the grounds as if there were no one there but himself."

Young as she was, Esther had distinct ideas as to how gentlemen should manage their estates. "Don't he take no interest in the place then?"

"Not he! There's an agent to manage it, you know. They say he has lost ever so much money, but that's not footman's business. Old Randall would know, I daresay. He and the master is very thick, sometimes."

But Esther was still puzzling over the notion of a squire who took no interest in his land. "But what does he care about then?"

"Oh, he's a great naturalist, you know. There's a stuffed bear in his study and cases full of eggs and such things, and none of the maids likes it a bit. I shouldn't care to go in there myself after dark, when the lamps are out. Here! We're coming to the house right enough."

She saw that the hedge path whose line they had been following for the past half hour had now begun to descend through high banks of summer foliage, knots and clumps of tall trees beyond which outbuildings and stable yards could now be glimpsed. After the heat of the level path, this downward progress was very pleasant to her: there were great outcrops of swollen ferns that seemed to conceal sunless woodland glades, dense interiors far below the tree canopy. The effect of this new landscape, and of William, who continued to talk of Mr. Dixey's dogs, of a great hound he had bred for the chase in Europe, four feet high, of all kinds of things both strange and familiar, was to produce in her a sense of dissociation, so that she might have been walking into some magical faery land altogether detached from the world she knew. The sensation was such that she clutched anxiously at the rough cloth of her dress and the pointing

D. J. TAYLOR

of her calico jacket as if to reassure herself that some vestige of the old world had come with her.

But it was so: the man at her side was simply another servant from the hall; her mother's books were in the bundle that he carried; the railway station lay three miles down the path behind her. There was no mystery, except that she comprehended that a certain part of her life— the life of nagging women in suburban villas, her mother's cottage and her brothers and sisters—was at an end, and that a new one whose lineaments she could barely discern was about to begin. Humbled by this realisation, she found herself taking a sharp, obtrusive interest in the unfamiliar territory into which they now passed, in the curve of the tall poplar trees that hung over the path and the plumes of smoke rising from unseen chimneys in the middle distance.

"What are those sheds beyond the stable yard? There seem a great many of them."

"Them? That's where Mr. Dixey keeps his dogs. You'll hear them in a moment, I daresay, as we go past. But it's not a place to linger. Jack Barclay, as was footman before me, lost his place on account of interfering with the master's dogs. But look here, it's past eight, and Mrs. Wates is just the sort to make trouble over a lost half hour. You had better say the train was late."

Esther knew that this was a falsehood, and was troubled on that score, but she consented to nod her head. They came eventually, by way of certain vegetable gardens and glasshouses, into a little cramped square, its surface made of bare earth stamped flat, abutting the back parts of the house. Here a stout, red-faced woman with bare, mottled arms stood shaking out a tablecloth while contriving to suggest by the attitude in which she stood that this arrangement was not to her satisfaction.

"So you are Spalding, are you?"

"Yes, ma'am, I am."

"But it is half past eight. You were to have been here on the hour."

"The train was late, Mrs. Wates," William cheerfully interjected. "Indeed it was."

"And you taking the girl idling out of her way, no doubt, William Latch. Well, it can't be helped. You had better come inside."

Meekly, Esther passed behind her into a long, low kitchen, its air made stifling by the heat of the range and the log fire that burned at its further end. She had an impression of squat, heavy furniture, a cat darting suddenly away from the hearth, muted light spilling from the half-shuttered windows. Standing on the flagged floor, the bundle silently returned to her grasp, she became aware of several persons seated around a vast mahogany table, all eyeing her with a profound curiosity. A grey-headed old man who had been reading aloud from the Bible stopped halfway through the verse, slotted his finger in the page and looked at her open-mouthed. A woman with a lined face, glistening black hair and an air of authority brought her hands, both of which had been extended onto her chair-arms, sharply together. A thin girl in a maid's dress and a lace cap bobbed up from her seat and then sat down again. Somewhere in the near distance a bell rang. And so Esther came to her new home.

(11)

Esther awoke in a room suffused with light: light that poured through the open window a yard or so from her head, bounced and reflected off the coverings of her bed and made bright patterns on the bare, distempered walls beyond. For a moment, half unconscious, she was unable to recollect where she was: a stump of candle, half melted upon a metal saucer at her bedside, seemed a thing of horror; the noise of birdsong from beyond the window jangled alarmingly in her ears. Gradually these apparitions passed, and she became aware of her surroundings. She lay in a narrow bed, with a second bed jammed hard against its side—the arrangement leaving a gap of no more than a foot between the adjoining walls—in an attic room with a sloping ceiling and a low beam from which someone had hung a nosegay of withered flowers. A sound—not the birdsong from beyond the window, nor yet the noise of her own breathing, to which she had become keenly alert— disturbed her, and with a start she sat upright against the bolster. Sarah the parlourmaid, whose quarters she had been bidden to share, loomed half-dressed in the space between the end of the beds and the door posts, washing her face and torso in a basinful of water.

D. J. TAYLOR

"Gracious," she remarked, acknowledging Esther's presence with a shrug of her bare shoulder. "In my last place the housekeeper would have been ashamed to have two girls squeezed together in a room where there's no space to swing a cat. I declare we shall smother each other in the night without knowing."

"I'm very sorry to be a trouble to you."

"Oh it's no trouble. Indeed it's a pleasure to have company. I have been alone up here for a month, and the last kitchenmaid was a mouse." Finishing her ablutions, she turned towards Esther and began to dry herself with a morsel of towel. "But, Esther, why did you quarrel with the cook last evening? Everyone remarked it, and she is sure to mention it to Mr. Randall."

In her curiosity at Sarah's conversation, and the novelty of her situation, Esther had forgotten the events of the previous night. Now a fount of remembered bitterness welled up inside her, and she gripped the edge of the bedspread with her hands.

"It was she that quarrelled with me! To expect a girl to set to work on the instant peeling potatoes, with no dress to change into on account of a donkey cart that never came."

"I don't doubt that you're right, but you must see it from her point of view. Cooks are cooks, you know. And now she'll have her revenge, you mark my words. Why, you'll spend a morning sanding saucepans if she has her way."

Judging her to be a friendly girl, Esther climbed out of the narrow bed and began to put on her own clothes. Her good opinion of Sarah was confirmed a moment later when the latter said, "Look, it is only six o'clock. I have not to boil the kettle until half past. Let us go downstairs, and I can show you about the place before Mrs. Wates is afoot. She is very bad in the mornings, you know, and rarely shows herself before eight."

They went silently along the passages of the upper part of the house to the back staircase. Here all was quiet. A mouse ran over the uppermost step and disappeared into the wainscot. Down below them, in the hallway, they heard a door close.

"That will be Mr. Randall. They say there are nights when he never goes to bed at all."

"Why should he do that?" Esther wondered.

"Oh, he is a sly one, always poking about the place and turning up when you least expect him. How many of you are there at home, Esther?"

"Why, my mother and my four brothers and sisters. My father's dead."

"Now, you see, there's another reason why you must be civil to Mrs. Wates. Even if she does wear a moustache and drink gin out of her teacup."

Presently, talking all the while in subdued voices, they came through the back part of the house to the servants' quarters. Whether or not the retreating figure seen from the stairwell had been Mr. Randall, the kitchen was empty. A fragment of the fire still glowed in the grate, and Sarah busied herself with its reconstruction. She had quick, agile movements but moved uncertainly on her feet, Esther noticed, on one occasion coming within an instant of toppling into the hearth.

"I have got a stiffness in my leg," she admitted, when Esther commented on this. "Indeed, at my last place the footmen used to call me dot-and-carry."

"If they did, then that was very cruel of them," Esther burst out.

"Cruel? Then I have known crueller things than that. But look, here are the knife drawers and the pots for the vegetables. The meat safes are in the back cupboard. If you wish to redeem yourself with Mrs. Wates, then you must give her your beer. We are allowed a pint each at lunchtime and dinner. And if she sends you to the far orchard for apples, say that the distance is too great and she should send the keeper's boy instead. She'll respect you for that."

"You are very kind," Esther said, blushing.

"No, not kind. But you should know these things, and there are others that will grudge you the telling."

In this way Esther and Sarah became very intimate. Indeed, by the time that the servants' breakfast things were laid out on the table and Esther, under Sarah's direction, had a crock of porridge boiling on the range, she had acquired a substantial stock of information bearing on her new position. Thus:

Mrs. Wates, the cook, drank.

D. J. TAYLOR

Mrs. Finnie, the housekeeper, was a tartar. Mrs. Finnie had got Sarah her place, but perhaps she might find that she preferred a place that Mrs. F. had *not* got her.

Mr. Randall, the butler, was a God-fearing man and the elder of a dissenting chapel nearby. "Indeed, we are given sermons morning, noon and night. And he has such a down upon the maids." A girl couldn't look at a young man without Mr. Randall finding out and making himself objectionable.

Margaret Lane, the housemaid, was a goose. "It is unkind to say so, I know, but indeed she is. Why only last week Jem Raikes, Mr. Dixey's gamekeeper, was with us at tea, and to quiz her he said that he had shot a seraph that happened to be flying across Easton Wood, and she believed every word."

As for William, Sarah informed her, "He is a nice fellow, but he don't mean anything. Why, he and I kept company for three months last winter and were ready to have the banns put up in church, but it came to naught."

Esther, wondering about William and what tasks he might be engaged upon that morning, found herself interrogated by Mrs. Wates, who, coming down to breakfast in a bad temper and seeing her stirring the porridge, wished instantly to know if it had been made according to her exact specifications. Having managed to satisfy her in this, Esther had hoped to escape to the scullery (this she had been given to understand was her private domain) and the peeling of the luncheon vegetables, but Mrs. Wates called her back.

"Now, Esther," she began. "I trust that you are truly sorry for your wilfulness yesterday evening?"

It was on the edge of Esther's tongue to tell the red-faced cook that she was not sorry, but she resolved to curb her temper. "Indeed I am, ma'am, very sorry."

"Very well. Then we shall say no more about it. I like all my girls to be hardworking girls. Are you a hardworking girl, Esther?"

"I hope I am, ma'am."

"Well we have been without a kitchenmaid for a month, and there is much to be done. You had better leave those vegetables for Margaret and come with me."

The consequence was that, as Sarah had foreseen, Esther spent the morning at the scullery table cleaning a quantity of saucepans greater than it seemed probable that any single kitchen could accommodate. They were copper saucepans of the previous century, whose interiors required scouring with chains and whose surfaces must be burnished until they shone. And yet Esther did not repine, for it seemed to her that there was much in her mind that she wished to consider. The scullery window looked out onto the earthen square, and she stood, as if rooted to the spot, gazing out at the patch of grass beyond, where two small boys—the sons of the keeper, whose cottage lay hard by—played with a dog and threw quoits at a peg in the ground. The sunlight fell over the long table, burning off the copper and the bundles of knives, and she was not displeased to be drawn back to her work, which now seemed to her a consuming thing of great seriousness and importance.

At eleven, very red-faced and perspiring, Sarah fetched her a cup of tea.

"You have quite melted Mrs. Wates's heart. What do you think? I just overheard her telling Mr. Randall that she thought you were a hard worker after all."

"Gracious, Sarah, you look tired. What have you been doing?"

"Oh, it is Mrs. Finnie. She always gives me disagreeable jobs. Just now I have been beating out carpets on the lawn."

A little later Margaret Lane, the housemaid, stole into the scullery to prepare the vegetables. She was a small, dark-haired girl with a face like a doll's, disposed, in the light of Esther's treatment of Mrs. Wates, to regard her with some awe.

"I declare," she said, giving a nervous little glance at Esther's strong arms as they moved over the copper, "that you are so fierce I quite expect to be eaten."

"But I am not fierce at all," Esther said, putting down the saucepan she was scouring. "Indeed I am not. And I am sorry you are to do my work."

"Oh, it is nothing," Margaret replied meekly. "This is not a big establishment, you know, and we're all girls together. There are some

D. J. TAYLOR

houses where the parlourmaid won't speak to the housemaid. But we are not like that here."

Watching the girl as she sat peeling vegetables, with her brow furrowed in concentration, Esther thought that she would like to talk to her, but Margaret seemed reluctant to speak further.

The servants dined at one. Mr. Dixey, being an old-fashioned man, had his dinner sent up at four. There were guests at the hall but twice in the week, the other servants said. Seated at the lower end of the table, between Sarah and Margaret, her plate filled with beefsteak pie and greenstuff, Esther let her mind wander over the events of the previous day: her arrival at Easton, Sarah, William, the light burning through the bedroom window. William was absent from the table, having accompanied Mr. Dixey into Watton in the gig. Before the meal began, she listened wonderingly as Mr. Randall, hands clasped in front of his face, offered up an extemporaneous prayer.

"Oh Lord, we're all sinners here. I'm a sinner. Sarah and Margaret, Esther, who has just joined us, they're sinners too. Protect us, dear Lord, from the wrong that we do, and the wrong that is done to us, and bring us all to your table that we may eat with you in safety, and lead us to your eternal rock that is cleft for us that we may shelter there in comfort. Amen."

After luncheon, Mr. Randall took himself to his parlour to smoke his pipe and, it was thought, to sleep. Mrs. Wates was driven into Easton in a dogcart by one of the gamekeeper's sons. Margaret was summoned to an upper chamber by Mrs. Finnie to sort linen. ("It's a precious hard time she'll have of it," Sarah explained to Esther, "with the old cat always finding fault.") Left to themselves, the two girls cleared away the lunch things and brought in fresh logs for the fire from the timber store in the yard.

"You must not think that anything happens here," Sarah told her, "for it does not. I never knew a duller house."

"Oh, but it is very beautiful," the other replied. "I think I should like to walk in the woods for hours at a time if I had the chance."

"Well, perhaps you shall. Look, there is a whole hour until Mrs. Wates comes back. Let us go to the orchard. It is my favourite place."

And so they walked past the kitchen garden and the glasshouses along a dusty path where the grass grew six feet high against the hedges to a sad little half-acre apple orchard, very ragged and over-grown, where last year's fruit lay rotting beneath the trees.

"Why is there no one to pick it?" Esther asked.

"Because there's no men left to work on the estate, you know. Mr. Dixey discharged them all last Michaelmas quarter day. They say he is pressed for money."

Esther made no comment. Of the resources required to finance a gentleman's estate, she knew nothing. Lady Bamber lived in a villa of the kind that Esther had seen on the station road, and bullied her servant. But Lady Bamber, she knew, was the widow of a naval com-mander, lived on three hundred pounds a year and had no property. The Dixeys, she had been led to believe, were an old county family. This paradox had the effect of quickening her interest in the solitary files of apple trees, some of them so choked with foliage that it was impossible to pass between them. Turning to Sarah, in search of fur-ther information, she found the other girl seated on a tree stump with her apron drawn up to her face.

"Gracious, Sarah, what is the matter? Ain't you well?"

"Oh, it is nothing. Indeed it is very nice here, and I am glad to have you with me." She dabbed at her eyes once or twice with the sleeve of her dress. "If Joseph were here, he would tell me not to take on, I know he would."

"Who is Joseph?"

"He is my brother. But he is in China with the army, and I have not seen him these two years."

"And have you no other family?"

"None to speak of. But he writes to me, and that is something. Look, there is that gaby Margaret Lane. Mrs. Finnie must have grown tired of sorting the linen and sent her out to find us. Hollo, Margaret! You would never guess what has happened to us since we sat here."

Margaret's face stared anxiously at them from the path. "What has happened?"

"Why a great swarm of bees from Farmer Mangold's hive across

D. J. TAYLOR

the field fell upon us. Indeed I think they would have stung us to death had not Esther here yelled at them and driven them away."

Seeing the girl's open mouth, Esther could not resist a smile.

Margaret frowned. "It is very bad of you to hoax me in that way. Mrs. Finnie says you are both to come instantly to the house."

"Cheek of Mrs. Finnie to send you her orders," Sarah muttered under her breath, "when everyone knows that the kitchenmaid answers to the cook. You should say you will wait to hear from Mrs. Wates."

Nevertheless, she made no move to prevent Esther from accompanying her back along the path. As they came through the kitchen garden, a slither of displaced gravel and the noise of hoofs announced the return of the gig. A moment later William's tall figure, his arms laden with parcels, could be seen in the kitchen doorway.

"Let us not go into the kitchen," announced Sarah, who had stopped to adjust the pinafore of her dress. "Look, there are the shutters of the dairy half-open. Ten to one the cat has got in. Will you come with me, Esther?"

Wondering, Esther followed her. There was no sign of the cat.

That evening after supper Mr. Randall read from the Psalmist:

Behold, he travaileth with iniquity,
And hath conceived mischief, and brought forth falsehood.
He made a pit and digged it,
And is fallen into the pit which he made.
His mischief shall return upon his own head,
And his violent dealings shall come down upon his own pate.

VI

SINGULAR HISTORY OF MR. PARDEW

There are some men whose lives are altogether mysterious. How do they come by their daily bread? No one knows, and yet they are always respectably dressed, seen stepping briskly out of hansoms or into their box at Astley's. Their very wives, perhaps, are ignorant of the paths they tread in the course of a morning's business, the company they keep and the hour at which they are likely to return to their familial hearth. They are glimpsed at the opera, at race courses, at boxing matches, at all the genteel diversions that England affords its citizenry, and yet the friends gathered round them are as mysterious as they. Their absence—should they cease to appear in these public amphitheatres—is seldom remarked, for there is no one sufficiently near to them to remark it. They bring legal suits, occasionally, and win them, they sit in Parliament or are active at the patent office, without one iota of this mystery ever separating itself from their elusive forms, and their fellow citizens can spend twenty years in their occasional company without ever forming a clear idea of their character, opinions and temperament.

Such a one was Mr. Pardew. At the time of which I write he was a man of perhaps fifty years of age—but there had been no one with him at a school or a college or a regimental mess to confirm this speculation—tall, long-jawed, his hair still jet-blacked and with a hard grey eye that suggested its owner would brook no interference in any scheme on which he was legitimately engaged. As his voice assumed at moments of emphasis a somewhat curious intonation, it was thought that he had spent some time on the Continent, and might even have been born there, but this, as in the matter of his age, was the merest conjecture. As for the other appurtenances by which a man's stature is generally judged, scarcely anything could be said. He had a house in Kensington, but it was not thought that he was often at home there, and when he entertained his friends it was at a public room or at a theatre. There was a Mrs. Pardew—at least he spoke of such a lady—but no one had ever seen her. Of his antecedents, his business and the nature of the ravens that fed him, all was as dark as pitch. And yet it was said at clubs, and in drawing rooms, by those who if they did not know him well at least knew of him, that Mr. Pardew was a warm man and that he knew what he was about.

At the same time, a man cannot spend half his adult life on the margin of polite society without one or two incontrovertible facts arising from his dealings, and so it was with Mr. Pardew. The sum of what was known about him may have been unconscionably small, but there was at least *something*, and what there was encouraged Mr. Pardew's fellow men to regard him with a certain circumspection. Ten years ago he had featured in the commercial directories as a stockbroker with an office in Pump Court EC and a certain Mr. Fardel as his associate. Of this Mr. Fardel even less was known than his partner, and yet his notoriety was, for a brief moment, altogether remarkable. In short, Mr. Fardel was found one morning lying dead in an obscure alleyway not far from Pump Court with the back of his head stove in by some blunt instrument—a life preserver or bludgeon, it was suggested by Captain McTurk of the City Police Force, who attended this melancholy scene. It was first presumed that Mr. Fardel had been robbed, until a search of his person disclosed that neither his notecase, nor his diamond tiepin nor his gold watch-seals—not even the silver-knobbed cane that lay by his side—had been disturbed.

Some enemy, then, who had waylaid him in this dark corner at dead of night—the hour of Mr. Fardel's demise was put at between one and two in the morning—to prosecute a personal vendetta? And yet Mr. Fardel's existence, diligently investigated by Captain McTurk and his men, proved to be the most blameless that ever a man had lived. A bishop, as the inspector observed, would have been flattered by the encomia pronounced over his catafalque. And here the matter would have rested, had it not been for a statement offered to the police some months later by a gentleman who had been abroad and only lately returned to hear news of the murder.

This person alleged that, walking in the vicinity of Pump Court on the night of the murder—very late it was, he believed—and passing the office of Pardew & Fardel, he heard loud voices coming from within. It was then suggested by persons who had had professional dealings with Pardew & Fardel that the two principals had for some little time been in dispute about certain matters relating to the firm's business. A clerk summoned to give evidence to Captain McTurk deposed that on the day preceding Mr. Fardel's murder, during the course of an argument in the doorway of the office, he had seen Mr. Pardew raise his fist and shake it at his partner's retiring back. All this was very bad, but it was not perhaps conclusive.

Mr. Pardew, in the course of his several questionings, replied in his blandest manner. Certainly he and his late partner, the absence of whose capital he very much regretted, had had their differences. Certainly they had quarrelled that day in the office. Certainly they had remained there until a late hour on the evening that Mr. Fardel had met his end. Equally certain, however, was that between one and two in the morning, and indeed for two hours before that, he had been playing cards at his very respectable club on Hay Hill in the company of half a dozen very respectable gentlemen, all of whom were ready to swear to his never having left the room.

And there, inevitably, the matter had to rest. Captain McTurk declared himself satisfied—more or less—of Mr. Pardew's innocence. The office in Pump Court continued to trade for some months and then shut its doors, and no more was heard of Mr. Pardew for the next half-dozen years. It was thought that he had engaged himself in commercial speculations on the Continent—some said at Leipzig, others at Prague—but whatever commercial speculations they were no hint of their nature was ever breathed in London. There were one or two people—possibly the gentlemen with whom Mr. Pardew had been playing whist on the night of his partner's misfortune—who said that he had been harshly done by, and that base calumny and foul slander had conspired against his reputation, but these defenders were not notably numerous. When Mr. Pardew returned into the public gaze, whether from Vienna, Prague or some other foreign capital, it was as the proprietor of a manufacturing process which, various quidnuncs had asserted, might altogether revolutionise certain aspects of commercial engineering. No one quite knew how Mr. Pardew had come

D. J. TAYLOR

by his expertise, or his capital, but for a short time at any rate his stock was in the ascendant. And then there came another gentleman, a professional engineer, which Mr. Pardew was not, who alleged that in the course of their association, at some manufacturing works in the north of England, Mr. Pardew had . . . defrauded him of a patent? Appropriated some idea to which he was not entitled? The legal point was obscure, but it was generally held by those who knew about such things that Mr. Pardew had behaved badly. A Chancery suit was brought at great expense, whose result was not quite satisfactory, either to Mr. Pardew or to his former associate, and the manufacturing process altogether lapsed. All that had taken place four years ago, after which no more had been known of Mr. Pardew's whereabouts, or his undertakings, than Captain Franklin's.

On this particular morning—it was a raw, brisk morning in the early part of the year—this Mr. Pardew could be found seated in an office in the modest thoroughfare of Carter Lane, London, EC. It was a somewhat humble premises—no more than a single room with a couple of tables crammed together and a fat, shabby clerk grooming his nails with a paper knife in the corner—but Mr. Pardew's demeanour suggested that it was his to order and command. Beyond the window, which looked out onto the lane itself, the great dome of St. Paul's spread across the skyline, and Mr. Pardew, lounging on his tilted chair at such an angle that it seemed he must topple over and go sprawling in the dust, regarded it sardonically, as if he altogether saw through it and declined to be hoodwinked by its bulk and solemnity. The clerk, whose attitude to Mr. Pardew suggested a familiarity not often found in City functionaries, completed the paring of his nails and flung the knife down onto his desk, where it rattled ominously and lay quivering for a full half minute.

"Are you a-going out this morning then?"

Mr. Pardew continued to stare sardonically at the cathedral dome. "I may very well do so. What is it to you?"

"Nothink. Nothink at all. I mind my business like anyone else. But what am I to say if Donaldson comes?"

"You may give him a civil answer, show him the paper and remind him that it's due three weeks hence."

"Shall I now?" exclaimed the clerk with a horrible, bogus enthusiasm. "And I don't doubt he'll pay us the fifty sovs on the instant. Cash down, I shouldn't wonder. Oh yes indeed."

From which conversation it may be gathered that whatever business Mr. Pardew had previously undertaken he now dealt in discounted bills—the discounted bills, moreover, of people who were very anxious that they should not be redeemed. The look which Mr. Pardew gave his clerk at the conclusion of this exchange was a curious one, for it spoke, on the one hand, of a very definite obligation to him which Mr. Pardew could not ignore, and, on the other, of an absolute determination to have done with this indebtedness, and it was perhaps as well that the clerk did not see it.

It was now about midday, the time when men of business, if they are to perform any useful activity, are generally about it, but still Mr. Pardew sat, swaggering, it might be thought a little uneasily, on his chair. Once or twice he took a letter from his waistcoat pocket and read its contents through very thoroughly, made various abstruse calculations on a second piece of foolscap and then pushed the first document into the pocket of his coat. Once, again, he picked up a walking stick that lay against the table, weighed it in his hand like a man who tests a weapon and then replaced it.

The clerk, meanwhile, ate his luncheon out of a paper bag while regarding his master with a vigilant eye. Finally, in a movement that for all its purpose seemed to suggest some inner uncertainty, Mr. Pardew rose to his feet, jammed his hat on his head and thrust the stick under his arm.

"I'll not be back. If Carey calls, you had better have a message sent to me at the club."

The clerk having signified that he would do this, Mr. Pardew opened the office door and stepped out into the street. Very spruce he looked in his grey morning coat and tall hat, with the cane wedged under his shoulder like a swagger stick, and several passersby remarked him as they went along Carter Lane in the direction of the City. Had any one of them continued to stare, they would have observed him walk in a leisurely fashion along the lane and its adjacent thoroughfares until he came to New Bridge Street. Here, in

D. J. TAYLOR

sight of Ludgate Circus, he boarded an omnibus, tendered his two-pence to the conductor and was conveyed along High Holborn to the vicinity of Lincoln's Inn. A further walk of two minutes brought him to the chambers of Mr. Crabbe, where he sent up his card via the clerk and asked if he might have the pleasure of speaking to that gentleman. Had there been a third person present in Mr. Crabbe's sombre vestibule, that person might have deduced from their famil-iarity that Mr. Pardew had had previous dealings with the clerk, and that they were sufficient to admit the transfer of two sovereigns wrapped in a twist of paper.

Mr. Crabbe, sitting in his room, with its fine view out over the gardens—very frosty now, with the trees altogether black and leaf-less—and the wall of books surrounding him on three sides, knew all the little there was to know about his visitor, did not like it at all and had half a mind to send back the card with a short answer. By chance, however, a great nobleman who had intended to spend that morning at Lincoln's Inn had found himself unexpectedly detained at the House, and Mr. Crabbe, tired of poking his fire and bullying his clerk, was eager for diversion. Accordingly, he sent down word that he would be happy to see Mr. Pardew, and, having done so, placed himself before his bow window, the better to receive his visitor.

If Mr. Crabbe had expected that Mr. Pardew would be awed or made otherwise respectful by this piece of condescension, he was mis-taken, for Mr. Pardew stalked into the room as if Mr. Crabbe's deign-ing to see him was a simple acknowledgement of his genius. Upon my word, Mr. Crabbe thought to himself, he is going to hit me with that stick! However, having exuberantly flourished his cane practically under the old lawyer's nose, Mr. Pardew secured it beneath his arm and bobbed his head.

"It is very good of you to see me, Mr. Crabbe. Truly I am obliged."

Mr. Crabbe, bobbing his own head, and silently acknowledging that it was good of him and that Mr. Pardew in considering him-self obliged spoke only the truth, looked carefully in front of him. He noticed the shine of Mr. Pardew's hat and coat, the jut of his jaw and the grip of his fingers on the walking stick, but he did not as yet form

Kept

any judgement save to wonder idly what possible errand, or request, or supplication could have brought Mr. Pardew to see him.

"I believe, Mr. Crabbe, that we have a mutual friend. His Grace the Duke of —— has mentioned your name to me."

At this, Mr. Crabbe pricked up his ears. He was indeed a friend of the Duke of ——, knew every secret of the great man's that there was to be known, had presided, in fact, over the ducal family's affairs for thirty years. In addition he was jealous of his friendship, and it irked him that such a man as Mr. Pardew (a man who, as he reflected, was supposed to have murdered his own partner!) should presume to allude to it. At the same time, such was the discretion with which Mr. Crabbe conducted his affairs that he had an idea that the only way in which Mr. Pardew could have come by this information was if he had been told it by the Duke himself. Consequently, he did not bristle in anger but contented himself with smiling rather stiffly.

"His Grace is very kind."

"His Grace," said Mr. Pardew, "is a d——d old fool. He has a great heap of money which he will not invest, an estate which is falling around his ears and some highly expensive habits which he will not curb. But doubtless you know him better than I."

And here Mr. Crabbe's eyes opened very wide indeed—not merely because he was shocked at hearing his noble friend, the proud bearer of sempiternal strawberry leaves, jocularly abused in this way, but because Mr. Pardew's estimate of his foolishness was so manifestly correct.

"You must forgive my asperity," Mr. Pardew went meekly on. "But I find that in dealing with persons such as His Grace, one is always being pressed to offer advice, whereas advice is generally the last thing that is wanted."

"That may well be the case, Mr. Pardew. It may well be the case indeed. What is it that I can do for you this morning?"

"I shall be perfectly frank, Mr. Crabbe. I have money, rightfully mine, in the hands of others, that I need to reclaim."

A prudent man—and Mr. Crabbe was such a man—knowing something of his visitor's history, and hearing this pronouncement, would have taken the opportunity to bid Mr. Pardew good morning. And yet for some reason—it may have been the ghostly presence of

D. J. TAYLOR

His Grace, or some greater fascination of which he was not perfectly aware—Mr. Crabbe did not ring the bell for his clerk or go and stand by his fire in such a way that even so thick-skinned an animal as a rhinoceros would have understood the interview to be at an end.

"Am I to understand, Mr. Pardew, that you are asking me to collect a debt?"

"In a manner of speaking. I am asking you, in the first instance, to write a letter."

"But the retrieval of a debt is your ultimate aim?"

"Certainly."

"But surely, Mr. Pardew—you will forgive my bluntness—any attorney of your acquaintance could write such a letter. And might indeed be better suited to its execution than such a person as I."

Mr. Pardew bared his teeth ingratiatingly in a manner that suggested he forgave Mr. Crabbe the bluntness entirely. "If you will permit me to say so, Mr. Crabbe, there is no one better qualified to execute such a commission as yourself."

"That is all very well."

Mr. Crabbe was aware that all this was very mysterious, and that he did not quite like it. Most men, in visiting a lawyer's office, are specific in their desires. They wish a document to be drawn up, or a transgression punished, or a claim pursued. Mr. Crabbe fancied—nay, Mr. Crabbe knew—that something was amiss. Still, though, he did not voice his suspicions but stood on his Turkey carpet with his thin back to the fire considering what had been placed before him. Mr. Pardew sensed something of his disquiet and turned in his chair to face him.

"Perhaps I had better explain myself, Mr. Crabbe. I am at present engaged in the trade of bill-discounting"—Mr. Crabbe nodded his head at this—"but until fairly recently I was active in a branch of commercial manufacture. At the commencement of this business, which I may say was not unsuccessful, I had several associates—men of a humbler station than my own—whose practical help I needed but whose financial means were necessarily limited. Accordingly, it was decided that though they might withdraw funds out of the business, my own capital should remain within it, with the prospect of future redress."

"No doubt there is documentary proof of these agreements?"

"No, there is not. Such was the closeness of our association that each of us thought our word sufficient. Doubtless it was very foolish."

- Mr. Crabbe nodded his head to signify that it was very foolish.

"But I am convinced," Mr. Pardew went on, smiling in a very suggestive manner, "of their essential good nature and their willingness to return what is rightfully mine. The business closed a year or two since, but the profits were considerable. It is my aim to retrieve a proportion of those profits."

"Trusting to your former associates' essential good nature?"

"And to lawyers' letters, Mr. Crabbe. Which are sometimes more efficacious even than that."

This was of course the moment at which Mr. Crabbe should have taken full possession of his Turkey carpet, turned his back on Mr. Pardew and wished his visitor good morning. The story about Mr. Pardew's debtors he did not believe for a moment, for he could think of no man so situated as Mr. Pardew—and certainly not such a man as Mr. Pardew—who would not have taken better steps to protect himself. It appeared to him, insofar as he could judge from the fragmentary materials before him, that Mr. Pardew was playing some game whereby money could be covertly transferred to himself, and in which the name of a lawyer, especially such a lawyer as himself, would be useful to him, but he could not be sure. Above all, he was suspicious of Mr. Pardew's manner, which, however deferential and respectful, seemed to him false. Still, though, he did not ring the bell, summon his clerk or intimate to Mr. Pardew that he would get better advice elsewhere. There was something about the situation, still more perhaps about the man himself, that intrigued him and that he wished in some manner to keep within his grasp. Consequently, he continued to stare at Mr. Pardew as he sat easily in his chair, wondering what could be done about him and what could profitably be said.

"Of course there is no guarantee that you would achieve your object."

"I suppose not."

"No guarantee at all."

"I have no doubt it is as you say."

"And you would wish to proceed immediately?"

D. J. TAYLOR

"No. That is, not quite immediately."

"Indeed! Then you have a very emollient nature, Mr. Pardew. I confess that if I were owed money over such a long period I should be pressing my debtors. I should be very pressing, indeed I should."

Again Mr. Pardew smiled his ingratiating smile. "It is a question merely of information. . . . I will admit, Mr. Crabbe, that there is one gentleman of whose whereabouts I am altogether ignorant."

Once more Mr. Crabbe hardly believed a word of what was said to him. Men, he knew, can usually be found, especially if the pursuer was such a one as Mr. Pardew. Yet he was aware that, having temporised in this way, it would be difficult for him to draw back. Without precisely acknowledging the fact, he feared that Mr. Pardew had been too much for him, and while this understanding irritated him it also served to quicken his interest. At the same time, he was determined, for these and other reasons, that the interview should cease forthwith.

Mr. Pardew, observing this, was aware of the workings of the old lawyer's mind. He realised that if he were to play his trump card, he had better play it now. Accordingly, he reached into his breast pocket and brought forth a sheet of paper folded into two, very grimy about its extremities and bound up with a red ribbon.

"Here is a letter," he said in the easy tones of a man who entreats his friend to examine the evening paper, "which I believe you once wrote. Perhaps you had better read it."

Mr. Crabbe accepted the proffered piece of foolscap and sniffed at it. If the set of his eyes betrayed the fact that its contents were a source of profound disquiet to him, the tone of his voice did not confirm this impression.

"Where did you get this?"

"Dear me, I hardly recollect. Let us say that it came to me in the course of my professional dealings."

"You are no doubt aware that it is a forgery—a most impudent forgery."

"No doubt. And yet I believe you are acquainted with the Mr. Dixey to whom it was written?"

"That, sir, is none of your business." And yet still, for some reason, Mr. Crabbe hesitated to ring for his clerk.

"Perhaps it is not." Mr. Pardew's smile was, Mr. Crabbe thought, the most infuriating thing he had ever seen. "But there is a deed box with his name on it in your strongroom, or I am the old Duke's ghost."

Something in Mr. Crabbe's eye divulged that there was such a box. But Mr. Pardew was a clever man and did not on this occasion press home his advantage. "It is a small world, is it not, where a client of yours may also be a connection of mine. These things must be expected, I suppose."

There was a silence, while Mr. Crabbe, absolutely outraged by this treatment, yet still calculating what had better be done about it, stared at his desk and at the letter, which Mr. Pardew now prudently retrieved and dangled between his fingers.

"You had better come to me again when there is anything to be done," he said eventually.

Mr. Pardew rose to his feet and bowed. If he felt that he had achieved a great object, he did not by the manner of his voice and eye betray it. Having flourished his stick once again, he placed it under his arm.

"I am very much obliged to you, Mr. Crabbe. Very much. One does not always enjoy dealing with lawyers, but when one does it is as well to find one whom one respects."

"No doubt."

"And perhaps you would do me the honour of conveying my compliments to His Grace?"

Now Mr. Crabbe did not like this at all. Mr. Pardew's observations about lawyers were, to one who had been in the profession for a half century, disagreeable to him. He was aware, too, that by dwelling once more on those ducal strawberry leaves, Mr. Pardew intended to signify that they had some bearing on what had passed between them. And invisible above their heads, yet burning all the while in the pale air, lay the outrage of the letter. Accordingly, he neither agreed nor disagreed with this request, merely nodding his head as he waved Mr. Pardew towards his staircase and the escort of his old clerk. Still, though, hearing the noise of Mr. Pardew's departing footsteps on the stair—jaunty feet, as they seemed to him, belonging to one who has attained some private goal—he thought that the matter was unsatis-

D. J. TAYLOR

factory to him, and rather than seat himself once more at his desk he remained on the Turkey carpet thinking hard and wretchedly on what he had done. There were various books lying to hand, thick tomes of the kind that decorate lawyers' offices, and he delved within them for a while, hoping that they might provide the reassurance he sought. Finding that they did not, he did take finally to his desk, but the letter he began to write seemed equally unsatisfactory and at length he flung its torn fragments into his wastepaper basket.

It was by now about half past one in the afternoon, the time at which most legal gentlemen are at their clubs or at legal eating houses near the Inns of Court or anywhere save inside their chambers. But Mr. Crabbe was not deterred by the obscurity of the hour. He had an inkling that the person he thought he wished to consult would be at home, indeed never was anywhere but at home, and that he could safely go and seek him out. Thus, having spoken a word or two to the clerk, he put his hat on his head, left his premises and walked along the gravel paths at right angles to each other until he came to a somewhat shabby building in the very far corner of Lincoln's Inn inhabited for the most part by youthful barristers fresh from their pupillage and that sad species of middle-aged attorney on whom the light of professional fortune has ceased to shine.

Here, at the very top of the utmost flight of stairs, in rooms that it was jocularly supposed had not seen a charwoman's broom since the days of the Chartist demonstrations, lived a gentleman named Mr. Guyle. Of Mr. Guyle, with whom it was thought that Mr. Crabbe had been at school long centuries before, it may be said that he was in his way quite as legendary a figure as his boyhood companion. And yet his celebrity was of an entirely different character to the man in whose company he was alleged to have been flogged when the two of them absented themselves from their desks to pick raspberries from a nearby market garden at about the time of the Battle of Austerlitz. Mr. Crabbe went everywhere in the world and was esteemed for his worldliness. Mr. Guyle, on the other hand, went nowhere and was equally esteemed for his detachment. Mr. Crabbe knew dukes and duchesses, dined at grand soirées and administered the affairs of landed estates. Mr. Guyle knew only his immediate neighbours, dined in a public house and had his most intimate conversations with the old woman who darned his shirts, and yet it was to Mr. Guyle—humbly and with a due sense of the latter's expertise—that Mr. Crabbe went when he needed an opinion.

Indeed Mr. Guyle's opinions were famous. The claim to an earldom, it was said, had perished on account of what Mr. Guyle had to say about it, and a bevy of old men quartered in a municipal almshouse had been awarded ten guineas a year for life as a consequence of an ancient will that Mr. Guyle had grubbed up in some overlooked depository. All this Mr. Crabbe gratefully acknowledged as he nodded at the lounging porter (who, knowing Mr. Crabbe of old, greeted him with the most reverential bow) and made his way up Mr. Guyle's four rackety staircases to Mr. Guyle's room.

Entering this sanctum, at whose door stood a jug that had pretty clearly contained Mr. Guyle's pint of midday porter brought across by a potboy an hour since, Mr. Crabbe was immediately conscious of an almost Arctic chill settling around his limbs. Mr. Guyle had never been known to have a fire, even in January, and disdained warmth as he disdained all social invitations. No coy blandishment, not one dispatched by royalty itself, had ever seduced Mr. Guyle. He sat now as he always sat, at a little desk beneath a great shelf of books— books differing from those in Mr. Crabbe's chamber by virtue of their shabbiness and torn bindings—with further books piled around him almost to the level of his knees, and a great tray of legal papers laid out on a second desk at his side, a little old man with a shock of white hair and a palsied hand that yet moved over the page beneath him as if pursued by Mr. Guyle and anxious to evade his grasp. There was dust everywhere: dust on the cracked and rheumy window; dust over the drugget that made shift as Mr. Guyle's carpet; dust on the framed portraits of my lords Eldon, Coke and other luminaries that hung on the wall; and dust, it may be presumed, in the ventricles of Mr. Guyle's ancient legal heart.

"How do you do, Crabbe?" Mr. Guyle enquired when he saw him, in a way that suggested that the exploits of their youth still lay before them, would not perhaps be referred to but could not altogether be discounted in any colloquy that they might undertake. "Keeping well,

D. J. TAYLOR

I take it? My clerk's ill, or I'd have him bring you tea." And he laughed mercilessly, as if to imply that this was the merest jest.

"It's a very cold day," Mr. Crabbe observed, gingerly availing himself of a chair that harboured some very ancient copies of the *Law Review*.

"Cold, you say?" Mr. Guyle's breath as he said this rose in a little cloud above his head. "I suppose you've a fire in your chambers, eh? And a young man to bring in the coal?"

Mr. Crabbe acknowledged meekly that he did.

"I never saw the need of such things myself. Never indeed. A lot of d——d nonsense. Well then, Crabbe" (it was alleged by certain young barristers that in a moment of conviviality Mr. Guyle had once addressed his friend as "Adolphus"), "what is it that I can do for you?"

And here Mr. Crabbe hesitated. He had come to Mr. Guyle not for a legal opinion but for advice—information even. And yet he knew from long experience that even should Mr. Guyle possess this information, and even should he care to divulge it, such intelligence would not be given up without a struggle, in which the yielding up would become a kind of triumph on Mr. Guyle's part. Accordingly, he decided to advance by stealth.

"I hear," he said, "that Lord —— was most heartily obliged by your opinion of the Darrowby affair. Indeed, I have heard it said that the case could not have been prosecuted without your aid."

As Lord —— was the gentleman who currently sat upon the woolsack, and whom Mr. Crabbe and Mr. Guyle each regarded as the leading luminary of their profession, this might have been taken for the prettiest of compliments. Mr. Guyle, however, was not to be won over by compliments.

"Hm . . . well! Darrowby was a fool to think that he could bring the affair off uncontested. And Lord —— was a fool to think the business could be concluded in a lower court. But come, Crabbe, you are not here to talk pleasantries, I'll be bound."

Mr. Crabbe, looking at his fingers as they lay in the lap of his black lawyer's suit, thought that they were nearly blue with cold, and that even minor humiliation at Mr. Guyle's hands was perhaps preferable to the discomfort of sitting in his room even a few moments longer.

"Very well. I merely wish to put a question to you. Have you ever heard of a man named Pardew?"

Mr. Guyle examined the quill pen he held in his right hand with apparent incredulity, as if he had never seen such an implement in his life before and rather doubted its function. "There was a judge of that name on the northern circuit in, when would it have been? Thirty years since, I don't doubt."

Mr. Crabbe sighed gently. Mr. Guyle was in one of his captious moods. "Your memory, Guyle, is really remarkable. No, I have just had this gentleman at my chambers. A bill discounter, stockbroker, that kind of thing."

Mr. Guyle placed the quill pen wonderingly down on the foolscap page beneath him and bent his hands over it as if he intended to worship it as a fetish.

"The man who murdered his partner? Farrell? Fardolf? McTurk came within an inch of taking him. He told me so himself."

"Nothing was ever proved."

"And nobody ever saw the poor wretch who shot at Her Majesty in the park, but when found he had a pistol in his shirt and a spent cartridge at his feet. Well, what did the man want?"

Again Mr. Crabbe hesitated. He was aware that he was not quite getting the better of this exchange, not quite indeed being treated with the respect that the Mr. Crabbes of this world demand from their Mr. Guyles. A part of him, consequently, did not altogether wish to reveal to Mr. Guyle why it was that Mr. Pardew had come to him. Accordingly, he once more moved the equipage of his conversation onto a subsidiary track.

"Well then, let us say that Pardew did murder his partner, although nothing was ever proved. Presumably, that would not debar him from taking legal advice?"

"The man who is due to be hanged tomorrow morning is not debarred from taking legal advice, as you well know."

"At any rate, he seems thoroughly respectable," Mr. Crabbe went on, thinking as he did so that he knew Mr. Pardew to be thoroughly unrespectable. "I believe him to be a friend of His Grace the Duke of ——."

"You may take it from me that His Grace keeps some pretty queer company."

All this, Mr. Crabbe acknowledged to himself, was hard. He had never boasted of his dealings with the Duke of —— to Mr. Guyle. Nevertheless, Mr. Guyle was as familiar with them as he was with the names of Mr. Crabbe's wife and daughters. He was aware, too, that in mentioning that nobleman, in advancing his name as the touchstone of Mr. Pardew's respectability, he had betrayed himself. The realisation made him bitter, more bitter than he perhaps cared to admit, and he shifted his neat little lawyer's boots uncomfortably on Mr. Guyle's dusty floor and resolved that at any rate he would stay no longer in this icehouse. Something of this resolve communicated itself to Mr. Guyle, for he shuffled the papers that lay before him, exhaled another mighty spout of condensed air and stared levelly at his friend.

"Now see here, Crabbe. I don't know what this man may have told you. He may very well not have murdered his partner. He may be head nursemaid to Lord John's grandchildren for all I know, though I must say I doubt it. All I can say is that a lawyer has a duty to be . . . circumspect. As for Pardew, I believe I heard that he had been at Prague or Vienna, though what he did there who knows? From what I hear of him, he would not be the kind of person to tell you. And now perhaps you'll excuse me as I have a deal of work in front of me. You had better give my regards to Mrs. Crabbe and the girls."

Mr. Crabbe, thinking that he had got off rather lightly in this exchange, nodded his head and made his way down Mr. Guyle's Arctic staircase and across the frozen garden to his own chambers, where he immediately ordered his clerk to stoke the fire to its fullest extent and instructed that a glass of brandy should be fetched from the public house beyond the Inn's gate, so great was the extremity of cold into which he had been plunged. And Mr. Crabbe, as he drank the brandy and sat with his feet practically in the flames, such was the chill that he had brought back with him from Mr. Guyle, and thought of Mr. Pardew, who had been at Prague or Vienna, but about whom nothing was known, was struck by a feeling of disquiet that he could not quite fathom, the thought that he had plucked from its shelf some container that had better stayed unopened.

Kept

Presently he fell asleep over the fire—the old clerk, stealing into his room, watched him for a moment and then crept silently away—but the dreams he dreamed were not pleasant ones. A cat that in fine weather sunned itself on the steps came loitering through the half-open door to curl up next his feet; a cracked old gentleman with a suppositious interest in a Chancery case who had been bringing Mr. Crabbe his petitions these twenty years or more got a quarter way up the staircase before being smartly repulsed by the old clerk, but Mr. Crabbe heard neither of them. When he awoke it was gone four o'clock, the fire had burned down, the cat was investigating the crevices of the wainscoting and there was snow falling beyond the window onto the dark trees. And Mr. Crabbe watched it in silent wonder, as he and Mr. Guyle had watched it fall on the turrets and pinnacles of old Windsor in the days of King George III.

* * *

Mr. Pardew, when he emerged beyond the high stone gate of Lincoln's Inn, did not, as he had suggested to his clerk, make his way to his club. Instead he boarded a second omnibus at the corner where Chancery Lane meets High Holborn and had himself conveyed along the Marylebone Road and then northwards in the direction of St. John's Wood. Once arrived at this desirable locality, and having brushed from his boots several pieces of straw that he had brought with him from the omnibus, he set off in a purposeful manner along two or three side streets until he reached an avenue of secluded villas, each set back from the road and established behind hedges of laurel and cedar. It was growing steadily colder, and Mr. Pardew as he walked pulled the collar of his coat up to his chin. An onlooker who had studied his passing, here on this grey January afternoon beneath a darkling sky, would perhaps have noted that he appeared to be in a remarkably good humour, smiling to himself and on one occasion, such was his apparent delight, stopping at the pavement's edge to laugh out loud. Turning in at the gate of one of the laurel-shrouded villas, and having been admitted by a servant girl in a white cap and a pinafore, he made his way into a drawing room, very daintily furnished, with pink and white paper

D. J. TAYLOR

on the walls and copies of pictures by Frith and Etty hanging in gilt frames, where sat a woman of perhaps twenty-nine or thirty years with a complexion as pink and white as the paper, reading, or perhaps only affecting to read, the *Pall Mall Gazette*.

"Why, Richard," this person remarked when she saw him—her friendly tone perhaps masking a faint anxiety—"you are quite a stranger here."

"I don't believe that I am quite . . . that," replied Mr. Pardew, standing on the hearthrug and jingling his money in his pocket. "It is but a week, surely?"

"Nine days. Ten days. But I declare, had you come only a little later you would have found me out."

"Indeed? And where would you have gone?"

"I had thought of going to see the people in Islington."

"Had you now?" Mr. Pardew's face as he said this was set in the same cast as when he had discussed the little matter of Donaldson's bill with his clerk. "You know I don't care for you paying such calls."

"It is only my sister, Richard. And besides, what else is there for me to do? I declare, since I last saw you I have left the house only once, and that was to visit the milliner in Marylebone High Street."

By way of an answer Mr. Pardew looked down his nose, took off his coat and scarf, both of which he placed on the sofa, and seated himself in an armchair. An onlooker who observed this scene—one of the cupids, perhaps, gazing down from the frame of Mr. Etty's picture of the Crystal Palace Exhibition—would possibly have drawn two conclusions from it: first, that the young woman with the pink and white complexion, though dressed in accordance with the latest dictates of fashion, was not what is generally known as a lady; second, that though his relation to her might not be outwardly clear, Mr. Pardew brought to his surroundings the same proprietorial air that had been in evidence at his office.

"But let us not say another word about that, Richard," continued the young woman, whose name was Jemima, "for I am very glad to see you."

Mr. Pardew did not reply, but the look on his face seemed to suggest that he, too, was glad. Jemima hastened to press home her advantage.

"You will take tea?"

"Tea? Certainly I will. Let the girl bring it in. Upon my word, Jemima, you're looking uncommon handsome."

Jemima laughed, but there was something in the laugh that suggested she did not find Mr. Pardew's compliment wholly to her liking. The tea having been brought by the very respectable maid, she busied herself with its infusion, rattling the tongs against the sugar basin and standing meekly at Mr. Pardew's side as he accepted his cup.

Drinking a certain portion of his tea off at a gulp, Mr. Pardew looked at her sardonically. "Upon my word! Anyone would think that you had been a parlourmaid once. There's a way they deal out the sugar, I have remarked it."

"That is very ill-natured of you, Richard. A girl can't help where she comes from."

"I don't suppose she can. I meant nothing by it, so don't take on. Shall I tell you what I have been about?"

"If you will." She hovered attentively by his side, not knowing whether he desired her to remain or to return to her seat.

"Well, today I hoodwinked an old lawyer. Well—not hoodwinked him. Played upon his vanity rather."

"Gracious, Richard! Do you mean you took his money?"

"Nothing so grievous. Let us say that I placed him in a position where he may be able to do a service for me."

"What kind of a gentleman was he?"

"Don't be a goose! The most respectable old lawyer in Lincoln's Inn. Lives in a big house at Belgravia and dines with half the Cabinet, I shouldn't wonder. Should you like to see him? Why, we could call upon him if you like."

"No indeed! I should like nothing less."

But there was a colour in Jemima's cheeks as she said this, over and above the pinkness of her complexion, that suggested she liked to hear such stories, and that Mr. Pardew's tales of the world he inhabited were among her greatest solaces. "But, Richard, how can he be of service to you if you have . . . hoodwinked him, as you say?"

"Why, he has a name, you see. That's the beauty of dealing with men who have names. Have a Treasury lord vouch for you and you've

D. J. TAYLOR

twice the credit you began with. It's a trick I wish I'd learned long before."

"But why is it that you need . . . credit, as you say?"

"Well . . ." Mr. Pardew was always circumspect in his dealings with the persons around him, but Jemima's pink and white complexion was so agreeable to him that he was perhaps less cautious than he should have been. "Let us say that I have a little scheme in mind, with which this gentleman may be able to assist me."

All this conversation was very pleasant to Jemima, and she hung upon it, wishing in fact that it could be indefinitely sustained. In truth she knew very little of Mr. Pardew's affairs—he was perhaps careful that she did not—but what she did interested her beyond measure, interested her, it might be said, rather more than did Mr. Pardew himself. But it could not, of its nature, be indefinitely prolonged, or perhaps it was merely that on this particular afternoon Mr. Pardew did not wish to prolong it. At any rate, when the servant girl had returned to the drawing room to clear away the tea things, he ceased to talk affably of his affairs and stood by the window looking out into the gathering darkness.

"I declare it is starting to snow. You had better tell the girl to go."

Jemima did as she was bidden. Soon there came the sound of a door closing and footsteps receding into the distance. Returning to the drawing room, Jemima placed herself in its very centre, in the manner of one who awaits some signal. Finding that Mr. Pardew continued to stand by the window, she angled her head in a gesture that he appeared to understand as he twitched two or three fingers of his left hand and she retired once more. Presently her movements could be heard in the room above.

Mr. Pardew continued to watch the snow keenly: soft, regular flakes of snow, beneath which the summit of the laurel hedge had already begun to disappear. In his mind he could see it falling elsewhere: down the river at Greenwich, up on the heath a mile or so distant from where he now stood, upon the strawberry fields at Hammersmith, piling up in drifts upon the islands of the Thames at Twickenham and Teddington. It reminded him of certain other snowfalls he had witnessed, several thousands of miles distant, and of times when fate had not smiled on him in the way it seemed now to be smiling and there were no grand schemes in his head on which to brood.

The noises from above him had ceased. The house was altogether quiet. Seizing a lighted lamp from where it lay on the sideboard next to the door, he began to move soundlessly up the staircase.

CURIOUS BEHAVIOUR OF MR. CRABBE

I will own that I am a curious man. And yet my curiosity is, as it were, of an altogether curious kind. A sealed casket holds no charms for me. A locked door seldom makes me yearn for a key and the right to admittance. Rather, my fascination lies with great people and the moment when their greatness has, albeit temporarily, been put aside. How does a bishop conduct himself when, retiring to the bosom of his family, he divests himself of his mitred hat? What does Lord John, coming back from the Treasury chambers, say to his wife, his butler or the domestic who hands him his tea? Half the charm of fiction resides in these imaginings. Write a novel about a ploughman in his field or a City Croesus striding about the floor of 'Change with his hands plunged into his trouser pockets and no one will read it, but let a distinguished nobleman, the heir to broad acres and the confidant of half the Cabinet, tell his wife that he has the gout or that he will lend no more money to her scapegrace brother and the public is instantly agog!

Say by some chance that a spyglass could be brought to bear on Mr. Crabbe's innocent recreations; what would it show? It is late, very late indeed, on a black January night in Lincoln's Inn, yet still a light burns in the upper storey of Mr. Crabbe's chambers. Three hours have passed since the sucking barristers and the high-collared young men went home to their families and their landladies, and all that time Mr. Crabbe has sat absorbed among his books and his solitary lamp so that even the old clerk, now waiting at the foot of the staircase and noting the crack of light under Mr. Crabbe's door, now descending to some bolt-hole of his own in the building's lower depths, marvels at it and thinks it odd. Lincoln's Inn is shut up and deserted, with the shadows marshalled under the great door and the wind bristling over the inky grass, and the old clerk wonders if his master has fallen asleep over the fire or some other eventuality. But no, here is Mr. Crabbe's footstep on the stair and the sight of Mr. Crabbe's fingers buttoning his waistcoat and the lamplight spilling from his room to illumine his downward passage to the door.

"Decidedly cold," Mr. Crabbe murmurs in his soft voice to the old clerk as he steps out into the night air, and the old clerk nods, for it is cold, decidedly cold indeed, and watches his master pad cautiously away in the darkness like an old ghost rising out of his catafalque until a black wall of shadow looms up to swallow him and he disappears. (Where does the old clerk sleep? I declare I think he doubles as nightwatchman and lives on the premises.) The great gate of Lincoln's Inn is shut, but Mr. Crabbe avails himself of a side door and emerges with his hat in his hand and his coat pulled up to his chin into a public thoroughfare dominated by a cab rank, a workmen's brazier and a baked potato stall. Given his age and eminence, Mr. Crabbe might be forgiven for resorting to a hansom, but no, he scuttles off, rather in the manner of his namesake, in the direction of High Holborn. On the corner of this thoroughfare there is an ancient law dining house named the Eldon—very sombre in its furnishings, with grim grey waiters in black stocks—and here Mr. Crabbe stops almost without knowing that he does it, scuttles inside, hangs up his coat and under the approving eye of the head waiter—Mr. Crabbe has been coming here since before that head waiter was born—orders a chop and a pint of watered sherry.

But something is agitating Mr. Crabbe. Why else does he pull a slip of paper from his waistcoat pocket, stare at it and replace it, only to repeat the operation two minutes later? An elderly legal acquaintance, so old and shaky in his movements that one almost expects to see a periwig on him and a pair of knee breeches, totters over to shake his hand, but Mr. Crabbe, though he is civil, has no eyes for him; his mind is bent entirely on the slip of paper, now lodged again in his breast pocket but soon brought out once more to be dandled in his white old palm. The head waiter notices that Mr. Crabbe don't eat much of his chop, the wine waiter remarks that he don't drink much of his sherry (excellent Marsala it is, that you or I would willingly entertain) and presently Mr. Crabbe rises from his table, leaving chop and sherry

D. J. TAYLOR

to be carried back into the kitchens, and sets out once more into the night.

It is very cold now, past nine o'clock—the legions of the street have all but gone away—and Mr. Crabbe's breath rises into the dark air in a veritable fume of condensation. There is a cab bowling along High Holborn towards him, and Mr. Crabbe considers it for a moment before raising his hand and with the slightest imaginable movement compels it to stop. Where to? the cabman wonders, and Mr. Crabbe tells him Grosvenor Square in a tone so mild and coming from so deep inside his coat that the man has to ask him to repeat the name of that very distinguished neighbourhood. But even now, in his cab, whipping off in the direction of Oxford Street, Mr. Crabbe does not seem at ease. There are workmen out on the road, grubbing up a portion of the pavement, with a stretch of lanterns suspended over their heads like the illuminations of the Chinese pantomime, and Mr. Crabbe stares at them altogether indifferently, as if to say, "So this is how the world conducts itself? Well, I neither approve nor disapprove," before returning to his meditations.

At Oxford Circus he takes an old lawyer's brief out of some inner pocket, very grey and curled up at the edges, and dabs gingerly at it with a pencil stub, and halfway down Bond Street he puts brief and pencil stub back into the same recess inside his coat, and that is the solitary diversion of Mr. Crabbe's journey. At Grosvenor Square the cabman puts him down in front of a grand house positively aswarm with carriages, policemen, bowing butlers, and Mr. Crabbe steps down from his chariot, sniffs the air like an old charger about to re-enter the fray after long years in the paddock and feels himself rejuvenated, tips the cabman threepence, to that gentleman's great disgust, and marches up the great steps to the vestibule, where amidst a chaos of human traffic—ladies in evening dresses, gentlemen furling and unfurling umbrellas, perilously borne trays and suchlike—a servant divests him of his hat, coat and scarf and murmurs that His Grace is in the drawing room. Mr. Crabbe nods his head at this intelligence, accepts a glass of champagne from a flunkey in a gorgeously damasked tailcoat, strides out across the wide hall, where so many ladies are standing fanning themselves that the candles burning on the marble tables about them are in danger of being extinguished, and proceeds up the great staircase.

Many of the great people clustered on the landing at its summit know Mr. Crabbe, and he them. Here he shakes a hand, there he listens attentively as a lady whispers something in his ancient ear. And thus Mr. Crabbe makes his way through the succession of rooms, past great glaciers of ice on which lie salmon sent down that morning from His Grace's estate in Perthshire, and hecatombs of fruit forced prematurely into ripeness in His Grace's glasshouses in Kent, through veritable ornamental gardens of fresh flowers purchased at I don't know what expense that forenoon in Covent Garden, until he comes at last to an inner sanctum, much smaller than its predecessors, with a red-faced footman standing guard and a mere half-dozen persons glimpsed dimly within its half-open door. And here a very great gentleman indeed rises stiffly from a chair, offers Mr. Crabbe two fingers of his right hand to shake, commands the red-faced footman to replenish Mr. Crabbe's glass and remarks that it is a fine night if somewhat cold (to which Mr. Crabbe dutifully replies that it *is* a fine night if somewhat cold) and—this in valediction—wonders, h'm, what Mr. Crabbe thinks of, h'm. Whatever Mr. Crabbe says in return is lost in a sudden swirl of conversation, the sound of music, faint yet distinct, starting up beneath the floor, a rattle of glasses on a newly emerging tray, and the great gentleman draws himself up, nods at Mr. Crabbe as if their recent colloquy had entirely escaped his memory, murmurs that he is exceedingly pleased to see him (a sentiment Mr. Crabbe heartily reciprocates) and that Her Grace is probably in the ballroom.

Whereupon Mr. Crabbe moves off once more through His Grace's anterooms, past the ranks of His Grace's guests, brought in that evening from Belgravia and Kensington, down His Grace's marbled staircase, and having retrieved his belongings in the hall—now a kind of pandemonium of gentlemen calling for their carriages and a lady overcome with faintness having sal volatile administered to her by the housekeeper—steps out once more into the street. It is ten o'clock now, early by the Mayfair timepiece—His Grace will not see his bedchamber until ever so many more hours have passed—but Mr. Crabbe, who had perhaps pondered the notion of a game of whist at his club,

D. J. TAYLOR

decides that the evening has afforded him sufficient diversion and that his own home were a better solace than rack punch and cigars at the Megatherium. Another cab is summoned, accordingly, by one of His Grace's footmen, and Mr. Crabbe is borne away—very small and pale he looks, staring out of the cab's dark interior—through the great squares to his house in West Halkin Street.

And yet what is it that continues to agitate him? What is it that Mr. Crabbe is muttering to himself as he raps on the front door, is smartly admitted by the butler, who knows his master's habits, and is divested once more of hat, coat and scarf, and why is it that his hand continues to play upon the slip of paper concealed in his breast pocket? The Crabbe interior is, to all intents and purposes, a cheerful one. There is a Mrs. Crabbe—Mr. Crabbe married late in life, it should be said—reading a novel and a pair of fine bouncing girls seated at the pianoforte, and Mr. Crabbe, advancing into the drawing room where these recreations are taking place, is consequently made much of, kissed, petted, asked if the fire should be poked up for his benefit and whether he will take a tea cake or a glass of negus. Has he spent a pleasant evening? his wife enquires. And Mr. Crabbe, very meek and humble—how astonished his clerk would be if he could but see him now—intimates that he *has* spent a very pleasant evening, very. His elder daughter, a somewhat high-minded and severe young person, hopes that Papa hasn't been to "that dreadful club," whereupon Papa replies that no, he has had the pleasure of attending upon His Grace the Duke of ——, causing his younger daughter to demand whether or not Her Grace was looking very beautiful.

This, it may be acknowledged, is the pleasantest half hour of Mr. Crabbe's day, and for a moment the slip of paper lurking in his waist-coat pocket is all but forgotten. It is a shame, avers his younger daughter (whom in his heart of hearts Mr. Crabbe prefers), that Papa should have to go calling on duchesses when he could be safe at home in front of his own fire with herself to bring his slippers, and Mr. Crabbe thinks, also in his heart of hearts, that it *is* a shame. An hour passes. The drawing-room fire is all but extinguished, and the lamps turned down. Mr. Crabbe's butler is nodding over his pantry table. The two bouncing daughters have retired to their boudoir, the elder to ponder a volume of the Reverend Rantaway's brimstone sermons, the younger to read one of Miss Edgeworth's novels. Mrs. Crabbe is fast asleep with her hair done up in a turban and a cambric counterpane pulled up close under her nose. What is it, then, that draws Mr. Crabbe to his study desk at this late hour, with a candle at his elbow and a nightcap resting on his grizzled old head? What letter can be so important that it requires to be written at eleven o'clock at night, and so troublesome the manner of its composition that half a dozen previous attempts lie in fragments in the wastepaper basket? To be sure, the butler, looking over his master's leavings the next morning with his customarily attentive eye, will wonder who this Mr. Dixey is and why Mr. Crabbe finds such difficulty in addressing him. Meanwhile, high in his eyrie Mr. Crabbe scribbles on into the night as the lights go out all around him, and there is no one awake in West Halkin Street, and no sound except the draw of his breath and the tread of the policeman's boots on the pavement thirty feet below.

JORROCKS'S CART

W ell, I have seen Mr. Crabbe," were John Carstairs's first words
that evening as he plunged into his mother's drawing room,
rather startling that lady by the force of his irruption.

"Indeed? And what did Mr. Crabbe have to say?"

"What did he say? What do lawyers ever say?" John Carstairs
glanced round the room, which was a kind of shrine to the memory
of the late Mr. Carstairs, culminating in a portrait of that gentleman
dressed in the uniform of the Suffolk Fencibles, satisfied himself that
there was no one else in it and continued: "It seems that poor Isabel
is quite deranged, living in seclusion in the country and that kind of
thing. At any rate, Crabbe explained it all."

John Carstairs was perhaps aware, as he uttered this synopsis of
Mr. Crabbe's opinion, that it would scarcely do. But if he expected any
close questioning from his fond parent, he was disappointed—or shall
we say relieved? Mrs. Carstairs, as she handed her son his cup of tea
and resumed her seat, merely remarked that it was very dreadful but
that she was glad to have an explanation. Of the little scheme she had
meditated during the day involving a Bradshaw and a directory of the
County of Norfolk, she wisely kept silent.

But Mrs. Carstairs was a woman of resolve. The next morning,
having ascertained from her son before he left the house that he
intended to dine at his club and would not be back until a late hour, she
dressed herself in her travelling clothes, instructed the parlourmaid to
step outside to Marylebone High Street and summon a cab, and had
herself taken off to Shoreditch Railway Station. Here she purchased
a return ticket to Watton, this being the stopping point suggested by
her researches to be nearest to Easton Hall. It was by now about eleven
o'clock in the morning. Mrs. Carstairs calculated that she could travel

down to Norfolk, achieve the object of her quest and return once again to Marylebone without her son being any the wiser.

It was a mild, windy day with great ragged clouds moving over the Essex flats, and Mrs. Carstairs, as the train moved eastwards, was sensible of a faint exhilaration. That she might not achieve her aim— might not even insinuate her way into Mrs. Ireland's presence—she thought very possible, but it would be something to have tried. Mr. Dixey might refuse to see her, might pretend, indeed, that he was not at home, but to bead him on his very doorstep would be to prove a point. And thus Mrs. Carstairs reassured herself as the train rattled on past Colchester and Manningtree, where the fog hung over the ships' masts in the estuary and the geese lay in great flocks on the riverbank, deep into the Suffolk plain. A gentleman seated on the farther side of the carriage, after an examination of the lowering sky, deposed very courteously that it might rain, and Mrs. Carstairs graciously assented.

At Ipswich she descended from her carriage and walked along the station platform to the refreshment room to recruit herself with a glass of sherry and a biscuit. Thus did she maintain her spirits, preserve them in fact almost to the moment when the outward part of her journey was done and the train deposited her at Watton in such a cloud of steam and soot that she might have been Bluebeard's sister in the play rising out of the orchestra pit to strike factitious terror in the hearts of her admiring audience. It was only then, as I say, that she experienced a faint misgiving. An unreasonable optimism had led Mrs. Carstairs to suppose that Watton would run to some kind of conveyance. It did not. It ran only to a long, low platform set forlornly in a field, to a solitary waiting room and an equally solitary porter in whom Mrs. Carstairs's enquiry about the existence of a station fly produced only a shake of the head. "A carriage then," Mrs. Carstairs persisted, having explained the object of her quest. "Surely there must be something that can take me to Easton?" "There's Jorrocks's cart, ma'am, I suppose." And so Mrs. Carstairs found herself absolutely compelled to climb into the back of a haywain, where with two bales of straw and an empty rabbit hutch she was despatched across the Norfolk backroads at a speed of perhaps five miles to the hour.

It was by now half past one in the afternoon, with a stiff wind

D. J. TAYLOR

blowing from the east and the roadside trees all blown back along one side as if they found the sight of Jorrocks's cart labouring along the little track beside them too objectionable to be borne and yearned to be away. Beyond the hedge the fields, bare and grubbed up, descended in a melancholy way towards a flat expanse of wood and heath. To be sure, the compilers of gazetteers and guidebooks always represent Norfolk as a picturesque county, but I confess that I have never found it so myself in spring. There are too many flat fields, too many dank little lanes, perilous to the feet, leading nowhere in particular; there is too much wind, too much mud, too much silence—except for the cries of birds that must be the most mournful in all England. Mrs. Carstairs, peering out between the slats of Jorrocks's cart, jolted almost out of her wits by the unevenness of the road, reckoned it a very desolate place.

By this stage, it need scarcely be said, her earlier exhilaration had altogether passed off. She was cold. The motion of the cart was torture to her. More especially she feared that the effect of the journey, should it ever come to her son's ears or those of anyone who knew the circumstances of the case, would be to make her seem foolish. There was also—a fact not perhaps intelligible to the reader who learns of her adventure in the comfort of a fireside armchair—something about her present situation, here on the rutted road with the high hedges towering on either side and the melancholy cries of the birds ringing in her ears, that she did not altogether like. Possibly as a child Mrs. Carstairs had lingered too impressionably over that engraving in which a man, journeying down a country road at night, finds himself pursued by a fearful fiend, but it is a fact that she more than once turned her head and regarded the road behind her with an expression of grave foreboding. Then the cart lurched forward into a damp, gloomy avenue of trees where the wind amidst the branches produced a sensation of unseen hands tugging at her skirts, and Mrs. Carstairs felt that she would give anything to be back in her comfortable drawing room in Marylebone with the fire to poke and the parlourmaid to bully.

"Dear me, this is a most lonely spot, is it not?" she enquired of the carter.

"Ef'n' you say so, ma'am. There is not many folks as comes here."

Presently the cart rolled out of its tunnel of trees into a road whose course lay westward through fields of spring wheat, and Mrs. Carstairs's spirits revived. Still, though, in her heart she was anxious. Twenty minutes or half an hour, she knew, would see her on Mr. Dixey's doorstep, and then how would she conduct herself? What if Mr. Dixey declined to see her, sent some answer bidding her to go away? As a young married woman she had once startled herself and her husband by giving her opinion of the bill of 1832 to one of Mr. Peel's young men who sat next to her at dinner, but Mrs. Carstairs knew enough of her character to admit that such irruptions of spirit were behind her now. She was still pondering her probable reception when she became aware that the cart had come to a halt at a point in the road where a path forged off to the right towards a distant lodge gate, and that the carter was awaiting his instructions.

"Is this the place?"

"It be so for zartin, ma'am."

Mrs. Carstairs took hasty stock of her surroundings. For the past half mile the road had followed the curve of an ancient brick wall, with dense evergreens tightly enclosed behind it. This, she guessed, was the boundary of the Easton Hall estate. Looking eastward, where the track ran away in the direction of the lodge gate, she saw signs of habitation: a cottage or two and an outhouse. Beyond this a gravel drive, soon disappearing into the wall of trees, and in the further distance the outlines of the house itself. Mrs. Carstairs asked herself whether she wished to be observed negotiating Mr. Dixey's driveway in a hay cart and told herself that she did not. At the same time, the hay cart must somehow be preserved. Descending onto the rough ground and depositing her reticule at her feet, she addressed herself to the carter: "If you will kindly wait for me, I shall give you half a crown."

Keeping the outline of the gravel drive directly before her, Mrs. Carstairs set off to walk to the house. She was conscious of several sensations: that the carter must think her a fool; that it had begun to rain and she had forgotten to bring an umbrella; that the grounds through which she now progressed seemed very rundown and wretched. As a child Mrs. Carstairs had possessed a venerable great-uncle with an estate in Kent which it had been her delight to visit. There had been flower beds and avenues and a certain walk by a river that even now, fifty years later, she remembered with affection. Easton Hall bore no relation to this juvenile Eden. The trees crowded up close to the path and quite defied you to wander beneath them. There was timber lying in piles on the grass that looked to have been cut ever so many years ago, and a great barn with dogs locked up in it, for she heard them barking as she passed. Not a soul was to be seen. In fact such a desolate prospect did the overgrown lawn before the house present—it was a great barrack of a place, Mrs. Carstairs thought, and must be very uncomfortable—that she feared she would find it shut up.

Happily, the door was opened, albeit by a servant girl—no more than a child the visitor judged—with a doll-like face who regarded her in a manner that suggested callers were very uncommon at Easton Hall. However, Mrs. Carstairs was used to dealing with servant girls. It had been the pastime of her adult life to command, bewilder and confuse them, and the uncertainty of the present situation, here on a gloomy doorstep in Norfolk with the afternoon light glowing through the distant trees, only served to strengthen her resolve.

"I wish to speak to your master. To Mr. Dixey. Is he at home?"

The girl, whom certain signs intelligible only to the female eye suggested to be perhaps seventeen years of age, continued to stare.

"Mr. Dixey. Is he at home?"

"What name, ma'am?"

Whereupon she disappeared hastily from view, leaving Mrs. Carstairs alone in the vestibule and wondering in her heart of hearts whether the enterprise was worth continuing with. And yet, if truth be known, she was not displeased with her endeavours. Whatever else might happen—whatever Bluebeards might subsequently be found lurking behind Easton Hall's wainscoting—she had at least gained an entrance to the place and could now form some slight opinion of its lineaments. She saw now that she was standing—no one had asked her to sit down—in a spacious lobby or entrance hall, shabbily decorated but genteel after its fashion, with prints on the wall and a profusion of walking sticks and pattens strewn in a heap. She had moved to the further wall and was inspecting a melancholy engraving of the battle of Culloden when the servant girl came running very breathlessly back.

"Ef'n' ye please, ma'am, the master says, would you care to wait?"

Kept

Signifying her assent, Mrs. Carstairs allowed herself to be conducted through the vestibule into a wider hallway and thence into a modest anteroom, halfway between a study and a parlour, looking out onto a ragged, unkempt garden. Here half a dozen logs burned in a small grate, and three or four chairs stood in random attitudes against the bookshelves. The general effect was not prepossessing, and Mrs. Carstairs knew it was not. She turned on her heel, but the servant girl had vanished again—apparently into thin air as no sound of her footsteps could be heard elsewhere in the house. As if to prove a point, Mrs. Carstairs seized a chair and took it over to the fire, which she then poked up with a vengeance, but she was not happy. Something about the window and the view beyond, the treetops dancing in the wind and the draggled grass, drew her eye constantly towards it, and she remembered the story of Mr. Le Fanu's in which the evil governess stands gesticulating in the twilight. Mrs. Carstairs edged her chair a little nearer to the fire and reminded herself that she was in a gentleman's house in Norfolk on a spring afternoon in the age of steam engines and the Crystal Palace, but still she remembered the evil governess signalling from the twilit garden.

What was to be done? There was a line of pictures—family portraits, she presumed—on the wall above the hearth, of old, dead Dixeys in periwigs and clerical bands. Mrs. Carstairs looked at them for a while, but they brought her no succour. They had pink and white faces and hard eyes and reminded her uncomfortably of cold boiled veal. The books in the bookcase were scientific and abstruse, the objects in a cracked display cabinet by the wall rustic and peculiar—old pieces of bone and rock, with Latin inscriptions beneath them in faded italic. In despair Mrs. Carstairs turned back to the window, where the rain was now falling in torrents. There was something about the scene, about the dismal little garden and the bygone Dixeys in their frames and the scientific histories on the shelf, that altogether disturbed and discountenanced her, but she could not say why. Presently footsteps sounded in the corridor, the doorknob turned—so sharply attuned was Mrs. Carstairs to these developments that the noise seemed to resound in her ears—and a man stood squarely in the doorway.

It had ever been Mrs. Carstairs's boast that she was, as she put it, "a good judge of a man." Perhaps there is no general agreement on how such judgements should be arrived at, but Mrs. Carstairs had made them since the days of her girlhood, the days of Lord Castlereagh and Mr. Canning, Mr. Chinnery's pictures and Miss Austen's novels. Military heroes in proud receipt of Her Majesty's commission, professional persons from lawyers' chambers and banking offices, divines and gentlemen of leisure: all these had risked the silent appraisal of Mrs. Carstairs's gaze. In a discreet and unexacting way she had even judged the late Mr. Carstairs. But something told her that she could not judge Mr. Dixey.

In appearance he was a tall, thin, rather elderly man—perhaps a year or two older than herself, perhaps a year or so younger—very pale-faced, with abundant grey hair and bearing such a sharp resemblance to the portraits on the wall that it almost appeared as if he had stepped down from them but a moment ago. And yet it was not in these particulars or his dress—he wore a thick jacket and countrymen's gaiters—Mrs. Carstairs thought, that his singularity lay. Where it did lie she could not quite be sure. He had restless blue eyes, which darted down upon the walking stick he held between his fingers and then towards the window before alighting on the visitor by the hearth.

"I believe I have the unexpected pleasure of addressing Mrs. Carstairs?"

If anything could have startled Mrs. Carstairs, it was the news that her journey, by subterfuge, across three counties, was an unexpected pleasure to anyone. Rising swiftly out of the chair in which he had found her, she said in a rather doubtful way, "Indeed, sir. I don't know that I regard it as altogether a pleasure, but—no matter."

Mr. Dixey's eyes darted across to the window once more. "I assure you, madam, that in this part of the world a visitor is a visitor and as such highly prized. But what is it that I may do for you?"

This, as Mrs. Carstairs silently acknowledged to herself, was very bad. She knew that whatever she believed—and she was not sure exactly what she did believe—about Mr. Dixey and the question of Henry Ireland's will, she could not say it to him outright. The man who meets another man on his doorstep at dead of night with a large sack under his arm does not instantly accuse him of being a burglar. And so it was with Mrs. Carstairs, keenly aware of the expression of curiosity on her host's face but quite unable to frame a satisfactory form of words for her thoughts.

"Mrs. Henry Ireland is your ward, I believe?"

Mr. Dixey looked up very keenly at the window and at the book-cases before answering.

"Mrs. Ireland is indeed my ward. Have you come to enquire after her?"

This, too, was very bad. But Mrs. Carstairs, like her son in the lawyer's office, satisfied that Mr. Dixey could not at any rate eat her, veered off at a tangent.

"We are related to Isabel—to Mrs. Ireland. She is a connection of my late husband. We had heard nothing since"—and here Mrs. Carstairs hesitated— "since those events of which the world knows."

"There has been very little to hear."

There was something in Mr. Dixey's articulation of these words which suggested that this was not a profitable line to pursue. Mrs. Carstairs understood this and marked it, yet at the same time she was not altogether quelled. No doubt the memory of Watton Station and Jorrocks's cart had a little to do with this. Mrs. Carstairs was a prudent woman, but she had been inconvenienced, put out, driven to a stealthiness that did not at all accord with her notion of how the world should operate. Consequently, she determined to say what she had come to say.

"I declare, Mr. Dixey, I do not think that I was ever in such a remote spot in my life. Is Mrs. Ireland here?"

"She is not. If she were, I regret that I could not let you see her. She is . . . deranged."

"Deranged!"

"You will excuse me, but how else would you have me put it? When I last saw her—it was in this very room—she did not recognise me, and she screamed because the girl who brought her wine had mixed too much water in it. Believe me, madam, that you would get no joy from her, nor she from you."

Still Mrs. Carstairs did not altogether quail. She knew that it would be another five hours before she saw her drawing room in Marylebone, knew, too, of the further subterfuges and concealments that would be

D. J. TAYLOR

required of her. Mrs. Carstairs was not afraid of her son, but she knew that were he ever to find out about her excursion to Norfolk, or rather were he to find out about it in circumstances that were not satisfactory to both parties, things would go very ill with her. So, and with the memory of Jorrocks's cart still hanging before her, she resolved to persist.

"Where is she then?"

"I do not know, madam, if even that is a question which I am obliged to answer, but I shall answer it. She is at present in the care of Dr. Conolly. You are familiar with Dr. Conolly's work?"

"I . . . that is, I have heard his name."

"As I say, she is under the care of Dr. Conolly. What would you have me do? You may write a letter, I daresay, but I very much doubt that she could read it. I have no wish to alarm you, but when she was first brought here it was all that we could do to restrain her. Would you wish to write a letter? I assure you that it shall be put into her hands."

There was something altogether reasonable about this, and Mr. Dixey's expression as he stood before the dreary window, against which the rain continued to fall, was one of grave attention. Once again, however, Mrs. Carstairs found herself placed in a quandary. The mystery of Mrs. Ireland's disappearance—to Norfolk, to Dr. Conolly's establishment, to wherever it was that she might be lodged—seemed to her so obviously a mystery that she could not believe that any other person could not imagine it so. And yet Mr. Dixey had greeted her courteously, given civil answers to her questions, done everything, in fact, save produce Mrs. Ireland for her inspection. Still, though, Mrs. Carstairs felt—she did not quite know why, but she felt it nonetheless—that she was being misled.

"But this is all so very mysterious, is it not, Mr. Dixey? You will forgive me for saying so, but there is poor Mr. Ireland dead and his wife not . . . not herself" (even now Mrs. Carstairs did not like to say the word *mad*) "and yet nobody has seen her."

"Mr. Crabbe has seen her. I have seen her. My servants have seen her. Would you wish to question them?"

"And now you say she is in the care of Dr. Conolly. That may be all very well . . ."

"My dear madam"—Mr. Dixey's face as he said this was as genial as Mrs. Carstairs had seen it during the course of their conversation—"I must disagree with you. If there is a mystery, I cannot see it. Henry Ireland was my very great friend. His wife is my ward. She is not of sound mind. That being so, she has been placed in the care of an eminent gentleman who may do her good. I am very sorry indeed that you should have come all this way to learn such a simple truth."

Mrs. Carstairs, hearing this, was conscious that there was not a great deal more to be said. She was conscious, too, of Jorrocks's cart waiting in the lane. And yet she was forced to admit that she had no idea whether she had won a great victory over Mr. Dixey or suffered a great defeat. Sensing this indecision, her host—who did not at any rate carry himself like a man who has suffered a defeat—became anxious to conciliate her. Would she take tea? He would have it brought in at once. Where was she travelling, and how might he assist her? One of his domestics would escort her to the village. Each of these offers Mrs. Carstairs declined, but in doing so she felt that she had conceded another point and that nothing remained for her to do save depart from Mr. Dixey's doorstep. She became aware now that the man was watching her as he stood by the window, not in any obtrusive fashion but in the way that a man gazes at a painting or a horse. There was no harm in Mr. Dixey's glance, but still Mrs. Carstairs felt that she did not like it.

And in the end, it being three o'clock in the afternoon and Mrs. Carstairs ever more conscious of Jorrocks's cart waiting in the lane, they did take tea together: brought in on a tray by the girl who had opened the front door and tasting, Mrs. Carstairs thought, unlike any Bohea she had ever chanced upon. Mr. Dixey drank his sitting down in his chair with the walking stick propped up against his side. A very benign and demure old gentleman he seemed now, as the housemaid attended to the fire and he blew on his tea to cool it.

"You will have to excuse me," he remarked as he performed this act. "The fact is that I have been so long out of society that I am quite unfit for a civilised drawing room."

And so, as will occasionally happen in such circumstances, if only for a brief moment while the tea was drunk and Mrs. Carstairs ate a biscuit, they became almost intimate with each other.

"Dear me," Mrs. Carstairs observed, with her undrinkable tea before her on her lap, "but this is a very lonely spot in which you live."

"Lonely? I suppose it is lonely. At any rate, I find that I can never get anybody to come and stay with me. I congratulate you, madam, on your persistence."

"But you have your studies, I believe? They must take up a deal of your time."

"Oh indeed, madam, a great deal." &c., &c.

Consequently, when Mr. Dixey escorted her to the front door and shook her hand on its sunken step ("I may write, I suppose?" Mrs. Carstairs enquired. "Yes indeed, write by all means," Mr. Dixey assured her), Mrs. Carstairs told herself that it could all have been a great deal worse. She had surprised the lion in his den—quite a benevolent lion, he now seemed—and emerged unscathed. At the same time, Mrs. Carstairs hardly knew whether she had achieved the object she desired. True, she had discovered Mrs. Ireland's whereabouts, or rather she had been told them, and yet hardly one of the mysteries that had attached themselves to her disappearance had been satisfactorily explained to her. Had she in fact done a foolish thing, merely intruded herself onto a situation that would have been better left alone? Mrs. Carstairs was not quite prepared to believe this of herself, but her mood as she traversed the gravel path that led to the dense coppices and woods of Mr. Dixey's estate was by no means sanguine.

It was by now perhaps half past three in the afternoon. The rain had ceased, although black clouds still hung low in the March sky. Retracing her steps across the gravel, with the first great hedges of evergreens rising up on the path on either side of her, Mrs. Carstairs reached a point in the path where a small subsidiary track branched off at a right angle through the trees and, insofar as she could judge, doubled back in the direction of the house. It was then that Mrs. Carstairs did something that, at a time when she could bring herself to think once more of the event, she could not satisfactorily explain. Perhaps it was that in her heart of hearts she did not believe Mr. Dixey, believed, if it came to that, that Mrs. Ireland was living under his roof and could be spied out by subterfuge. Perhaps it was merely that her curiosity was aroused by the great banks of trees and the lonely house behind her,

Kept

the thought that here, enveloping her in its scent, was a place where secrets were kept. Whatever the explanation, Mrs. Carstairs altered her course and set off between the trees and along the side track.

There was not, indeed, a great deal to see. Within a moment or two she came upon a clearing with a melancholy gamekeeper's gibbet, where a couple of shrikes and a weasel hung pinned up and mouldering on the board. It was a desolate spot, and she did not linger. There was a building behind her, she fancied, through the trees which she took to be the laurels she had passed on her incoming journey, but the hedges were grown up so dense that it was impossible for her to grasp her bearings. Mrs. Carstairs had just begun to assure herself that one of the several amenities lacking in the management of Mr. Dixey's estate was a regiment of gardeners, when the tail of her eye registered movement away and to the left behind her. She was now standing at a point in the track where a further subdivision crept away into hidden undergrowths of scrub and bracken. Here, half-concealed by shadow, thirty or even forty yards distant, a grey, long-muzzled creature was moving silently up through the wood. To be sure, Mrs. Carstairs had led what is politely known as a life of genteel seclusion. But its gentility had once admitted a visit to the Regent's Park zoological gardens, and she knew instantly that the creature she now saw before her was a wolf.

As has been said, Mrs. Carstairs was a resourceful woman. What seemed to be no more than a few seconds found her back on the gravel path, in sight of Mr. Dixey's outhouses and his estate cottages, and, in the further distance, Jorrocks's cart dimly visible in the lane. On tottering feet and with her breath coming in great exhalations, Mrs. Carstairs made her way to the lodge gate, ever fearful of what might leap out of the hedge beside her or be heard pursuing her from the rear. But there was nothing there, no living thing except the carter, whom she found hunkered down in the back of his vehicle between the hay bales regarding the world from beneath a piece of sacking. Greatly relieved, Mrs. Carstairs allowed herself to be carried off to Watton. And if his passenger seemed more than usually silent, and inclined to cast the most agitated and imploring glances back along the gloomy road, the carter did not remark it.

Part Two

22 November 1864

A year now past since I commenced my cure. The people civil and God-fearing yet, me judice, *credulous. Viz a woman dying this last week in Watton discovered to have carried on her abdomen a tumour weighing eleven pounds, shunned by her neighbours as* "the devil's mare." *I had this story from Mr. Stanhope, the surgeon. In truth, the winter evenings wear heavy on me. The tapers are brought in at four. Beyond that, all is dark and silence. Resolved to continue with my* Defence of Episcopacy, wh. *shall be my salvation.*

* * *

13 December 1864

A curious conversation with my parishioner, Mr. Dixey, whom I chanced upon in the churchyard roaming—there is no other word— among the graves. He began by enquiring, did I believe that madness was an affliction sent by God? I answered that all afflictions came from God, and all blessings too. Man could only endure the one as he embraced the other. Mr. Dixey admitted the justice of this. He then demanded, if madness were divinely ordained, did it then have supernal sanction? Thus, were an attempt to cure it not simple blasphemy? Again, I replied that God's purpose was necessarily beyond us, yet we had our Christian duty, that Our Lord himself had healed he who spoke in tongues. He seemed satisfied by this and shook my hand very warmly.

* * *

29 December 1864

Met Mr. Dixey in the fields walking with a pair of hunting dogs. On my remarking their great size and singularity—for I had seen nothing like them before—he declared that he bred them himself and that some people *would wonder at their parentage. The foregoing said with a very marked emphasis. . . . Later, a brace of pheasants sent up from the Hall. This, I fear, will please my landlady more than it pleases me.*

* * *

5 January 1865

Dixey calls. He seems eager for my company. He enquired, had I read Mr. Gosse's book Omphalos, *whose reconciliation of natural science and divine purpose seemed to him most ingenious? I replied that I had not, indeed that I made it my business to avoid such things, a* reconciliation *in matters spiritual being tantamount to a* capitulation. *Dixey most pressing, however, undertook to procure me a copy, or even to lend his own.*

[Later. The Gosse, as I suspected, arrant blasphemy. Viz. that if we accept the fact of absolute Creation, God becomes a Deus que *deceptus. It is not my reason but my* conscience *which revolts me. . . . Nevertheless, wrote a note to Dixey thanking him for his kindness.]*

* * *

22 January 1865

Met at my gate by Dixey's tall footman, very civil, with a cockade in his hat, bearing an invitation to dine. Mrs. Forester, my landlady, much impressed: "There's rarely company up at the Hall." Knowing my friend's solitary habits, I had supposed that we should dine alone. In fact a third gentleman was present, Mr. Conolly, the celebrated mad-doctor, late of Hanwell Asylum, whom I was interested to see. Much talk about the American war, condition of the Southern Negroes, &c. Conolly a well-conducted fellow, sober in his cups. Dixey offered me his carriage. It being a moonlit night, and wanting distraction, I purposed to walk. Dixey keeps some creature confined in his park. At least, passing a timber fence on the edge of the estate, I became aware of movement behind it and, I am ashamed to say, quickened my step not a little.

14 February 1865

No word from Dixey. A copy of this month's Cornhill *containing an article by Mr. Gosse that I had sent up to the Hall unacknowledged.*

* * *

27 February 1865

The days lengthening. I continue to work at my Defence. *No word from Dixey.*

* * *

11 March 1865

No word from Dixey.

D. J. TAYLOR

ESTHER'S STORY CONTINUED

(III)

Later Esther would remember her time at Easton Hall as being hedged about by numbers.

Fifty-six was the extent of the pieces of cutlery in the great mahogany canteen kept upon the sideboard in the dining room. Viz.: a dozen bone-handled knives, curved like scimitars and rising to sharp points at their ends; a dozen ancient two-pronged forks of a kind she had never glimpsed before; a dozen soupspoons with the Dixey crest engraved upon their backs; a dozen dessert spoons so small that you could lose one in the folds of a dishcloth and spend an hour searching for it; a half-dozen serving spoons, a great carving knife and fork full eighteen inches long. These must be cleaned each week with knife powder and polished with an apron end, for if the master found that one was not to his liking he would send it back.

Seventeen was the number of keys that hung from the brass ring in Mr. Randall's pantry. A key for the front door; a key for the back. A key for the pantry itself, and a key for Mrs. Finnie's storeroom. A key for the wine cellar and a key for the dairy. A key for the strongbox that lay in the master's study and contained the title deeds to the house. Keys for the laundry cupboard and the two glass-fronted bookcases in the drawing room and the box in the pantry where Mr. Randall kept his religious books and his copies of the *Missioner's Gazette*. A key for the lid of the drawing-room piano. A key for the empty parrot cage that hung in the hall. A key for the cover of Mr. Dixcy's field glasses, and a key for the cover of the great family Bible. A butterfly key for the grandfather clock in the hall. And a final key, of which no one, not Mr. Randall, not the master, not anyone else in the household seemed to know the use.

Twelve was the number of copper saucepans that hung on great hooks from the scullery wall. A great boiling cauldron in which Mrs. Wates made preserves. Nine for the cooking of vegetables, steak puddings and the like. Two for the boiling of milk. These must be scoured on the inside and burnished on the outside until their surfaces glowed, for a dull saucepan was ill luck to a kitchen and those that worked in it, Mrs. Wates said.

Nine was the number of engravings, each a foot square, that hung on the wall of the servants' hall. They showed ladies in voluminous dresses with their hair *à l'impératrice* and gentlemen with periwigs and knee breeches and square-buckled shoes, the ladies riding sidesaddle on great horses or being handed down from their carriages; the gentlemen walking together with their dogs or engaged about their occupations. And Esther wondered at them: in what century they lived, and how their hair was kept in such a way; and what the gentlemen talked about, their right hands kept carefully on their sword hilts, their square toes pointed neatly before them.

Six (this information came from Sarah) was the number of kitchenmaids that had come and gone during Mrs. Wates's time as cook at the Hall, having excited that lady's displeasure.

(IV)

The thing that Esther fancied above all that she would find in the country proved not to be there. That thing was silence. Easton Hall was a house filled with noise. The wind blew against the windowpanes. The carriage horses stamped their feet upon the gravel. A woman's voice laughed somewhere in a room far off. At night came ominous creakings and patterings and the sound of trees blown against each other in the wood beyond. With the noise, though not always a part of it, came movement: a fox stealing away from the corner of the kitchen garden in the half hour after dawn; a stoat bounding across the path at her feet as she walked with Sarah in the orchard; the rooks soaring above the elms. Amidst the noise and the movement lay things that were silent and solitary: a kitchen drawer pulled open to reveal a nest of squirming field mice; an earthenware

D. J. TAYLOR

pot a thousand years old and a handful of silver coins dug up by one of Mr. Dixey's men in a ditch; a signet ring glimpsed between the flagstones of the kitchen floor and brought winking into the light. Once, on a grey afternoon when Mrs. Wates and Mrs. Finnie were in Watton and Mr. Randall sat asleep in the pantry chair, Sarah took her to a room under the roof where there was a trunk full of high-waisted dresses with hooped skirts and tiny slippers that might have been worn by Cinderella.

"What are these?" Esther wondered, running the faded paduasoy and the rags of taffeta through her hands.

"Why, they are dresses great ladies wore. A hundred years or more since, I should say, that the mice have eaten. Did you ever see such things?"

"And what is this? It looks like the stuffing of a horsehair sofa."

"I believe it is a wig!"

Doubtfully—for it seemed to her that they were certain to be spied upon and rebuked—Esther allowed the ruin of false hair to be smoothed down over her head. It smelled of dust and decay.

"There! You see. You look like a duchess."

"I look very foolish, I am sure," Esther replied. Nonetheless, she was not displeased. They spent an hour trying on first one dress and then another, walking up and down the room and bowing to each other as they passed.

"What would Mrs. Wates say, I wonder, if we came down to supper wearing these dresses?" Sarah said.

"We should lose our places, I am sure we should," Esther said. "Listen! That is the church clock. It is five already."

And so the dresses were folded up and put back into the box.

(v)

"Hollo, Esther, is that you? It seems an age since we ran into one another."

Esther, on her way from the back lawn to the kitchen, her hands clasped around a bundle of folded washing, a heap of clothes pegs balanced upon the top, regarded William neutrally.

"An age you say?" She made to edge past him through the open door, but he lounged before it, one hand plunged into his trouser pocket, the other stretched out to halt her progress.

"Do stop now, do. There is something I badly want to ask you."

Esther looked carefully around her. It was four o'clock on an autumn afternoon with the light beginning to fade above the peaks of the elm trees and a damp chill, a chill that seemed to come from the very depths of the earth beneath it, pervading the air. There was no one about, either in the kitchen or in the servants' hall beyond. Cautiously, she placed the washing basket on the step at her feet.

"What is it then?"

In the time since Esther's arrival at Easton Hall she had learned a great deal. Nothing very much, perhaps, in point of view of the world and the manner of its working, but in her own private imaginings a great deal. Under Mrs. Wates's direction she had learned how to make quince jelly and construct a hollandaise sauce ("That is a sure sign that she likes you," Sarah had admiringly explained. "Usually she is afeared that the kitchenmaid is after her place.") She had also, through chance remarks let fall at the supper table and in the servants' hall, heard something of her employer's circumstances. The Dixeys were an old Norfolk family, it appeared, of immense antiquity—so old that they might have come over with William the Conqueror or have even regarded that gentleman as a usurper. A Dixey, it was said, had been barber-surgeon to the Confessor and perished at Hastings. Their good fortune, unhappily, had not endured so long. There had been a great many Dixeys—lord lieutenants, Cinque Port wardens and ladies of the bedchamber—and now there was only one. Thirty years or more ago a Dixey had fought a lawsuit against a neighbour, a lawsuit which, beginning in a quarrel over a covert, extended into every avenue that the law allows, fought it tenaciously and with no regard to expense, fought it and . . . lost. Another Dixey, a cousin of the litigant, had spent ever so many thousands of pounds opening up a mine in Cornwall which was found, at the conclusion of this labour, to contain nothing but water. And so thirty years later the fruit lay and rotted under Mr. Dixey's apple trees, and the farmers of

D. J. TAYLOR

the district came over his fields to shoot such pheasants as lingered there on the excellent grounds that he did not preserve.

The late afternoon sun was receding in flames above the elm wood. Somewhere in the distance a dog barked. Across the horizon, where the wood descended into fields of scrub and pasture, a wagon came trundling along the rutted path, and Esther watched a ray of sunlight catch off the carter's whip. Caught up in this picture, her gaze ranging far beyond the tall figure poised at her side, conscious of the pressure of his hand on her arm, she allowed a sharper note to come into her voice than she intended.

"What is it then?" she repeated.

"Gracious, Esther, you will bite a man's head off. It is just that we seem to have got out of the habit of talking to each other. Well then, there is a subscription dance at the hall in Watton next Saturday and a party being got up to attend. Do say you'll come."

"A dance?"

"In aid of the Volunteers, or some such. With a buffy and a string band promised. The master is a patron of the Volunteers, you know, so it's all regular and aboveboard. Even old Randall don't mind a dance, for all that he's such a down on folk enjoying themselves, and we are to have a wagon to go in. Come now, what do you say?"

Immediately there flew into Esther's head a vision, or rather several visions: of a dress, as yet unbought, in red merino and a pair of soft slippers rather than the boots she customarily wore; of gentlemen in stiff black coats standing up to dance. At the same time, there came a sensation of horrible uncertainty. Still she continued to stare into the further distance, where great streaks of sunlight lay in bars across the indigo of the sky. The carter and his wagon had all but reached the line of the horizon. Soon they would disappear.

"Come, Esther, say you will. It will make a change from sitting in the back kitchen listening to a sermon."

Looking at him as he pronounced these words, still leaning negligently against the door frame but with his hand now detached from her sleeve, Esther acknowledged that she was grateful for the offer. Easton Hall she had quickly divined to be a solitary house. Mr. Dixey himself she could not claim to have seen more than a dozen times. Visitors there were, but of a peculiar kind: a pair of rough-looking men, once, who were closeted with the master in his study; an old gentleman in black whom Mr. Randall bowed to as "Mr. Crabbe" and who might, she thought, have been a doctor or a lawyer. Mrs. Wates pined over her receipts for French sauces and sugared creams, for, as she put it, "If there is to be no entertaining, what is the point of anything?" Neither, it transpired, was the Hall a place where the servants were accustomed to fraternise. "Indeed," as Sarah tartly remarked, "I daresay it will take an earthquake before anyone talks to his neighbour at supper." Mr. Randall was cut off from the others by virtue of his religion; he could be seen each Sabbath forenoon walking demurely to his chapel in drab garments appropriate to the day. Margaret Lane occupied her spare time in cutting out pictures of great ladies from the illustrated papers and pasting them into an album. Only with Sarah, consequently, did Esther believe that she had established something amounting to friendship.

Once, at a time when the master was away and things grown slack, they had contrived to conjoin their free afternoon. They had wandered into Easton, patronised the village's solitary shop and taken tea in the parlour of the inn. Later they had stolen up the great staircase, turned along a corridor and stood on the threshold of the master's study regarding the stuffed bear and the great display cases whose polished surfaces gleamed through the dusk. This, Esther thought, had been a very pleasant time. And yet even Sarah's friendship came at a price. There were evenings in the tiny attic when she flung her face beneath the coverlet as soon as the candle was extinguished with a declaration that she didn't "care to talk." Thinking that she knew the source of Sarah's melancholy, Esther decided to widen her attack.

"I think you will find Sarah in the drawing room."

"Now that's underhand of you, Esther, I declare it is. You know there's nothing between Sarah and me. Now, say you will come to the dance."

From within the kitchen there came a sound of heavy but haphazard footsteps, which signalled that Mrs. Wates had arrived to commence

D. J. TAYLOR

her preparations for supper. Esther retrieved her washing basket from the step and began to count up the pegs.

"Very well then."

"Now, Esther," came Mrs. Wates's mournful voice from inside the house. "Half past four and not a morsel ready for tea. You had better look sharp, my girl."

And Esther looked.

(VI)

One raw November morning, when a fine dusting of hoarfrost lay upon the stable roofs, Esther looked up from her work and found Sarah standing silently before her.

"Esther! Sam Postman has brought me a letter!"

"Has he now?"

Esther put down her paring knife, washed her fingers in the bowl of chilly water and wiped them on her sacking apron. She was tired, having been up at six to light the drawing-room fire and sweep the hall, Margaret, whose duties these were, being confined to bed with a quinsy. Nevertheless, she regarded her friend with interest.

"Who is it from?"

"I—that is to say . . ." Sarah hung her head. "Would you do me a great kindness, Esther, and read it for me?"

"We had better go into the drawing room, where there is a light. Is the master at home?"

"No, no. He has gone out with William in the dogcart."

The letter lay unopened in its stout white casing. Reaching the drawing room, where the fire she had laid five hours before blazed cheerfully, Esther busied herself with the paper knife.

"Who is it then?" Sarah wondered in a paroxysm of nervousness. "It cannot be from Joe, for I know his hand. Oh do tell me, Esther!"

Esther scanned the single piece of foolscap beneath the glare of the gas lamp. Written in the flowing copperplate of an official hand, it begged to inform Miss Sarah Parker that her brother, Lance-Corporal

Joseph Parker of the ———th Regiment, had died at Canton on the twenty-ninth of August, of enteric fever, that the Secretary of the Army Office had heard of this sad fact with regret, as he was sure would Miss Parker, &c., &c.

"Oh, Esther," Sarah said. "It is bad news about Joe, I know it is. He is dead in battle or crushed by an elephant, I know it."

For some reason that she could not fathom, Esther hesitated.

"No, he is not dead. But he has been injured."

"Thank God for that. Poor Joe. Poor boy. But what else does it say?"

"Only that he is recovering, though not fit to write himself. That is why you have been sent this letter."

"I see. Thank you, Esther."

When she had gone, Esther sat and looked at the letter, which in her excitement Sarah had forgotten to take with her. The words burnt into her brain. She could not imagine why she had done this thing, other than that in doing so she hoped to spare her friend pain. But what should she say if another letter came, or, worse, no letter at all? Her mind could frame no answer. She sat brooding in an armchair for a long while, as the wind rattled the panes in their sockets and the ivy beat upon the glass, until William, coming into the room with a sherry decanter and a tray of glasses, found her there staring into the depths of the fire.

"Here, Esther," he said, "this won't do. The master will be back in a moment. Besides, Mrs. Wates is wondering where you are."

Esther made to rise up from the chair, taking care to conceal the letter in the folds of her dress. William stared at her keenly.

"Is there anything the matter, Esther? You look as if you had seen a ghost."

Esther shook her head. Silently, she allowed herself to be escorted back to the kitchen and the righteous wrath of Mrs. Wates. "Well," that lady remarked, "I never knew such girls as there is these days. There is Margaret Lane ill in bed and the doctor to be sent for and Her Ladyship here taking her ease in the drawing room by all accounts." Knowing that there was little point in defending herself, Esther merely bobbed her head and retired to the scullery, where last night's crockery

{ 124 }   D. J. TAYLOR

lay in an accusing pile. Not, however, before she had crushed the letter into a tiny ball and cast it into the depths of the kitchen fire.

(VII)

Winter came early to this bleak hinterland. Each morning Esther awoke to find a thin blanket of mist extending beyond her window to the tops of the trees. Laying the fire in the kitchen grate, her hands grew stiff with cold. Once, while she was hanging washing to dry, a gust of air plucked a kerchief from her fingers and sent it flying fifty feet above her. The wind blew down from Jutland, Mr. Randall said, and there were no mountains to take the edge off its chill; certainly not the fields of the West Norfolk plain, full half of which lay below the level of the sea. Though the house was perched on a hill, their lives seemed governed by water. Moisture dripped ceaselessly off the gables of the house. Fish and elvers, caught in the great dykes to the west, were brought up for them to eat. The pond beyond the kitchen garden swelled to such a size that it was no longer safe for the keeper's children to splash through it in their long boots. It would be a hard winter, Mr. Randall said, for the rain presaged it. A travelling packman, speaking a dialect that could scarcely be understood, came and spread his wares on the kitchen table: handfuls of pins, green and yellow embroidery thread, an illustrated Bible over whose garish leaves Mr. Randall shook his head (here Jonah clamoured vainly from the whale's mouth, and the sun smote off Abraham's dagger as he bent to murder his son). It was but blasphemy, Mr. Randall said, to treat the Lord's devisings in this way. "Ef'n' your honour says," the packman demurred, "and yet them gays is onnerful instructive. Look, there's the Devil a-temptin' of Ave, and Balaam's dicker a crunching of his master's fut." The maids bought cotton reels and ivory combs, and Mrs. Wates, as a preventative against indigestion, a tincture of peppermint oil that smelled suspiciously of gin.

In the evenings the old people sat by the fire in the servants' hall and talked of past times.

Mrs. Finnie said: "When I was a girl I was kitchenmaid to Lady Ardley. This was in King William's time, you understand. Half a dozen footmen, and venison sent up each day from the estate. But gentlefolk were gentlefolk in those days. It is all very different now."

Mrs. Wates said: "In my young days a girl that went into service wouldn't think to get wages. No indeed. Her father would pay money himself for the comfort of knowing she was well apprenticed. There was a nursemaid at my first situation who had been with the family sixty years and remembered seeing the German king in his coach."

Mr. Randall said: "My father was pantryman to a duke, and that is the truth. But I thought I could do better, fool that I was. I was apprenticed to a seedsman in Waterloo year, set up my own shop and failed. Times were hard in those days. Many's the day I worked eight hours for a plate of bread and cheese and been thankful for God's good mercy that I should get it."

After this all the old people felt better. And Esther, sitting silently on the great window seat with only her face palely visible in the shadow, thanked providence that she lived in an age of railways, Miss Nightingale, Viscount Palmerston and Lord John.

Once, as they sat in the inglenook of the kitchen fireplace, Sarah said, "Did you ever think, Esther, that you should wish to be married?"

"It is what every girl wishes, I suppose."

"I used to wish it. More than anything." Esther noticed that Sarah's fingers gripped white on the flat stone as she said this. "But now I think I shall be a companion or a cook. Indeed I shall have the best of both worlds, for cooks are Mrs. by courtesy, you know."

"I should not care to spend all my life in service, I think," Esther said seriously.

"And yet you may do so and not like it."

Remembering the crushed ball of paper in the kitchen fire, Esther said nothing.

It would be a hard winter, Mr. Randall said.

(VIII)

Only once in these first months did Esther see her employer for any length of time. One autumn afternoon as the twilight fell over

D. J. TAYLOR

the wood, she was standing in her scullery with her hands plunged in a basin of dirty water when she heard Mr. Randall's voice in the hall. Seeing her through the open door, he came rapidly into the room, clasping and unclasping his hands as he walked.

"Esther, is that you? Where are Sarah and Margaret?"

"It is Sarah's afternoon off, Mr. Randall. The last I saw of Margaret Lane she was at the linen cupboard with Mrs. Finnie."

"Well, it cannot be helped. You had better bring a brush and pan and come with me now."

Wondering at his agitation, Esther supplied herself with these items and followed the butler up the great staircase and along the corridor where she knew lay the master's study. Halfway through its half-open door, Mr. Randall stopped and addressed her nervously.

"There has been an accident. A great deal of smashed glass. You must take care, Esther." And then, raising his voice as they came into the room: "Here is Esther, sir, who can help set things to rights."

Standing in the doorway, Esther saw immediately what had happened. A display case resting on one of the brass cabinets had become dislodged and crashed to the floor. Pieces of broken glass lay everywhere about with, here and there, the stuffed birds that the case had contained. Mr. Dixey stood a little way off with his back to the window. When he saw her he said, "You must take great care. Randall, we shall need a broom. You had better fetch one."

Esther remarked the irritation in his voice, which seemed to her disproportionate to a shattered display case and half a dozen stuffed birds. Instinctively, she dropped to her knees and began to gather up the glass. She did not care to touch the birds but swept round them.

Mr. Dixey noticed her reluctance. "You should not be afraid of a dead bird. Look here!"

He laid one of the feathery bundles in his palm for her to inspect.

Esther thought that his voice croaked and was reminded of the rooks in the elm trees. Thinking that something was expected of her, she said: "Which kind of bird is it, sir?"

"What kind?" Mr. Dixey seemed surprised. "Why, it is a ruff. See the feathers bunched at the neck. Like a gentleman in an old painting.

And this"—he indicated a tiny orange corpse a yard away—"is *Upupa epops*. It is rare in these parts."

He looked as if he wished to say something more, but the sound of Mr. Randall returning with the broom drove him to silence.

The glass was swept up and the cabinet taken downstairs to await the summoning of the carpenter.

"Ugh! A nasty thing to have to do," Sarah remarked, when the incident was reported to her. "Gentlemen should not keep such things. I hope you told Mr. Randall so."

Esther said nothing.

(IX)

Sarah," Esther began, "who is the woman in the upstairs room?"

"I do declare, Esther, you say the strangest things. Which woman?"

"The woman who sits in the attic and has her food taken up to her."

"Really, Esther, I shall think you are making fun of me, indeed I shall."

They were sitting on the oak bench in the orchard, well wrapped up in their shawls against the wind and with pattens on their feet, for it was an afternoon in late November. Mist hung over the distant fields and the church tower, and the grass was wet underfoot.

Sarah looked hurriedly back in the direction of the house. "Look, here is that Margaret Lane come to find us." She rose to her feet. "Poor Margaret. You know she has been making sheep's eyes at Sam Postman, and him spoken for these two years since?"

Esther followed her glance but could detect no sign of Margaret. The kitchen garden and the patch of land that abutted the rear of the house were quite empty. Seeing no reason to move, she sat still on the bench and began to retie the strings of her bonnet.

"No, it is quite true. Last Tuesday I was coming through the front hall after I had been to help Margaret Lane move the table in the drawing room, as I was bidden by Mrs. Wates, and I saw Mr. Randall going up the back stairs with a tray with a lunch plate on it and a jug of water."

"Really, Esther!"

"And then an hour or more later I happened to be passing back through the hall—it was you I was coming to find, I recollect—when I saw William coming down the stairs with the tray and the plate and the jug empty."

"Why, Esther, what a goose you are! Hasn't Mrs. Finnie been ill all week in bed and Mr. Randall taking up her meals?"

"Yes, but I remarked Mr. Randall as he climbed the stairs. When he reached the top, he turned not to the right, where the servants' rooms are, but to the left. The west wing where nobody lives."

"Well, if nobody lives there, how can there be a woman that never comes out?"

"And then again the other day I was walking around the eastern side of the house to take a message from Mr. Randall to the keeper when something caught my eye and I looked up towards the rooftops, and there was a woman's face at the window. And yet when I came back five minutes later it was gone."

"Or had never existed at all. I am surprised at you, Esther. How could a woman live in a house and nobody know?"

"Mr. Randall must know. And William. And Mrs. Wates, for it is she that prepares the food."

"Well, you had better ask them then. Now, look, there is that Margaret Lane by the kitchen gate, really it is. And if you'll take my advice, Esther"—and here Sarah gave a sharp look of a kind that Esther never remembered seeing in her face before—"you will forget about women in rooms and William with a tray, for it is an absurd fancy and will do you no good."

(x)

U pon my honour, Esther, you are looking uncommon fresh in that bonnet and dress!"

Esther pursed her lips but said nothing. Privately, having inspected herself in the mirror that hung in the servants' hall before they set out, she agreed with William's judgement. The dress, produced by Mrs. Finnie out of an ancient cupboard, was not new, but it had been worked up to look as if it might be; the bonnet had been similarly refurbished.

"I declare that when I saw you and Sarah Parker sat next to each other, I thought she looked a dowdy thing beside you, indeed I did."

With this, too, Esther privately agreed, though she thought it unkind of William to say as much. Lifting her head from where it had been sunk in reflection on her breastbone, she said, "It is very ill-natured of you to say that of Sarah."

"Oh, I meant nothing by it. You mustn't have a down upon a fellow, Esther, because he speaks his mind."

The wagonette having deposited them at the end of Watton High Street, they were proceeding along that thoroughfare to the rooms where the subscription dance was to be held. It was about eight o'clock on a Saturday night, and many of the shops were still open. A grocer's window passed before her eye, lit by a flaring gas jet. Many of them, Esther knew, would not shut their doors until midnight in the hope of an order from one of the big houses in the district. Behind them, but some way further down the street, walked Sarah and Margaret Lane, together with Mrs. Wates, who had come, as she said, "to see fair play" and might, it was thought, stand up with a butler from one of the neighbouring establishments if such could be found.

"Now, Esther," William said again, "you are going to dance yourself, I hope. I can't abide those girls who sits in the corner and drinks negus and blushes whenever anyone comes near them."

Esther smiled an answer, but in truth she was somewhat perplexed about the evening that lay before her. She could dance, after a fashion, yet she feared to make herself conspicuous. At the Hall, prior to the party's departure and in celebration of it, she had been induced to drink a glass of wine, the first she had ever taken. This, too, had contributed to the expectant but vaguely troubled manner in which she regarded the world. Abruptly, she looked back to where Sarah and Margaret came trailing behind her, wondering whom they would find to dance with. She would dance with William, that much was certain, who had sworn to escort and protect her for as long as the evening continued.

At the end of the high street, where the road bent round towards the churchyard and the almshouses, they came to their place of entertainment. Here lights blazed in the windows, and a noise of music and resonating feet could be heard from within. A knot of idlers standing at the roadside regarded them incuriously. "There's a nice-looking girl," Esther heard a man say to his fellow as they passed in through the gilt swing doors. Pleased at this acknowledgement, which she knew must refer to her, Sarah and Margaret still being some way behind her, she quickened her pace and arrived, more rapidly than she had intended, in a vestibule full of girls and women divesting themselves of cloaks and hoods. Within she glimpsed a room whose atmosphere, allowing for certain incidental changes, was familiar to her from her girlhood.

At its further end, adjacent to a roaring log-fire, a banner proclaiming the Volunteer Movement had been ceremoniously unfurled and leant against the wall next to a table on which rested a framed daguerreotype of Her Majesty. On a raised dais by the near side, variously disposed in cane-backed chairs, three rustic musicians sat over a fiddle, a bass viol and a little drum. Through an archway on the further side could be seen a circular buffet and a trestle topped with a cloth at which waiters in white jackets presided over an urn and a tray of punch glasses. Of the persons in these two rooms, whose number amounted to perhaps four dozen, Esther calculated that she knew nearly half by sight: tradesmen from Watton and their wives, a squire or two standing talking at the bar, other servants from the neighbouring houses. Correct ideas of female evening wear being no means standardised in the locality, she marvelled at the varieties of apparel on display. Some of the servant girls had merely put on their best pinafores and caps. One girl wore her grandmother's wedding dress. A plethora of improvised black gowns testified to the ingenuity of the local seamstresses. Looking at the crowd, as the fiddler struck up his tune and the men at the bar glanced up hastily into the other room, Esther felt a sudden satisfaction at the nature of the thing and her place within it. The others had come up by this time, and they stood in the doorway exclaiming at the room and its decorations.

"Now, Esther," William began, but she shook her head. She would not dance yet. Instead she walked with Sarah to the end of the hall, stepping over the feet of those dancers who strayed too far from the circle, and admired the banner, alive as she did so to the spectacle around her.

Margaret Lane was sulking, Sam Postman having arrived with his intended, a large young woman in a canary-yellow dress who clung to his arm with such vigour that he cried out, "Mary! 'Tis all very well to hold on to me, mawther, but I can scarce move with your clinging!"

It occurred to Esther that she ought to say something good-natured to Margaret Lane, so she caught hold of her hand and remarked, "Why, Margaret, how nice you look in your dress."

Margaret's small pinched face broke out into a smile. "Why, you are a good sort to say so, Esther. It is my mother's dress, that she gave me when I went into service."

There were several young men standing around the buffet, grooms from the gentlemen's houses and the like, who asked Esther if she would dance, but she shook her head. There was an exhilaration within her that made her quite content to stand here in sight of the white-coated waiters and the buzz of the other room, waiting for such time as William should come to claim her. Sarah, approaching through the crowd with her game leg dragging a little, stopped when she saw her and gave an inquisitive look.

"Why, Esther, are you not dancing?"

"I am waiting—that is," Esther said hurriedly, "nobody has asked me yet. But what is the matter, Sarah?"

"Oh, it is nothing. It is only that there is that goose Margaret Lane quaking in her shoes because Sam Postman's young woman shook her fist at her and called her a hussy. But look, here is William come to fetch us."

Plunging through the buffet room, full half a foot taller than the men on either side of him, William assumed an air of conspicuous gallantry. Seeing Esther, he brought his heels sharply together and bowed. There was a waltz beginning. Would she waltz? Esther did not waltz, but she consented to be brought a glass of lemonade and admire the fierce look and the sharp rebuke that William directed at a man who knocked into her as she bent to receive it. However, William's good humour was not abated. This was capital lemonade, but would she try something stronger? Esther would not, but she listened to William's account of the wine's inferiority to that served at the Hall with interest.

"The master may be an old screw," William declared, "but there is

D. J. TAYLOR

no wine in the county like that served at the Hall, old Randall says, and he should know."

The memory of her conversation with Sarah strode into Esther's imaginings, and she glanced up shrewdly at him.

"William. If I ask you a question, will you answer it?"

"If it's in my power to do so, Esther, I shall. Fire away."

"Who is the woman in the upstairs room?"

William laughed. "Why you are a-hoaxing me, Esther. Which woman in the upstairs room?"

"The one that has her meals taken up to her. That you bring down."

"Now see here, Esther. This is some stick you have the wrong end of, I can tell."

"No, I have seen her. A woman sitting at a window. Dark-haired and with a staring face. *I have seen her.*"

Esther realised that in repeating these words she had raised her voice above the ordinary level of conversation in the room and that one or two people were looking curiously at her.

"You'd best be quiet," William said, almost roughly. "Indeed you had, Esther, and not mind things that don't concern you. What would the master say if he knew his affairs were being talked of in Watton High Street?"

"Then there is a woman?"

"There is nothing. Nothing and no one. As to the tray, you must have seen me coming from Mrs. Finnie's room."

"But Mrs. Finnie does not live in the west wing. Besides . . ."

"Besides what, Esther?"

"The other morning when Sam Postman knocked on the door and gave Mr. Randall the letters, he was called away sudden and left them on a tray, and I looked at them." Esther did not say that her principal object had been to spy out any further communications regarding Sarah's brother. "Who is Mrs. Ireland?"

William's eyes, Esther saw, were smarting with anger. "The last cook had that name."

"And Mrs. Wates in her place these ten years past. I think you must take me for a fool, William Latch."

Kept

There was a sudden skirl of music from the room beyond and a whoop of laughter as a fat woman in a pink dress tumbled over, bringing her partner with her. William glanced nervously over his shoulder.

"Now see here, Esther, you're not being fair to me. I came here to dance with you, truly I did, not to have you asking me questions that you should know better than to think of. A fellow should be better treated, I tell you."

Esther found that words altogether failed her. A part of her wished to dance with William, to be carried up in his arms and borne away past the admiring glances of the people around them. Yet another part of her resented what she saw as his dissimulation, the keeping of a secret that she could only guess at. Crossly she said, "If you've a mind to dance you had better ask Sarah. When I last saw her, she was warming herself at the fire."

Without answering, William turned on his heel. Esther watched him go. In his absence she was quite at a loss as to what she should do. The people standing next to her at the refreshment tables, seeing that she had had some disagreement with the tall footman, regarded her sympathetically, but she would not meet their glances. There was a window at the back of the room over which the shutters had not been drawn, and she moved instinctively towards it, arms folded before her, and looked out absently into the little street, down which occasional groups of revellers bound for the ball came moving swiftly, and at a great gibbous moon which lay above it, irradiating the fronts of the houses and the shop windows with eerie red light. How long she remained in this attitude, oblivious to the noisy traffic of the buffet, she did not know—it might have been ten minutes or even twenty—only that it was a period of time brought to an end by a vague awareness that the music in the ballroom had descended first into raggedness and then into silence, that this descent had been punctuated by a scream, or rather a series of screams, and that someone had come running towards her through the crowd and begun to shake her by the shoulder. Gradually, the trancelike state into which she had subsided began to pass, and she saw that the person before her was Margaret Lane.

D. J. TAYLOR

"Oh, Esther! You must come quickly! Sarah has had a dreadful accident."

Scarcely hearing her words, but knowing only that she must do as she was bidden, Esther ran before her into the ballroom. Such was the speed of her entrance that what she saw presented itself to her eyes in a series of fragments: one of the musicians, rising from his chair with his bass viol clutched under his arm; a look of alarm in the face of a young girl standing with her hands held up to her chin; a gentleman in a shooting jacket and long stockings saying something behind his hand to a waiter; and beyond them all, at the very end of the room, a yard or two from the glowing fire, a group of people bent over a recumbent figure that lay awkwardly across the floor with one arm over its face and did not move.

"She was a-dancing with William," Margaret stuttered, "a-dancing of a polka, and then her leg seemed to give way beneath her and she pitched forward into the fire."

The Easton Hall servants knelt or stood at Sarah's side. William, Esther saw, had positioned himself a yard or so beyond them and, very white-faced and sober, was staring at the tips of his boots. A medical man in a black coat, in fact the doctor who attended the Volunteers, was examining Sarah's hand and forearm across which ran a deep scorch mark. Sarah herself had fallen into a dead faint.

"A terrible thing to have happened," a man standing nearby and wearing the scarlet sash of the Volunteers remarked to William. "There ought to be a rail before the fire to prevent such accidents."

Mrs. Wates pulled herself to her feet from where she had been squatting at Sarah's side. "Accident," she said. "You may call it an accident, I suppose, with him a-taunting of her and calling her names. I heered him do it, indeed I did, let him deny it if he will. It's my belief that she threw herself in the fire a purpose."

"It's a lie!" William exclaimed, still not lifting his eyes from the tips of his boots but with his face flushing scarlet. "I won't stand here, Mrs. Wates, and have you say such things about me. The master shall hear of it, indeed he shall."

"The master shall hear of a good many things," Mrs. Wates briskly retorted.

Kept

By this time quite a group of men had gathered around the fire-place, several of them regarding William with looks of hostility. The medical man, feeling now for the pulse on Sarah's forehead, said, "This is all very well, but the girl must be taken home. She isn't badly injured, I daresay, but the shock has to be considered. Someone had better get a stretcher."

"I tell you, it's a d——d lie," William said again, "and anyone who says otherwise had better tell me to my face."

"I'll tell you," Mrs. Wates said. "And the master, too. But we had better do what the gentleman says. Look, the girl's stirring. Take a hand, will you, Margaret Lane. Esther! Go to the wagon and ask the man to drive up to the door."

With some difficulty, for her legs dragged heavily beneath her, they brought Sarah to her feet and half propelled, half carried her to the vestibule. Turning around to look for William, Esther saw that he had disappeared. Hastening back along the street as Mrs. Wates had directed, she found the wagon driver and his cart and explained the situation to him. A quarter of an hour found them trundling back in the rickety hold through the pitch-dark, silent back route. Lying next to her in a resting place improvised out of shawls and travelling blankets, with her arm done up in a sling, Sarah cried quietly to herself.

"Oh, Esther," she said once. "I've gone and brought him into trouble, isn't that it?"

"No one has brought him into trouble but himself, I think," Esther replied. Nonetheless, she was conscious of a great disappointment, of some scheme in her life, momentarily grasped at but unfulfilled. How splendid it would have been, she thought, if she and William could have danced together in the brightly lit room before the crowd of ball goers. Calling the scene into her mind for a moment, she remembered a particular air that had caught her fancy and softly hummed it under her breath. The wagon trundled on. From time to time, when they moved out of the avenues of trees and hedgerows to a crossroads where the moonlight fell directly onto the path, she peered into the gloaming, searching for the sight of a tall figure plodding in the wagon's rear, but there was nothing there, only the black trail of the trees and the mist rolling in across the distant fields. A church clock struck the hour,

D. J. TAYLOR

the wheels creaked beneath them, the carter coughed stertorously into the dark, and by degrees they made their way home.

(xi)

It was very soon agreed that William must leave the Hall. The upper servants sat in judgement, the master was consulted, the medical man who had attended Sarah at the ball drove up in his gig and the deed was done. Mrs. Wates, although several times questioned by Mr. Randall and the other servants, stuck to her story: that she had observed William and Sarah as they danced, overheard a scornful expression pass William's lips as the latter fell clumsily against him and watched as Sarah flung herself forward onto the burning logs. Sarah, who might have corroborated or denied the account, kept to her bed, where Mrs. Finnie administered drops of laudanum to her and dressed her burns, and said nothing. In her absence a terrible air of gloom descended upon the house. William, seeing that the general feeling of the servants' hall was against him, took himself to his own quarters and was rarely seen about the place.

"It is always the same when a servant is given notice," Margaret Lane explained, as she and Esther laboured in the scullery one winter afternoon. "William won't see out his month, you mark my words."

Beyond the window dark shadows were already hastening across the square of beaten earth and the kitchen garden. In the upper storey of the keeper's cottage an oil lamp flickered and then went out.

"I think it is very unfair," Esther said. "If anyone knows truly what happened it is Sarah, who will not speak."

"I know what is unfair," Margaret replied. "It is us two girls having to clean out this scullery and attend to the lamps at twilight."

Esther acknowledged the truth of this. In the absence of Sarah and William, most of the work of the establishment had devolved onto Margaret and herself. Each afternoon at four, consequently, she followed Mr. Randall about the house with a tray on which lay the tapers used to light the oil lamps and a brush and pan with which to sweep up the debris that fell from the ancient wooden shutters. The rooms seemed very melancholy to her at these times, and there were afternoons when she quailed at the prospect of the Dixeys in their gilt frames staring across the darkened rooms while Mr. Randall went about his business.

The old man seemed to sense her disquiet and to sympathise with it, for there came an afternoon when, as they returned to the pantry with the tray and the unused tapers, he enquired, "Are you happy in your work, Esther?"

"Indeed, I have nothing to complain of, Mr. Randall."

"Another girl would reckon it hard to do another person's work. I think she would. Tell me, Esther, is there any religion in your house at home?"

Though she went in awe of him as a source of authority second only to Mr. Dixey, Esther had hitherto taken little notice of Mr. Randall. He seemed to her merely a futile and occasionally querulous old man, debarring himself from conversation and society by virtue of his religious observances. Looking at him now as he sat in his easy chair with the amenities of the butler's pantry arranged around him, she was suddenly thankful for the question.

"My father went to chapel all his life. Although my mother used sometimes to mock him for it. He is dead now, a long time."

"Indeed? There are always those that will mock the servants of the Lord. I am not speaking of your mother, Esther, but of the world in general."

And after this Mr. Randall favoured her, conferred certain duties that had previously been hers onto Margaret Lane and implored her occasionally to drink a glass of Madeira on the grounds that it was "especially suited to ladies," and Esther was glad of the impulse that had led her to talk of her father and the old days at Lynn.

Finally, though, there came a day when William's trunk lay by the great door in the hall and the carter's wagon stood in the driveway waiting to carry him to the railway station. The sight of the trunk, bound up with lengths of twine, and with his things folded up and placed in a bundle on its surface, was poignant to her, for it reminded her of the day she had come to Easton Hall and their walk home through the shadows of a summer evening. It was a dreary day towards the end of December with the clouds streaming in above the bent-back trees and a curious air of restlessness about the house and its grounds, as if people moved there unseen and the rattling at the windows and doors was made by invisible hands. For an hour that morning, as the trunk lay in the hall and the carter sat stoically under his cape and the rain fell over the weeping elms, Esther looked in vain for him. Greatly daring, she stole up to his room under the eaves, but the door was open, the bed stripped down and the only trace of him a few twists of tobacco and a snuffed-out candle lying on a table by the bedstead. She picked up one of the twists of tobacco and put it in the pocket of her apron. Downstairs in the hall Mr. Randall passed her with a copy of the master's newspaper pressed under his arm.

"*Let me not be ashamed, O Lord,*" he said, "*for I have called upon thee: let the wicked be ashamed and let them be silent in the grave.* Do you know the psalm, Esther?"

"No, Mr. Randall, but I should like to read it someday."

In the servants' hall an air of tension prevailed. Mrs. Finnie was in a black mood, advertised the disappearance of a sheet from the laundry cupboard and spoke of giving notice. Margaret Lane dropped a dinner plate and was roundly upbraided by Mrs. Wates: "For I don't know what girls is coming to these days," Mrs. Wates remarked in vexation. "There is that Sarah Parker still lying abed and no work to be got out of her, and Esther here mooning about the place all on account of some young man who were better gone six months since, and Margaret Lane fair to play at ninepins with the master's crockery."

"Indeed, Mrs. Wates, I am truly sorry," Margaret cried bitterly, for she regarded the cook as her protector in the house.

"You are a silly girl," Mrs. Wates told her, "and should go away from here and marry some man whose dinner plates you can smash, and his dinner burn, rather than the master's."

And then Esther felt sorry for Mrs. Wates, with her waxen face and her shaking hand and the grey hair coming adrift from its pinioning down her broad back, who would never marry anyone.

In the end, when she had all but given up hope, she met him in the kitchen garden, coming back from the keeper's cottage. He had taken off his footman's clothes and was wearing an old suit of black with a cracked billycock hat jammed down over his head.

"Now, Esther," he said, seeing her mournful expression. "You did not think I would go without saying good-bye, surely?"

"It is hard to know what to think sometimes."

"But it's not as you suppose, Esther. I am still Mr. Dixey's man, even though I am going from here, and have his commission. You may tell that to the old cat in the kitchen if you like."

"I shall say nothing of the sort."

"But see here, Esther, I shall miss you, and I don't mind saying so. You watch out for a letter, do you hear? It takes more to part folk than distance, you know."

Then, perhaps thinking he had said enough, he moved off around the side of the house to the waiting cart. Esther stood for a long while in the kitchen garden with her head held down, hearing the wind rush in her ears and the bending of the trees until there came a raised voice from within the house calling her name and she moved inside.

(XII)

Esther sped up the staircase. The letter that Sam Postman had put into her hand ten minutes before lay pressed into the pocket of her apron. Reaching her bedroom, she closed the door behind her, sat down upon the bed, took the letter from its hiding place in her lap and laid it facedown upon the coverlet. Her heart was beating very fast, both with the effort of her run upstairs and a greater agitation that she was unable to disguise, and for a moment she clasped her hands around her waist to steady herself. But there was nothing to be done, no agency that would take the letter away from her or return her to the tranquil state in which she had existed before it had arrived, and so she tore it open and stared eagerly at the single sheet of paper that lay within.

Seven Dials
London W.

Dear Esther,
I said as I should write to you, and I hope you'll grant that I'm
as good as my word, which is more than some are. How are
the people at the Hall? I wonder. They have no love for me, I
expect, nor I for them. As for me, I'm faring tolerably, with a
snug little billet and a place that suits me well. Not in service,
you understand, for I have done with all that, but in the commercial line. There are kinds of business that I put in folks' way
and kinds of business that they put in mine—I can't say more
than that. Just at present I'm a-nursing of my face, on account
of a fellow who was shy of paying me a debt, but it's nothing
to cry about, I daresay. Mind you, be a good girl and drop me
a line if you have anything to tell and I shall write again soon
with more news from

　Yr. obedient servant,
　Wm. Latch

This brief paragraph Esther mused over for some time, not understanding the half of it and alarming herself very much over the half
that she did understand. The references to commerce and business
escaped her entirely, but she fancied that William had begun to draw
apart from the world that she and others like her inhabited. This
realisation disquieted her, for she knew that she remained in the place
he had left, but she approved what she saw as his progress through
the world. She had seen pictures of fashionably dressed persons in
the magazines that lay around the servants' quarters—gentlemen in
high hats and natty topcoats—and she wondered if William, moving
about the city in this great adventure of his, wore these things. His
being hurt—bruised about the face—scared her, but she supposed that
it was something that men, or a certain kind of man, did, and the
thought of William's great height and strength caused her to reflect
upon his assailant with scorn. "The idea of anyone hurting him," she

said to herself as she brooded over the sheet of paper. The brooding was pleasurable to her, and she sat quite still on the bed for some moments, first musing over one sentence, then another, then dwelling on William's signature, inscribed with a great flourish at the foot of the page. So engrossed had she become that she altogether failed to notice that the door had swung open and that someone was regarding her from the portal.

"What have you got there, Esther?" came Sarah's voice sharply. "What is it you are looking at?"

"I suppose a girl may look at a letter if it is sent to her," Esther remarked mildly, folding the sheet of paper into a square, pushing it into her apron pocket and turning to face her visitor.

Since her accident Sarah had gone into a decline. Esther had hoped that once she had been pronounced cured by the doctor, she would return to their shared bedroom, but Sarah had preferred to remain in the attic room to which they had conveyed her on her return from the ball at Watton. Staring at her now as she stood in the doorway, a curiously pursed look about her lips, Esther was conscious of how strange she seemed.

"Why, Sarah, you do look queer. Whatever is the matter with you?" On the instant a memory of the girl flitting around Mrs. Wates's kitchen the previous day gave her the answer. "You have been drinking vinegar again! I am sure it is very bad for you to take such stuff. And Mrs. Wates would say so too, if she knew."

"You are very hard on me," Sarah said disconsolately. She sat down on the bed and ran her fingers over her parched mouth. "There are few enough things that a girl can take comfort in." She glanced about her once or twice, as if grasping at a thought that had eluded her. "Who is your letter from?"

"It is from William."

"What does he say?"

"That he has a place. Not in service. A business."

"I had a letter once," Sarah went on. "About Joe. But I never saw it again. Did you take it, Esther?"

Esther said nothing.

"I know I could not read it, and that is very stupid of me. But it would have been a comfort to have it near me. Like your letter from William, I daresay."

"You must not drink the vinegar, Sarah. It will make you ill, I know it will."

Sarah rocked gently backwards and forwards, her arms clasped around her knees. "I have such a pain. Not in my arm. That is all healed now. In fact I never think of it. But in my head."

"You should see Mrs. Finnie," Esther said sympathetically, "and ask her for some drops of laudanum. She has a bottle, I know."

There were beads of perspiration on Sarah's forehead, though the air in the bedroom was chill. Her face seemed grey with fatigue.

"It is all right. I feel better now, indeed I do. But there is a message for you, Esther, from Mr. Randall. He says you are to go to him immediately. Gracious, Esther!"—and here Sarah gave a laugh that was not at all pleasant to hear—"What a thing it would be if you were to marry Mr. Randall. Why, I should have to call you 'ma'am,' and Mrs. Finnie and Mrs. Wates would have to be civil to you at supper and help you to the pudding."

"It is wrong of you to say such things, Sarah, and I shan't listen to you."

"Why is it wrong of me? I think I should like to be a butler's wife. I should have as many headaches as I liked and no one to scold me." And here, somewhat to her surprise, Sarah put her head in her hands and began to cry. Esther stood over her for a while, uncertain as to which of these demands had the greater claim on her time. Then, with the fingers of her right hand still clutched around William's letter where it lay in her apron pocket, she sped back down the stairs.

(XIII)

In William's absence an air of dereliction had fallen over the place. It was as if his departure had brought some greater upheaval amongst the lives of those who remained there that none of them could fathom. Mr. Dixey went on his errands alone; the hot water for his shaving was taken up by Margaret Lane in a teakettle, for, as she said, she could not manage the great china ewer with which William had ascended the stairs each morning a half hour after dawn. An occasional gentleman or lady came to call or to eat luncheon, even more rarely two of them together, but the dishes that Mr. Dixey ordered up were of the plainest kind, and Mrs. Wates despaired, for, as she truly remarked, what was the point of having a receipt for a hollandaise sauce if one was never allowed to make it? Hastening down the back stairs and into the servants' hall—very desolate in the daytime with the fire unlit and the last night's crockery still lying on the table—Esther found Mr. Randall in his pantry. He was seated in the big armchair, comfortably enshawled in a wolfskin rug, so comfortably in fact that he might almost have been asleep, but when he saw her he pulled the rug from his shoulders and rose to his feet.

"I am glad to see you, Esther. Will you sit down?"

Esther did as she was bidden, wondering what Mr. Randall wished to say. He had a doubtful look on his face—very creased, it seemed, from his half slumber—and his fingers turned over an iron key that he held in the palm of his hand.

"Now, Esther," he said, moving the key between his fingers so that, try as she might, Esther could not but look at it. "Here is a question for you. How many people reside in this house?"

"There are six. Now that William has gone."

"There are seven," Mr. Randall corrected her. "How are there seven? I shall tell you, Esther. You shall not think you have been deceived, I hope, for there has been no deception. You know the west wing of the house?"

"I have never been there."

"No. The rooms are empty and shut up. They have not been used since before I came here, and that is many years ago. But see, one of them is not empty and not shut up. Or rather . . ." The key was very ancient and antique, Esther saw, with a large, much-ornamented hinge. "There is a lady lives there. Mr. Dixey's ward. An invalid."

Feeling that something was expected of her, Esther said, "What is the matter with her?"

"What is the matter with her? It is hard to say. The master has had doctors to see her. Their opinion is that her mind is troubled, that

D. J. TAYLOR

she does not know herself. That is why she lives as she does. Do you understand me, Esther?"

Esther nodded.

"Naturally, it is Mrs. Finnie that looks after her. Who attends to her wants. But we are shorthanded, Esther, and there is need for another. . . . I wish you only to take up Mrs. Ireland's meals and attend on her. Just as if she were a guest in the house."

"Her name is Mrs. Ireland?"

"Did I not say so before? Yes, that is her name."

As Esther listened, Mr. Randall explained the nature of her duties. These were that:

Thrice a day, at eight, one and seven, she should take a covered tray supplied by Mrs. Wates to Mrs. Ireland's chamber.

On reaching the chamber, she was to knock at the door. If Mrs. Ireland did not answer, she should wait a short time and then unlock the door.

Once inside the room, she should lock the door behind her.

The key should at all times be left in her pocket and returned to Mr. Randall when not in use.

If, at any time, Mrs. Ireland seemed disturbed, alarmed or in any other way altered from her usual manner, she should leave the room immediately, locking the door behind her, and inform Mr. Randall.

Any questions put to her by Mrs. Ireland that were not immediately answerable should be referred to Mr. Randall.

The door should be locked at all times.

Any suggestion by Mrs. Ireland as to leaving the chamber should be referred to Mr. Randall.

Twice a day, at two and eight, she should return to the chamber and collect the tray. Again, she should knock at the door. If Mrs. Ireland did not answer, she should wait a short time and then unlock the door.

The key should be kept in her pocket.

The door should be locked at all times.

* * *

Kept

(XIV)

O ne spring morning, when the wind blew crazily against the upper storeys of the house, Esther went into Sarah's room and found her gone. For a moment, standing in the doorway with her hands plunged into the pocket of her sacking apron and the light spilling over her face, she saw nothing strange in the vacant bed, the half-open skylight window and the patch of angry blue sky beyond, supposing that Sarah had already gone downstairs to light the fire or, as was sometimes her habit, risen early to perform some mysterious errand of her own. And yet there was something about the room that seemed to her odd, beyond the roar of the wind and the neatly drawn coverlet. Not altogether knowing why she did it, Esther tugged open the top-most drawer of the chest in which Sarah kept her clothes. It was quite empty. So, she discovered, was the drawer beneath it. Instantly, half a dozen other tiny vanishments and discrepancies became apparent to her—the square of mirror that had hung on the wall, the portrait of the Crystal Palace Exhibition cut out of an illustrated paper, Sarah's pattens gone from beneath the bed—and the room's secret declared itself. Carefully shutting the drawers of the chest and hauling the sky-light window to, Esther considered the implications of this discovery. It occurred to her that Sarah might still be in the house—it was, she calculated, barely half past six—and with this expectation growing in her mind, she rushed downstairs into the hall, practically colliding with Mr. Randall, who, very white and shabby at this early hour, was winding up the grandfather clock with his butterfly key.

"Why, Esther! Whatever is the matter?"

"It is Sarah, Mr. Randall. It's my belief that she's gone."

Together they moved around the ground floor of the house open-ing doors and throwing open closets, but there was no sign of anything save the kitchen cat, who looked up resentfully from its slumber on the parlour sofa as if to say that it very much deplored the intrusion. Then Mr. Randall discovered that the bolts of the kitchen door had been drawn and that the door itself lay half-open on its hinge.

There was no doubt about it, Mr. Randall said, standing uncertainly

D. J. TAYLOR

in his shirtsleeves, with the wind rushing into the kitchen through the open door, but that Sarah had gone.

Subsequently, Mrs. Wates bustled downstairs with her hair done up in curlpapers, conducted a rapid inventory of the kitchen and confirmed that a two-guinea piece left in a box by the outer door and intended for payment of the butcher's bill had also vanished in the course of the night.

The master had best be told, Mrs. Wates suggested.

At lunchtime the remaining servants sat in conclave over the absentee.

Mrs. Wates deposed that Sarah was a bad girl, who in the manner of bad girls would undoubtedly come to a bad end. It was not for her to judge, for judgement lay in the hands of the Lord, but a girl of that sort, who crept out of the house in the middle of the night without a word to anyone, would certainly have a baby, and the baby would die, or be taken from her, and this was on balance a good thing.

Mrs. Finnie said that she was a sly one and no mistake, that she had had a look on her face this past week that was a sure clue to her intentions to anyone experienced in these matters, that it was a wonder, what with people sneaking downstairs in the middle of the night and opening doors, that they had not all been murdered in their beds, and that Mr. Randall ought to unlock his strongbox and ensure that the plate had not been stolen.

Margaret Lane said that she did not wish to speak ill of anyone, least of all those that were not there to defend themselves, but she had always thought the way that Sarah had made eyes at William downright shameful.

Mr. Randall said that it was all a great pity, and that he hoped Sarah would be happy.

Esther said nothing.

That afternoon Mr. Randall went into Watton to make enquiries, asked at the railway station, put his head into the bar of the Bull and returned empty-handed. It was not, he explained to the audience of the servants' hall, and notwithstanding the missing two-guinea piece, as if Sarah had committed a criminal act. She had merely quitted her situation, albeit in mysterious circumstances, and there was nothing that could be done.

"Oh Lord," Mr. Randall prayed aloud that evening as they sat before the fire, "we commend to thy care thy servant Sarah, and we hope that we may remember her as we should and have no cause to repent of the treatment we allowed her, and that no harm shall come to her on the path she treads. Amen."

And that was all that was said of Sarah, the parlourmaid at Easton Hall, who could not read and whose brother had died in China.

D. J. TAYLOR

THE CONFIDENTIAL CLERK

It will perhaps be allowed by those who have gone into the matter that in late years our idea of London has altered somewhat, and that a metropolis previously known for its stink and its monotony has blossomed forth in all kinds of unexpected colours. In short, the place has been taken up and turned romantic. Somers Town, as sketched by Mr. Dickens, stands revealed as the most charming of localities; Islington is a sooty paradise; even Limehouse Hole has declared itself full of the most interesting byways and peculiarities that polite society had formerly not imagined to exist. A penny gaff, beneath the gaze of these new explorers, is the most delightful refuge for the curious seeker after pleasure, and a threepenny theatre with a conjuror and a line of young ladies in Turkish trousers practically the acme of popular entertainment. Neither must it be supposed that this transmogrifying hand, once directed at a Clerkenwell, a Whitechapel or the vicinity of the Borough, can be stayed from touching the inhabitants of these respectable purlieus. The very beggars and the street acrobats have grown suddenly picturesque and behave as if they wished to appear in those representations of "London Characters" that decorate the print sellers' windows, and the coster-women have the vanity of artists' models. For myself, I altogether abhor and repudiate this false alchemy, whereby base metal, wrested out of the foulest pits and mines, is brought forth as human gold. Limehouse Hole, where Rogue Riderhood dwelt deep and dark, is no doubt a fascinating and fashionable place, but I for one would not go there, and one were as likely to meet a footpad in High Holborn as a soft-voiced old apple-woman with a sentimental eye. Dirt is dirt and squalor is squalor, that was what I was taught, and a waistcoat held together by one precarious button less efficacious than that secured by three. The number of persons rendered more humorous and idiosyncratic by their privations is a dismally small fraction of gross humanity.

Certainly, the eye that lingers in St. John's Square, Clerkenwell, on a fierce morning—fierce, that is, in point of view of rain, fog and other elements—in early February will be hard put to distinguish any redeeming features. For a start, there is the general aspect of the place: a great ragged confluence of shabby thoroughfares quite cut in half by the Clerkenwell Road, the whole bleakly laid out and disposed beneath a flint-coloured sky suggestive of impending cloudburst, such light as there is dissolving into misty radiance. Then there is the teeming throng of people: each omnibus that clatters by is laden with passengers; tarpaulins gleam over the knees of those who sit outside. Labouring men in mufflers and shabby jackets, with billycock hats pulled low over their brows, go shambling past to their places of work hard by in Goswell Road or Aldgate; small boys with pieces of wet sacking drawn over their already wet shoulders slip past bent on God knows what errands, darting out of the little shops and places of manufacture. The commercial genius of Clerkenwell, it may be said, does not hanker after the grand scale. Warehouses, factories and the like are there none. Rather, each dwelling house and shop is divided into a myriad of individual concerns, three or four at a time. The house that stands yonder, within a yard or two of the public wheel track, squeezed in between a corn chandler's and an ironmonger's and looking like a very small man quite domineered over by two burly companions, a house that in Kensington might harbour a family of five plus a cook and a maid of all work, contains, in Clerkenwell, beginning at its uppermost storey, a dye-stamping business, a sign painter's, a glass and enamelling establishment, a mysterious enterprise engaged in the distillation of black lead and, in its basement, a room in which six children are employed twelve hours a day manufacturing colour-paper fans at three-halfpence the dozen. Thirty-seven persons pass in and out of these premises on a given day (there is an old woman, dying of the dropsy, locked up in a gaunt back bedroom who goes nowhere at all), all of them liable to tumble head over heels amongst the corn chandler's stock or scarify themselves upon those of the ironmonger's wares proudly displayed on the narrow pavement. There is no space, you see, in Clerkenwell, and a shop is not a shop until half its contents are on view beyond the doorway, and a house not a house until two

D. J. TAYLOR

dozen people are crammed into its five rooms. No space, only dirt and decay, and ash-ridden streets, and a blackness of night which no lamp can penetrate, and nocturnal policemen going two by two, and poverty and pestilence taking turns as to which shall more advantageously dispose itself.

Loitering keenly along the corner of the square, a dilapidated umbrella allowing a miniature cataract to descend on his uncovered head, Mr. Grace, Mr. Pardew's confidential clerk, was in no way discountenanced by what he saw. He had been dealing with Clerkenwell and its regions for the greater part of his professional life. Clerkenwell, it might be said, was in his blood. Set down in it, he knew exactly where he was bound, what he might find there and what in strict monetary terms might be the issue. In this spirit, forgetting the particular errand that brought him here, he browsed impressionably for a moment on the crowded pavement, put his head in at a pastrycook's and reluctantly withdrew it, stood for a while before a down-at-heel stationer's displaying copies of the *Raff's Journal*, the *Larky Swell* and other publications, and took a determined interest in the back part of a sofa, from which the horsehair had begun to sprout in little melancholic tufts and follicles, that some enterprising dealer in furniture had crammed into his window. The sound of a bell, clanging from the tower of St. James's Church, cut short this reverie, and negotiating his way past the lower outcrops of a kind of Parnassus of willow-pattern crockery, over which the rain dripped and tumbled, he passed around the western edge of the square into a street of tall, nondescript houses dignified by the name Clerkenwell Court. A casual observer who monitored his progress might have remarked that he examined not the house numbers but the brass plates set at head height next to their doors. An apothecary's, a day school and a dealer in hides and tallows—from whose frontage came a reek that made even Mr. Grace, Clerkenwellian that he was, shy his head—were rejected, until finally he stopped before a plate whose inscription read *J. Snowden, Dial Painter*. Having ascertained that this was the place he sought—for he was a nearsighted man—he rolled up the tattered umbrella, gave a couple of smart raps on the dusty front door with the ferrule and stood back from the step the better to appraise whoever might appear upon it. The door having been opened by a young woman in a shawl carrying a baby on her hip, Mr. Grace bared his teeth and enquired, "Name of Dewar?"

"Second floor back."

Experienced enough in these visitations to know that the woman's sullen tone denoted not impertinence but the dignity of proprietorship, Mr. Grace raised his umbrella by way of a salute and proceeded across a negligently swept hallway to the staircase. He was a calculating man—long years in the service of Mr. Pardew had taught him the value of calculation—and as he ascended he looked diligently about him and calculated both the degree of the squalor that he saw and the likelihood of his errand's proving successful. That there was a connection between the two, Mr. Grace well knew. "No stair carpet anyhow," he said to himself as he gained the first landing. "Not that one expected it anyway. But holes in the timber big enough to put your foot into, and not even the sight of a coal scuttle"—this observation was provoked by a heap of coal piled up on a sheet of newspaper—"dear me, that's bad." Proceeding up the second flight, he grew suddenly conscious of the noise his boots made on the bare slats and wondered proudly at the effect such irruptions might have on the equanimity of persons inhabiting second-floor back bedrooms in Clerkenwell Court. Standing finally on the second landing, he beat a miniature tattoo on the door, which caused it to rattle dangerously in its frame, and then, barely pausing for the weak cry of acknowledgement that came from within, pushed his way inside.

He stepped into a room that was not disorderly or unclean but presented merely the chill discomfort of poverty. The bare boards of the floor space were decently swept. Upon them could be found a high brass bedstead of the old-fashioned type pushed back almost to the window, a wash-hand stand, a couple of cane-backed chairs and a small occasional table. A tiny fire burned in the grate, composed of three glowing coals and so insubstantial that the air by the door where Mr. Grace now lingered seemed quite unwarmed. On a shelf affixed to the nearside wall sat a beer jug, a white china cat from whose mouth issued a spray of coloured paper, and a copy of *All the Year Round*, so dusty and timeworn that it seemed that, in deference to its title, it

D. J. TAYLOR

had always lain there from January through December. A few miscellaneous items—a plate, the half of a quartern loaf and a teapot—lying in the grate completed the picture. All this, Mr. Grace's beady eye took in as he stood in the doorway. So fascinated was he by the meagre inventory that it was a moment before he could begin to appraise the room's human populace. This consisted of a thin, pale-complexioned woman who, although dressed, lay on the bedstead in an attitude of extreme fatigue, and a pasty-faced, unhealthy-looking man wearing a dressing gown over his frayed shirt who sat awkwardly on one of the cane-backed chairs. Seeing from their faces, in which curiosity combined with great alarm, that he was master of the situation and that no voice would be raised against him, Mr. Grace brought his hands smartly together and made a little bow.

"Name of Grace. That put you in the way of Lewis Dunbar. Recollect me?"

Receiving no answer, other than a vacant nod of the head from the man, he delved into the inner pocket of his coat and brought out a wad of grimy paper, much folded and secured with a piece of ribbon.

"See this? Bill for thirty pounds in favour of Hodge, dry-goods merchant, Pentonville. Know anything about it?"

Dewar turned a doleful pair of eyes towards him. "On my honour, sir, the money was paid."

"Very likely! Very likely indeed, with me standing here a-holding of it in my hand. Did I say thirty pounds? More likely thirty-five, what with the interest owing. More like thirty-seven pound ten shillings, I shouldn't wonder. Question is, Mr. Dewar, what do you mean to do about it?" He stopped for a moment, his attention fixed on some incongruity in the room, in the set of Dewar's face even, that he could not quite fathom. "Great heavens, man! What have you done to your hair?"

"He's dyed it." The woman spoke for the first time, indistinctly, with her hand drawn up to her breast.

"Dyed it, has he?" Grace rocked back on his heels, as if this were the most singular thing he had ever heard. "Now why should he want to do that?"

The woman coughed, in a way that brought a crimson flush to her otherwise pallid cheeks. "He thought one of the reasons he couldn't get work was his looking so old."

"And so it was!" Dewar interjected. "Once your hair's turned, there's no chance for you. The governors don't want old men, or them that they think is old. I was working in a chophouse in Hanover Street, first job I'd had in a month. Come the second day I saw the man who owned it talking to the head waiter. 'We don't want no old men,' he says. 'Better turn him off.' So they turned me off, and I went away and had my hair dyed, though precious little good it's done me." The woman began to cough again, and he broke off and regarded her helplessly.

"Had to dye your hair?" Grace wondered. "Dear me, that's bad. That's bad indeed." Although he continued to stare around the room with benign amusement, as if the sight were a kind of tableau expressly designed for his entertainment, he had already begun to recalculate his strategy. His original scheme had been to browbeat Dewar, threaten him even, and thus to secure some small portion of the debt contracted to Mr. Hodge of Pentonville some eighteen months before and now transferred to his own master. Experience told him, however, that such a game was not worth the candle. Accordingly, he began upon a second scheme, which Mr. Pardew had suggested to him earlier that morning in Carter Lane.

"Now see here, Mr. Dewar. I don't doubt there's paper of yours all over the City. There may be a dozen Mr. Pardews after you. I don't know. P'raps there's more. However many there are, it's no good to me. Still, there's a way we might help one another, indeed there is. If the lady don't mind, perhaps you could come along of me to somewhere we could talk more private-like?"

·   Dewar looked at him curiously for a moment, but in the end assented, muttered something in an undertone to his wife, drew off the tattered dressing gown and replaced it with an equally threadbare topcoat, which he took from a pile of clothing heaped at the end of the bedstead. Thus arrayed, he stood uncertainly in the doorway for a moment while Grace, tipping his finger to his forehead in salute to the occupant of the bed, led him out onto the landing.

"Your wife's bad, ain't she?" he remarked conversationally as they descended to the level of the street.

"Don't take no nourishment from her food," Dewar gloomily assented. "Thin as thin."

"Consumption, I should say. I seen that kind of cough before. When the spots come to their cheeks. She'll die on you, I shouldn't wonder. I means no harm," he admonished, catching the look in his companion's eye. "Neither does Mr. Pardew, for all he's a hard man. But there's truth and there's lies, you know. Now, from the look of you I should say that you could do with something 'ot. Am I right?"

Dewar nodded his head. Glancing sideways at him as they passed through the door of the house into Clerkenwell Court, Grace satisfied himself that he seemed to shuffle rather than walk.

"Here," he said. "How long since you had a square meal? Come on, you can tell me, you know."

"Yesterday. That is, the day before."

"And that bread and tea, I shouldn't wonder. Never mind. Just step along this way."

On the corner of Clerkenwell Court, where it verges on the green, there was a public house, empty now against the anticipated dinner hour, but emitting gusts of beer and spirituous liquor from its half-open doors. A potboy, one of those insouciant, devil-may-care potboys with a black eye and a cap pulled down low over his forehead, looking as if he had lately escaped from Mr. Egan's *Life in London* and needing only the attentions of a beadle or two to drag him back, stood at the entrance polishing the dark windows and whistling horribly through his teeth. They passed into a dark, cavernous chamber, lit by a blazing fire which winked and glinted off the pewter mugs as if it were having a kind of round game with itself and these utensils were in the habit of passing the message on, where Grace, leaving his companion at one of the tables, went to the bar and returned from the bar carrying two steaming tumblers of brandy and water.

"You'll find this warm enough," he observed, jangling the change from the transaction in his palm and turning over the coins as he did so. "D——— it, will you look at that?"

"I don't see anything amiss," Dewar commented, examining the florin that Grace threw down on the tabletop between them. "What's the matter with it?"

"Coiner's silver," he elucidated. "See the colour of the metal next to a real two-bob. Probably made of one of them pewter pots. Now, as to our business. I daresay you're finding the wind blows just a trifle cold around your legs at the moment. Would that be the case?"

"It does blow cold—very cold."

"Well now." Grace brought his face to within a foot of Dewar's. "What would you say if I were to offer you a week's work as could strike out Hodge's bill *and* leave you with five pounds in your pocket? You'd be agreeable, I take it?"

"Naturally I should."

"Very well. But there's one or two particulars that I need to assure myself of, see. Mr. Pardew"—and here Grace paused, as if he somehow expected that his employer would take visible shape in the spirit fumes that rose above their heads—"Mr. Pardew don't like sending good money after bad. It's a thing he can't abide. First point: have you a decent, respectable set of clothes as you can set your hands on?"

"I think I have."

"In quod I suppose?" Grace deduced, more or less sympathetically. "How much needed to take them out?"

"Twelve shillings . . . twelve shillings and sixpence. I haven't the tickets with me."

"Very well again. Second point, and no offence meant or taken in return: can you play the gentleman? Meaning, if you was sent into a bank and asked to collect money that was due, could you act the high feller, come across haughty-like, and that kind of thing?"

"I suppose I . . ."

"Come along! You've kept a shop in your day. You'll have made a particular study of the breed, I'll be bound. Yes or no?"

"Yes."

"Excellent! Couldn't be beat. Now, there's one or two peculiarities of the case as you should know of. First item, for the purposes of this job your name ain't Dewar, it's Roper. *R-o-p-e-r*. Got that? James Roper. Second thing: you're a gentleman of means. Three days from now you'll get a letter with a banknote in it. You're to take that note to Bulstrode's Bank in Lothbury—as Mr. Roper, mind—and open an account. Know the place?"

"I think I do."

"Excellent again! I knew as we should be able to do business. Now, there's one other thing. When you're opening the account in Lothbury—and it'll all be quite in order, no fears on that score—you're to say that you're paying a visit to Yarmouth (no, not the one on Wight, Yarmouth in Norfolk!) and that the money should be transferred to Gurney's, as are their agents in the town. Once that's done, you're to go to Yarmouth—as Mr. Roper, mind—and make believe as you're taking the sea air."

The look on Dewar's face as he stared up into his companion's eyes suggested that this was a piece of jocularity too far. "You are making fun of me, Mr. Grace. Indeed you are."

"I was never more serious in my life. Listen to me. You're a gentleman that's on holiday—well, on business then. Anything as looks respectable. You takes lodgings somewhere, and pays for them cash down. You go for walks along the promenade. Take a look at the sands—I b'lieve they're very fine. And await our communication."

"A letter?"

"That's the ticket. A letter giving full particulars of what you're to do. Couldn't be easier, hey?"

It now wanted but a few minutes to midday, and the tavern in which they sat had lost its recherché air. Half a dozen workmen, come from manufacturing shops in the vicinity, now clustered by the bar ordering pots of porter. The musicians of a German band, their instruments propped against their feet, were regaling themselves with faggots purchased from a metal plate kept hot by jets of steam that surged beneath it, and a villainous old woman in a shawl and a poke bonnet was going amongst them selling exceedingly waxen apples. Seeing the crowd of people—none of whom, as is the habit of the Clerkenwell work horde, took the slightest notice of him—Grace grew taciturn, replying to Dewar's questions in monosyllables and affecting a great interest in some sporting prints that hung from the far wall.

"See that Silver Braid? Now that was an 'oss, that was. Ten guineas I've won on that animal in my time. But perhaps you aren't a betting man?"

"I confess I'm not."

"And with the Derby coming up again too! Well, never mind. Now see here, Mr. Dewar"—and here Grace lowered his voice significantly—"all this is going to cost money. Naturally it is. Couldn't not. Now, what I suggest is that we go somewhere a bit out of the way of the generality."

At the rear of the tavern there was a small anteroom set aside for the benefit of gentlemen who might wish to wash their hands or engage in other ablutions. As, however, very few gentlemen seemed eager to avail themselves of this amenity, the room was generally vacant. Here, beckoning Dewar to follow him, Grace unostentatiously repaired.

"Stinks to high heaven, don't it? Never mind. Now, a sovereign to take your things out of quod and spruce yourself up—for you must look the part, you know, be able to tip your tile to the quality. Then there's travelling expenses, lodgings and so forth. Five pounds should cover it." And to Dewar's astonishment—for there was a part of him that still believed their colloquy to have been an elaborate game, got up to mock him—he produced a battered purse from his pocket and counted out this much in gold coins. Then, abruptly, his manner changed.

"There you are. I don't need no receipt—ha! You'd best go away and do what needs to be done. Ain't no need to seek me out, for I shan't be found. One more thing: anyone asks if you know anything about me or Mr. Pardew as employs me, you're as silent as the grave. Anything goes amiss, and we never met, never spoke, never so much as nodded in the street."

Seeing the look on Dewar's face, he brightened and clapped him on the back. "Never say die, though, eh? Why, we shall see the Derby together maybe, you and me. Now, don't cling so tight as all that while we make our way out of here, do you see?"

Grace's anxiety appeared to be misplaced. Certainly no one—not the workmen, now conversing animatedly among themselves, or the members of the German band, or the old woman selling apples—so much as raised an eye as they made their way to the door. Outside the sky retained its singular, slate-grey shade. The dolorous bells of St. James's, pealing across the square, disclosed that the midday hour had come. At the tavern door Grace halted, plunged his fist into his trouser pocket to jingle his change, and caught the eye of the potboy, who, having completed his polishing, was pushing a wretched broom listlessly across the flagstones.

"Here," he said, producing a florin from his pocket and flinging it across in what Dewar, who followed the coin's arc, registered as a single movement of his arm. "Something to remember me by."

At the street corner he turned and brought his face, now grinning from ear to ear, to within an inch or two of Dewar's. "Ha! Fancy the look on his face when he goes a changing of that, eh?"

Dewar shook his head. "Why should that be?"

"Why? For it was the snide that I gave him, don't you see?"

He laughed again, turned his head and was gone, and Clerkenwell knew him no more.

* * *

Dewar's behaviour, once he became aware of his companion's disappearance, was of a very singular kind. Having witnessed the trick played upon the potboy, which seemed to him in his mild way a very cruel piece of spite, he was struck by a sudden anxiety that the coins given to him might be similarly false. For a moment this possibility affected him so forcibly that, standing alone on the street corner, with the midday crowd flowing around him, he began to shake with fear. Yet a glance at the five sovereigns, which he now took out and arranged in his palm, reassured him. Indisputably, the coins were real. Still nervous of his good fortune, he put one into his mouth and bit down on it, but no, all was as it should be. For a brief second the action reminded him of other experiments, carried out behind the counter of his grocer's shop, and his frame shook once more. Then, in an instant, his head cleared and he realised—something that had scarcely occurred to him in the time since he and Grace had passed out of the tavern—that he was standing on a street corner in Clerkenwell, very wet now, to be sure, yet with money in his hand.

Several thoughts now crowded in upon him: that the nature of the business that Grace wished him to transact both now and in Yarmouth had altogether escaped him; that he was exceedingly hungry; and that he was now in a position to assuage at least some of the sufferings of his wife. However, for some reason that he could not properly fathom, it seemed to him that it was inadvisable for him to return home at the present moment, that there were things that he needed to establish to his inward satisfaction and that, above all, more pressing than any of these concerns, he needed food.

There was a luncheon bar ten yards down the street—a poor place, his eye told him, catering to the lowest navvies and street women, but no matter. At this moment it seemed to him the most delightful refuge on earth. In a few seconds he was inside it, pressing his fingers into the breast of his coat to feel the outline of the coins within its thread-bare lining. A cup of tea or coffee? the proprietor, a gaunt man in an extremely dirty apron, proposed. No, he was half starved. He must have something to eat. What was there? Seeing the fearful, flustered look in his eye, the man regarded him suspiciously for a moment until he saw the glint of gold in his hand. Why, what—sweeping his hand above the giant urns and the metal trays kept hot by various patent apparatus—would he have? Within a further few seconds, it seemed, Dewar found himself at a table at the rear of the shop dining off a plate of fried ham and eggs, the luxury of the poor. No sooner had the last morsel passed his lips than he called for a second plateful. He ate with relish—no food he had ever tasted seemed so good—and yet he was aware, as he did so, that his thoughts were not pleasant ones, and that the figure of Mr. Grace, with his smile and his fascinating jargon, wandered through them like a ghoul. By now he had finished his second meal, and the proprietor was bearing down on him again. Would he take anything else? Let him say the word, and a dessert should be brought. But Dewar's euphoria had altogether evaporated, to be replaced by a feeling of the deepest trepidation. He rose from his table, paid the man and strode out into the street, there to brood on the tasks to which he had committed himself.

It was by now about half past twelve—early still for Clerkenwell, much of whose business, it may be remarked, takes place in the hours of darkness. The rain had ceased; a ray or two of watery sunshine pen-etrated the flint-hued cloud wall to the north. All of this Dewar ignored. His duty, he knew, directed him to Clerkenwell Court and the woman to whom he had bade farewell an hour or so before. Such, though, was the pitch of Dewar's disquiet, a paroxysm of nervousness that could only be quelled by the rapid movement of his limbs, that he began to walk not westwards towards his home but northwards across the square and to the dim and even less respectable regions beyond. With the food that he had eaten he felt better, physically, than he had for many a day, and yet inwardly his mind was altogether restless. He saw Grace everywhere—on every street corner, grinning from every omnibus, his coattails descending every area step. He moved on rapidly, taking due care of such hazards that lay in his way but, it later seemed to him, blindly, with no thought of the direction he took. In this way he traversed great areas of the northern city. He walked to King's Cross and stared at the railway work. He wandered through Somers Town, along shy, empty streets where it appeared that no man before had ever trod. All sorts of queer things caught his attention and held him mesmerised: a street clown turning lugubrious cartwheels; a bolting cab horse that had overturned hansom and driver into the road and now lay quivering beneath the press of onlookers; a white-faced prisoner, with a grim woman pulling at his arm, led out of a house by three policemen.

All this Dewar saw, or rather did not see, for his mind was lost in ceaseless calculation. He knew little of the money world, the world of Grace and his master, but he knew sufficient to be aware that the tasks he had been commissioned to perform could not, of their nature, be legitimate. He knew, too, that should he prove unsuccessful—should some authority take an interest in his masquerading as "Mr. Roper"— his protestations of ignorance would be altogether disbelieved. At the same time, he was conscious that having taken Grace's money, spent two shillings of it and having nothing with which to replace it, he had, perforce, incriminated himself already. Seeing that he could not go back, he could only go forward. And meanwhile what was he to tell his wife? How to explain the five sovereigns, the requisitioned suit of clothes, the "playing the gentleman" and the going to Yarmouth? On this he brooded fruitlessly, yet not altogether unhappily, as the afternoon wore on, the sky darkening by degrees as he did so, until at length, scarcely knowing how he had come there, he found himself on the summit of Primrose Hill looking down on the distant city.

A Londoner for half his forty years, he swiftly identified the various landmarks that lay before him. Far away, rising from the lower masses of buildings, there stood in black majesty the dome of St. Paul's. Scraps of murky vapour, softening its outlines as they flew around it, gave it the appearance of something less than solid, floating almost on a sea of penumbral brick. Nearer, amongst a myriad of spires and steeples, lay the bulk of Newgate, its countless little windows glittering out of the shadow. Nearer still Smithfield, St. Bartholomew's Hospital, the glimmer of the railway line, like an enormous artery, which spreads between Clerkenwell Road and Charterhouse Street.

The enormity of the scene, and his own insignificance in the face of it, impressed him, and he began rapidly to descend the slope, reaching decisions of which he had not formerly thought himself capable as he went. He would find some form of words that would satisfy his wife without telling her the exact truth. As for himself, he would shut his mind to all extraneous thoughts and fix his concentration on the task in hand.

Reaching the foot of the hill once more, he plunged southeastwards into more familiar territory. Dusk had fallen now, and the pavements—garishly illumined by the flaring gas lamps—were crowded with costers' barrows and roadside shops. Here he wandered for a while, his hand tightly clutched once more in the pocket of his top-coat, in search of some inexpensive delicacy that might be a comfort to his wife. A handful of shrimps and a tin of salmon having completed his purchases, he moved off in the direction of the Farringdon Road. The house in Clerkenwell Court was quite dark. Entering his room he found it unlit, the fire extinguished in the grate; only the sound of his wife's breathing denoted that any living thing inhabited it. Presently, although he had been silent in his movements, merely squatting by the hearth and with infinite patience attempting to rebuild the fire, his wife stirred.

"Is that you, John?"

"Yes, but don't trouble yourself. Look, here is the fire nearly alight. And there shall be supper presently."

"I declare I do feel that bad. As if my head would tumble off my shoulders. Supper, you say?"

D. J. TAYLOR

The lamp lit and the flames taking hold in the grate, he displayed his purchases to her.

"But I thought the gentleman had come after a debt?"

"Well . . . yes. In a manner of speaking. But there is money, too. And work, of a kind. Let me explain it to you."

"Well, John!"

The fire rose in the hearth. With an effort, his wife hoisted herself from the bed and began to decant the shrimps into a saucer. Let it be hoped that, between them, the Dewars did not spend an altogether comfortless evening.

* * *

Somewhat to his surprise—for there was a part of him that still believed his dealings with Mr. Pardew's clerk to have been entirely chimerical—Dewar discovered that the events of the succeeding days fell out largely as Grace had predicted. On the next morning he proceeded to an establishment in the Clerkenwell Road, with whose proprietor he had in recent weeks become exceedingly intimate, and for the sum of thirteen shillings and sixpence took his suit of clothes out of pawn. It was a good suit, purchased shortly before the end of his grocering days, and examining it as it lay on the brass bedstead in Clerkenwell Court—where it seemed to flaunt its superiority to every other garment in the room in a very vulgar and indiscreet way—Dewar thought that it would do. He was not sanguine enough, however, to imagine that this would be the limit of his expenditure. His boots, as he knew from his excursion to Primrose Hill on the previous afternoon, were falling into pieces, and his tall hat, run to earth in a cupboard that contained the fragments of a defunct mangle, proved to be rent nearly in two. Accordingly, taking one of the four sovereigns that remained, he went out again to an emporium in Rosamon Street and laid out a further ten shillings on a pair of shoes. A hat, seen in the window of a secondhand shop, subjected to the most devious negotiation and eventually knocked down to him for five shillings and ninepence, completed his wardrobe.

"How do I seem?" he demanded of his wife, having struggled into these garments and, finding no mirror, being forced to make do with his reflection in the teakettle.

"Indeed, John, you look very well."

"A band for the hat? But no, that's scarcely necessary. What about gloves?"

In the end it was decided that a pair of gloves could be procured from Mrs. Hook, a seamstress who inhabited the room above. Throughout this investiture Dewar's expression, which he was careful to disguise from his wife, was of the most melancholic cast. He knew that, however ignorant he might be of the ultimate purpose of Grace's scheme, he was engaged in what he had assured himself inwardly was some kind of "dodge." This feeling was made doubly worse by the clothes in which he was now caparisoned and the silk hat that hung from his hand. It seemed to him that he could scarcely venture into the street beyond his house without risking exposure, that the very policemen who directed the traffic would look upon him with eager eyes. Gradually, by slow degrees, this feeling left him. He had, as far as he knew, not yet committed any crime. It might be—and to this hope he clung like a condemned man who has been offered one last hope of pardon—that the task before him was less suspicious—more honest—than it seemed.

It was inevitable that something of this disquiet should communicate itself to his wife, and on the evening of the day in which his sartorial transformation was complete, Mrs. Dewar observed somewhat gravely, "It does not seem to me, John, that you are happy about this work that you've to do."

"Well . . . no. Perhaps I am not. Not very. You see," he improvised, conscious of his inability to communicate any of the fears that burned within him, "it is such a deuce of a way. And of course I don't like to leave you."

"I shall do very well." (Mrs. Dewar's face, which was chalk-white, belied this assertion.) "Mrs. Hook has promised to see after my meals. And, you know, John, it is important that you should make a success of this chance."

"Well, yes, there's that of course." But Dewar's countenance, as he

D. J. TAYLOR

said this, did not make it appear as if he regarded success as a very probable outcome.

Two days passed, at the conclusion of which Dewar's nervousness had reached such a pitch that he had almost determined upon selling the suit and other appurtenances with a view to returning the five sovereigns. Then, on the morning of the third day after his encounter with Mr. Grace, the postman—not an official seen very often in the vicinity of Clerkenwell Court—could be heard ascending the rickety stairs to deliver a letter. Sent from an address in Carter Lane, it contained, as Grace had promised, a banknote for fifty pounds, a summary of the instructions previously tendered and an injunction to convey himself to Great Yarmouth as speedily as he could. The letter was received at nine in the morning. At ten, dressed with a punctiliousness that won the instant approval of Messrs. Bulstrode's commissionaire, which gentleman swept open the vestibule door with a respectful flourish, Dewar presented himself at Lothbury. Nothing, it appeared to him from the warmth of his reception, could be easier than the opening of a bank account in the name of Mr. James Roper or the concluding of an agreement with Messrs. Bulstrode's East Anglian agents, and by eleven he was on his way to the Shoreditch Railway Station. Here he paid eleven shillings and threepence for a return ticket to Great Yarmouth, surrendered his valise to a porter and was installed in a second-class carriage curiously impregnated with the scent of aniseed and containing an old woman with a Pekinese dog in a wire travelling basket.

"He's a very good dog, sir," this lady said. "Never bitten a person yet. Not even when he was a puppy."

Dewar remarked that he was very glad to hear it.

"And yet it's a fact, sir, that he can't abide travelling. Never could, and never will yet."

Dewar observed that this was very surprising.

Eventually, in a great hiss of vapour and disturbed air, the train bore them away out of Shoreditch into a queer hinterland of smoke-blackened chimney stacks and meandering tributaries of the river, their surface rainbow-hued with oil, past warehouses whose sombre frontages hung low in the water, and ancient manufactories whose windows had known no glass and whose roofs had known no slates, beneath great, black-bricked viaducts tilted monstrously against the sky, alongside immense, sprawling cemeteries where the gravestones lay all tumbled together under fantastic outgrowths of sooty foliage. Everything—the chimney stacks, the greeny-black skirts of the warehouses, the ledges of the viaducts and the gaunt palings of the cemeteries—dripped rainwater, off which the rays of a weak sun intermittently flashed, so that the effect was of a dozen little candles suddenly gleaming into life out of a fog of greyness and being just as suddenly extinguished. The old lady sucked caraway comfits for a while and then went to sleep with her mouth open, exposing a row of yellow teeth the colour of pianoforte keys, and the dog, howling a little at this abandonment, burrowed deep into his basket as if he genuinely believed that he might contrive an escape through the square of tin sheeting that constituted its base.

All this Dewar watched, without finding any salve for his dissatisfaction. There was a conspicuousness about his position that he wholly distrusted. It seemed to him that, clad in his black suit, silk hat balanced on his knees, he was a kind of exhibit at a public gallery that men might be invited to step forward and appraise. This self-consciousness preyed upon his mind and made him nervous. Were the guard to come tramping along the corridor, he would shrink into the corner of the carriage like a man pursued. Were, at the several stations along the line, an old woman to put her head in at the window offering newspapers and trays of hardbake, he started up in his seat in terror. At Ipswich the old lady woke up, pronounced a final encomium over her wire basket and was escorted away across the platform by a female relative, but her successor, a dark and silent man who trimmed his nails into a pocket handkerchief, Dewar did not like at all, believing him to be a police inspector travelling incognito who desired only the obscurity of a tunnel to leap up and apply a set of handcuffs.

It was no better at Norwich, where he was compelled to wait two hours for a connecting train and skulked miserably around the city in the grasp of a zealous porter, examining an ancient cathedral and a castle-cum-prison whose gardens were tended by men in zebra clothes with equal indifference. It is a scant twenty miles from Norwich to Great Yarmouth, across a great bare flat covered by a myriad of wind-

D. J. TAYLOR

mills, and yet Dewar wished the distance were two hundred. However, on reaching his destination he was pleased to discover—something that would have seemed impossible to him four hours before—that he was at any rate alive, that no lions had eaten him, or attempted to eat him, and that the porters, railway men and tourist touts whom he encountered treated him with an agreeable civility. In this way his spirits improved, and carrying his valise out of the station—it was by now about four o'clock in the afternoon—he absolutely stopped to ask an old man in a smock holding the bridle of a dray horse where in Yarmouth he might stay and if, in addition, there were anything in the town worth seeing? Finding that persons of quality generally put up at Bates's Hotel and that the beach contained a wonderful houseboat that Mr. Dickens had put into one of his novels, he determined to be taken instantly to the former and to spend a part of the next morning examining the latter.

Alas, Great Yarmouth out of season is a dreary place—at least I have always found it so. There is a promenade, running in parallel to the sea for nearly a mile, over which the spray gusts with unappeasable ardour; there is a north wind which blows directly down from Jutland; there are a couple of theatres which, though displaying the most inviting notices of past and forthcoming attractions, are always shut up; and a Thursday bazaar, always threatening to break out into a rash of "sixpenny sales," "shilling auctions" and the like, but, in point of fact, closed on all seven days of the week. Quite how the inhabitants of the town may be thought to occupy themselves between the months of October and March I do not know, for the shops are always shut and the streets always empty.

Having risen early the next morning, proceeded to the telegraph office, where he communicated his address to Carter Lane, investigated the sailors' reading room, which contained a rheumy-eyed copy of the *Yarmouth Mercury* and a cannonball supposedly discharged at Trafalgar, and examined the exterior of the houseboat on the beach that Mr. Dickens had put into one of his novels (the interior proving unnavigable as it contained a family of nine persons), Dewar felt that he had exhausted the town's possibilities.

On the next day, however, there came a further letter from Carter

Lane. This he examined with great alarm, for it disclosed to him the precise nature of his business in Great Yarmouth. Specifically, he was to visit that morning in the character of Mr. Roper the offices of two of the town's solicitors. At each he was to represent himself as the creditor of a gentleman named Nokes, living at an address in Peckham, and request that a letter be written soliciting the payment of debts to the value of £150. He was then to retire to his hotel and wait until such time as the solicitors communicated with him. All this—and in truth there was not much more than a page of it—Dewar read half a dozen or even a dozen times, so anxious was he to commit these instructions to memory.

Then, with his hat in his hand and the gravest foreboding in his heart, he stepped out into the high street with the aim of executing his commissions. Again, though, as with the bank at Lothbury, nothing could have exceeded the civility that greeted his appearance at these legal portals. In each case he was swiftly admitted, inducted with the merest delay into the presence of a partner in the firm, heard respectfully and assured that the letter would be written forthwith. He was staying at Bates's Hotel? Well, it would be their pleasure to communicate with him there. At the second of these offices discreet mention was made of the need for a reference. Dewar, though he felt sure that the beating of his heart could be heard by passersby outside in the street, gritted his teeth, referred the questioner in his blandest manner to Messrs. Gurney, with whom he believed his own bankers corresponded, and was bowed out onto the staircase in the manner of a modern Croesus. All in all, Dewar reflected, as he made his way back to his hotel, through air that now seemed to carry a rank odour of fish, it could all have been a great deal worse. Again, no lion had eaten him, or even attempted to eat him. In all his undertakings he had met only lambs.

It was in this spirit that, stepping out of the hotel after luncheon with the aim of taking another turn along the beach, he met with a calamity of such a nature as to send all his former fears flying once more about his head. Idling in the lobby, having transacted some minor piece of business with the desk clerk—a certain shovel of coals that might or might not have been added to his fire, a certain dish that

D. J. TAYLOR

might or might not have been added to his supper menu—he became aware that a man who had just entered the vestibule was regarding him with the keenest of looks. Dewar turned aside, intending to return immediately to his room, but in an instant the man, whose features Dewar now believed that he half-remembered, was at his elbow.

"Now here's chance. I said to myself when I came into the place that it was you, and d——d if I wasn't right."

"Well, yes indeed. How are you?"

Searching the man's face, Dewar recognised a commercial traveller with whom he had had dealings in his Islington days, one, moreover, to whom every detail of his commercial misfortunes would be known. Striving vainly to compose himself—for he was conscious that he had gone very red in the face—he became aware that the commercial traveller was observing him with more than usual interest.

"Here on business, I suppose? Well, you look as if the world was treating you pretty comfortably. By the way," the other continued, "didn't I hear the fellow at the desk call you Roper or some such name?"

It was an innocent enquiry, but to one of Dewar's febrile state of mind sufficient to goad him almost to frenzy. Stammering some excuse—he could not subsequently remember what he had said—he rushed from the vestibule into the street and, having ascertained that he was not being followed, took himself off to the promenade. Here, aided by cool air and the absence of onlookers, his head became clearer. He had met with a misfortune, he assured himself, but there was no reason why it should prove fatal. Doubtless he could no longer remain in a hotel where his assumed name might come to be generally known, but there were other establishments where the name "Mr. Roper" would attract no such suspicion. Accordingly, having allowed the greater part of an hour to elapse, he returned to Bates's Hotel and, having made sure that the commercial traveller was nowhere to be seen, presented himself at the desk with the intelligence that a letter recently received required him to leave town instantly. Five minutes saw the matter concluded, and Dewar found himself out in the street once more with his valise in his hand. Fear, he now perceived, had made him cunning. Rather than transferring himself to a rival hotel—the thoroughfare in which Bates's lay contained two or three—he walked to a rather out-of-the-way part of the town, somewhat beyond St. Nicholas's Church, and engaged a room in the house of a fisherman and his wife. Here he straightaway wrote to the two solicitors' firms and to Carter Lane informing them of his removal, though not, in the final letter, offering any explanation for it. He spent the remainder of the day walking the shoreline (a presentiment having told him to avoid any region where he might chance upon the commercial traveller) and eating the frugal supper of sprats with which his landlady had seen fit to provide him.

Alas, Dewar's troubles were far from vanished. Time hung heavy on his hands. Dull, rainswept mornings, which might have been tolerable in a commercial hotel, with a fire and the society of other men, were infinitely tedious to him in a fisherman's cottage in Southtown. He took to wandering the beach, far down by the water's edge beneath the flight tracks of the gulls and the murky sky, and in this way walked solitary miles along the coast path. There was a town to the south named Gorleston, full of picturesque cottages built of stone from the beach, and a lonely lake—the Breydon Water—populated only by herons and silent trees, but in neither of them did he find any solace. He had got into the habit—he remarked it during the course of these excursions—of muttering to himself as he walked, and the realisation was not pleasant to him. At the same time, labouring through the wind with his collar turned against his face, hands plunged deep into the pocket of his coat, he assured himself that his ordeal was nearly at an end, that another day—two days—would see him home. The tenement in Clerkenwell Court now seemed a kind of Elysian field and the clanging of the bells of St. James's was celestial music when set against the endless sand and the harsh cries of the gulls. He was a Londoner, he told himself, and the placid Norfolk faces that dogged his every step mystified him.

On the third day of his sojourn in the Southtown cottage, two letters arrived for him by the first of the morning's posts. Each was from one of the firms of Yarmouth solicitors he had engaged. Each begged to inform him that £150 had been received from his debtor, Mr. Nokes of Peckham, and that the money, less the firm's commission, was there for him to collect. This intelligence, which Dewar

D. J. TAYLOR

had calculated would only raise his spirits, had, curiously enough, the effect of deflating them still further for they offered proof—if further proof were needed—that the scheme in which he was engaged was altogether fraudulent. No creditor, he reasoned, having experience of creditors in his own line of business, would remit a sum of such magnitude in such a brief space of time. Surely such rapidity would arouse the deepest suspicion in those he had employed to collect it. There was nothing to be done, however, save to obey the summons, and into the town, carrying himself very circumspectly and with his hat pulled down over his eyes, Dewar went. Again, at both establishments, he—or rather Mr. Roper—was greeted with the greatest deference. In each case he was invited to read a letter in a fine italic hand, signed by Mr. Nokes of Peckham, berating him for his exigence but nevertheless acknowledging the extent of his obligations. In each case he quitted the premises with a cheque, drawn on the firm's account, for slightly less than £150.

There remained only a single task to perform. Dewar's money was by now nearly expended. Only a shilling and a few pence remained of the five sovereigns that Grace had given him a week and more ago. Yet each of the Yarmouth solicitors had, in addition to the cheque, presented him with a bill for six shillings and eightpence. Further funds would be required to pay his rent in Southtown. Following the advice of the most recent letter from Carter Lane, Dewar resolved to apply to Messrs. Gurney for some portion of the funds lately transmitted to his account from Lothbury. Calculating that half an hour would see him gone from the town, arming himself with the two solicitors' bills by way of a reference, he stopped a passerby to enquire directions. Gurney's Bank? Yes indeed, Gurney's Bank lay in the very next street.

It was by now nearly midday. Knowing that the businesses of Great Yarmouth, such being the case in provincial towns, clung to the habit of a dinner hour and that the doors would soon be barred against him, Dewar made haste. Whether it was the flustered state into which he was thrown by his rapid transit or the general air of light-headedness which had afflicted him for some days past that was responsible for what now befell him is perhaps arguable. Nevertheless, it is certain that on reaching the teller's desk, the following exchange took place:

"I should like to draw on some funds which I believe have been transferred here by your London agent."

"What is the name?"

"Dewar."

He corrected himself in an instant, but the instant was too late. The clerk's eye was already raised in enquiry. Worse, a senior clerk with a beard and an eyeglass who happened to have overheard the exchange from his own desk to the rear now rose and made his way across the room. Another man might perhaps have brazened it out, made a joke of his absentmindedness, produced incontrovertible proof that he was Mr. Roper, but Dewar was not that man. He merely took to his heels and fled. Making his way wretchedly back to his lodging, he cursed himself for his incompetence while demanding of himself the question: what am I to do? A search of his pockets realised the sum of fifteen pence. There was only one thing that he could do. Reaching the house at Southtown, he made the welcome discovery that his landlady was absent: a moment later and he and his valise were once more out into the street. Sweat pouring from his forehead, looking wildly around him as he went, he walked hurriedly to the station. Four hours later, followed only by a fog that had risen in the Norfolk fields and pursued his train westwards across the flat, he was back in London.

* * *

MR. THACKERAY'S TOUR

Norwich—Hingham—Watton

Within, except where the rococo architects have introduced their ornaments, the cathedral is noble. A rich, tender sunshine is stealing in through the windows and gilding the stately edifice with the purest light. The admirable stained glass is not too brilliant in its colours. The organ plays a rich, solemn music. Six lady visitors, each with her guidebook and her attendant gentleman, were parading up and down the nave in the company of a fierce-looking verger whose eloquence was such that I declare I felt ashamed of my ignorance of my ecclesiastical history and slunk away to the gate of the cathedral school hard

D. J. TAYLOR

by. Here half a hundred young gentlemen in tight black jackets and trowsers were playing tag or cockshies or purchasing hardbake off a tart woman's tray, watched over by a kindly young master in a stuff gown who clearly envied them their relaxations—I know I did.

At noon we left the city by its western approach, passing the great house of Earlham, seat of Mr. Gurney, and the pretty village of Colney before emerging once more onto the hard Norfolk road. This is, I believe, a charming country, where the river winds through water meadows and osier beds, with little neat churches rising here and there among tufts of trees and pastures that are wonderfully green, and yet the whole curiously empty and forlorn. Where the people had gone, unless it were to help with the harvest, I do not know. At any rate, I saw none, except a solitary boy playing by the roadside at Wymondham, who enquired, "Would your honour like to see a big pig?" "Titmarsh," I said to myself, following him into a sad little maze of allotments and yards of scuffed-up earth, "you shall observe the agricultural delights of the county and be a farmer yet," but I must confess that the animal, found staring complacently from its sty, seemed a very unremarkable specimen. Still, it was a pleasure to hear the rascal prattle of the thirty shillings his mother would get for the carcass and the plate of pig's fry he would have on slaughtering day and I confess quite reconciled me to the twopence which constituted our fee for the viewing . . .

Beyond Hingham—a neat town with a fine mere rippling at the wood's edge—the land turned morose and dreary. A cart rattled by bearing half a dozen old men and women with shabby luggage piled up at their feet and not a tooth between them—paupers, said my friend, who knows the county well, bound for the workhouse at Watton. A brewer's dray passed us, drawn by two great stamping horses, and I thought of its journey's end: mine host in a white apron standing at his door, the barrels rolled down into the dim, cool cellar, the pretty barmaid drawing the drayman's tankard. No such welcome, alas, awaited the old paupers. Towards Watton we came to a big house half hidden by trees with its boundaries fenced off by a high flint wall. This I was interested to see, being the abode of Mr. Dixey the celebrated naturalist. A smart lodge lay at the gate, with white ducks and stockings hung up to dry on the currant bushes, but there was no sign

Kept

*of life. The gates themselves were locked and barred, and it seemed to
me that Mr. Dixey, however strong his ardour for butterflies, does not
care much for visitors.*

*Indeed this part of the country has a desolate aspect: tall trees
shading the roadside, a horrid old ruined house that could have been
the setting for one of Mrs. Radcliffe's romances, and always the great
brooding flat stretching on into the distance. A wind had got up and
came soughing through the reed beds in the most melancholy way.
Passing a gap in Mr. Dixey's wall, where the stone had crumbled, I
could not resist taking a peep into his parkland, but there was nothing
except a pack of hounds chained up in an enclosure and a woman's
figure fluttering silently in the meadow before the house . . .*

*And so at length to Watton, a wide old marketplace with ostlers
attending to their beasts at the rails and the George Inn, with its fragrant beds and the liveliest parlourmaid I ever saw, and an imperious
old housekeeper to whom I would only say, "Madam, my chop would
have been sweeter still had the serving girl's thumbprint not stared up
at me from the plate."*

—W. M. THACKERAY,
"A LITTLE TOUR THROUGH THE COUNTIES OF EAST ANGLIA,"
Cornhill Magazine, 1862

D. J. TAYLOR

⚝ XI ⚝

ISABEL

Whenever I think of the life I led before I came here, it is always Papa to whom my thoughts return. Indeed, I sometimes imagine that of all the things I have seen & all the people I have known, it is only Papa that is real, that all the others are mere ghosts tapping at a door through which they shall never be admitted.

Papa has beautiful white hands with pink knuckles & long nails. His eyes are soft & large. His voice is slow & gentle. He holds down his cheek to kiss & he presses my forehead.

I can see him passing his hand through his hair laughing at the children pouring out his tea.

I can see him swinging his arms as he walks. I can see him looking out over the ship's side & replacing his spectacles that are always slipping.

When Papa wrote his stories, he would draw the pictures for them as he worked: gentlemen on horseback, fine ladies conversing, all upon the margins of his manuscript book. Once when we were at tea, there came a tap at the window & looking out we saw Mr. Hannay, that Papa knew, waiting on the step. "That is the man I need," Papa cried & set to work at once with his pen. And that is how the face in Papa's *Cromwell* is not Cromwell's at all but Mr. Hannay's as he stood on our doorstep.

When I was one-and-twenty, Papa gave me a birthday dinner at Richmond. Such a bad dinner, Papa said, but we liked it so much, the two of us. When the things were cleared away, Papa called a little carriage & we drove home past the river through clouds & clouds of mist, & came through Barnes & over the bridge, & all the people were out in the street at Kensington, & I was so very happy.

All this is very vivid to me, very particular in its dimensions, as if the years that followed had never been. And yet I know that had I foreseen them then, I would have wished them gone.

*　*　*

"When I am an old man," Papa used to say, "you shall be married to a grand gentleman, & living in a fine house with company calling in carriages & footmen in powdered wigs, but perhaps I shall be allowed to sit & drink my glass of claret & watch my grandchildren grow."

But now Papa is gone, there is no grand gentleman & no fine house, no company calling in carriages or footmen in powdered wigs, & the claret is all drunk up.

*　*　*

This morning Mr. Conolly comes. He is brought to my room by the butler, who waits outside until he is done.

I am sure that I saw Mr. Conolly before. But there is so much that is gone from my mind that however long I dwell on those old pictures I cannot find his face within their frames. Papa & Mr. Hannay, & Mr. Smith that was Papa's publisher coming up to see him in a cab, but not Mr. Conolly. Who is a white-haired, civil, old, thin-legged gentleman of a kind I do not like. Who presses my hand and looks very searchingly into my eyes as he speaks.

I would that Mr. Conolly's eyes looked elsewhere. At the butler waiting in the doorway, or the water jug & the teacups (they do not allow me a drinking glass, tho' I have often asked for one). Anywhere but at me.

How do I find myself? Mr. Conolly begins by asking.

"I am perfectly well, sir, I believe," I tell him.

You will excuse me, madam, he next says, if I ask you a question or two.

"If I can answer you, sir, I shall."

I do not mean to answer Mr. Conolly. Who still presses my hand as he looks into my eye. Who is very impertinent.

　　　D. J. TAYLOR

"How long has the Queen reigned?"

"A dozen years. A hundred. I am sure the Queen would know, if there is a doubt."

"If I wished to journey from London to Bristol, through which counties would I pass?"

"Indeed, sir, I should travel by air balloon. It is said to be most agreeable."

I am surer now than ever that I saw Mr. Conolly before. Who proceeds in this manner for some time. Who finally takes his eyes, and his soft hand, and his thin little legs away from me and shuts the door behind him. Whose carriage, shortly afterwards, can be heard grinding up the gravel in the drive.

I am Isabel Ireland.

I am twenty-seven years old.

The Queen has reigned twenty-eight years.

If I wished to journey from London to Bristol I should pass through Berkshire, Oxfordshire and Gloucestershire.

The number of states of the American Confederacy is thirteen.

The Prince Consort is four years dead.

How do I find myself? Alas, I am altogether lost.

*   *   *

A conversation with my guardian, Mr. Dixey.

"Have you diversion enough, madam? Is there anything that can be got for you?"

"I should much like to read Miss Brontë's novel *Agnes Grey*," I say to test him.

"I believe we have it in the library. Randall shall bring it up to you. But something other than a book?"

"Indeed, sir," I tell him, "I should like to see company."

To this he says nothing. The book comes with my supper. I fall on it as hungrily as the food.

*   *   *

Papa hated to see me idle. If he found me in the drawing room with my feet among the sofa cushions, he would say, "Come, miss, let us take a walk around the gardens" or bid me to fetch a block from the study floor (it was on these that Papa did his drawings before they were taken away to the engraver). So I am always careful to occupy myself. I read my book. I mend my clothes—that is, when they are in need of mending. I study my situation. A man should make an inventory of any new place in which he finds himself, Papa used to say, and this I have accomplished. Thus:

I have two rooms for my private use: the one a sitting room, the other a bedroom.

The dimensions of the sitting room are twenty-four feet by eighteen feet; the dimensions of the bedroom fourteen feet by nine feet.

The dimensions of my sofa are six feet by two feet; of my desk four feet by three feet; of my table the same.

I am brought my breakfast at eight, my luncheon at one, my supper at seven.

I read my book. I mend my clothes. I study my situation.

* * *

Papa and I often talked of the man I should marry.

He will be an archdeacon living in the country, Papa would say, & you will have ten children, & write his charges, & make puddings, & be very severe on the dissenters.

Nonsense, I would say in return, he will be a navy captain with only one leg, & a great telescope fixed to his eye, whom I shall see but once a year when his ship is in harbour & who will shock me with his oaths.

Nonsense again, Papa would say. He will be Professor of Greek at Oxford & you will turn bluestocking & have solemn parties for the undergraduates & be very down on ladies who have not read Homer.

I think that Papa joked in this way because he feared that I should leave him, & that I joked with him because I feared it too. "Alas," he would say, whenever a young lady's banns were read in church, "another

D. J. TAYLOR

old gentleman turning his face to the wall and wondering who shall bring in his slippers."

"The old gentleman," I would say, to twit him, "should bring in his slippers himself."

All that was five years since. And now all those that I loved are gone from me, & there is no power on earth that shall bring them back.

* * *

I have been very ill. That is what they tell me, & I daresay it must be true, for there is so much that has vanished from my mind that only sickness could have dragged it from me. It is not for want of thinking—oh no, not that! Once, indeed, I tried to set down on a sheet of paper all that has passed since Papa's death, yet found myself altogether defeated. The essentials were there in my head, I knew, but it seemed to me that I could not grasp at them & that they drifted through banks of vapour whose depths I could never penetrate.

I remember Papa dying, and the silence in the bedroom above our heads, and the servant rushing in crying, "Oh he is dead, miss!" and myself running to fetch Dr. Collins from his breakfast.

I remember the motion of a boat upon the water & Henry's face very white and grave—next to mine, & a ribbon fastened about my waist that, try as I might, I could not undo.

And—much later it seems to me—a woman's voice saying, not unkindly, "Now put on your bonnet," and I, very meekly, putting on my bonnet & stepping out into darkness & a jolting cab, tho' where it took me I could not say.

For I can be good—oh so very good—when I wish it.

* * *

When I was a child, I had scarlatina. It was in Italy, with Papa, who was unwell too, & the two of us lay on our backs in adjoining rooms overlooking the sea with our arrowroots & our lemonades & were, I think, very comfortable together. Now I lie on a sofa with a view of Mr. Dixey's wild garden, & my treatment is this:

I have a draught of medicine, brought to me morning & night, which I am bidden to swallow.

I have Mr. Conolly to press my hand & ask me how I find myself.

I have the door locked behind me, for fear that I should injure myself.

I am glad that the door is locked behind me, for I should not wish to cause inconvenience.

Not to myself or to anyone else.

* * *

As for Mr. Dixey's establishment, seeing that I have never been permitted to explore it, I have scarce an idea of its design. There may be a dozen rooms or a hundred; I have no means of knowing. And yet I have a vision of myself stealing about the place at night, a candle in my hand, opening doors that should not be opened, prying into chambers where Mr. Dixey would not have me go. No doubt it is very wicked of me to think these thoughts. But they have crept into my head unbidden, while there are other thoughts I would have kept there that have stolen away.

Yet though I may not turn keys & steal down staircases, I have eyes & ears, & there are things that I may deduce within the confines of a locked room. Thus, I calculate with certainty, there are nine of us in this house.

Mr. Randall, the butler, brings me my meals. He does not speak, except to ask if the food is to my liking (it is not!). Once, indeed, he pressed upon me a small book, saying that I should do well to take its contents to heart. When he had gone, I looked & saw that it was a tract, *Some Paths for the Craven Spirit*, of the kind that Aunt Charlotte Parker favoured. And which, knowing it to be dull, I did not read.

William, the footman, Mr. Randall's viceroy, says not a word. Indeed, he lays down my tray and refills my water jug, scurries to the door and scrabbles with the key in such hot haste that I believe he fancies me to be a young sorceress ripe to turn him into a toad.

Mrs. Finnie, the housekeeper, attends on me each morning at eleven, there being certain feminine wants that a butler and a footman cannot between them be expected to supply.

Who is a sour old woman with hair of such a blackness of jet that it cannot be her own.

Who declines to be drawn by the most amiable pleasantry.

"It is a fine morning, Mrs. Finnie."

"Indeed, ma'am."

"But not so fine, I think, as it was yesterday."

"Perhaps not, ma'am."

There is no conversation to be got from Mrs. Finnie.

Then there is a cook, Mrs. Wates, on whom I never set eyes, & three maids, whose voices I hear about the house & whose figures I have glimpsed at a distance in the grounds. I confess that I should like to speak to them, to sit in a parlour with them, even, & listen to them as they talk. Yet such are the ways of this house that I know they would not wish to speak to me.

Sometimes I hear the scrunch of gravel on the drive & the sound of voices far below & know that visitors are come. Once there came a clergyman, for I stood on tiptoe to look out of my window & saw his shovel hat. Another time an old lady came walking at a great distance through the gardens & passed round the side of the house. What business she had I cannot imagine.

I am forbidden company, Mr. Conolly says, for there are foolish fancies in my head that conversation may excite. I confess that this makes me very unhappy.

But perhaps it is for the best.

This evening Mr. Dixey again comes to visit me. He says nothing at first, but merely regards me as if there were some question he wished to put but could not bring himself to ask it.

"I have finished *Agnes Grey*," I tell him. "Are there other books I might see?"

"I shall have some brought to you," he says. "Is there anything else you would wish?"

"Indeed, sir," I say, greatly daring. "I should like to write a letter."

"A letter! To whom would you wish to write?"

Alas, so hastily was the thought plucked out of my mind that I cannot immediately answer him. "I should like to write to my husband's lawyer."

"There is nothing that he can tell you that cannot be told by me."

"Nevertheless, I should like to do so."

He bows but says nothing. Later, with my supper, Mr. Randall brings me two books. They are Mr. Trollope's *Framley Parsonage* and Mr. Jerrold's *The Story of a Feather*. Knowing how much Papa disliked Mr. Jerrold, I leave the latter unread.

* * *

A dull morning, overcast & with rain. Mrs. Finnie arrives punctually at eleven.

"It is a fine morning, Mrs. Finnie."

"Indeed, ma'am."

"Even finer, I think, than yesterday."

"As you say, ma'am."

There are other fools in this house than I!

* * *

I confess that I have begun to make a study of Mr. Dixey. A study of the set of his features. Of the way he stands before me. Of the way he sits in his chair.

What is there to say?

My guardian is a tall man, somewhat elderly yet vigorous in his demeanour. He has grey hair & grey eyes that sit in his head like pieces of flint but conceal, I judge, a kindly & industrious nature.

He is very active in his pursuits, wears a pair of gaiters, seems ever to be returning from some walk, has on riding boots or carries a dog whip, &c.

There is no Mrs. Dixey, nor I think ever was.

He has read Papa's books & indeed those of other literary gentlemen that Papa knew.

Yet there is something mysterious about him. Viz: his habit, when asked some question, of not replying; his habit of regarding me as if I possessed some piece of information of which he was dearly in want; his habit of casting his grey eye around my chamber as if something was hid there that he could not discern.

Henry, as I now recollect, used to talk of him occasionally, saying he was a man to whom he owed much, that the Dixeys were thought to be "queer people," whatever that might mean, that this Mr. Dixey had some reputation as a naturalist & scholar, &c., that his name could be found in the catalogues at the British Museum and so forth.

This is all that Henry said, & having little interest, I asked no more.

My guardian's face is clean-shaven with deep lines etched into the loose skin. He has long, delicate fingers and a way of saying "That will do very well" or "I had not remarked it" when something is drawn to his attention—trivial expressions, no doubt, but as they are part & parcel of the man, I set them down.

As to his interests, the other day he fetched a slowworm that he had found on the path & concealed in his pocket for his amusement; the week before, a bat nestled in moss upon a saucer that he believed he could nurse back to health. When I shrank from these objects—the bat with its pinched little face & evil claws I could scarce stand to look at— he expressed surprise, saying that he supposed certain things were not to others' tastes. This I thought very singular, but somehow characteristic of him.

And then last evening a most curious encounter, whose elements will long remain with me.

It was very late—gone eleven indeed—pitch-dark outside with a high wind blowing, but I had been amusing myself by singing snatches of old songs—it was something Papa and I used to do in days gone by—& had not thought of going to bed. Just as I assured myself that I absolutely must retire, there came a knock at the door, very loud and distinct, & in answer to my enquiring a turning of the key & my guardian's tall figure standing in the doorway. Again, he stared at me for a full half-minute without speaking, went to the window & stared into the night, & finally remarked:

"The hour is very late."

Kept

"I had not noticed it," I lied.

"You are quite comfortable here?"

"Indeed, sir. Very comfortable."

"I cannot offer you company. But there is conversation, if you wish it."

"I do wish it."

I had thought he would seat himself on one of the armchairs in my chamber. Instead he bade me follow him through the open door—he had a lighted candle set near the wainscot which he now retrieved. In this way—he leading, myself following, with my skirts gathered up in my hand to guard against the dust of the bare boards, our two shadows in monstrous relief against the wall—we proceeded along a corridor to a great silent landing, with moonshine streaming through the window onto the balustrade, climbed a flight of stairs & came eventually to a far-off room where lamplight glowed under the door.

His study, my guardian explained. He seemed very anxious that I should explore it and stood by my shoulder, indeed, as I examined it, like a small boy with his boat that his female relatives are bidden to admire.

Indeed my guardian's study is a very singular place, unlike any other gentleman's room that ever I saw. Picture, if you will, two or three great high bookcases extending almost to the ceiling, so that it must take a stepladder at least to ascend to their topmost shelves. And then a number of squat glass cabinets, all agleam with the light from the fire, and filled with the queerest objects: a stuffed pine marten poised on the bough of a tree; several animal skulls and pieces of bone; lichens and ferns set under squares of glass. Several of these exhibits I confess I did not overlike—viz., a wolf's head on a plinth, a stoat preserved so ingeniously that he seemed ready to strike the grey mouse that lay at his feet. Turning from them, I all but fell into the arms of a great brown bear who stood in the corner of the room in such a lifelike attitude that I could scarce prevent myself from crying out.

I must not mind old Bruin, my guardian said. Who in life craved but tender shoots and honeycombs.

There were, in addition, several little tables set against the wall on which lay trays of what I could not fail to remark as birds' eggs,

D. J. TAYLOR

all neatly labelled, thus: *Philomachus pugnax, Rallus aquaticus, Circus aeruginosus*. These, I will admit, took my fancy & I browsed among them for some time.

"What, pray, are these, sir?" I enquired of a pair of reddy-brown specimens, reposing on a saucer of moss.

My guardian seemed gratified by my interest.

"They are osprey's eggs. A bird the Scots call the eagle fisher, and very hard to come by in these times."

Much as I admired the eggs, there seemed something sad in this admission. That it were a great tragedy for the hen bird who returned to her nest to find them gone.

"It is a pity," I said, "that they could not have hatched, and allowed the world two more ospreys."

"As to that, madam," he remarked, "I fear that I cannot agree with you."

After that no more was said about eggs.

I suppose that I must have remained in that room an hour. I remember that there was a moon shining on the garden & an owl that flapped at the window, & the warmth of the fire being very pleasant.

My guardian is a restless man. He does not sit easy in his chair but stands up repeatedly to poke the fire, take down a book, inspect one of his cabinets, &c.

He is the possessor of a great fund of curious information, so that I should now think myself tolerably able to answer the most searching questions on the breeding habits of the lynx, the manufacture of otter snares, &c.

One very droll incident occurred, which I must not omit. By my guardian's chair, as he sat, I noticed there lay a saucer of milk. This I supposed the perquisite of some cat that I had not yet seen. Presently, though, a tiny mouse popped its head through a hole in the wain-scot, darted forth to the saucer & began to lap up the milk, apparently oblivious to the fact that great people were talking above its head. When I drew my guardian's attention to this—for I confess to a slight horror of mice—he smiled & said Sir Charles (he is named after Sir Charles Lyell, the great geologist) was a pet & had the run of the place, & stooping down put out his forefinger, which the mouse saw

Kept

& scrambled up almost the length of his shoulder, so that I could not help but laugh, it being so very humorous to hear a gentleman talking while a mouse ran in and out of the folds of his coat.

* * *

A very curious aspect of our conversation, which I here set down as fully as I can recollect it.

"Who made the world?" my guardian asks.

"Why, God made it."

"And yet there are those who say he did not."

"Indeed then, who else would be able to form us in the manner that we are and give us life?"

This was the answer that Papa always gave his friend Mr. Lewes in debates of this kind. My guardian acknowledges it with a nod of his grey head.

"Some men would say that the world made itself."

This seemed to me such a blasphemy that I cried out, "But out of what materials? And who placed them there?"

At this my guardian seizes Sir Charles, who has been polishing his whiskers in the region of his master's collar, and continues: "And mice? Did God make them? Or were they once some other thing?"

"A mouse is a mouse."

"But he might not always have been so. The rocks are older than the Bible."

"And yet, sir, they are all a part of God's purpose."

As am I, & my position here, & what will become of me, of which I would know more, when it pleases God to tell me.

* * *

And then a greater mystery even than my guardian's questionings.

Waking early this morning, at six of the clock, with the wind still beating against the eaves and a grey dew beyond the window, I entered my chamber to find a white rose upon the desk. A single white rose lying upon a silver dish, the thorns neatly trimmed from its stem.

D. J. TAYLOR

I enquired of the servants—Mr. Randall, who fetched me my breakfast, Mrs. Finnie, who came to me at eleven, the tall footman who brought my lunch—yet none of them could account for it.

* * *

I have been thinking of Mama.

Although, to be sure, it is twenty years since I saw her & fifteen since she died. Which I remember above all, the funeral at Kensal Green, and Papa in his black coat, and Sir Henry Cole, Papa's friend, standing at the grave, & all of us quite broken down with our grief. At the thought of poor Mama, who would never again laugh or comb out her red-gold hair as she sat on the terrace, or kiss me & tell me to be a good child, & all the other things that we recollected her for.

Papa and Mama met at Worthing, where he had gone to write his book & she to take the air with Aunt Charlotte Parker. Their carriage broke its axle on the Brighton Road & Papa was very gallant, summoned a cab & escorted them to their hotel, which I thought a very romantic story. When they were married, they lived in an old brown house in Kensington. One day when I was a girl, Papa told me to put on my hat & I walked with him across the gardens to a house where a gentleman in a travelling cloak with a great beard coming down over his shirtfront sat at breakfast over a silver teapot. This, Papa said, was Mr. Tennyson.

I remember Mama reading to me from the beautiful silk books that lay on the round drawing-room table.

And Mama sitting on the terrace with all her hair tumbling about her shoulders & our servant Brodie combing it out.

And Mama putting me to sleep in a dear little room with two little beds & some pictures. One was of a good boy doing a sum & another of a sleepy boy yawning on his way to school, & then over the door hung Daniel O'Connell, who I fancied would make the most horrible faces to frighten me.

And Papa's figure in the doorway as he regarded us & his shadow in the firelight as he stooped down to bid us goodnight.

And then we were at Paris & Mama was ill & she went to live

Kept

with a doctor in a big house with a great garden full of little paths, &
sometimes I would spend the day with her & run after her down the
long slopes. And Mama would become quite like a girl again & play
with me for hours at a time until Papa & the nurse came out to find
us. And Papa would say that we were his two darlings & that the hap-
piest moment of his life was when he came along the Brighton Road
(Mama said that he had his head in a book & scarce noticed her) &
saw the carriage with its broken axle.

Sometimes Mama would fly into a temper & throw the cup that
she had in her fingers to the ground or beat her hands upon her chair
in a passion, tho' it was a puzzle to me that anything could distress her.
Yet I was never frightened of Mama at these times, for I knew that she
loved me & would not bring me to harm.

Mama herself said as much.

Then the doctor said it was better we should not go to see her
anymore & we came away to England. I remember Papa's face in the
diligence that fetched us from Paris, & the lamp swinging from the
jolting road, & Papa scolding me for some trick I had played, & thinking that I should see Mama again & be consoled.

And yet I never did.

And when she died—I was twelve then & had a great friend called
Tishy Cole, & Papa was writing his life of Sir Thomas More—it was
as if someone I had known long ago & then forgotten had come back
to haunt me. And I resolved never again to forget Mama, & her red-
golden hair, & running down the slopes of the doctor's gardens. Which
I have not done to this day.

It seems to me that I am very like Mama.

I too have a room where I sit & am brought things & people are
very kind to me.

I too have my tempers & my frets.

I too have my red-golden hair, which is like Mama's, altho' I think
not so long.

And yet Papa, & all the others on whom I might rely, are gone
from me forever.

*　*　*

　　　　　D. J. TAYLOR

Once, before Henry & I were married, I tried to explain to him about Mama, & the doings at the French doctor's house, & other things—of Mr. Farrier, even, & what had passed between us—but he shook his head, smiled & said that it did not signify.

* * *

Of all flowers, there is nothing I detest so much as a rose.

* * *

And now, all unexpected, there is *an addition to my circle* (as Mrs. Brookfield, who we knew in the old Kensington days, & was very kind to us, would say when she had some lion to tea).

This lunch hour, instead of the tall footman who never speaks, there comes bearing my tray one of the maids, the yellow-haired girl whom I recollected seeing from my window. Very sturdy & carrying her burden before her as if it weighed no more than a teacup.

"Where is William?" I asked, the tray having been set down & the girl bobbing her head.

"Please, ma'am, he has gone away."

I fancied that William's going away was not to her liking.

"And you are to take his place?"

"If you please, ma'am."

Upon which she gave me a look such as I have often seen in the faces of those that serve me: as if she were wary of what I might say or do & wished that the door were open behind her.

"You must not be afraid of me," I said. "Indeed you must not, for I mean no harm. What is your name?"

"Esther, ma'am."

She would not say more but busied herself about my desk & shook out a sofa cushion that had disarranged itself, in such a way that I was very grateful to have her company. Plainly my situation—the room, my papers, &c.—interested her for I saw her dart several eager looks as she went about her work.

When she had gone, I listened to her footsteps tripping along the passageway until there came a moment when I could not distinguish them amidst the other noises of the house, & then another moment when they were altogether gone.

D. J. TAYLOR

XII

DEALINGS WITH THE FIRM OF PARDEW & CO.

15 MAY 186–

Wm Barclay, Esq.
Director
South-Eastern Railway Company

Dear Sir,

I refer to the meeting of the 11th inst, at which it was desired by the directors that our position regarding the conveyance of bullion to the French banks should be formally set down. The arrangements, which I have examined with the aid of representatives of the firms of Abell, Spielmann and Bult, and of Mr. Sellings, stationmaster of the London Bridge terminus, are duly summarised herewith.

As you are no doubt aware, the company's overnight mail train departs for Folkestone each evening at 8.30. The ferry service is naturally dependent on the hour of high tide, when the steamer may be brought further in to embark heavy cargo. It may be observed that the safe may even be lifted aboard the steamer, should this prove necessary, such is the vessel's proximity to crane and gantries at high water.

Naturally, our dealings with Messrs. Abell, Spielmann and Bult are of the most confidential nature. Mr. Spielmann informs me that Mr. Sellings, a most trusted and respectable employee of the company, is kept ignorant of their intentions until such time as a representative declares himself at the station office. Under Mr. Sellings's express supervision the bullion chests are escorted by the railway police to the stationmaster's office. Here each is weighed. Subsequently the chests are taken under escort to the baggage van of the ferry train.

I must here emphasise the strenuous efforts of both ourselves and Messrs. Abell, Spielmann and Bult to guarantee security. Mr. Chubb has provided the company with three copies of his patented "railway safe," constructed of steel plate to a depth of one inch and with dual locks. (It may be noted that at a recent exposition Mr. Chubb fixed one of his patent locks to a hotel door and invited the assembled company of locksmiths to pick it. None could do so.) As a precaution, copies of the keys are held by separate individuals of the company at London Bridge and Folkestone. Further, although all three safes are opened and closed by the same keys, only one is in use at any given time. The bullion boxes—each of these contains perhaps a hundredweight of gold—are of course locked, each additionally bearing the merchant's individual wax seal.

The company's engine having arrived at Folkestone, the railway safe remains under constant guard until such time as the bullion boxes can be removed for checking and shipment. One key is held by the station superintendent; the other is kept under lock and key at the company's office on the harbour pier. The weight of each chest is checked against its measure in London. Additionally, the station superintendent has been instructed to conduct a close inspection of the seal. Once placed in the care of the captain and crew of the steamer, the bullion is thenceforth conveyed to Boulogne. Here it passes into the custody of the Messageries Impériales and is once again checked with regard to its weight before proceeding to the Gare du Nord and the Bank of France, where the boxes can be collected by the Paris merchants.

I should add that Messrs. Abell, Spielmann and Bult, with each of whom I had some private conversation, professed themselves thoroughly satisfied with these arrangements, Mr. Bult in particular being convinced of the impossibility of any larceny being perpetrated while the shipment was in the company's hands. The merit of Mr. Chubb's safe, I am assured, is that a cracksman has nothing to work upon save the keyhole. Further, a fully loaded bullion box requires two men to carry it. In the unlikely event of any theft being committed, the outrage would become apparent as soon as the safe was opened at Folkestone. To lay hands on the stamps of merchants such as Messrs. Abell, Spielmann and Bult would, as Mr. Bult asserts, demand nothing less than the burglary of their vaults.

I trust that this information is of use, and would be glad to supplement it with any further details that may be required.

Having the honour to remain your most obedient servant,

I am, sir, yours most faithfully,

JAMES HARKER
Secretary to the Board

* * *

Spring had come, finally and after much hesitation, to Lincoln's Inn Fields, and there were daffodils out upon the green grass and gillyflowers blooming in the window boxes of the ground-floor sets. This being Lincoln's Inn, where an air of general severity prevails, they did so with an unconscionable meekness, as if they feared that some legal eminence—Mr. Crabbe perhaps—would descend in wrath from his chambers and present them with a writ for unlicensed blossoming or occupying too great a proportion of space. Mr. Pardew, hurrying through the great black gate on his way to see Mr. Crabbe, saw neither the daffodils nor the gillyflowers, saw nothing, in fact, other than the several phantoms that rose up and stalked through his imagination. Though he strode with his customary vigour, had walked all the way to High Holborn from his office in Carter Lane brandishing his stick as if all manner of unseen enemies were about to leap up at him, Mr. Pardew was not happy in his mind. There are some men who pride themselves on their autonomy, of having their progress through the world laid out in a manner that they themselves have arranged, and Mr. Pardew was such a one. He was the kind of man who, if he wished to have the pleasure of dining with a certain gentleman, would make sure that the invitation came from himself, or if he wished to pursue a certain course of commercial action would insist that the business was of his own devising. Such a resolve to follow his own inclinations had perhaps contributed, some years before, to his falling out with the late lamented Mr. Fardel.

Just at this moment, on the other hand, Mr. Pardew was on his way to an engagement to which he had been summarily bidden not once but twice, and he did not like it. To be sure, he had begun by treating the affair with his customary insouciance. A letter had come from Mr. Crabbe suggesting that he might present himself at the former's chambers at such and such a time, and Mr. Pardew had . . . ignored it. Then a second letter had come repeating the suggestion advanced in the first in such a way that it became a request. This too, after a certain amount of reflection and calculation, Mr. Pardew had ignored. Finally, a third letter had come, whose tone was so unambiguous that not even Mr. Pardew, however insouciant the remark he pronounced over it to his clerk, could deign to throw it in the wastepaper basket. This, consequently, was the chain of events that brought him to Lincoln's Inn Fields on a bright March morning with the breeze springing this way and that through the newly risen grass, gnawing savagely at his finger ends and waving his stick at the shifting air in a manner quite worthy of Don Quixote with the windmills.

In truth Mr. Pardew was not greatly alarmed at the prospect of facing Mr. Crabbe in his den. He had taken up arms against Mr. Crabbe before and knew that he had had the better of him. The letter whose production had so enraged and cowed Mr. Crabbe lay still in the pocket of his coat. This repeated summons to the old lawyer's presence was but a consequence of that victory. Moreover, he had an idea of what Mr. Crabbe might say to him and what he himself might say in reply. Yet there were other anxieties revolving in his mind, other schemes on which he hesitated to embark but which could not long be postponed, which agitated him to a much greater degree. The conflict that these precipitated in his mind became so great that at the door to Mr. Crabbe's chambers he halted, made a great slash with his cane at some chimerical adversary and muttered to himself something to the effect that he could not be eaten by Mr. Crabbe, and that this gentleman might, if he did not take care, be eaten himself. Having taken himself in hand in this way, he rapped noisily on Mr. Crabbe's brass knocker, was admitted with such alacrity that it appeared the old clerk had known of his coming and been expressly stationed behind the door, divested himself of his coat—the stick he retained in his hand—and whipped smartly up the stairs to Mr. Crabbe's room.

Mr. Crabbe was awaiting Mr. Pardew. In fact, having seen him coming across the grass from his window, he had been able to make certain preparations in advance of his visit. In particular, he had envisioned a ruse not uncommonly thought up by gentlemen who wish to interview other gentlemen and appear to some advantage: he had with his own hands taken the chair that stood in the centre of his room for the use of visitors and propelled it behind a screen that faced onto one of the bookcases. This meant, according to Mr. Crabbe's reasoning, that Mr. Pardew would be compelled to stand in front of him and should, additionally, find it very difficult to avoid Mr. Crabbe's gaze. In this assumption Mr. Crabbe was, as it turned out, altogether wrong. Mr. Pardew, coming into the room with the old clerk panting at his heels, saw immediately the nature of the ruse and decided that he would have nothing to do with it. Shaking hands with Mr. Crabbe and muttering some civility, informing the clerk that, yes, he would have a cup of tea if such were procurable, he took himself first to the fireplace, where he stood for a moment warming his hands, and then to the window, where he appeared to take a very keen interest in a cherry tree whose burgeoning upper branches could be seen perhaps twenty yards away. Mr. Crabbe, seating himself behind the desk from which he had risen to shake Mr. Pardew's hand, was not quite put out by this cavalier treatment, but he was aware that his preliminary stratagem had failed and that an advantage could only be secured by the ingenuity of his tongue. Accordingly, he shuffled the papers on his desk—papers which related to his recent dealings with the firm of Pardew & Co.—and did his best to attract Mr. Pardew's attention.

"A very fine day," Mr. Pardew observed from the window, where he was still engrossed in the cherry tree. "Upon my word, I think I never knew it so fine for March."

"I don't doubt it is a fine day," Mr. Crabbe deposed, with a blandness that he did not at all feel.

"By the by, I saw His Grace the Duke of —— the other night. He seemed to be in extraordinarily good spirits."

Mr. Crabbe, staring at his visitor's back, the front half of him still being turned towards the window, felt that this allusion was too much to be borne. He laid the papers down on the desk in front of him with a little crash of his fingers and coughed.

"Mr. Pardew. I have asked to see you because a very serious matter has arisen with regard to your affairs."

Mr. Pardew turned abruptly from his station by the window. "Indeed? Anything that concerns my business is serious to me. By all means say what you have to say, and you shall find me a willing listener."

Mr. Crabbe nodded at this courtesy, which was far more like the kind of thing to which he was accustomed, but at the same time he hesitated, for there was a difference between what he knew or suspected of Mr. Pardew's affairs and what he could decently insinuate. A gentleman, after all, does not invite onto his premises another gentleman with whom he had business dealings and accuse him of being a thief. On the other hand, he may very easily introduce into his conversation a presumption of thievery which the presumed thief can either acknowledge or deny as he chooses, while being aware that this presumption exists. Mr. Crabbe, to be blunt, remembering the course of their last meeting, was wondering how far he could go and what might be the consequence if, in a manner of speaking, he went too far.

The facts of the case were these. In the course of the past two months, relying solely on information provided by Mr. Pardew, Mr. Crabbe, or rather Mr. Crabbe's clerks, had written letters to perhaps half a dozen persons at addresses in the north of England requesting payments of debts owed to the firm of Pardew & Co. Somewhat to Mr. Crabbe's surprise, these debts had all been paid, either by cash, cheque or a combination of the two, the payment being made either by post (the letter generally lamenting Mr. Pardew's exigent attitude towards his debtors) or by emissary to Mr. Crabbe's office. In each case the money or moneys having been received by Mr. Crabbe and transferred into Crabbe & Enderby's bank account, where all the firm's receipts were customarily deposited, Mr. Crabbe, having first deducted his commission, had written a further cheque in favour of Pardew & Co. How Mr. Crabbe now regretted having written those cheques! For in the fullness of time word had come back from Mr. Crabbe's bank that one of the cheques had been inscribed on a form that, it was alleged, had been stolen from the person on whose account it was drawn, and that two of the banknotes were forgeries. All this was necessarily a source of horror to Mr. Crabbe, for he knew that he had been the party to a fraud. The loss to the bank had been instantly made good out of his own pocket. The circumstances—the promptness of the payments, a certain consistency in the tone of the letters lamenting Mr. Pardew's harshness—made him deeply suspicious. But still he had accepted Mr. Pardew's instructions in respect of his debtors—something that he now greatly deplored—and there was, he thought, a limit to the crimes of which Mr. Pardew might legitimately be accused.

Divining something of the thoughts that were oppressing the old lawyer's mind, Mr. Pardew, prowling now in the region of the fire, determined to make them work to his advantage. Smiling in the friendliest manner imaginable, he remarked, "I suppose it is something to do with those debtors of mine. I presume one of the cheques has not been honoured, or something of the sort?"

"It is worse than that," Mr. Crabbe told him grimly, wishing for all the world that the interview was over and he could go back to his copy of the *Times* and the devising of errands on which to send his clerk. "One of the cheques was written on a stolen form, and two of the notes were false."

At this Mr. Pardew opened his eyes very wide. "Indeed? How very provoking. But then I suppose a man to whom a debt is owed can scarcely be held responsible for the honesty of his debtors."

"Perhaps not." To allow even this concession was a source of pain to such a one as Mr. Crabbe. "Naturally the police have become involved."

"Oh indeed?" said Mr. Pardew again, with perhaps rather too studied a nonchalance. "And what have they managed to discover?"

"Only that the address from which the forged notes were despatched was a poste restante."

Despite his nonchalance, Mr. Pardew, standing on Mr. Crabbe's

Turkey carpet with his legs opened against the warmth of the fire, was engaged in a rapid calculation. He knew, of course, that the banknotes were forgeries and the cheque was written on a stolen form because, in an assumed hand and using anonymous messengers, he had sent them to Mr. Crabbe himself. But that such transactions could be traced back to the office in Carter Lane he thought unlikely. Should anybody—the famous Captain McTurk, say, or any representative of Mr. Crabbe—take it upon himself to investigate any of the addresses to which Mr. Crabbe had been directed to write, Mr. Pardew was confident that he would find nothing in the least incriminating. Having assured himself of this, but reminding himself that there was still one favour he required of Mr. Crabbe, he drew himself up to his full height, made a little feint with his stick at the fire and said in a meditative tone, "Indeed? This is very shocking. I can only apologise, Mr. Crabbe, for the inconvenience to which you have been subject."

This was too much for Mr. Crabbe. "Inconvenience, sir? It is more than inconvenience! Why I have had a man from the bank absolutely asking me—asking *me*, sir!—if I knew of the money's provenance."

"And how did you reply, I wonder?"

"I said what I believe to be the truth. That I had been requested to write a letter in connection with a debt, quite in the usual way, and this had been the result. I tell you what, sir"—and Mr. Pardew observed that Mr. Crabbe was genuinely angry, much angrier than he had been at the start of their interview—"this had better be the end of any dealings between us, indeed it had. If you have any further debts to be collected, you had better take them to some other firm and see what they say."

Hearing this opinion, which would have had many a legal colleague with whom Mr. Crabbe dealt positively abasing himself on the carpet, Mr. Pardew hesitated. He did not believe, in the last resort, that Mr. Crabbe would altogether throw him over, for he knew—and he knew that Mr. Crabbe knew—that if questions could be asked of himself regarding the stolen cheque and the forged notes, then they could also be asked of Mr. Crabbe. Behind their conversation, as ever, lurked both the stupendous figure of His Grace the Duke of ——, and the letter that Mr. Pardew had waved in front of Mr. Crabbe's face on

D. J. TAYLOR

their previous encounter, but Mr. Pardew acknowledged that there was a limit to both the power of His Grace's ducal strawberry leaves and the power of the letter. He might threaten to drag Mr. Crabbe down, but he fancied that Mr. Crabbe might wish to drag him down also. He needed to appease Mr. Crabbe, but he could not afford to leave him conscious of any triumph.

"Well, if it is any consolation to you, Mr. Crabbe, that money from my former business associates is pretty much in. There is no need for me to trouble you with any further labour in that line. But there is a chance that in a month or so I shall require you to write me another letter."

"There is, is there?"

"It may not be necessary. Indeed I trust it will not. It is a client of mine who has been sadly neglectful in the restitution of his obligations. Perhaps you have heard of him. It is the Earl of ——."

Mr. Crabbe, brooding savagely in his chair, looked up at this. He had indeed heard of the Earl of ——, and from what he had heard imagined him exactly the kind of gentleman likely to fall into the hands of Mr. Pardew. Instinct told him to request Mr. Pardew to leave his chambers immediately, and yet something stayed him from issuing this demand. Mr. Crabbe could not exactly locate the source of this unease, but he told himself that he did not quite like the look in Mr. Pardew's eye, which seemed to him both mocking and complicit, as if Mr. Pardew knew other things about him, things quite beyond those contained in that awful letter, while being altogether indifferent to any revelations that Mr. Crabbe might make with regard to his own dealings. Therefore Mr. Crabbe did not summon his clerk and have Mr. Pardew ushered away. He merely sat and stared at the fire and at the papers on his desk and at Mr. Pardew (who was now swaying luxuriously from one foot to the other like a cat that is getting ready to pounce), finding solace in none of them and feeling older than he had felt for many a year.

"As I say," Mr. Pardew continued, with an unmistakable note of deference in his voice, "such a course may not be necessary. It may not indeed. And even if it were not, I should of course be delighted to return that piece of property of yours of which we spoke . . ."

Mr. Crabbe made some feeble motion of assent with his hands and muttered something. It was not intelligible to Mr. Pardew, but its meaning was clear. Mr. Crabbe, if absolutely entreated and compelled to, would write the letter. For the moment, however, he would do nothing other than to have Mr. Pardew take his leave at the earliest possible juncture, would be glad, in fact, if he never had to set eyes on Mr. Pardew again. Mr. Pardew understood this as well as he understood the rates of interest in that morning's *Financial Gazette*, and was quick to depart, shaking the single finger that the lawyer extended to him from behind his desk and stalking down the staircase into the vestibule at such a rate of knots that he altogether forgot his overcoat and had to be followed out of the door by one of the clerks with that garment gathered up in his arms. Mr. Crabbe, watching him go, felt so wretched that he flung a pen wiper into the fire and sent his clerk out to a law stationer's in Carey Street to fetch a copy of the *Legal Review* that he did not in the least want to read. Such was the wretchedness of Mr. Crabbe.

Mr. Pardew, now striding away across the green grass towards the gate, congratulated himself on the result of his dealings with Mr. Crabbe, but he did not linger on this congratulation. Having gained his immediate object, his mind was bent on the greater purpose which he had been considering half an hour before and on which, it is fair to say, his mind had been bent for many months. Mr. Pardew was not a timid man, and yet the boldness of the scheme greatly alarmed him. It was an enterprise, he was aware, that might crash without warning over his head, one that would involve extraordinary risks and dangers, the principal danger being to Mr. Pardew and his liberty. Half a dozen times, as he sped over the grass, past the daffodils, through the great gate and into the street beyond, Mr. Pardew declared to his inner self that he would not do it, that the risk was too great. Half a dozen times, too, he corrected himself, slashed at the thin air with his stick, settled his hat more advantageously upon his head and plunged on again. In this way, arguing furiously with himself, at one point calm, confident and assured of his abilities, at another cast down, unhappy and sure that all would fall instantly into ruins, he walked back down the long expanse of the Farringdon Road and bent his steps in the direction

D. J. TAYLOR

of Carter Lane. It was midmorning now, and the streets, especially those side streets through which Mr. Pardew walked, were not unduly crowded. Turning into the lane, he saw on the other side of the pavement from his office door, smoking a pipe and staring up and down the street, an exceedingly ill-favoured man in threadbare clothes with a cotton handkerchief tied round his neck. When this gentleman saw Mr. Pardew, he gave the faintest perceptible sign—no more than a movement of his eye—that he recognised him. Mr. Pardew, even less perceptibly, acknowledged this and then turned into his office.

Here he found Bob Grace, feet up on a chair, hat pulled low over his eyes, eating his lunch out of a pastrycook's carton. Seeing his employer, he removed his boots from the chair and cocked up his hat, but did not otherwise salute him. Mr. Pardew smote his desk hard with the ferrule of the stick.

"Upon my word, Grace, I never knew such a one as you for eating. Well, has anything happened?"

"Davidson undertook to pay ten now and renew for another month. Here's the stamped paper. And that Pearce is outside. Brought a letter here, which he says you'll want to see. I told him as you'd want to see the letter first and him second, most probably."

"Most probably is right. Where is it?"

Grace flicked across the desk a piece of rough white paper, which Mr. Pardew immediately picked up and smoothed beneath his fingers. He knew, as soon as the paper passed into his hands, that it was not in fact a letter but a copy of one, or rather the first attempt of a clerk working to dictation, for there were several crossings-out and emendations by a second hand. Nonetheless, the paper was entirely sufficient for Mr. Pardew's purpose, and he examined it with great interest. The letter was signed by the secretary to the South-Eastern Railway Company and addressed to its directors. Such was the care taken with the alterations that Mr. Pardew declared himself certain that the information contained in it was accurate and that a final document would soon after have been prepared.

Much of what it had to say was known to Mr. Pardew, but a certain proportion was not. These parts of the letter he read over two or three times, committing them to memory as he did so, before placing the piece of paper on the table before him. As he did so he became aware, once again, of his surroundings, the shabby room in which he sat and the saturnine figure of his clerk, and resolved to himself that whatever steps might be necessary to remove himself from Carter Lane, its bleary window, the piles of stamped paper and Bob Grace would be worth the taking. Again he picked up the paper and read through it once more, lest there were some detail that had escaped his eye. But there was nothing, and having assured himself that he had the words by heart, and thinking such a course of action prudent in the circumstances, he crumpled the paper quickly between his fingers and flung it into the wastepaper basket. As he did so his gaze fell upon his clerk, who had ceased all pretence of eating his lunch and was sitting with his hands drawn up over his chest regarding him keenly.

"Now," said Mr. Pardew, looking up again at the bare, distempered ceiling of his office and thinking that he hated it. "Now, Grace, what hour would you say it was?"

Grace licked some gravy from the ends of his fingers, staring all the while at these appendages as if he fancied that they might serve as his dessert. "It's a few minutes after midday, I daresay."

"Where is Latch?"

"Out collecting. Gone after the swell in Monmouth Street as was supposed to have renewed this day fortnight."

"You had better go and find him. You needn't trouble to come back this afternoon."

"Not come back! Why, who's to lock up the shop? I should like to know?"

"I think you'll find," Mr. Pardew observed tartly, staring at the bleary window and hating it, "that I can turn a key in a lock if I have to. Now, be off with you. And ask Pearce to step in on your way out, if you please."

With the expression of one greatly wronged, Grace rose to his feet, scattering a fine spray of crumbs negligently on the desk as he did so, jammed his hat as low over his brow as it would go and took his leave, taking care to slam the door smartly behind him as he went. In truth he was not unduly displeased by the turn that events had taken, having grasped the opportunity to read the letter before it passed into his

D. J. TAYLOR

master's hands, and also to have spoken several words to Pearce when that gentleman first presented himself in Carter Lane. Armed with this information, and with certain other hints that Mr. Pardew had let fall, deliberately or otherwise, over the past month, he had a fair idea of what his master was about, and the advantages that might accrue to himself from this knowledge. "He is a sly one and no mistake," he said admiringly to himself as he lumbered out into the street, "and yet I'll be even with him too."

Left on his own in the office, Mr. Pardew got up immediately from his desk and performed several rapid actions. First he took a small notebook from out of a drawer and laid it open before him. Then he inspected the contents of a metal cash box that sat upon his clerk's desk, replaced the lid but did not lock it. Finally, he took Grace's chair and, lifting it easily in one hand, placed it in the centre of the room. This done, he returned to his own chair just as Pearce, following the instructions given to him by Grace, came through the street door.

Mr. Pardew laid his hands out squarely on the desk before him, stuck his chin up at an angle and gave his visitor a glance. On close inspection, he seemed even more haphazardly attired than he had appeared in the street. The cotton handkerchief looped round his neck was stiff with grease, and his hands, half protruding from his trowser pockets, were extremely dirty. Seeing Mr. Pardew, he raised his eyebrows slightly in a gesture that spoke of an intelligence greater than that suggested by his outward demeanour and accepted the proffered chair. He smelled very strongly, Mr. Pardew now noticed, of beer and tobacco smoke.

"It's a Friday afternoon," Mr. Pardew said, without preamble. "Why ain't you at work?"

"Sick," Pearce rejoined, hoisting one leg over the other so that Mr. Pardew could take better notice of a pair of exceedingly patched and battered boots. "Left word at the orfice. Expected back Monday."

"You'd better take care, else you'll be out of a situation," Mr. Pardew told him with a familiarity that suggested he had perhaps met Mr. Pearce once before and perhaps even enjoyed with him a previous conversation of this nature. "Now, you'll oblige me by telling me where this letter came from."

Kept

Pearce opened one of his eyes, having for some reason closed both of them during Mr. Pardew's earlier remarks. "Fellow named Tester as is assistant to the superintendent."

"A young man?"

"Four- or five-and-twenty. I daresay you'd call that young."

"I daresay indeed." It may be seen from these remarks that Mr. Pardew was not altogether certain of the man who sat before him. The problem was that he disdained to attempt any intimacy with him and yet he fancied that scant progress could be made until at least some kind of intimacy had been established. Accordingly, he went off on a different track.

"As to the letter, I can't say that it contains anything altogether startling."

Pearce opened both his eyes to their absolute limit in a way suggesting that had he not been employed by the South-Eastern Railway Company, he could have made a fair living at the dramatic entertainments that are staged at penny gaffs. "That may be your opinion. It ain't mine."

"No? Well no doubt it will be of some use, let us say. Oblige me, Pearce, by walking over to that cash box there"—he indicated the metal tin on his clerk's desk—"and telling me what you find in it."

Pearce did as he was bidden.

"A ten-pun' note."

"Very well. I never saw it there. The box was empty when you came into the room. You take my meaning? There is another box here in this drawer. You take my meaning in that respect? Excellent. Now, about the letter, which to be sure contains nothing altogether startling. The days on which bullion is to be shipped are not generally known to the company's staff?"

"Stationmaster himself don't know until the van drives up."

"In how many safes are they generally contained?"

"There's three safes. Only one of them is ever used, though."

"And how many keys to lock it?"

"Two. Superintendent and the stationmaster has one each at the bridge. There's two more the same down at Folkestone."

"And who has charge of them?"

"Folkestone superintendent has one. Other one's kept in the office on the pier."

"Very well. Is the safe only in use when there is bullion to be shipped?"

"No. It travels down in the luggage van anyhow, whether there's things in it or not."

"Is there ever a time when the two keys are kept together? Either in London or Folkestone?"

For the first time since their conversation had begun, Pearce looked if not uneasy then reluctant to vouchsafe the information that had been demanded of him. He took a little turn around the portion of the room in which he stood, peered through Mr. Pardew's window at the great dome of St. Paul's, shuffled his feet uncomfortably and looked at the door behind him. Mr. Pardew saw all this and was encouraged by it.

"I assure you we are quite alone. Now, is there ever a time when the two keys are kept together? For an hour even?"

"Last week," Pearce began, speaking in a low voice and addressing his remarks not to Mr. Pardew but to the inkwell on his desk, "one of the Folkestone keys went missing." He lapsed into reverie once more and was silent for such a long time that Mr. Pardew felt it necessary to sharpen the tone of his voice: "And what did the directors have to say about that? Come now!"

Pearce, looking up, thought that he did not like the expression on Mr. Pardew's face, that it seemed to have grown larger and more oppressive in proportion to the rest of his figure, and that he would have given much not to have had it trained upon him.

"Office turned upside down to find it. And when they didn't find it, the talk is that it's 'mislaid.' All the safes to go back to Chubb. New locks, new keys, everything."

"So at some point two keys—that is, two sets of two keys—will be returned to London Bridge? And to whom will they be sent?"

"Tester, I suppose. He had the writing of the letter."

Having vouchsafed this intelligence, Pearce looked so enquiringly at the cash box that Mr. Pardew decided to halt his interrogation. He was in any case confident that the man had told him all he needed to know. Ascertaining from him that Tester lived with his mother at an address in the Borough, he dismissed the man from his office and sat down again at his desk. There was a copy of a financial newspaper before him, which he picked up and affected to study, but I do not think that its contents interested him very much, for his mind was far away brooding savagely. Outside in Carter Lane the promise of the morning had given way to an overcast sky. Rain fell against the window, and Mr. Pardew watched it fall, hating it and the things that lay beyond it. He had reached, he acknowledged, a crisis in his affairs. Either he could proceed with the plan that had been occupying him for the past three months, ever since he had walked into Mr. Crabbe's chambers and asked him to write a letter, or he could put it aside and make to believe as if it had never been. For the moment, he knew, he had taken no decisive step. He was like a man who, resolving to burn down his enemy's house, lights a lucifer, holds it to the thatch and then withdraws it. Thinking of his conversation with Pearce, of the opportunity that the mislaid key seemed to offer him, of half a dozen other courses that he must follow if he wished to be successful in his plan, Mr. Pardew found even now that his mind drew back from the task. There was a sudden noise at the door and he started up guiltily, taking his stick in his hand, but it was merely a circular falling airily through the letterbox and he stood looking at it stupidly as the rain fell against the window and somewhere near at hand a clock chimed the half hour. The room in which he sat, he now discovered, had become intolerable to him. Its mass of papers, its unswept floor, the discarded carton from which Grace had eaten his lunch: all these, though glimpsed a dozen times before, oppressed him in a way that he now found almost painful.

On the instant an idea came to him. Lying in a drawer of his desk was a letter addressed to the Earl of —— outlining that nobleman's melancholy dealings with the firm of Pardew & Co., and it occurred to him that it would be a relaxation to deliver it to the Earl at his club. Accordingly, he placed his hat on his head, drew on his coat, seized his stick, placed the letter in an inner pocket and stepped out into the street. Here Mr. Pardew did what for him was an unusual thing. He walked to the cab rank on Ludgate Hill and had himself carried

{ 206 }   D. J. TAYLOR

away by hansom along Fleet Street and the Strand towards Trafalgar Square and the West End. Almost immediately, though, having seated himself in the cab's interior, with his stick drawn up under his chin, he found that this mode of conveyance was no relaxation at all. He tried fixing his gaze on the people milling by in the rain—on an immensely tall man who rose a foot or more above the crowds, on a very miserable street clown dancing a hornpipe near the crossing opposite St. Bride's Church—only to find that his eye continued to bore inward and that he scarcely saw the sights that lay before him. Constantly, his mind turned on the information that Pearce had given him, devising half a dozen little schemes by which he might press his plan forward. Then, almost immediately, he would acknowledge to himself that it would not do, that half a dozen different stratagems were likely to prove more successful. Then again, shifting his attention to these new possibilities, he would decide, again on the instant, that they too were flawed in conception or beyond his power to execute. In this way Mr. Pardew spent a thoroughly miserable quarter of an hour, gnawing on his stick, staring out of the cab window with such ferocity that the passers-by might have thought him a madman being carried off to the Bedlam on the instructions of his heir, and altogether wishing that he stayed at his office where there were letters to write and work in which he might have immersed himself thoroughly. Reaching Trafalgar Square, he could stand his situation no more and so, paying off the cab, walked hastily along Pall Mall before turning into St. James's Street, where he knew the Earl of ——'s club was to be found.

It was by now perhaps half past one, the sky turned slate-grey and the rain continuing to fall. Having walked a brisk half mile in which he had concentrated on the transit rather than the problems that oppressed him, Mr. Pardew felt somewhat more at ease with himself. Yet a second, more immediate, difficulty now presented itself. It was Mr. Pardew's intention to mount the steps of the Earl's club, where experience told him that his lordship would most probably be found, and absolutely confront that nobleman in the card room or the library or wherever he might have taken refuge. And yet Mr. Pardew was not a member of this establishment (his own club was a modest affair in Covent Garden, where he went to play whist with six or seven retired

Kept

barristers and discreet tradesmen), and he rather fancied he would have difficulty in gaining entry. Nonetheless, having ventured all this way, he would have despised himself had he not made the attempt, and so, with the letter in his pocket, he fairly skipped up the steps and plunged into the club's hallway. It was Mr. Pardew's hope that he might pass through this entrance undetected. Almost immediately, though, a majordomo in livery and with a tremendous floured wig came stalking across the tiles to enquire how he might assist him.

"I was hoping very much to have a word with the Earl of ——," Mr. Pardew said blandly. "That is, of course, if His Lordship is available."

The majordomo, regarding Mr. Pardew as he stood there on the marbled floor with the letter in his hand, did not quite like the look of him. He rightly suspected that Mr. Pardew was up to no good in the matter of the Earl of ——, that he had come, additionally, from the City, and that the envelope in his hand contained a bill. Therefore he placed himself squarely in the path that Mr. Pardew imagined that he might have taken towards the staircase and remarked that he didn't believe His Lordship was in the club.

"Not in the club!" Mr. Pardew exclaimed. "Why, he told me himself that he would be here this afternoon."

The Earl of —— was, as it happened, at this moment smoking a cigar with certain pleasure-loving acquaintances in the billiard room. However, something in Mr. Pardew's manner of expostulation suggested to the majordomo that the Earl would not wish to be troubled by such a one as Mr. Pardew. Therefore he repeated his denial, at the same time nodding his head to a footman, who now came and stood ominously a yard or so from Mr. Pardew's side.

Mr. Pardew saw that he was defeated. He saw also that nothing was to be gained from an outburst of temper in the hall of a grand gentlemen's club in full view of several of its members. "Perhaps, then, you would be good enough to see that this is placed in His Lordship's hand," he remarked, extending the letter as he did so.

The majordomo flicked his forefinger in the direction of the footman.

"If you give it to Jeames here, he will see that His Lordship gets it."

D. J. TAYLOR

Mr. Pardew, having been relieved of his burden, very shortly afterwards found himself once more upon the steps of the club. He was by this time quite furious. The Earl of —— refuse to see him! Who did the Earl of —— think he was? Was his money not as good as the Earl's, seeing that a goodly proportion of the Earl's was got from other people? Such was the extent of Mr. Pardew's rage that for a moment he almost raised his stick and beat against the door of the club with it. Indeed he might have done so had he not noticed that a policeman standing on the street corner to which the steps of the club descended was regarding him with more than usual interest. And so Mr. Pardew put away his stick, contenting himself with a sardonic glance at the club's bow window, behind which three fat gentlemen were staring benignly out. Mr. Pardew knew one of these gentlemen—knew, too, how much he owed—and the recognition fuelled his contempt. The Earl of ——! The Earl of —— should be damned, and Mr. Pardew stand on the edge of the fiery pit cheering on his judges.

Thoroughly exasperated, he made his way down the steps of the club and into St. James's Street, aware as he did so, yet not perhaps connecting the two, that the events of the previous five minutes had made the subject of his former brooding clearer in his mind. He continued up St. James's Street to Piccadilly, where he waited irresolutely for a moment, staring into the doorways of the great shops, into Messrs. Manton, in whose window lay a pair of pistols with which he would quite happily have shot the Earl of —— had that gentleman been to hand, and Fubsby's the confectioner, where a demure young woman presided over a gigantic bridal cake, but coming to no speedy conclusion as to what he ought to do with himself for the remainder of the afternoon. There was his house in Kensington, but Mr. Pardew did not often present himself at his house in Kensington. There was his office, but Mr. Pardew had forsworn his office for the day. There was his club, but all clubs, whether his own or anyone else's, were anathema to Mr. Pardew in his present mood. "D——n it!" he said to himself, passing a window where a couple of gentlemen in evening dress leaned forward and looked as if they might be about to engage him in conversation but that they were tailor's dummies, "I shall go and see Jemima, indeed I shall!"

There was a cab rank twenty yards away, but Mr. Pardew had had enough of cabs. Instead, picking his way carefully over the greasy pavement and avoiding a pertinacious crossing-sweeper in search of a penny by almost jumping over his broom, he proceeded to Piccadilly Circus and stepped onto an omnibus. Seated on the lower deck, next to an old lady with a goose in a basket and behind a couple of men discussing the prospects of the Tutbury Pet in the next great sporting contest, Mr. Pardew found himself comparatively at ease. The subjects on which he had brooded on his way along the Strand came back to him, but they did so in a manner that enabled him to deal with them to his satisfaction. And in this way he mulled over certain of the pieces of information conveyed to him by Pearce until he had arranged them into a structure of which he could approve. "I could do that," he said to himself occasionally, or "But then that would not do at all." On these occasions his lips moved silently and he shook his stick, and the old lady wondered at him, grasped her basket more tightly to her and edged up nervously into her corner. The sporting gentlemen got up and went away, leaving a newspaper behind them, and Mr. Pardew, picking it up and cursorily examining it, saw that it contained news of a daring burglary recently committed in the metropolis, the burglars now apprehended through the agency of Captain McTurk, and read on with intense interest. If there was one name that Mr. Pardew hated and feared, would not allow to be breathed inside his head while he meditated his schemes, it was that of Captain McTurk, and yet the deliberations of the past few minutes had given him courage, and he fancied that, if the occasion permitted it, he could deal even with Captain McTurk.

By the time he approached St. John's Wood, Mr. Pardew's mood was altogether placid. There was a little row of genteel shops in the street abutting the row of laburnum-shrouded villas, and he strode into one of them and made several little purchases and had them packed up nice and neat in a paper bag. On his reaching the house, the glimpse of a female face through the window of the drawing room told him that some entertainment was in progress, and opening the front door with his key, he stepped into the parlour, beckoning the servant girl, who had bobbed her head into the hall, to follow.

D. J. TAYLOR

"Who is it that your mistress has with her?"

"Indeed, sir, it's her sister," replied the girl, who shared Mr. Pardew's views about the people in Islington.

"Would you tell her that I would like to speak to her immediately?"

The girl did as she was bidden. Mr. Pardew went and stood in the corner of the room, beneath a very fanciful etching of a young lady on a swing, looked at the etching and at his boots, found pleasure in neither, opened the pianoforte and touched a note or two with just enough force to make them resonate and then straightened himself and clasped his hands behind his back. Near at hand he heard the sound of a door closing sharply, a rustle of silks in the passage and then Jemima was standing before him, somewhat flustered and with her complexion even more pink and white than ever.

"Upon my word, Richard, I did not expect you, indeed I did not. You said Thursday forenoon, I am sure of it."

"What is that . . . person doing in the house?"

"Indeed, Richard, it is very hard if a woman cannot see her own sister."

"I suppose she wants money. Isn't that the case of it?"

"No more than a trifle. It is not her fault. They have shut the factory where Ned was working, and there is rent owing."

"An idle, good-for-nothing scapegrace."

"It may be as you say"—Jemima's voice as she said this was studiously respectful—"but would you have me sit by and have my own flesh and blood starve?"

Mr. Pardew shrugged his shoulders and jingled his money in his pockets. This was not a question that he could decently answer, and he knew it. In fact it would not have disturbed him in the least to learn that Mrs. Robey—this was the name of Jemima's sister—had starved to death, but gentlemen are generally shy of saying such things.

"Will you not come and have some tea, Richard?"

"No, I will not. The girl may bring me some here if she likes."

Somewhat to his surprise, Mr. Pardew found that his ill humour was ebbing away. It occurred to him that, with the problem on which he had expended so much mental energy settled to his satisfaction, he could afford to be polite even to Mrs. Robey. He would not unbend sufficiently to see Mrs. Robey, but he would be . . . polite.

"See here, Jemima," he said. "I have had a great deal to trouble me today, and these things turn a man sour. I mean no harm to your sister, indeed I do not. You had better give her these two sovereigns"—he extracted the money from a little heap that he brought out of his trouser pocket—"with my compliments and ask that she will take herself off."

Wondering a little at such largesse, Jemima took the sovereigns in her outstretched hand and retired into the passage. Presently there came the sound of a door closing, and gazing from the parlour window—having first chosen a vantage point from which he could not be seen—Mr. Pardew saw a stout, red-faced woman in a black coat and bonnet making her way hastily towards the gate. Once she was out of sight, the nervousness that had affected him since the beginning of the day began to recede. He looked around the parlour and its furnishings and remembered that he had paid for them. He recalled the morning's interview with Mr. Crabbe and fancied that once again he had got the better of the old lawyer. He thought of Jemima and told himself that should events fall out as he proposed, there were certain things he might do for her: a house, perhaps, up the river in Richmond, far away from the base intimacies of Islington; a carriage in which she might be driven of an afternoon with himself beside her. In this way, standing on the parlour carpet with his hands in his pockets, Mr. Pardew built up numberless airy castles round whose battlements he stalked, until a soft step interrupted his reverie.

"Gracious, Richard, you have been a very long time."

"Eh? Well, perhaps I have been. I shall come now, at any rate."

Whatever resentment might have been bred up in Jemima's pink and white bosom by Mr. Pardew's remarks about her sister had been softened by receipt of the two sovereigns. Leading her lord and master to the drawing room, she administered tea and certain of the delicacies he had brought home in the paper bag with a humility that Mr. Pardew found very agreeable. Beyond the window the rain had ceased to fall and a weak sun was shining across the mottled grass and the laburnums, and Mr. Pardew rather thought that he liked it. In this

D. J. TAYLOR

way he passed a very pleasant half hour drinking his tea, staring at Mr. Etty's cupids and supposing that the day had turned out largely to his advantage.

"What was it that you had to trouble you today?" Jemima wondered meekly as the servant girl came in to clear away the tea things.

"To trouble me? I don't know that there was so very much. There is a gentleman—the Earl of —— in fact—whom I was compelled to go and see at his club to remind him that he owed me money."

"Gracious! And you told him so to his face?"

"Well . . . I left a letter there for him, which is much the same thing."

"I should think that it was," replied Jemima, who loved talk of this kind.

"His Lordship spends too much on horses, that is my opinion of it. By the by," Mr. Pardew persisted, whose benevolence knew no bounds, "how should you like to go to the Derby this year?"

"I should like it very much."

And so they sat and talked some more about your young fashionable sprigs of aristocracy and their weakness for the turf—Mr. Pardew meditating once more on the decision he had reached, Jemima thinking of the Derby and what she might wear and what might be the outcome of things—and eventually had supper over the fire and were very comfortable together.

* * *

In the course of the next few days, when not engaged in discounting his bills or sitting in his office devising tasks for his clerk, Mr. Pardew undertook a number of useful and prudent activities. Arriving at Carter Lane early the next morning, so early as to precede Grace by a full eighty minutes, he wrote a letter, in a disguised hand and signing himself "Elias Goodfellow," to William Tester, Esquire, of Fairfax Street, the Borough, and caused this missive to be taken off immediately by a messenger boy whom he found lurking by the side door of an inn twenty yards farther down the lane. If Bob Grace, arriving at his customary hour of ten, wondered at his master's presence behind his desk, he did not say so but contented himself with whistling under his breath and laying out fresh sheets of blotting paper in a very significant manner. "Upon my soul, Grace, you are very cheerful this morning," Mr. Pardew observed at one point. "Indeed I am, sir, as cheerful as may be," Grace told him, even going so far as to buff the bleary window with a piece of rag he produced from a basket.

All this took place quite early in the morning. Subsequently, having left his clerk in charge, Mr. Pardew betook himself to Clerkenwell and to a little alley in the vicinity of Amwell Street, where lodged a gentleman named Mr. File. Mr. File was a demure little man of about sixty with a bald head and a very powerful pair of spectacles who some ten years before had been greatly celebrated in the City of London as a locksmith. It was said at the time that Messrs. Chubb, by whom he was employed, could do nothing without him, and that the safes of half a dozen of the great banking houses had been secured by his agency alone. A champion cracksman, arraigned at the Old Bailey, confessed that Mr. File's skill had altogether defeated him and was chided for this failing by the prosecuting barristers. And yet somehow Mr. File's reputation had not thrived in the wake of these accomplishments. It was rumoured that the company he kept was not of a kind that Messrs. Chubb, or indeed the City police force, would have liked had they known of it. Towards the end of the year in which the champion cracksman had stood at the dock of the Old Bailey and testified to Mr. File's ingenuity, there was a robbery at Messrs. Collingwood, the City tallow dealers, in which a quantity of bullion was got out of a safe and spirited away into thin air, the doors of Messrs. Collingwood's establishment remaining bolted throughout, and it was said by those who knew about these things that Mr. File had something to do with it. Naturally, Mr. File had protested this libel, which appeared in an evening newspaper, but it was noticeable that no action was brought and that very soon after, Mr. File's employers decided that they would dispense with his services. Thereafter Mr. File retired into private life, in which capacity Mr. Pardew, who had perhaps had some earlier dealings with him, sought him out and talked to him for upwards of an hour. Their conversation concluded with Mr. Pardew shaking his head and enquiring of Mr. File if he thought it could be done and Mr. File

D. J. TAYLOR

nodding his and remarking that he thought that, given fair weather, if not with odds so great as Lombard Street to a china orange, it possibly might.

Two days later, Mr. Pardew could be found at London Bridge Station, very spruce in a green travelling cape with a bag under his arm and looking for all the world like a man who intends to avail himself of the amenity of the boat train. In this capacity he could be seen, by anyone who cared to look, prowling in a very interested manner up and down the station concourse, examining the timetables and generally immersing himself in the life of the place. A wagon came rattling up from the City as he stood there, and Mr. Pardew looked on with apparent nonchalance as a couple of policemen came forward under the stationmaster's eye and superintended the transfer of a large crate, bound around with red and black tape, into that gentleman's office. In short, there was nothing that Mr. Pardew did not see. He peered into the gentlemen's cloakrooms and satisfied himself of their salubrity. He went and had his boots shined by the bootblack, took a cup of coffee in the refreshment rooms and purchased a newspaper at the bookstall. Then, when perhaps half an hour had passed, he proceeded to the ticket office and, emerging from it some few minutes later, stepped onto the Dover train. Here, seated in a third-class compartment, he took quite a lively interest in his surroundings: in the attentions of the guard who moved up and down the train, in the number of stations through which they passed and the time it took to pass them. At Redhill, through which the Dover train in those days passed, he got up from his seat and took a little saunter, walking as far as the guard's van, into which he surreptitiously peeped, assuring himself that it contained a safe, and then wandering back, passing the guard as he did so, that official very courteously holding a connecting door between two carriages open for him as he went by.

Arriving at Folkestone, where a spring breeze had got up, causing him to press the collar of his cape more tightly around him, Mr. Pardew, in common with those of his fellow passengers who alighted from the train, made his way to the harbour pier. He did not, however, purchase a ticket at the shipping office. Instead he amused himself by observing preparations for the departure of the Boulogne steamer, noting as he did so the location of the railway office and the behaviour of the railway superintendent, who several times emerged from it to conduct some piece of business before returning to the room and locking the door behind him. For an hour Mr. Pardew stood on the pier amidst the crowds of people watching the steamer make ready. At length there was a crunch of iron wheels and a vehicle rolled up to the harbour from which was lowered the safe that Mr. Pardew believed he had seen in the guard's van. And Mr. Pardew marked down in his mind the manner in which it was picked up, set down and examined before being deposited out of sight in the ship's hold. The wind picked up and drops of rain blew in from the grey clouds massing beyond the arm of the sea, and Mr. Pardew walked to the end of the pier and stood looking at the waves with keen satisfaction as the ship's bell rang and the gangways were gathered up and the idlers and the venerable gentlemen in oilskin suits stood back from the pier rail and went in search of some fresh diversion. The ship passed by, its prow dipping into the waves and then rising again, with the gulls wheeling in its wake and black smoke disgorging into the shifting air above, and Mr. Pardew, seeing all these things, went off to eat his dinner in the Folkestone Harbour Hotel, where he pecked up a beefsteak, drank off a pint of porter and was as comfortable as a man can be who finds himself in a seaside hotel out of season when the wind is up.

D. J. TAYLOR

XIII

"NOT IN EARNEST!"

Upon my word, Mother, I think you have been very imprudent!"
     "Imprudent! I suppose that is one way of looking at it."

"You will not mind my saying that it is the only way of looking at it. To arrive at a gentleman's house in the middle of nowhere, unannounced, in absolute defiance of his wishes and the advice of his lawyers—well!"

"Gracious, John. You talk as if I had wished to walk off with his plate or—or had asked to see the deeds to the house."

Neither of the participants in this exchange, who were Mr. John Carstairs and his mother, took part in it with the least enthusiasm or with the merest semblance of personal ease. Just at this moment they were both in the back parlour: John Carstairs seated at the table behind his breakfast cup; Mrs. Carstairs standing in an uncertain attitude by the mantelpiece. A parlourmaid, half in and half out of the doorway, completed the scene.

"All I can say, Mother, is that I should like to know what you meant by it."

"Meant by it! I simply determined—there is no need to leave the room, Jane—that as you would do nothing about the matter, I should do something."

"After I had expressly gone to discuss it with Mr. Crabbe!"

"And got a very unsatisfactory answer for your pains."

The presence of the parlourmaid leaning over the table to retrieve the breakfast things now preventing any harsher expostulation, mother and son fell silent and looked at one another again. Each was crosser with the other than at any time in their previous dealings: Mrs. Carstairs because she believed that her son had been weak; John Carstairs because he believed that his mother had wantonly meddled in affairs that were quite outside her proper sphere. Each, though, was quietly resolved to conciliate the other: John Carstairs because he hated all disputes and disagreements, whether with his mother or anyone else; Mrs. Carstairs because she was aware that a united front with her son offered the only means of settling the business to her satisfaction.

The parlourmaid now having left the room bearing the breakfast things before her, John Carstairs became conscious that his mother's last remark had left him at a disadvantage, and that it behoved him to say something more, something that would, as he saw it, clinch the argument in his favour. As he could think of nothing, was in fact desperate to leave the room and present himself at his office, he picked up the letter that had been the cause of this dissension and poked it across the table with his forefinger.

"Well, here is Crabbe's letter. You had better read it."

Mrs. Carstairs pulled the piece of foolscap out of its envelope, placed her lorgnettes before her eyes and read the following:

Dear Sir,
We are instructed to communicate with you by our client, Mr. James Dixey of Easton Hall, Watton, in the county of Norfolk.

Mr. Dixey begs us to inform you, presuming that you are not cognisant of this fact, that on the 16th inst. he was visited at his residence by a lady representing herself as Mrs. Carstairs, whose object was to discuss with him the matter of his ward, Mrs. Ireland.

Mr. Dixey also begs us to inform you that he can entertain no further communication on this subject, and that any subsequent enquiries, whether of a personal or written nature, will be ignored.

Yours very faithfully,

CRABBE & ENDERBY
Solicitors and Commissioners for Oaths

"Well, that is plain enough, is it not?"

"Very plain. As plain as a pikestaff," John Carstairs remarked. "Look, there is another note in here from Crabbe. Deep regret at having to write in these terms and that kind of thing. A trifle mealy-mouthed, I dare say. You had better see it too."

Mrs. Carstairs picked up the second letter, which contained additional remarks on the delicate state of Mrs. Ireland's health and the fiat on disturbance pronounced by her medical men, and made a pretence of reading it, but her mind was already deep in consideration of the first. In her heart she was not displeased by this exposure: on the one hand, because she was an honest woman who deplored duplicity, especially when it was practised on those she loved best in the world; on the other, because experience had taught her that affairs of this kind have a habit of breaking out into the public gaze. And yet on two counts she was afraid: of her son's displeasure, certainly— although she knew that this was likely to be short-lived—but also that he would regard Mr. Crabbe's letter as a final prohibition of her involvement in the case. Her task, as she saw it, was to stimulate John Carstairs's interest in the matter of Mrs. Ireland's disappearance but to do so indirectly, or at any rate in such a way that he would mistake this prompting for something else. Thinking of all of this she continued to stare at the letter while John Carstairs drummed one set of his fingers on the tablecloth and shook the seals of his watch with the other.

"Upon my word, Mother. There had better be an end to this. As it is I do not know how I shall be able to look old Crabbe in the face again when I see him at the club."

"Very well. Perhaps you are right," Mrs. Carstairs replied with a meekness that would have surprised a less unobservant person than her son. "All I can say is that it is a great pity."

"Well yes, no doubt it is." As Mrs. Carstairs had anticipated, this hint of contrition produced an immediate softening of her son's tone. "The fact is, Mother, that questions of this kind must always be carried on through the proper channels. Imagine what would be the result if every time that a gentleman had a question to ask of another gentleman he simply called at his house to ask it. Now"—he began to pull on his gloves in a way that suggested he thought the interview was at an end— "I should be obliged if we could no longer discuss the matter, or at any rate"—and he went so far as to give his mother a smile—"not in quite the manner that we have been doing, eh?"

Mrs. Carstairs was conscious that she had succeeded in the first of her endeavours, which was the drawing of her son's wrath, but that she had yet to lure him into the second snare. Accordingly, and nervously aware of the risk she took, she changed tack.

"But John, it is all so very mysterious. To think of Isabel Ireland simply vanishing in this way. And then there is this Mr. Farrier that everyone talks of . . ."

"Richard Farrier! A man that nobody seems to know anything about!"

"But that he is her cousin, and was supposed to have been in love with her, and has now disappeared too."

"Upon my honour, Mother!" John Carstairs had succeeded in drawing on his gloves and was now reaching for his walking stick and newspaper. "It is this d——d female hankering after sentiment that confuses everything—excuse me, I did not mean to be so candid. Richard Farrier, wherever he may be, no more loved her than I did. As for the poor girl, she is, well . . . not in her right mind, and we had better leave her to those who have a duty to care for her."

"That is all very well, John, but . . ."

"But what, Mother?"

"It is just that—you will not mind my saying this—it comes from love of you, indeed it does—I would wish you were not so, so . . ."

"So what?" He was looking at her keenly now, with his walking stick in his hand and his hat halfway to his head.

"So . . . so lacking in resolve."

"Lacking in resolve!" Fortunately for Mrs. Carstairs, it seemed from his tone that her son was prepared to treat this remark as a joke. "Let me tell you, Mother, that when a man is informed by a lawyer that someone for whom he is . . . hm . . . responsible has behaved foolishly, and he chooses to mention that foolishness, then he can scarcely be accused of being lacking in resolve. No, don't trouble to see me out."

And with that, making a great show of haste and eagerness to attend to his duties, Mr. John Carstairs pulled on his hat and quitted the house. It may be said, though, that his mother, left alone in the empty parlour, was confident that she had achieved the second of her objects.

D. J. TAYLOR

* * *

Indeed, had Mrs. Carstairs been able to observe her son's conduct over the next half-dozen hours, she would have congratulated herself still further. John Carstairs, as he made his way from the Marylebone Road to Whitehall, found that his mind turned—*burned* were not too strong a verb—upon a single question. Did he, as his mother had suggested, lack resolve? Was he, to use a yet more objectionable word, *weak?* Mr. Carstairs was disposed to think that he did not and that he was not. A matter had been offered for his consideration, he had meditated on it, taken the most prudent advice and reached a decision. He had subsequently been embarrassed by one very dear to him and had sought to prevent a repetition of that embarrassment. All in all, it seemed to him, turning the question ceaselessly over in his mind, that he had done what he ought to have done and that his actions could not seriously be faulted by anyone with a knowledge of the case. At the same time, John Carstairs was aware that there is a difference between acting in a way that does not incur reproach and acting well. Perhaps, too, the memory of those earlier episodes in his life when he might have been thought to lack resolve played upon him. At any rate, the half hour that he occupied between leaving his, or rather his mother's, house and arriving at his place of work was not pleasant to him and may explain certain of the events that very quickly followed.

The public, perhaps, has a somewhat exaggerated idea of the amenities enjoyed by young men who work at the Board of Trade. The public, perhaps, imagines an environment of high-ceilinged chambers, soft carpets and crackling fires, in which damask-coated attendants steal discreetly to and fro while in inner sanctums noble lords gravely attend to the affairs of the nation. The public, if it imagines this, is altogether wrong. It can be stated, by way of correction, that the office in which John Carstairs laboured with his colleague the Honourable Mr. Cadnam, was about twelve feet square, consisting of two japanned desks joined together, an immense bookcase and a recess in which sat, or did not sit, an inky clerk, that on his arrival the fire was unlit and the papers on his desk untidied, and that his first action was to fling

Kept

his hat on its peg and to ask in an aggrieved voice, where the devil was that boy with his coffee?

"I sent him out for some," observed the Honourable Mr. Cadnam, who was a somewhat dandified young man of about twenty-six. "Indeed I did. But there's no dealing with the boys they send us these days."

Replying with an oath that he didn't suppose there was, Mr. Carstairs seated himself at his desk, where he discovered, to the further ruin of his temper, that there was a letter from the Undersecretary, Mr. Bounderby, requesting attendance in his room at the hour of noon.

"Damnation! And here is a note from old Bounderby, too. What on earth does he want?"

The Honourable Mr. Cadnam looked up from his desk, where he was now perusing a sporting newspaper, with an expression of languid horror. "Upon my word, I couldn't say. But he has been here not half an hour since searching for you. I should say he looked exceedingly fierce."

"Hm. Where did you say I was?"

"I said I thought you were with the Earl of ———." And here Mr. Cadnam named a gentleman who was great in the counsels of the Board of Trade and to whom it was known that Mr. Bounderby, who was reputed to be the son of a Manchester manufacturer, habitually deferred.

"Well, that was very sporting of you, Cadnam. Now where is that boy with the coffee?"

It will be seen from this conversation that John Carstairs was used to getting his way at his place of work, that he enjoyed the esteem of his colleagues and was well able to fight any battles that needed to be fought with his superiors. The morning, or what remained of it, brought further proofs of his enviable position in this regard. At midday he was closeted with Mr. Bounderby, and if he did not exactly say that he had been attending on the Earl of ———, gave the former gentleman to understand that he was detained on the most pressing official business. A noble lord passing through the building nodded to him in the most friendly way, and another gentleman, the private secretary to a cabinet minister no less, asked him whether he would be attending a certain soirée in Mayfair that evening and whether he thought a certain unmarried lady would be present. All this was very gratifying to John Carstairs's sense of what the world owed him and what he in turn owed the world, as well as comforting him greatly as to that charge of want of resolve, and he ate his luncheon with the Honourable Mr. Cadnam in a chophouse in Whitehall Place in excellent high spirits.

"Upon my honour," Cadnam remarked, as they returned to their room and the glance of the inky clerk, "I feel most dreadfully fagged. We were dancing at Lady Jane's until two, you know. I think I should feel better if I could sit down, indeed I should."

It was the Honourable Mr. Cadnam's invariable habit to spend the hour between three and four of an afternoon in secret slumber at his desk.

"Very well, Caddy. Have no fear. You sit down, and I shall go and attend upon the board."

All this was breathed in an access of the high spirits that had enlivened John Carstairs's chop and his half pint of sherry. Unhappily, the remainder of the day offered two proofs that the satisfaction with which he regarded his prospects was not wholly shared by other people. As he had promised Mr. Cadnam, John Carstairs did indeed attend upon the board—this was not, it should be said, the Board of Trade itself but a subsidiary board which was thought to be the exclusive property of Mr. Bounderby and over which he tyrannised—for he had a special reason for wishing to ingratiate himself with its members. A certain high official—not so highly placed as Mr. Bounderby, but high nonetheless—was awaiting transfer to another department, and it was known that a vacancy existed. Now, much as he enjoyed the society of the Honourable Mr. Cadnam and the somewhat lax hours tolerated by his superiors, it was John Carstairs's ambition to prosper in the service of his country and at the very least to acquire a room that would accommodate only himself, where the coffee was, so to speak, on tap and where there were no Mr. Bounderbys to enquire of his whereabouts. Accordingly, he was very kind to that gentleman this afternoon, and to the Earl of ——, who was also present, handed their respective papers to them with an exquisite courtesy and played his own smaller part in the proceedings with a modest punctiliousness.

And then there came one of those unfortunate mischances that no amount of civility or discretion can ever quite forestall, when a man happens to overhear something said of him which it were better that he should not. It happened in this way. The meeting of the board having broken up, John Carstairs and certain other gentlemen had quitted the room in which it had been held, leaving Mr. Bounderby and the Earl of —— and two or three other persons talking at its further end. Halfway down the staircase leading back to his own room, Carstairs realised that he had left a certain document, a document moreover that he should not let out of his keeping, in the committee room. Hastening back to retrieve it, he arrived in the doorway at the precise moment when Mr. Bounderby remarked to the Earl of —— that he felt Mr. Carstairs would hardly do and that there was a want of—what there was a want of, Mr. Carstairs did not linger to hear. He knew that the men inside the room were not yet aware of his coming and that it was best for all parties that it should remain so. Therefore he went back downstairs with as cheerful a smile as he could muster and rallied the Honourable Mr. Cadnam about his attendance at Lady Jane's ball, but I do not think he liked it. At first he tried to make light of his eavesdropping, assuring himself that the subject under discussion was something merely trivial, but a precise recollection of Mr. Bounderby's words, which had been spoken with absolute clarity, served only to convince him of the futility of this exercise and he grew gloomier still.

And then there came the second jolt at his arm, which was administered by a gentleman named Dennison. Now, as has been mentioned, John Carstairs was a political young man. Just at this moment he had his eye on the borough of Southwark, where a sitting member had died and the writ for a by-election was shortly to be moved in the House. The late Mr. Jones had been a Liberal, but it was reckoned by those who knew about such things that now was the moment when a Conservative, nailing his colours to the mast of Queen, Country

D. J. TAYLOR

and Constitution, could rise up and drive the armies of Southwark Liberalism into the Thames. John Carstairs had for some time thought that he might be that Conservative, and in this way he had contracted if not an alliance then an understanding with Mr. Dennison, who, though employed as an attorney, was known to act as the party's agent in the Borough. Mr. Dennison was a short, ill-favoured man of fifty with a pronounced air of cockney in his speech and a habit of cracking his knuckles when he talked. Nonetheless, he was esteemed in the circles in which John Carstairs moved as an infallible barometer of the Southwark political weather. If Mr. Dennison said that such and such a thing would do, it would do. If he said that it would not do, then it would not. While Mr. Jones, MP, had lived, Mr. Dennison had frankly despaired of unseating him. Now he was dead, he gave it to be known that he thought his Liberal successor would not have it all his own way.

All this necessarily made Mr. Dennison a source of great fascination to John Carstairs. Mr. Disraeli himself would perhaps not have been received with the deference extended to the Southwark attorney when he arrived at the Board of Trade that afternoon. The fire was instantly poked up, the inky clerk despatched on a fictitious errand and the Honourable Mr. Cadnam positively compelled to go and kick his heels in the newspaper reading room downstairs. Mr. Dennison was not insensible of these courtesies and sat smoking the cigar that John Carstairs had offered him and kicking his little legs beneath his chair in a state of some satisfaction.

"Well now," he said at length, casting his eye once or twice around the room, "this is all very pleasant, is it not?"

"Yes indeed—if you like that kind of thing."

"You'd have to give it all up, you know, if you were elected." And here Mr. Dennison's knuckles went off like a pair of nutcrackers. "Gentlemen as works in public offices can't sit in the House as well. But no doubt you're aware of that."

John Carstairs signified that he was, smiling keenly as he did. In his heart of hearts he abominated Mr. Dennison's locution and his knuck-lecracking, but knowing the man to be an embodiment of Southwark

Conservatism, he was anxious to humour him. In fact, had Dennison wished to be introduced to Mr. Bounderby or taken to dine with the Earl of ——, I think John Carstairs would have managed it somehow. Now, however, he merely nodded, shifted his eyes from their contemplation of the cuff of Mr. Dennison's shirt and remarked, "I suppose we are all right for—for the Borough?"

"Well," said Mr. Dennison, very affably and turning round his chair until his feet were very nearly in the fire. "It depends on what you mean by all right. There is Sir Charles Devonish, as used to be the member for Chatteris, that is spending a deal of money."

"But Sir Charles has no connection with the place!"

"I don't say he has, and I don't say he hasn't. I was merely saying that he was a-spending of a great deal of money. And then there's that Mr. Honeyman—you'll have heard of him no doubt, sir—as is a brewer, which the publicans always like."

"D—— all brewers!"

"Quite so, sir. But it's the publicans that win elections as you very well know." Here Mr. Dennison's knuckles cracked like a pistol shot. "And then there's yourself, sir."

"Certainly there is myself."

Dennison examined the young man shrewdly. Although he enjoyed John Carstairs's society, appreciated the fire that was stoked to warm his feet, the cigar that was proffered for his relaxation and even the occasional glimpse of the Honourable Mr. Cadnam, he was at heart a realist.

"We-ell," he remarked eventually. "There is yourself, sir, as you say. And if the honour was mine to dispense, sir, you should have the nomination straightaway, indeed you should. But there are folk in the Borough that say you are not quite . . ."

"Not quite what?"

"Not quite in earnest." And here Mr. Dennison cast the root of his cigar regretfully into the fire and shifted his toes ever so slightly away from its fulcrum.

"Not in earnest! You may take it from me that I am very much in earnest!"

"That's what I have told them, sir. Time and again," observed Mr.

D. J. TAYLOR

Dennison, who was not of course under any obligation to tell the exact truth in his dealings with his young friend. "But there's that Sir Charles a-spending of his money so very free, and they do say of Mr. Honeyman that he owns some of the publicans' leases."

After this remark it was clear to John Carstairs that his chances of capturing the Borough's nomination were almost nil, and that Mr. Dennison knew they were nil. He was also aggrieved at the thought of the various moneys previously advanced to Mr. Dennison under the guise of "expenses" and the idea that he had, in effect, been hoodwinked. Nonetheless, it behoved him to be civil to the man, and Mr. Dennison, consequently, was waved out of the room with all the deference due to his position, nearly colliding as he did so with the Honourable Mr. Cadnam, who, his intellect exhausted by the pleasures of the newspaper reading room, had determined to make his way back to his desk.

"Upon my honour," Mr. Cadnam observed, a few minutes having elapsed after Mr. Dennison's departure, "but I should say that you were in the most devilish bad temper."

"I should say that you were probably correct."

After this nothing more was said between them. Yet seated at his desk, his eye fixed on the chair from which Dennison had pronounced his verdict, John Carstairs seethed with vexation. To have private misgivings over your want of resolution is one thing. To have them confirmed, twice, by others in the space of a few moments is another. The consequence was that he was perfectly savage to those employees of the Board of Trade who crossed his path for the remainder of the afternoon, snapped at the messenger boy, frowned at the clerk and was even frosty to Mr. Bounderby when that gentleman arrived in the room with some chance enquiry.

"I say," Mr. Cadnam remarked, as they strolled together down the staircase at the conclusion of the day's business, "you look dreadfully fierce, you know."

John Carstairs laughed. "Do I? I imagine I shall probably eat some-one before the evening is done. But don't worry, Caddy, it shan't be you."

And yet John Carstairs did not eat anyone. Instead he went off to his club, listened very meekly to the advice of the steward and ate his dinner in silence, musing all the while on his opportunities. It was his duty, he told himself, to make some bold stroke, and yet he did not at all know how to proceed. Reviewing each of the areas in which he imagined that he had failed—the matter of Mrs. Ireland, his position at the Board of Trade and his prospects for the Southwark nomination—he could conceive of no step that it would benefit him to take. Thinking again of these annoyances, he began to brood, curiously enough, on the morning's letter from Mr. Crabbe. This, in truth, he had not quite liked, feeling that gentlemen who met in society should not address each other in this peremptory way. Quite by chance, as he sat pondering this injustice, a legal friend—not one who hailed from Lincoln's Inn, but one who at any rate would know of Mr. Crabbe and his doings—passed by his table.

"Carstairs! How are you? You are coming out for Southwark, I hear."

"Well . . . perhaps. It is not quite settled. Look—have you a moment? There is something I particularly wish to ask."

"Very well—fire away."

And so, rather to his own surprise, John Carstairs found himself outlining the tale of his mother's visit to Norfolk in pursuit of Mrs. Ireland and his dealings with Mr. Crabbe. It was not by any means the whole tale, but it was sufficient to interest the legal friend, who further excited John Carstairs's regard by appearing to know certain of the details already.

"The beautiful widow languishing with her Bluebeard? Then I have heard something of that."

"And what do you think is Crabbe's game?"

John Carstairs's friend smiled a smile of the blandest legal diffidence. "Crabbe? Crabbe, my boy, is the most respectable old legal gentleman who ever pulled on a wig or took a marquis's instructions. All the same, I heard a rumour—just a rumour, mind—that he was sailing rather too close to the wind in one or two quarters. But I had better say no more."

"No, perhaps you had better not," murmured John Carstairs, wishing on the contrary that he would say a dozen things.

The friend drifted away, the club began to fill up with people and

D. J. TAYLOR

the air turn blue with tobacco smoke, and John Carstairs found himself playing whist with three or four men whose company he would customarily have shunned. Nonetheless, beneath the placid exterior presented to his fellow cardplayers, he was exultant. If the enquiry about Mr. Crabbe was not a display of resolve, he asked himself, then what was?

Part Three

﹏ XIV ﹏

THE DEAN AND HIS DAUGHTER

**FROM THE DIARY OF THE REV. JOSIAH CRAWLEY,
CURATE OF EASTON**

21 November 1865
*The winter has set in early. Holly berries &c. well advanced, which
the people say is a sure sign. Today, walking in the lanes, I saw a
shrike pecking out the brains of a dead mouse which it had conveyed
to the top of a fence post. I am not, I believe, a credulous man, but this
sight—the solitude of the place, the eager, repetitive motions of the
bird's beak—filled me with superstitious dread.*

* * *

25 November 1865
*To my surprise, a note from Dixey inviting me to call. The year has
brought a great change in him: he seems altogether more bowed and
grey-haired than I remembered. On my enquiring why I had not
seen him at church, he replied ambiguously. Having drunk a glass of
Madeira, we sat in his study: a most curious place attesting to Dixey's
scientific interests. At one point, drawing to my attention the corpse
of a toad which lay on a dissecting tray, its limbs pinned back and the
vital organs exposed, he asked: did I believe that animals were sen-
tient? I replied that it seemed to me that animals perceived the world
as we did ourselves, though in necessarily diminished fashion, that an
ox, for example, could mourn the loss of its master but that its grief
was not a human grief. The Hall very silent and gloomy, I find, the*

D. J. TAYLOR

pathways ragged and overgrown, a great howling of the wind forever rising at the glass.

*   *   *

27 November 1865

I have resolved to put aside my Defence of Episcopacy, *which avails me naught.*

*   *   *

1 December 1865

To Ely this forenoon, at the invitation of Mr. Marjoribanks. A dull journey by long, narrow roads, the fens stretching out on all sides as far as the eye can see. Much oppressed, I fear, by the bleakness of the region. The Deanery decidedly feminine in its accoutrements, though I believe Mr. Marjoribanks to be a widower. Much good talk, an oasis of sweet water after the desert in which I have lived of late. Great crowd of persons, most of them unknown to me. Amongst the women, Miss Marjoribanks by far the most agreeable.

*   *   *

5 December 1865

Again at the Hall. Dixey confined to chair by some unspecified ailment (arthritis? Certainly his hands are very gnarled and swollen) yet received me civilly. The footman much in evidence, plumping his cushions, arranging footstools, &c. Pressed to examine several of Dixey's specimens, viz., the body of a mart, very lithe and dextrous it must have been in life, which Dixey said had been procured for him lately in Inverness-shire. Also two eggs of the osprey, from the same source. Apparently Dixey pays as much as five pounds for such things, wh. seems to me robbery. Dixey enquired, did I not admit the value of science? I replied that with any branch of study seeming to exalt our understanding of God's universe I was, of course, in sympathy, but

Kept

*that there were some things it were better not to know. More talk of
Mr. Gosse, Lyell, the secrets of the stones, &c.*

* * *

6 December 1865

*Fearful that I had offended Dixey, yet a civil note from the footman
bidding me to dine. He is much recovered from his afflictions.*

* * *

9 December 1865

Saw Dixey out walking in the lanes. Quite on our old footing.

* * *

26 December 1865

*Ely. Afternoon service. Deanery party. Blind man's buff. Miss
Marjoribanks.*

* * *

3 January 1865

Ely.

* * *

10 January 1866

*I waste my time in this place. A congregation of a hundred peasants,
and not one who attends my discourse. My heart elsewhere. Resolved
to write to Cousin Richard, to see if he may do something for me.*

* * *

13 January 1866

A. in London, visiting her aunt. Took out my prize poem, "Alaric,"

D. J. TAYLOR

wh. I wrote at Oxford, and meditated on sending it to a publisher. It has a spirit that, in my present state, is quite intolerable.

* * *

15 January 1866

To luncheon at the Hall. Found there Mr. Conolly, the mad-doctor, with whom Dixey seems very intimate. A bleak, mournful day, the air filled with the cries of Dixey's hounds, a sad-looking maidservant hanging out washing above the currant bushes, &c. The interior smelling strongly of damp. Dixey says that no fire can ever heat the place. I was pleased to find that Mr. Conolly recollected me, enquired courteously of my prospects. The talk at luncheon, concerning Conolly's professional occupations, somewhat abstruse. He believes that the insane, rather than undergoing forcible restraint, should rather be confined with the maximum freedom of movement, &c., that such comparative liberty is an essential part of their cure. Dixey greatly interested in this, providing several illustrations from his own experience, the effect curiously resembling a couple of medical men talking shop. Yet such was their enthusiasm that I did not feel in the least excluded.

All this—the luncheon itself, professional talk, &c.—necessarily cast into shade by an event that occurred during the dessert, one that, even now, I find myself curiously reluctant to set down . . .

* * *

Mr. Marjoribanks, the Dean of Ely, was a man approaching sixty, very hale, somewhat austere in the view of himself that he offered the world but, it was said, of a kindly and charitable disposition. He had been Dean for a dozen years and, living frugally yet not meanly, with an eye for those ecclesiastical perquisites which were his by right, was thought to have amassed a considerable fortune. If Mr. Marjoribanks was immediately conspicuous in the neighbourhood, it was not for the excellence of his sermons, or for the disinterestedness of his patronage, but for the doctrinal position he occupied in the church he served.

Kept

The Dean was a clerical conservative, and of such a deep-dyed and Imperial blue that more than one clergyman whom the world names as a conservative quaked in his shoes when led into that gentleman's presence. Catholics he necessarily detested, indeed the prospect of any kind of Roman emancipation filled him with horror. Methodists, Congregationalists and Quakers, any worshipper, in fact, existing beyond the confines of the Anglican communion, he would, I think, have had prohibited by law. And yet the Dean's vigilant eye was turned as much on his own congregation as on those outside it. Ritualism, Puseyism and the Oxford movement he held in the deepest contempt. It was the same with the albs and copes and birettas in which the contemporary clergyman so innocently delights. Mr. Marjoribanks conducted his services in a plain Geneva surplice and made very savage remarks about "weak minds engrossed in coloured scarves." All this, while tolerated and indeed approved in the fastness of Ely, was nonetheless thought to have wounded his chances of greater preferment in the Church, and it was said that the Dean was not only a hale man and a wealthy man but also a disappointed one.

Mr. Marjoribanks's wife had died early—a circumstance that was thought to have contributed to his austerity—leaving him with the care of two infant daughters. He had not remarried, believing that their upbringing was a task best accomplished according to his own design. All this had happened twenty years ago, and the daughters were now grown into blooming young women. The elder was by this time married to a brewer in the vicinity of Cambridge and rarely seen at her father's house, but the younger, now aged five-and-twenty, remained its solitary female ornament. Seeking to describe Miss Amelia Marjoribanks, I can only say that she was everything that a dean's daughter should be: pious, God-fearing, discreet, attentive to her father's wants and tolerant of his prejudices. She was also, having had the domestic affairs of the Deanery in her hands since the age of eighteen, not a little imperious, or at any rate used to having her commands obeyed, and in addition was doted on by her clerical parent. Some observers of Mr. Marjoribanks's dealings with the fair Amelia—and fair she undoubtedly was—would have gone further even than this and maintained that the Dean was afraid of his daughter. This, no doubt, was an exag-

D. J. TAYLOR

geration—Mr. Marjoribanks was not a man disposed to fear anyone, and certainly not the young woman who stirred his tea in the morning and brought him his slippers at night—but it was noticeable that he consulted her in everything and in general deferred to her opinion in much the same way that, twenty years before, he had deferred to the opinion of his late and lamented wife.

The Deanery at Ely was not in those days very commodious, but it was certainly very comfortable. In particular, there was a rose garden extending half the length of the back terrace, in sight of the great cathedral spire, whose blooms Mr. Marjoribanks delighted to inspect as he looked out each morning from the window of his breakfast parlour. He was looking out of the breakfast parlour window now, although the month was February and there were no blooms to be seen. His daughter sat before him at the breakfast table with a piece of crumbled toast in her hand, which, it must be said, she had ceased to eat some moments before. Whatever else her expression may have hinted, it did not suggest that her father was afraid of her.

"Do you intend to marry this man, my dear?"

"If it comes to that, Papa, he has not asked me."

"Perhaps he has not." As he said this, the Dean made a little motion with his hands, implying that men who asked and men who did not ask his daughter to marry them were each guilty of the gravest discourtesy. "As you know, I am the last person in the world to interfere in matters of this kind. (This was not true. The Dean had interfered repeatedly in the affair of the elder Miss Marjoribanks and the brewer.) "But people will talk. Why only yesterday I had Mrs. Delingpole"—Mrs. Delingpole was the wife of the Precentor—"ask me what I thought of dear Mr. Crawley, and could not something be done for him."

"Well, it is very disagreeable of people. Mr. Crawley has not spoken a word to me that he might not have spoken with perfect propriety to any other woman."

"Nevertheless, my dear . . ."

"Nevertheless, fiddlestick, Papa."

Notwithstanding the spiritedness with which Miss Marjoribanks, into whose face a fine red colour had come, pronounced this remark, it was clear to her, as it was to her father, that the conversation could not be allowed to stop at this juncture. Accordingly, she poured herself another cup of tea, disposed of the toast onto her plate and searched about in her mind for another means of defending herself.

"It is especially disagreeable of people, Papa, when one thinks of Mr. Crawley's position. He is the kind of man whom most young women would be glad to marry. To be sure, he is only a curate, but he was a Fellow of his college and, I believe, highly thought of, and they say that his cousin the Earl may very well do something for him."

"His cousin the Earl has no more benefices to dispense than you have, my dear."

"Gracious, Papa! As if an earl couldn't do something for his cousin if he had a mind to."

When he heard this, Mr. Marjoribanks knew in his heart that his daughter was going to marry Mr. Crawley. However, he was careful not to say as much. He merely remarked what he believed to be the truth, that Mr. Crawley appeared to be an able young clergyman and an excellent minister to his flock. Whereupon the breakfast table colloquy broke up, the Dean retiring to his study and his daughter departing to the kitchen and a half hour's conversation with the cook, which I fear that lady did not much enjoy.

Mr. Marjoribanks was, according to his lights, an honourable man. He knew that it required him to make various enquiries concerning this suitor of his daughter's. He was, at the same time, honest enough to admit that his principal objection to any suggested match was his own convenience. Austere though he was, the Dean liked very much having his daughter to stir his tea, fetch his slippers and scold his servants, and though the tea might be stirred and the slippers fetched in her absence, he told himself that the hearts that accomplished these tasks would not be as true. A less honourable man would have proceeded by subterfuge, but this was alien to the Dean's nature. He began, consequently, by taking down a certain clerical directory from the shelf above his desk and seeing what it had to say. Here he learned what he might very well have expected: that Mr. Crawley came of good family, had earned high honours at Oxford, been elected to a fellowship at his college and was, in short, a paragon. Still, though, Mr. Marjoribanks laid down the directory with a sigh. He felt that in the matter of Mr.

D. J. TAYLOR

Crawley, and his visits to the Deanery, and his cousin the Earl, he was being outmanoeuvred.

It happened, however, that the next hour brought a visitor to Mr. Marjoribanks, one of the dozens who waited on him during the course of his working day. This was a gentleman named the Reverend Dalrymple, who, by chance, inhabited a parish on the east side of the county, a dozen miles from Mr. Crawley's cure. Accordingly the Dean welcomed Mr. Dalrymple with the greatest cordiality, attended to whatever matter he had brought before him, and then said:

"What, pray, do you think of your neighbour Mr. Crawley?"

"Mr. Crawley of Lower Easton? A very amiable young man, I should say. But I believe I should congratulate you, Mr. Dean."

"Congratulate me? Why should you want to do that?"

A bishop would probably have quailed before the look in Mr. Marjoribanks's eye. Mr. Dalrymple, being a parish clergyman with a stipend of four hundred a year, looked as if he wished the ground would swallow him up.

"I am very sorry if I have spoken incorrectly, Mr. Dean. But I heard that there was an engagement."

"There is no engagement, Mr. Dalrymple, and you will oblige me by not referring to it again."

"Certainly. If that is what you wish."

Then Mr. Marjoribanks knew that he had been discourteous, that this was not the way in which Deans spoke to clergymen of their diocese, nor indeed the way in which gentlemen spoke to other gentlemen, and he felt ashamed of himself. He would have liked to be alone with his resentments, which now extended to his daughter, Mr. Crawley and the quidnuncs of the cathedral close, but he was conscious that Mr. Dalrymple still sat timorously on the further side of his study desk and so he raised his hands in front of him in a gesture of mock exasperation.

"You must forgive me, Mr. Dalrymple, for speaking as I did." The Dean was a subtle man, who usually got what he wanted in conversation or debate, but on this occasion he had only the vaguest notion of how to proceed. "That is . . ." he began again. Still Mr. Dalrymple sat silently watching him. "We were talking of Mr. Crawley."

Kept

Mr. Dalrymple, too, was a subtle man in his way, who, additionally, had no great love for Mr. Crawley. "A very amiable young man," he repeated. "And well thought of in his parish. I believe he is an intimate of Mr. Dixey's."

"Mr. Dixey?"

"Mr. Dixey of Easton Hall."

"Oh indeed, Mr. Dixey," said the Dean, who knew a great deal about Mr. Dixey, none of which he imagined to redound to that gentleman's credit. "Well, as you say, Mr. Dalrymple, a very amiable young man. And now perhaps I could ask your opinion of the plans for Hiram's Hospital?"

Mr. Dalrymple had enough wit to be able to see what was expected of him and said what he thought of the plans for Hiram's Hospital, Mr. Marjoribanks listening to him the while. And thus their interview concluded on a much more harmonious note than it had begun.

* * *

MISS A. MARJORIBANKS
C/o Mrs. Browning
18 Wimpole Street
London W.

My dear Miss Marjoribanks,
On the occasion of our last meeting you were kind enough to suggest that I might enliven your stay in the metropolis with some account of our undertakings here in your absence. Alas, I fear there is little that can be rated enlivening, for we have all of us been horribly dull. To particularise: this morning I preached on Isaiah to three dozen slumbering rustics, my discourse latterly punctuated by snores, returned to my lodgings to eat a dinner that I think no man ever ate before, so meagre was its extent, thereafter presiding at a Sunday school at which I dare-say many surreptitious apples were consumed by my youthful auditors but very little wisdom. Or perhaps I am mistaken, and you are just as dull in London as we are in our rural fastness.

D. J. TAYLOR

Do your fashionable London congregations lie asleep in church with their mouths wide open, I wonder, crowd out the porch with hay-carts, wagonettes and the like and then go home to dine off fat pork and parsnips—this being the only vegetable obtainable at this time of year? I think not.

And yet not all has been rank tedium and solitary rumination. Yesterday, for example, I dined with Mr. Dixey, of whom I believe you have heard me speak. Mr. Dixey lives at Easton Hall, where I don't think you ever went, three miles from here: a spacious house, though I think not kept up with the punctiliousness that its interiors warrant. Knowing that feminine mania for precision in the matter of describing gentlemen's appearances, demeanour, &c., I realise that it behoves me to give some account of Mr. Dixey, and yet I am not sure that I can do him justice. He is a tall, spare man, perhaps sixty years of age, rather stooped and grey about the temples, but still vigorous: very kind, obliging and courteous, but, in consequence of his living out of the world, somewhat rough-edged. Of ladies' society, I should judge, he sees only a very little. Mr. Dixey's great interest is the natural world. Certainly his study, in which I have been received on more than one occasion, is very like a taxidermist's shop—one hardly dare lay down one's arm for fear of what one may find beneath it.

Our companion at luncheon was Mr. Conolly, of whose reputation you may perhaps know, formerly superintendent of the asylum at Hanwell: a polite gentleman, some years older than Mr. Dixey, I should say, but owing nothing to him in point of intellectual vigour. The extent and substance of my host's connection with Mr. Conolly I can only guess at, but I should say that they had known each other for some years, for Mr. Conolly has a habit of referring to "that case in '59," or "that fellow I had taken out of irons against his father's wish," as if he expected Mr. Dixey to know all about it. Certainly Mr. Conolly is a walking casebook of the afflictions to which many of our most noble families are subject: to hear him talk, one could sometimes believe that there is scarce a marquis in the country who does not have some weak-minded son living in ghastly seclusion with his keeper, whose only concern is that his wine at dinner shall not be diluted. All this may suggest that Mr. Conolly is merely a professional man, whose profession happens to be mad-doctoring, and yet I confess I find him very sympathetic, sensible of the pathos of his charges, alive to the individual tragedies that had brought them into his care and the misery of the homes they left behind them.

But all this is by the way, and I should not have served you this preamble had it not some bearing on what was to come. Dixey's dining room is very large: a great, high-ceilinged chamber with an elliptical dining table taking up nearly the length of the room. Naturally the three of us made a poor show at filling this immensity. In fact we arranged ourselves comfortably at the further end, leaving perhaps seven-eighths of the table in disuse. It was a gaunt, miserable day outside—though cheerful within—the wind beating against the panes, the trees bending ceaselessly over Dixey's wild gardens. (They are all overgrown, with no one to keep them up.) Indeed, such was the continual interruption from beyond the glass that my senses were not at first alerted to a crashing sound coming from the upper part of the house. Nonetheless, the noise was repeated not once but twice, as if a giant had commenced to hurl items of furniture around in a corridor. At first I imagined that Dixey, who is somewhat deaf, was unaware of this disturbance. Then I divined that he was contriving to appear oblivious to it, drumming his fingers on the table top, enquiring loudly of Conolly if he would have any more wine, &c. Conolly, too, I noticed, saw that there was something amiss, glanced once or twice at the door, thereafter addressing to me some very inconsequential remark.

Eventually, the sounds died away, to be replaced only by the soughing of the wind. Indeed our conversation had all but resumed its even tenor when suddenly there was a determined rattling at the door handle. Dixey was on his feet in an instant, but before he could proceed more than a couple of steps the door burst open to admit a wild-eyed and dishevelled young woman, her face ablaze, her hair very much disarranged, who moved towards us in a kind of paroxysm of distress, beating her arms against her sides and talking very loudly as she came. I at first assumed this apparition to be one of the maidservants, yet concluded that I did not recollect her, and that indeed her voice—though I could not decipher many of the words she spoke—was genteel. Whosoever this person was, and whatever her complaint, Dixey was equal to the occasion. In a trice he had seized her firmly by the forearms, imploring her all the while to contain herself, and propelled her out of the room; she meanwhile conveying the most imploring glances back to where Conolly and I sat transfixed. He (and she) were gone a long time, full half an hour. In their absence, Mr. Conolly, who seemed not a whit abashed by the disturbance, explained that the young woman was a relative of Mr. Dixey, in plain fact deranged and living in his care, who through some mischance had evaded her keeper. Though, being naturally interested, I pressed him further, he would say no more, the two of us lapsing into an uncomfortable silence, after which we were joined once more by Mr. Dixey, who remarked that he was sorry, very sorry indeed, and called for a bottle of port. The afternoon was by now well advanced, and being somewhat disquieted by these events I very soon took my leave.

In sending this account of lunch at Easton Hall, Mr. Crawley omitted only two particulars. One was that the young woman who burst into the room with her face blazing and her hair awry was, in addition, stark naked. The other was that in the brief second when she brushed against him he felt the pressure of her hand in his, discovering subsequently that she had pushed into it a crumpled scrap of paper, on which had been printed two words: *help me*.

XV

DOWNRIVER

To: The Directors
South-Eastern Railway Company

Dear Sirs,
It is my regrettable duty to inform you that Joseph Pearce,
formerly a ticket printer at the London Bridge office, has been
dismissed from the company's service with immediate effect.

Having the honour to remain your most obedient servant, I
am, sirs, yours most faithfully,

JAMES HARKER
Secretary to the Board

* * *

To: The Directors
South-Eastern Railway Company

Dear Sirs,
I am disturbed to learn that the man Pearce, recently dismissed
from the company's service, should have compounded his
original offence by presuming to address—both by letter and, I
gather, in person—individual members of the board.

The facts of the case may be briefly stated. Pearce had been
known for keeping bad company. Indeed, Mr. Sellings informed
me that he had himself observed Pearce entering a public house
of low repute in Tooley Street. On another occasion it was
reported among the clerks that he claimed to have won a substantial sum of money betting on the St. Leger. A month previously Pearce absented himself from his duties without leave.
The clerk despatched to his lodgings alleged that, such was his
poverty, he had been obliged to pawn his work clothes.

Clearly, such behaviour could not be thought compatible with the discharge of an office of trust, and Pearce was dismissed forthwith.

Having the honour to remain your most obedient servant, I am, sirs, yours most faithfully,

JAMES HARKER
Secretary to the Board

* * *

To: Joseph Pearce, Esq.
Roupell Street SE

Dear Sir,
I am instructed by the directors of the South-Eastern Railway Company to inform you that they can entertain no further communications from you either in the matter of your dismissal or indeed on any other subject.
 Yours faithfully,

JAMES HARKER
Secretary to the Board

* * *

And always there is the river.

Just at this moment—two of the clock on an afternoon in March — the river is at slack tide. Very sluggish around Temple Pier, somnolent at Blackfriars and at London Bridge positively sedate, so that an intrepid boatman paddling east in the shadow of the Tower might think that he had strayed by accident into a lagoon, a kind of Sargasso Sea of murky water, cast-off rubbish bobbing on the swell from the lighters and the cargo boats in midstream, old hawsers washed up on the Middlesex shore, gulls swinging south towards the factory chimneys of Bermondsey and Deptford. On the further side from the Tower, a few mudlarks digging in the ooze and bringing forth who knows what stained and inky treasures. At the Tower itself a general air of battening down, of three-quarter-closed doors, feet hastening away lest they be called upon to perform some duty and a preponderance of ravens ambling this way and that across the stone pavement and wondering to themselves, like landlords in a holiday town out of season, where all the people have gone. Very cold, very flat and dull, with a raw east wind ruffling the pennants that hang in the Tower gardens and the awnings of the refreshments shops that stand now tenantless and empty, for the season of visitors has not yet come. A few tall ships in the middle distance sliding inexorably out of view, so that each glance sees another mast and another mainsail vanish over the horizon. Rowboats, cutters and launches clustering around the wharfs whose blackened fronts hang down low in the water like the skirts of bombazine-clad old ladies. Grey sky above, brown water beneath, so that Fauntleroy, RA, whom the fashionable world admires, setting up his easel by the Tower gateway, would despair at the chance of intruding a little colour into his composition.

A little further downstream—were that intrepid boatman still bent on making his way east—much the same conditions prevailing. At Wapping Old Stairs, where a swirl of black water washes around the grey steps, a man hanging out of a police launch with a boat hook to prod at something unidentifiable in the depths below. The cherry gardens on the further side very cheerless and cherryless and desolate, the trees huddled up against the wind as if no blossom would ever flourish there again. Then in quick, or rather slow, succession—for nothing moves here with any rapidity—a patch of waste ground with a fence and a little shed and a sign saying *T. Myerson, Merchant,* no clue at all being offered by these bare appurtenances as to what it is in which T. Myerson, Merchant, deals, a street of fantastically tiny houses in pink stucco, so small that you might wonder how the people squeeze themselves in through their exiguous front doors, and finally a dismal-looking pleasure garden, somewhat retired and secluded, with a gaunt refreshment room and a disconsolate proprietress seated in its window and a general air of having opened its gates this raw March afternoon in defiance of its best interests and judgement and of being about to shut them up again.

Here on a windswept terrace, at a solitary table whose four legs had been fastened to the ground—perhaps with the idea of preventing the wind from spiriting them away—two figures sat, with whom

D. J. TAYLOR

we have some slight acquaintance. The former, very big and burly in a thick topcoat, was eating zealously at a plate of shrimps; the latter stared at a pot of beer from which he did not drink. The first man, pausing occasionally in his negotiations with the shrimps to take a pull at his own tankard, seemed in high good humour; the second, casting wary glances at his companion and into the gloomy sky beyond them, seemed thoroughly miserable.

"'Pon my word," Bob Grace remarked, with his fork half out of his mouth and a brace of shrimps snaggled up in his teeth, "I never saw such a chap for not eating his vittles. Just say the word now and the girl shall bring you anything you fancy."

"Indeed, I ain't hungry."

"Some of these shrimps now, or a pie brought up hot and hot. No? Well, a man's the best judge of his own appetites, I suppose. Did they feed you in Yarmouth? I wonder."

"I hadn't anything to complain of."

Grace seemed to find the rejoinder amusing, for he put the fork down on his plate with a clatter and guffawed loudly. "No? I don't suppose you did." Fork in hand once more, he speared another shrimp from the plate, inspected it closely and fondly decapitated it with his teeth. "Nothing to complain of! Tell me now, how are things at home? Have you been in work?"

Dewar, who had been following the motion of his companion's jaw with a fascinated horror, hunched his shoulders more deeply into the folds of his flimsy jacket.

"I . . . I had two days at an eating house in Drury Lane. But it is casual work, you know, and if you aren't a favourite with the head waiter you are pretty soon discharged."

"And you weren't a favourite, I suppose. Well, never mind. And how is Mrs. Dewar?"

"No better. It's all she can do to rise from her bed."

"Can't get out of bed, eh?" Grace said affably. "Sounds to me as if you had a deal to complain of. Sounds to me as if your life was one long round of misery. But then Mr. Pardew has something to complain of too, wouldn't you say?"

Dewar said nothing.

"Bless you! You needn't look at me as if I meant to eat you. Oh no. It's nothing to me. What do I care as long as I gets my wages and the time to spend them? But Mr. Pardew now, he cares a great deal. Indeed he does. You might not think it, but the business at Yarmouth with you not remembering your right name took an unconscionable time to set straight. Why Mr. Pardew had to send a feller into the bank at Lothbury pretending to be you, and all the time was feared that Gurney's in Yarmouth might have written saying what had come about. In which case there'd have been the devil to pay, indeed there would, for there's a police captain, name of McTurk, as is very down on the likes of us."

The look on Dewar's face registering only blank incomprehension, Grace beat a little martial tattoo with his fork on the bare plate and struck his other hand on the tabletop.

"Bless us! You mean to say you weren't up to the dodge? You are a green 'un and no mistake. Let us say that a man has been put in the way of some cheques he'd like to put into ready money. No good just presenting them to a London bank, no good at all. The clerks these days have eyes like hawks. No, the trick is to get a man to go to some lawyer—some lawyer a good way out of town if you can find one—and tell him he means to recover a debt. The lawyer writes the letter to the debtor, only the debtor's you, if you take my meaning? You send the cheque, signed in the name as the lawyer wrote to. After a bit the lawyer takes off his commission and pays your man. If it's cash, well and good. If it's by cheque, with a signature, well there's another little game to begin. Mr. Pardew knows all about it. Now do you understand me?"

"I believe I do." The wretched expression on Dewar's face insisted that he understood all too well.

"That's the spirit! Debt collecting in the provinces—there's nothing like it! But see here"—and Grace bent his head low over the table—"there's another debt owing, and that's from you to us. Don't look at me! I'm a nice man, I am. I won't see you come to any harm. But Mr. Pardew, he's a regular tartar. He'll chew you up and spit out the bones if he's a mind. Others too. Why, there's a gentleman in Norfolk with ever so many acres who's beholden to us, and whose paper we have and other knowledge that I won't speak of. And if Mr. Pardew asks him for a thing, why he'll give it." And here Grace gave a short laugh as if by this he intended to make Dewar understand that a thing had been asked from this gentleman and that this gentleman had produced it. "Now, I make it half past two of the clock. What might you have been a-doing, eh, if I hadn't come to Islington and ferreted you out from that reading room where you'd gone to hide?"

"I daresay I'd have been out searching for a job. Or setting by my wife."

"Who won't miss you this once," Grace asseverated, slapping one palm upon the other with such force that the very gulls scavenging beneath their tables backed away in alarm. "You'd best come along with me, Dewar, indeed you had."

"Where should I come?" There was a plaintive note in Dewar's voice. "And what would you have me do?"

"You ought to understand," Grace said, grinning hugely, "that none of this is my doing. Indeed it's not. Neither does it bear on the gentleman in Norfolk nor on anyone else. I want no favours returned, I tell you, for I'm a nice man that wants to stand easy with his fellow creatures. But if Mr. Pardew says to me, 'Take this fellow Dewar, who owes us such a debt, down to Greenwich and introduce him to a couple of gentlemen as might be an advantage to him to know,' then what am I to say? Only that I'm Mr. Pardew's man."

"But what is there at Greenwich?"

"You shall see. You shall indeed. At any rate, you shall come to no harm. There shan't be no crocodiles to eat you if I'm there to prevent them. And a situation, too, as you might find agreeable."

"A situation?"

"That's right. For being a parrot as repeats everything that's said to him. No, I'm only joking. I'm a nice feller, I tell you, not one of those stick-at-nothing characters that take advantage of men that don't pay back what they owe."

Taking Dewar's mournful silence as an assent, Grace laughed his short laugh, beat another tattoo with his fork that would have had any military man in the vicinity snap to attention, and pushed his plate to one side. By degrees they made ready to leave. It would not be true to say, as these preparations were made, that Mr. Pardew's clerk exactly stood guard over his companion as the latter got to his feet and wound a threadbare scarf around his throat, or that his eye altogether strayed over various gates and doorways through which an exit might have been effected. Neither would it be true to say that Dewar, very pale-faced and rheumy-eyed in the cold and casting anxious little glances about him, was altogether unaware of these attentions. Nevertheless, the two men made their departure from the pleasure garden without incident.

In the half hour that they had sat there it had grown colder, very much colder; the wind was dying down. Beside the gate of the pleasure garden there was a flight of ancient steps, very mottled and briny, leading down to an equally ancient and crumbling jetty, very much cluttered with rope ends, barrel staves, metal pins and other nautical accessories. Again, it would not be true to say that Grace positively propelled his companion, as the latter picked his way through this maritime debris, or that he altogether stood in the way of a second flight of steps that led back up to the tide wall. Neither would it be true to say that Dewar ignored this second pathway or that his eye didn't rest somewhat longingly on its grey aspect. Reaching the water's edge, where there was a pair of wooden posts and a chain suspended between them, they stood staring downriver. In the distance, towards Deptford Reach, mist was beginning to rise, giving the ships' masts that crowded the foreshore an eerie particularity, as if their topmost points emerged out of nothing and were somehow suspended on the shifting air. Beyond, stray flashes of light broke intermittently out of the grey surround.

"Ha! They are firing the cannons down at the arsenal," Grace remarked. "A mile downstream and we shall smell the powder."

Presently a brisk little steam launch, very spruce and well burnished, with a white flag in its bow and a brace of streamers trailing from its stern, came toiling up to the jetty and, by means of a couple of planks laid lengthwise to form a gangway, disgorged a number of persons and a crate containing several live chickens from its front deck. Grace, leaning over the rail, took the most benevolent and scientific interest in this unloading. "The things people carry about with them,"

D. J. TAYLOR

he observed to Dewar. "See that old lady with the valise?—How are you, ma'am?—Must weigh three stone if it weighs an ounce. And the old gent with the mattress—A hand, sir, with your luggage?—You wouldn't catch me carrying such stuff." That Grace seemed altogether familiar with the boat and its navigators was confirmed by the practised way in which he bounded across the gangway, nodded at the attendant who stood by the cabin door and set his feet down easily on the listing surface of the deck.

"Greenwich Pier, I suppose, Mr. Grace?" said a tall man with a nautical beard and a metal hook in place of a hand, giving Grace the hook to shake.

"That's about the size of it," Grace agreed. "And my friend here too."

There was an inner cabin where they were invited to sit, tenanted by an old woman with a small terrier in a basket. Here Grace's good humour continued. He produced a green apple from the folds of his coat, polished it upon his shoulder and ate it with evident relish, following this refection with a short pipe, which he tamped down with macabaw and puffed in fragrant clouds, having first asked the old lady's pardon if smoke offended her. The old lady said that she didn't mind, but she would be obliged if they would close the window as it made her ear ache. This courtesy having been performed, Grace began to rally the old lady. That was a fine-looking dog she possessed; could he guard a house, and, if so, could Grace have the borrowing of him? The old lady replied that he *was* a fine dog and it was gratifying to her how many people remarked it. Not too sure of his sea legs, though, Grace deposed. Not sure of them at all, sir, the old lady replied with dignity, but then sea legs were not always an advantage to a dog.

In this way the half hour of their voyage passed very pleasantly, though I fear that the pleasure was mostly Grace's. Dewar sat silently at his side, watching the mist steal up beyond the cabin window and the lanterns of the cargo ships signalling to each other in midstream. He had reached an interior state not unlike the one in which Grace had left him at their previous meeting, his mind full of random impressions through which Grace, though still sitting beside him, seemed to move in a very sinister manner, his eyes caught by the most peculiar details of the cabin and the dimly glimpsed world without. The basket in which the old lady kept her dog had a metal fastening that protruded in two great snaps, and he stared at them blindly until they seemed to grow to an enormous size and frighten him with their immensity. The dog itself had a habit of butting repeatedly at the material that confined it, and this he found recalled to him a mechanism he had once seen at a manufactory in the City, a revolving piston that had struck endlessly at some metal plate until it made him sick to look at it. In the end he decided to stand up, simply so that the physical act of rising to his feet might bring some less unpleasant sensation, but the sway of the boat defeated him, he rocked uncertainly on his heels for a moment and then fell back into his seat, thoroughly miserable and ashamed of himself.

"Your friend don't say much," the old lady observed, noticing him almost for the first time.

"Indeed he don't," Grace told her. "Now, what would you say if I told you I was taking him to Greenwich to get married in the morning?"

The old lady remarked very sapiently that he would be a-gammoning of her, whereupon Grace riposted that she was not so green as she was cabbage-looking and he was delighted to make her acquaintance.

By the time the launch came in sight of Greenwich, Grace had tired of the old lady. His good humour had given way to restlessness. He sat back with his hands clasped behind his head and his feet planted squarely before him and looked first at a clock that hung on the far wall and registered the time as ten minutes past three, then at an engraving of a whale spouting in some Arctic sea, then at the toes of his boots. Finally, these diversions altogether failing him, he turned to Dewar.

"You ever hear of a party named Dixey?"

"I should think I did."

"Great house in the country, stuffed full of birds' eggs. Big in the taxidermy line. That kind of thing."

"Is he"—Dewar marvelled at his daring as he framed the words— "is he bound to Mr. Pardew?"

"Dixey?" Grace drummed his feet, but with an oddly muted report, as if he feared what havoc they might wreak in this confined space. "There's more there than I have the knowing of. But he and him have come across each other, and money owing and all, if you take my meaning. Here, you had better stir your stumps unless you mean to go on to Gravesend."

When they arrived at Greenwich, where the old lady and her dog were met and driven off by an equally old man in a donkey cart, Grace's manner became sweetly proprietorial. Taking Dewar by the arm, he showed him the naval buildings and the tall ships with such gravity that he might have designed them himself, regretted that the lateness of the hour prevented a walk up the hill to the observatory, spoke of half a dozen amenities that the place possessed and which he, Dewar, would no doubt come to relish. Then, with Dewar's arm still firmly pinioned in his, so firmly that Dewar, try as he might, could not detach it, he led his companion off along the high road, where from the doors of public houses and billiard rooms nautical gentlemen in striped jackets and top boots regarded them incuriously, and away into a region of mean little streets where the houses came crammed so tightly together that it seemed a wonder that some of them were not altogether squeezed out of existence by their more overbearing neighbours.

It was by now late afternoon, with the wind altogether quelled and the fog altogether descending, so that the lights from the riverbank, now steadily receding from view, seemed muffled and innocuous in the haze. Dewar, loping along at Grace's side, his tendency to saunter instantly corrected by a jerk from Grace's wrist, was subject to the most terrible premonitions. He was conscious that he was bidden he knew not where, that the only person who knew his destination was Grace, and that additionally he was bound to Grace and beyond him to the unseen Mr. Pardew without at all knowing how this binding might be unravelled. These fears worked within him to such an extent that when, reaching a crossroads where several streets converged, Grace made a sudden movement away to his right, he altogether shrank from the man and came within an inch of crying out. Curiously, Grace appeared not to notice this distress. He was in high good humour still, stamping his feet down smartly on the cobbled stone, darting inquisitive glances into the windows and doorways that they passed and whistling little fragments of tunes through his teeth.

At length they stopped in front of a mean little house with a door all tilted to one side and a plaster covering a crack in its gloomy front window. Here Grace halted, relinquished Dewar's arm, which the latter immediately found he had to rub to restore its circulation, and delved elaborately in his trouser pocket for a key. Extricating this implement from a heap of coins, pieces of wire and paper fragments, he turned it in the lock and admitted them into a dirty, dusty vestibule, very sparsely furnished and so dimly lit that the eye, travelling towards the rooms that it abutted, could discern nothing but the grey outlines of furniture, altogether ghostly and phantasmal in the murk. Some thought seemed to have occurred to Grace as he stood in the hallway, for he waited for a moment with his head half-cocked as if trying to make out some sound amidst the enveloping silence. Finally, he shuffled his feet once or twice on the exceedingly shabby carpet and remarked, a shade less high-spiritedly than before, "My mother is very bad about lighting the lamps, you know. She positively won't attend to them until it's pitch-dark."

Stepping gingerly into the body of the house, he called out suddenly, "Mother! Here, Mother, there is company come."

After what seemed an eternity of waiting a little old woman, attired in what appeared to be a dress of black crepe with a black bonnet secured to her head by strings under her chin and little black boots sticking out from beneath her skirts, came silently down a staircase that rose from the rear part of the vestibule. So silent was her descent that Dewar, not looking up and not apprehending her until she had reached a point three-quarters of the way downstairs, shrank back a second time. Grace, on the other hand, regarded his parent warmly.

"Company? Nothing was said about company."

"This is Mr. Dewar, Mother, of whom I spoke, come for his supper."

"Well, he shall have to take such luck as he finds."

Having made this speech of welcome, the old lady put out her hand, prompting Grace, with a great show of dexterity and good nature, to convey her from the bottommost step of the stair to the hall carpet. Having reached level ground and reconnoitred it once or twice with the toe of her boot, she said, "In my day lamps were never lit until dusk. But it is all very different now."

With the old lady leading, Grace darting occasionally before her to open a door or to implore her to watch her tread on the carpet, they negotiated a long, gloomy corridor and went down a flight of steps to a subterranean kitchen, very low-ceilinged and inconvenient, with the pots and cauldrons hung from hooks along the far wall. As they drew closer Dewar became aware that he could hear the sound of violent movement, as of some live thing beating itself against something else that was unquestionably inanimate. On the further side of the kitchen, quite shrouded in the half-dark, a tall window looked out onto a grim little garden of bushes and stunted trees. Here, on the kitchen side of the frame, a blackbird was dashing itself repeatedly against the glass.

"Dratted thing," said the old lady.

Dewar moved towards the window and reached for the fastening, but Grace stayed his arm.

"No indeed, that would never do. Here, light this lamp and don't trouble about what doesn't concern you."

Doing as Grace had bidden, Dewar now saw that a tiny chain was fastened to the bird's leg, the other end secured to a metal ring sunk into the wall, and that additionally a wooden birdcage hung from the ceiling among the pots and pans.

Eventually, the lamps were lit and the kitchen fire stoked into life and some faint beam of conviviality illuminated the place. The old lady clattered mournfully among sundry utensils, all of which had a habit of falling to the floor at a second's notice, while her son sat himself down at the kitchen table, took off his hat and looked about him with a satisfied air. Even the blackbird, whom Grace addressed as Sammy, ceased to fling itself against the window and consented to perch on the back of a chair and be fed a sugar lump which Grace crumbled for him in a saucer.

"Now, Mother," Grace said, drumming with his feet on the floor, "what have you got for us, eh? Something good and hot, I'll be bound."

There being no reply from the range, where the old lady now struck two saucepans together as if they surrounded some invisible enemy whose escape she was very anxious to prevent, Grace murmured in an undertone, "Mother is quite remarkable for her age. Why, would you believe that she cleans and dusts the place herself with no thought for any help? She says it would shame her to have a girl sweeping dust under the carpet. And she is much respected. You won't hardly credit it, perhaps, but only the other week an alderman of the borough with a carriage and a house on the hill proposed that she should come to him as housekeeper."

Grace's respect for his parent was beautiful to see. As they sat at the broad table, with the firelight casting monstrous shadows on the wall behind them and the blackbird chittering on his perch, he continued to dilate on her virtues: the excellence of her temper, the sagacity of her views and the impartiality of her judgement. "Why," he explained, "a year ago last Michaelmas there was a young woman as I was keeping company with. As nice a piece of brisket as a man ever stuck a knife into. The banns was to have been read in church on Christmas Day. But Mother wouldn't stand for it. And I don't doubt, having weighed the matter and considered the young woman's points—which were excellent ones, no doubt about that—that she was right!"

However extensive the list of Mrs. Grace's accomplishments, culinary skill was not amongst them. They dined very frugally off a plate of sardines and some boiled cabbage into which an unconscionably large quantity of vinegar had for some reason been mixed. Their repast ended and the plates stacked upon the wooden square next to the sink, where the old lady belaboured them with a stiff brush as if they were young women who had designs on her son, Grace took an envelope from his inner pocket, a very elegant envelope on whose back there might even have lurked the suspicion of a coronet, and stared at it suggestively.

"Now," he said, "a fish supper and pickled cabbage with it is all very well, but there is business to attend to. Mr. Pardew, through me—and I'm Mr. Pardew's man, which is something I urge you never to forget—has a proposition to make. This here"—he tapped the envelope, which now lay on the table before them—"is a testimonial to your character from a *dook*, no less. Take a look at it if you like."

Wondering, Dewar examined the sheet of foolscap that fell into his grasp. Here he read that His Grace the Duke of ——, having had occasion to employ Mr. J. Dewar in his service, initially as *valet de*

D. J. TAYLOR

chambre, latterly as underbutler, was pleased to recommend him for any position for which his undoubted talents might cause him to apply.

"Who is this Duke of ——?"

"Never you mind. That's down to Mr. Pardew, who has dukes and earls enough to fill a dinner table if such is wanted. Now, tomorrow you're to go to the London Bridge Station, which is the office of the South-Eastern Railway Company. Know of them? Good. There you are to ask for Mr. Smiles, as is the supervisor, and you're to give him this. There is a vacancy there, and you shall fill it."

Looking from Grace to the figure of the old lady going intently about her chores and back to the blackbird, who had flown back to the window ledge and perched there in a state of apparent dejection, Dewar felt that he might faint with fear.

"How . . . how will this help me repay my debt to Mr. Pardew?"

"That's for Mr. Pardew to say. But you working for the South-Eastern Railway Company is a start, indeed it is. But not a word about the Duke, mind. Mr. Pardew don't like his friends' names being bandied about, and that's a fact."

Half a dozen questions sprang unbidden to Dewar's lips, but Grace brushed them aside. He could say nothing more, for it was Mr. Pardew's doing and he knew nothing of it. Dewar had better take the letter, for there was further company expected and this was not a thing to leave lying around, indeed not. There was gin or whisky. Which would he take? His mother should bring a jug of hot water, that she should. The bird hobbled and fretted at his hand.

* * *

A dozen hours later Dewar awoke upon a mattress in a bare-boarded upstairs chamber which he could not remember having entered the previous night. He was fully clothed, save for his jacket, which lay atop the rough assortment of bedding piled around him. The room was empty except for a three-legged chair on which rested a water jug, an empty glass and a spent candle. He was not in such a condition that he could recall precisely what had happened to him in the later stages of the evening, but his first thought was for the letter, which he searched anxiously in the pocket of his coat to retrieve. There it was, still in its envelope, and he took it out and examined it once more, marvelling a little at the sonority of the words and his own name lodged inexplicably within them. There was a dryness in his throat, and he drank off a glass of water from the jug—very musty and stale it was—with trembling hands. Certain other remembrances of the previous night now crowded in on his mind with such speed that he could scarcely separate one from the other: of two very tall and silent gentlemen named Pearce and Latch arriving at the house very much muffled up in coats and scarves; and of his being introduced to them by Grace; and of one of them—he could not remember which—laughing and saying that he would "do"; of a great deal of talk he could barely fathom about Mr. Pardew's affairs and schemes; of a solemn handshaking intended to seal some compact of which Dewar had only the faintest comprehension before the gentlemen took their leave; of Grace leading him up the back staircase and grinning at him beneath the light of the candle; of the footsteps and whisperings that seemed to resound through the house after he had pressed his head against his makeshift pillow.

There was weak sunshine, he saw, falling into the room through a skylight above his head. Seizing his coat and stowing the letter back into one of his pockets, he made his way onto the landing, looked to right and left but found only closed doors, and so made his way down the creaking stairs. There was a little closet at their foot, and there he made water, washed his face, combed his hair and repaired the damage to his costume consequent upon a night spent in his clothes. The house seemed to him extraordinarily quiet. There was no sound that he could determine, save for a wheel turning in the street outside. A clock fixed to the wall beyond the closet door told him that it wanted a few minutes until the hour of nine. Grasping the lapels of his coat in his hands, so nervous now that his legs shook beneath him, he turned into the hallway, put his nose into the parlour and the drawing room and, finding no one there, took it out again. A giant ulster, which he supposed to be Grace's, hung on a peg by the door, but of Grace's hat, which he remembered seeing placed there the previous night by its owner, there was no sign.

D. J. TAYLOR

Supposing that he would find the household at breakfast, he descended the second flight of stairs to the kitchen, making a purposeful noise with his boots as he did so in order to announce his coming, but here, too, all was silent and empty. Beyond the gloomy window a wind had got up and was blowing the bushes back against each other and causing one of the stunted trees to bend at a very uncomfortable angle, and he became aware—how he had not noticed it when he first came into the room he could not tell—of a furious scratching somewhat above the level of his head made by the blackbird, the length of chain taut against its neck, dashing itself against the pane.

Something stirred within him, and he reached out and seized the chain in his hands, gave it a twist and broke it—it was flimsily made and came apart in his fingers—then released the catch and pulled the upper frame halfway down. He had an idea of removing the chain from the bird's neck, but before he could move closer, in a great rush of feathers and beating wings the creature was aloft, chain and all, into the rush of air. He saw it in flight for a moment, high above the chimney stacks and the distant gables, and then it was gone. It seemed to him that he had done something very foolish and which he would regret, but he was conscious, too, that he was glad to have done it. A few moments later he let himself out of the house and began the search for an omnibus that would take him to London Bridge.

XVI

"THE BLACK DOG KNOWS MY NAME"

In the corner of the paddock, from behind the oak rail, Mr. Dixey watches the wolf. The oak rail is five feet high, above a fence of corrugated metal, though once already the wolf has jumped the fence and been found wandering in the wood. How it made its way through the thorn hedge, which is impenetrable to man, and the locked gate, Mr. Dixey does not know, but he has resolved to be vigilant. He can leave nothing to chance. Wolves—this he knows from experience and study—are resourceful creatures.

From above his head, tumbling crazily out of the pale sky, a crow descends onto the grass and turns a beady eye over its surroundings. There are always carrion here. The trees are black with rooks. Jackdaws nest in the eaves above the dairy. The wolf, Mr. Dixey believes, leaning now on the rail—he is a tall man and can do this without discomfort—is no longer nervous of him. Or rather he has ceased to notice him. Mr. Dixey thinks that the wolf imagines him to be part of the landscape, a kind of moving tree that marches alongside the rail, the corrugated metal fence and the thorn hedge. Do animals have a sixth sense? Mr. Dixey thinks not, and yet even when he moves towards the rail in silence, stealing up to some vantage point from which he knows the beast cannot see him, the wolf is always anxiously regarding the space in which his head appears. It is uncanny, Mr. Dixey thinks.

Just now the wolf is huddled down in the shadow of the paddock's further end, tail curled over its forepaws, looking for all the world like a very large dog, sniffing at a strip of rabbit hide. It is extraordinary what it eats. Rabbits. Hares. Chickens from the farm. It is indiscriminate in its tastes but not, Mr. Dixey thinks, greedy. Food thrown into the paddock when it has eaten its fill will, like as not, be left for the crows. Mr. Dixey is impressed by this prudence. It confirms certain of his deductions about natural law while denying others. This interests him.

Silently, one hand shielding the other as it rests on the rail, Mr. Dixey sketches the wolf. He reproduces the high arch of the spine, the curve of the muzzle, but the set of the head—the grin when it raises itself up—eludes him. Mr. Dixey believes—long years of studying animals have told him this—that we see in nature what we wish to see. Nonetheless, the wolf's grin intrigues him. It speaks of fairy-tale children run to ground in dark forests, ransacked graves, rawhead and bloody bones. The Scots of Sutherland used to bury their dead in island cemeteries a mile from the shore, so persistent were the attentions of the grey gentlemen. Mr. Dixey wonders if his own wolf, now hunkered even further down in the shadow of the fence, is becoming faintly domesticated. It is a timber wolf from Norway, brought across the North Sea in a fishing boat three months since and landed on the quay at Lynn in a crate, snarling with such venom that at first the porters Mr. Dixey had engaged to carry it to his wagonette refused to go near. Though quiet, for the most part, it was not a docile beast. A fortnight after its arrival, thinking that he might see some sport, Mr. Dixey introduced a bull mastiff into the paddock. It is not an experiment he intends to repeat.

In some parts of Britain it is still considered unlucky to call a wolf a wolf. The Scots, in particular, have a horror of this. But then it is not much more than a century since the last in Scotland perished, wrestled and stabbed to death by the great Highland hunter MacQueen of Poll a'chrocain in the glens of the Monadhliath. A large black wolf which the previous day had killed two children crossing the hills with their mother. The timber wolf, Mr. Dixey thinks, is similarly coloured—grey as it wanders into the pale sunlight but with a darker tint showing through. His dogs loathe it, are reduced to paroxysms of unease even from the further side of the thorn hedge.

There is a squire in the West Country—Mr. Dixey has corresponded with him—who has a scheme to run wolves at stags on the downs or to make them quarry for his own hounds. Privately Mr. Dixey thinks this madness, but he is content to lend his ear. The timber wolf has risen to its feet now, stands staring at him incuriously before turning to examine the long curl of its tail. Mr. Dixey stares back. The crow, which has been quietly searching through the long grass, reemerges with something red and glistening held in its beak. Reluctantly, Mr. Dixey folds up the scrap of paper that is his sketch, sees that the paddock gate is securely fastened, passes through the low door in the thorn hedge and locks it behind him. There are other things that demand his attention: lawyers' letters, estate business and the stables' disintegrating brickwork. He has his own grey gentlemen, he thinks, gnawing at his vitals.

* * *

Mr. Dixey sits in his study. In the half-light—for the shutter is still pulled across one of the windows—the room seems ghostly: the display cabinets and the bookcases gathered up in shadow, the stuffed bear somehow insubstantial, like an oversized children's toy that might skip suddenly away to the chimes of a musical box. A mouse runs up over the pile of legal papers and bundles of foolscap, a bold, confident mouse that sits washing its whiskers in the shade of the inkwell and wringing its paws like some supplicant come to beg a favour, and Mr. Dixey puts down his pen and regards it, makes soft, encouraging noises with his tongue against his teeth, finds the fragment of a biscuit in his trouser pocket and crumbles it up.

There are black dogs everywhere in Norfolk, Mr. Dixey knows. When scudding storms hide the moon on a winter's night, then Odin, mounted on his eight-legged horse Sleipnir, leads the Wild Hunt across the sky with a pack of yammering hounds at his heels. In the time of Henry I, when an abbot that the monks of Peterborough did not desire was foisted on them, black huntsmen on black horses were seen, followed by hounds as black as jet with huge staring eyes. To meet Black Shuck and to stare at his solitary, blazing orb is to meet a portent of your own death. One summer Sunday morning in the time of Queen Bess, did not ominous storm clouds loom over the town of Bungay, whereupon there rose up *a great tempest of violent raine, lightning and thunder, the like whereof hath been seldom seine. With the appeerance of an horrible shaped thing, sensibly perceived of the people then and there assembled.* Already that morning a fiery demon had laid waste the church of Blythburgh, leaving two men stark dead. Here the demon took the shape of a black dog with eyes of fire, killing and burning every person in its path. Passing between two men, it *wrung the necks of them bothe at one instant cleane backward, insomuch that even at a moment where they kneeled they strangely dyed,* seizing a third *in such a gripe on the back, that therewithal he was presently drawen together and shrunk up, as it were a peece of lether scorched in a hot fire.*

In Mr. Dixey's study:

a tray of legal papers, over which Mr. Dixey looks and ponders and broods

a mouse washing its whiskers and drinking milk from a saucer

a morsel of paper, very much scratched and half obliterated, on which he, or someone, has written: *the black dog knows my name.*

XVII

MR. RICHARD FARRIER

It was at about this time that the name Mr. Richard Farrier began to be spoken of by those persons with an interest in the Ireland case. Quite how this came about was a mystery and yet, it seems to me, a mystery of a very common sort. Such is the strength of the public thirst for information, that a gentleman who at the beginning of the week lives a life of blameless anonymity can often discover by its end that half the world seems to be intimately acquainted with his affairs and likes nothing better than to discuss them with the other half. So it was with Mr. Farrier, of whom, a month or so before, nothing had been known, and who now, a month or so later, was spoken of in the most confidential terms by men and women who would not have recognised him had he arrived in their drawing rooms bearing the tea things before him on a tray.

At the time when people began to talk of him, he was in his twenty-seventh or twenty-eighth year, of a good family supposed to come originally from the West Country. He was, additionally, a cousin of Mrs. Ireland's, and by no means so remote a one as John Carstairs, being in fact the son of the great-niece of the former Miss Brotherton's great-grandmother. And here the most delicious scent of romance could be found wafting across the pathways of Mr. Farrier's early life, for it was said—no, it was known—that with regard to Miss Brotherton he had wished to be something more than a cousin, and that to this end he had proposed marriage to his relative when he was no more than eighteen years old. As to what had occurred between them, given that no one else had been present in old Mr. Brotherton's rose garden on the afternoon when Mr. Farrier pressed his suit, nothing very profitable could be said. Within a year, in any case, Miss Brotherton had absented herself upon the Continent with her papa, and her suitor went off to console himself in whatever manner young gentlemen of eighteen with broken hearts may hope to be consoled.

It is commonly supposed that if a man's romantic aspirations are known he cannot be altogether mysterious, and yet over Mr. Farrier's career, ambitions and even his whereabouts mystery continued to hang in an impenetrable cloud. His parents had died young. In their absence he had been brought up by an old clergyman in Devizes and then, at seventeen, prepared for admission to Oriel College, Oxford. Of Mr. Farrier's undergraduate doings, a certain amount was known, but not all of it was creditable. In particular he was thought to have got in with a set of sporting young gentlemen, spent astonishing sums on top boots, bridles, saddles, tailcoats and other equine appurtenances, altogether neglected his books and been compelled to quit university life before the completion of his second year.

As for Mr. Farrier's subsequent progress through the world, gentlemanly, upstanding and courteous though he doubtless was, I fear that the Dean of Oriel, who had ultimately pressed for his superannuation, must be granted a certain amount of prescience. At twenty he had been put into a public office, and for six months it seemed as if a great career awaited him there. And then people began to say that there was a certain want of . . application in his dealings with the great men who administered the office and that a certain noble lord on whom he had been bidden to attend, while acknowledging his gentlemanliness, courtesy, &c., had complained bitterly of his neglect. It was said also that he owed money, and to the kind of person to whom money should not be owed, and was more often to be found at a prizefight than attending divine service. The result was that he was removed from the public office, his debts were paid for him, a young woman who proposed that he was the father of her child was somehow placated and he was sent to read with a very respectable barrister in Thavies Inn with a view to entering at the bar. Here, once more, at the commencement of his studies he won golden opinions, was smiled upon by Mrs. Barrister and her daughters (the story of the young woman had not perhaps drifted as far as Thavies Inn) while even Mr. Barrister, to whom all young men were anathema, was supposed to have nodded his head and said that he would do. And then one morning as this Telemachus sat in his chamber with a copy of Coke open on his desk before him impatiently awaiting his pupil, he received instead a visitation from a knowing old gentleman with only one eye, in a shabby greatcoat, who produced from his satchel an equally shabby pocketbook from which he extracted a bill for fifty pounds with Mr. Farrier's signature —a fine, upstanding, gentlemanly signature it was, with all manner of flourishes and underlinings—appended to the stamp. "This is no business of mine," Mr. Barrister observed, having dangled the piece of paper between his fingers for as long as was consistent with civility. "I daresay not, sir," the old gentleman said, grinning, "but it's a thing as we always try with young gentlemen that reads in barristers' chambers, you know." And after that it was all up with Thavies Inn, Mr. Barrister, Mrs. Barrister and the latter's highly eligible daughters.

Still, though, all was not over with our young Apollo. It was at about this time, having achieved his majority, that he came into a certain sum of money left to him by his father. This being a circumstance that infallibly encourages an independent-minded and free-spirited attitude, he took rooms in Clarges Street, engaged the services of a valet and an old woman to do his laundry, displayed a row of stiff-backed invitation cards on his mantelpiece and was inducted into a gentlemen's club named the Megatherium, where it was his delight to remain until four o'clock in the morning on at least three days in the week playing whist. There were those who maintained, at this juncture in his life, that Richard Farrier was going to the dogs, that respectable mammas should not deign to have him in their drawing rooms and that the old gentleman in Devizes was greatly to be pitied. Still, I think, and the world tended to think also, that all was not lost with him. He was very civil in his manner, very courteous in his address and very prompt in the payment of his club subscription.

At twenty-two he grew meekly reflective over the errors of his early life. The public office and Mr. Barrister's chamber had been a torture to him, he declared, had stifled him into a misery from which he had pined to be released, but there was much that he might do—would do—to inspire some pride in the hearts of those who took an interest in him. For myself, I think he was sincere in this. Within a year, at any rate, he was gone from London, the rooms in Clarges Street were let out to the Honourable Mr. Popjoy, Lord Clantantrum's son, who furnished them with gauzy prints and portraits of Taglioni in the appropriate Parisian manner, and the blear-eyed waiter at the Megatherium, shuffling into the card room at dawn to take orders for breakfast, saw him no more. Nobody quite knew where he went for—and this was a peculiarity in him—he had no intimate friends. There are some gentlemen whose progress around the world is as well known to the public as the holders of government offices—one week they are at Paris, the next they have moved on to Munich preparatory to an excursion down the Rhine—but Mr. Farrier was not among them. His doings were his own, and his tracks were not of the kind determined by Mr. Cook.

All this was enough to make Mr. Richard Farrier a figure of consuming interest to those concerned with the fate of Mrs. Ireland. A gentleman who was her second cousin and in addition had been in love with her ten years! (The fact of Mrs. Ireland's marriage was conveniently forgotten.) There was a general feeling—no one quite knew where it had arisen, but it waxed powerfully nonetheless—that Mr. Farrier should be sent for, even unto the ends of the earth, and what he had to say be respectfully listened to. Sadly, this proposal, to which half a dozen genteel drawing rooms keenly assented, fell at the hurdle of Mr. Farrier's exact whereabouts. A man may be both everywhere and nowhere in particular, and so it was with him. The goldfields of the Cape; California; Moscow; Samarkand—all these were confidently proposed as places where he might be found, and to none of them, ultimately, could his scent be traced. The old gentleman in Devizes, to whom application was made, knew nothing about it. An old woman who kept rooms in Sackville Street which he used as a poste restante could offer only an accommodation address in Paris. It seemed that Mr. Farrier had vanished entirely, wandered to the very precipice of civilisation and then stepped off, only that he had a lawyer, a Mr. Devereux, with offices in Cursitor Street, to whom some account of these wanderings was presumably communicated.

On this Mr. Devereux, several pairs of eyes were instantly turned. "You should step along and see him, John, indeed you should," Mrs. Carstairs had remarked to her son. "Really, Mother," John Carstairs had replied, "I don't suppose it will amount to anything in the least." Nevertheless, John Carstairs was still nursing the wounds of that dreadful afternoon at the Board of Trade, and step along he did.

Mr. Devereux, it appeared, was a lawyer in a very humble way—at least he had no clerk, was seen to open his office door himself and at one point was absolutely compelled to go down on his knees and attend to a fire that was in danger of extinction. However, what he had to say proved to be of considerable interest to John Carstairs.

"Well, yes," he observed to that gentleman, "I don't doubt that it's a most interesting affair. None of Mrs. Ireland's friends able to communicate with her. Supposed to have lost her reason into the bargain. Yet I don't for the life of me see what it has to do with my client."

"A man may want to see a woman to whom he is related."

"Certainly he may. And there may be perfectly proper legal instruments that prevent him from so doing."

"He might apply to the lady's lawyer."

"Indeed he might. And yet you had no very great luck there yourself, I believe?"

"Well . . . no. Perhaps not."

Seated on the further side of Mr. Devereux's tiny hearth, his head practically pressed against a mantelpiece whose only adornment was a bust of the late Lord Eldon, John Carstairs was not cast down by this exchange. If he was to be compelled to spend his afternoons in lawyers' chambers, he much preferred that his host should be Mr. Devereux rather than Mr. Crabbe. Mr. Devereux was a youngish man, within a year or two of his own age. More than this, something in Mr. Devereux's manner—he was a dark-haired man with brisk movements and a pair of very knowing grey eyes—suggested that he would not be averse to the betrayal of . . . not secrets, but at any rate information that Mr. Crabbe would not have yielded up about his client in a hundred years. Consequently, John Carstairs determined not only to win his way into Mr. Devereux's confidence but to satisfy his curiosity in certain areas of the case that had always interested him.

"It's all true, I take it, about their former association?"

"If you mean by that: did he propose to her when they were both

D. J. TAYLOR

eighteen, then the answer is yes. But I don't suppose very many tears were shed on either side."

"No doubt it's as you say. And what about the story of the child he had from that other woman?"

"What about it indeed? I don't doubt that five miles from here there is an eight-year-old boy with exactly the same colouring to his hair as Richard Farrier and with Richard Farrier's exact habit of casting his eyes into the sky as he talks to you. But young men will be young men, I take it."

And Mr. Carstairs, who had been, and indeed still was, a young man and additionally recalled a similar accident from his own younger manhood, nodded his head very vigorously.

"But the thing is, Carstairs"—it will be seen how very intimate Mr. Devereux and John Carstairs had grown in the half hour of their acquaintance—"this is all very fascinating and so forth, quite a magazine serial in its way, but what is one supposed to do about it, eh? I can't write a letter on my client's behalf for I have no instructions. I can't write a letter on my account for where the deuce is my right to go interfering in things that don't concern me?"

"Even so," John Carstairs interjected.

"Even so. As for obtaining any instructions, I might as well ask you for your opinion as to where I might direct the letter for all the good it might do."

"Surely you, of all people, ought to have some notion of Mr. Farrier's whereabouts?" observed John Carstairs, who had not quite appreciated the very caustic ironies in which Mr. Devereux habitually dealt.

"But I do! He is in Canada. When last heard of, he was at Montreal with an earnest predisposition to travel to Vancouver. That is three thousand miles distant if you don't happen to have an atlas before you. Other than that, it is impossible to say."

"But there is an address?"

"There is an address."

In the end, after certain other items had been divulged, it was agreed between them that Mr. Devereux should write a letter to his client in Canada outlining such facts of Mrs. Ireland's history as might seem pertinent to him and that John Carstairs, much to Mr. Devereux's satisfaction, would undertake to pay him for his trouble and for all the expenses incurred. "For as you can see," he explained, with an engaging candour, "there are no legal Dives quartered here. In fact business is deuced hard to come by."

"In what branch of the law do you specialise?" John Carstairs wondered.

"Oh, testamentary dispositions, tenancy disputes—the full range of domestic and commercial practice. But to be perfectly frank, I spend most of my time in pursuit of defaulting bill signatories, which is not exactly work for a gentleman, don't you know?"

John Carstairs signified with a nod of his head that he did know and made his way out onto the pavement, where so much mist had descended in his absence that the corner on which Cursitor Street meets Chancery Lane had all but vanished into the gloom. There were pale lights beginning to shine in the windows of the law stationers and the copying shops, a young woman's startled face appeared suddenly behind a curtain ten feet above his head and drew it shut, a great clatter of milk churns being rattled downstairs rose from a dairy hard by, and John Carstairs wrapped his muffler about his face, secured the fastenings of his great coat and set off in the direction of Whitehall and the society of the Honourable Mr. Cadnam. He was thinking about a young woman to whom he had once behaved very much in the way that Mr. Farrier had done to the mother of his natural child, and the thoughts, though they at first awakened in him an agreeable nostalgia, were not in the end pleasant to him. In Cursitor Street, meanwhile, the afternoon wore on without further interruption in Mr. Devereux's chambers, and their tenant, having spent half an hour recruiting himself over a copy of *Punch*, went out searching for tapers, there being nothing with which to light the candle and no clerk to send out in his stead.

D. J. TAYLOR

XVIII

SUB ROSA

There is much that I would remember that I have forgotten. And there is much I remember that I would forget.

* * *

Last evening I had a curious presentiment that my guardian would come to my room & indeed it was so. He came bearing an ulster thrown over one arm & said if I wished it he would take me into the grounds & show me his dogs. Tho' I have no great liking for dogs—certainly not of the kind my guardian breeds—& no great liking for my guardian's company, I said I wished it very much. This seemed to please him, for he remarked that they were unusual dogs & I should not regret my choice.

"But you must be very quiet," he instructed. "Indeed we must be altogether silent while we are in the house."

I said that I would be very quiet.

Such a queer excursion! First we stole down the back staircase, where the moon shone through a great window & enveloped us in white, ghastly light. Passing through the servants' hall, we came upon a room behind whose door a lamp still burned. "That is old Randall's pantry. He has fallen asleep in his chair, I'll be bound," my guardian explained. Making not the least sound, he drew open the pantry door—I could see the old man fast asleep with his head on the table—& returned with a key that would admit us to the gardens.

I confess that I am of a singularly nervous disposition—altogether frail & fearful, Papa used to say—& that had I not had my guardian beside me & his arm to lean on, I should have been very much afraid. Viz., the trees rattling above us in the wind, a dark, cloud-strewn sky

& not a spark of light to be seen. As to where the dogs might be kept, I had no need to enquire, for we could hear them howling from afar. They are housed in a great barn, a full half mile from the house. This we approached—my guardian taking up a lantern which lay in one of the anterooms—whereupon the barking & snarling rose in a crescendo, & I wondered that the people in the house did not think there were burglars on the property.

For myself, I did not care for the dogs, which seemed to me great wolfish beasts, of a kind I never saw unless they are some breed of mastiff. My guardian, however, exulted in their company, reaching his hand through the bars of their kennels—they are all chained up against the hours of darkness—flinging them biscuits, &c., which he had brought in his trowser pocket.

I enquired—for it seemed to me that such animals must take a deal of labour—did Mr. Randall or any of the servants engage in their care?

My guardian said no, that he would not have the servants *interfering*—that was his word—in such business.

Seeing that I shivered at the cold, he immediately became solicitous. Would I take his coat to add to my own? Would I return to the house? Hearing that I should, he locked the door of the kennel room behind him, extinguished the lamp—the dogs seemed subdued & silent at his going—& set off across the darkling lawn. Next to the barn, I noticed, a high thorn hedge grew up in a square, with a wooden gate set into it, curious to see, yet even in daylight, I should guess, impenetrable to the eye.

"What is that?" I asked, as we passed there.

"It is nothing," he said. "A part of the wood that I keep shut up."

And yet it seemed to me that others of my guardian's hounds must be kept there, for I am certain I heard a noise of movement & a snuffling that did not come from the barn.

And so we returned to the house, taking ourselves once more to my guardian's study, where a fire still burned (for which I confess I was very grateful) & I was bidden to recruit myself with a glass of wine. It was by now very late—half past midnight—yet my guardian seemed disposed to talk, showed me a pair of avocets under glass. They are curious birds with turned-up bills, which he said had been taken at the Breydon Water and set up for him by Mr. Lowne, the Yarmouth taxidermist.

I thought the avocets pretty birds but did not see why they should not remain at liberty on the Breydon Water. However, I said nothing of this.

Neither—though it was on the edge of my tongue—did I speak to him of the rose.

Sir Charles came out of his hole in the wainscot & ran silently about the floor, coming rather close to my skirts, which I did not like.

My guardian continues to observe me in the most marked manner. Looking once more at his display cases, at his insistence, I caught for a moment in the reflection of the glass his face regarding me. The look Papa's face had when he drew his portraits, only, it seemed to me, less agreeable.

"Sir," I said, when half an hour had passed, "I wish very much to write the letter of which I spoke."

"Which letter was that?" he enquired, affecting forgetfulness.

"The letter to my husband's lawyer," I replied.

"Why do you wish to write to him?" he asked, by no means unkindly.

"There is much that I wish to ask him," I faltered.

"You may ask me."

"I would ask him."

"Then you may do so."

Nothing more was said. Presently he escorted me back to my chamber, pausing only to bow as he quitted me at the door.

It occurs to me that I am another of his avocets, set up by Mr. Lowne, for him to inspect at his leisure.

*　*　*

And then this morning another flower. The same white rose on the same silver salver. With no hint as to how it came here.

Yet I am not without resource in these matters.

Thus, when Esther arrives with the lunch tray, having first secured

Kept

the rose in my desk, I enquire, "Were any flowers brought to the house yesterday, Esther?"

"Indeed, ma'am, the master brought some from Lynn."

"And what kind were they?"

Esther looks up from setting down the tray. "Why, roses, ma'am. & grown under glass, too, for there be none outside in this weather."

I see. Or rather, I do not see.

* * *

Esther & I are very confidential. Indeed we talk for as much as ten minutes whenever she fetches my tray or retrieves it: I sitting in my chair; she performing certain little duties around the room for which I am exceedingly grateful. Thus I believe I can state with confidence of Esther that:

She is twenty-one years old.

She earns twelve pounds a year.

She has never left the county of Norfolk.

She has a mother & four brothers & sisters living in Fakenham.

She has read the Bible, & *Foxe's Book of Martyrs* & *Maria Monk*, but little else.

To be sure, her manner of speaking often bewilders me. She says "mawther" when she means "girl" & "du" when she means "do" & "dicker" when she means "donkey."

But I must not mock her, for she is very kind to me, sympathises with my wants & wishes to ameliorate them.

The footman, who is her admirer, has gone away to London. Where, she says, he will write one day & "send for her."

What should she do, I asked, when this summons came?

"Why," she said, "go and do as he bade me."

"What?" I said. "And give up your situation here?"

This, however, she would not answer. Feeling, perhaps, that I am confederate with Mr. Randall.

Once I asked her, "What should you do, Esther, if you could leave here & do exactly as you chose?"

"Why, ma'am," she said, "I should take a husband, & have six children, & live in a cottage, & be happy I hope. Only I should take care that I wasn't poor."

And where should I go if I left here & could do as I chose?

I have not the least idea in the world.

* * *

I am lying in bed in the old house at Kensington, though it is not yet dark.

It seems to me that I have lain there for hours, waiting for the light to fade & the noises around me to cease.

Then I see that, though I have not been aware of her coming, Mama is standing at the door watching me. Mama, in a brown dress with her red-gold hair standing out from her face, & something in her hand which the light catches & plays with. How long she stands there I do not know, until Papa, coming briskly into the doorway, catches her in his arms & whatever she has in her hand tumbles down to the floor.

And Papa smiles at me.

I set this down exactly as it came into my head this morning, at about half past ten, as I sat at my desk with bright sunshine—for the spring is come—pouring in through the window.

* * *

Esther is my spy.

No, that is not quite true. Rather, there is much that Esther tells me, all incautious, that I would not otherwise know. It is like Papa, who would come back from the meetings of the committee at his club (which proceedings were of course secret) & talk endlessly of them from sheer amusement.

Of the other servants. Of the house. Of my guardian & his habits.

Thus I learn—something I might have guessed—that Mr. Randall, the butler, is a religious man, constant at his meeting, &c., pressing tracts both on those who would have them & those who would not.

That Mrs. Wates, the cook, was found dead drunk in her room

last Sunday; a great scandal that was somehow kept from the master, despite there being no dinner that night.

That Mrs. Finnie, the housekeeper, "gives herself airs," is very hard upon the maids & in consequence much disliked.

I enquired of Esther: had she ever seen my guardian's dogs? She said no, "but we hears them, ma'am, whenever we are about in the gardens or on the paths, & 'tis not a sound you would want to hear close by you."

Esther says that she is happy in her work. That she has known worse. That she has been able to buy a dress out of her wages—she has promised to show me this dress!—& that a complement of six servants is better than a solitary employment. "For then, ma'am, the mistress is always around you, finding things for you to do, & making tasks where none existed just for the pleasure of it."

There is a Lady Bamber, who got Esther her place, "but I do not see her now, for she does not come here. Indeed, Mr. Dixey sees no company."

My guardian, I hear, is pressed for money. Indeed the men who worked in the gardens have all been paid off & William the footman has no substitute (much to the other servants' annoyance, Mrs. F., in particular, thinking it a disgrace to occupy a situation "where no footman was kept"). Last week, it seems, there was very near an execution in the house, for a bailiff came from Lynn in pursuit of some debt & could only with difficulty be begged to leave.

Esther says that it is "well known" that my guardian owes eight hundred pounds in London, & that the servants worry that their quarter's wages will not be paid.

"In which case, ma'am," Esther says, "what will become of us all?"

And to the untended gardens, & the dogs in their kennels & Sir Charles Lyell in his hole in the wainscot.

And what will become of me?

*　*　*

Not all is lost from the world I once knew.

Thus in the recess of my desk there is a little japanned box that

　　　D. J. TAYLOR

Papa once gave me. How it came there I know not, for I do not recall its being with me in the days before I came to Easton. And yet it must have been, for the contents are such that only I could have put them there. Viz.:

the old, blunt-nibbed pen with which Papa wrote his *Marlborough*

a silhouette of me as a little girl, done by Papa's friend Sir Henry Cole & framed on a square of white card

a lock of Mama's hair, placed in an envelope, still rust-red & dated 17 May 1848

a jet brooch that I had from Henry when we were married

Henry's ring, the seal from his watch chain, the locket with his mother's portrait, &c.

a receipt that Aunt Charlotte Parker wrote me once for hardbake & which I always kept

a set of verses that Richard—Mr. Farrier, that is—gave me ten years since, & which ditto.

To place these objects on the desk before me is to fall prey to the queerest sensations, as if I stood at a little window looking in upon a crowd of people who smiled at me, waved & spoke all manner of things that I, alas, could not hear.

I see Papa writing at his book, with the ink staining his white fingers, & calling out for tea & bread and butter, & a printer's boy waiting in the hall for some paper that Papa had promised.

I see Sir Henry cutting the silhouette & exclaiming, to quiz me, "Why, her nose is so snub that I shall never match the set of it, try as I may!"

I see Mama once more, seated on the terrace, with her hair tumbling around her shoulders & Brodie combing it out.

I see the jet brooch in Henry's hand & the ring on his finger, the watch chain peeping from his waistcoat pocket.

I see Aunt Charlotte Parker's white curls & her cap above them, which she says was very fashionable, only she meant the fashion of Queen Adelaide.

Kept

I see Mr. Farrier standing at the garden gate in his cutaway coat—being what the young men then used to call a "swell"—with the paper in his hand.

And then I see the room in which I sit, with its desk & its window & its locked door, & a little japanned box with a trinket or two & an old pen & some scraps of paper—nothing of the least consequence in the world.

* * *

The estate is in sad decline, Esther says.

The timber, cut two years ago & seasoned now, lies rotting in the woods for there is no one to take it away.

The grass grows up six feet high in the gardens & the panes in the glasshouse window crack in the winds & are never replaced.

The rats run wild in the barns & the keeper no longer preserves.

Mr. Dixey cares only for his dogs, Esther says.

* * *

When I was a girl I flew into the queerest passions. A drawing that I could not frame to my satisfaction, the thought that Tishy or some other girl did not love me—such things would anger me beyond measure & Papa would say that there was a devil in me & that at these times I knew not what I did or said. Dear Papa, who meant only kindness & would not blame me if he could.

Last night I flew into a passion.

All evening as the twilight faded into darkness & the wind buffeted the eaves, I had been thinking of the roses & how they must be placed in my chamber while I slept in the other room, struck all the while by a presentiment that this morning I should find another, mocking me on its silver dish, burning into my skin. Finally, as the clock came near to midnight I could bear this apprehension no longer & resolved to combat it as best I could. In the corner of my bedchamber there was a ball of twine, which I fancy had once secured the cover of my trunk. Taking this, & greatly surprised by my own ingenuity, I seized a chair

D. J. TAYLOR

& placed it to one side of my door, took up the fire irons & placed them to the other side, connecting the two by means of a piece of twine stretched across the doorway at a height of six inches. Anyone crossing the threshold, I assured myself, would perforce tumble over it, or at the very least greatly inconvenience himself. This done, & making sure that a candle & a box of lucifers (these are kept in the recess of my desk next to the japanned box) were to hand near my pillow, I retired to bed.

Naturally, being plunged into a state of nervous exhaustion, I was scarce able to sleep. Half a dozen times in that first hour of slumber I was awakened by what I conceived to be some stirring in the other room, only to find that it was the merest phantom of my imagination. Once indeed, so definite did the noise appear, that I rose up in my nightgown & went in my bare feet into the other chamber, but there was nothing there, only the tap of some branch against the window & the rush of cold air beneath the door, together with those creak-ings & groanings of timber in which the house customarily abounds. I confess that I felt more than a little foolish that these imaginings had crumbled into dust, but not I think frightened, for the passion was still upon me & an ogre from a fairy book lumbering into the room would merely have excited my scorn. Still there was no ogre, only the wind & the tap-tapping of the twigs, & so I retired to my bed, pulled the covers around me & once more lay down to rest.

How long I lay there I do not know, but the hour cannot have been much before three or four. Half-wakeful & half-asleep, I was yet conscious of being able to *see* very wonderfully (this I supposed a further consequence of my nervous state) & that I fancied Papa was there in the room making little remarks & observations that I strained to hear, that several other persons known to me were present but just a little way out of reach. It was then, again with a presentiment that it was *about to happen*, my senses all stimulated by the novelty of the situation, that I heard with utter distinctness the creak of a footstep & the turning of a key in the lock. Scarce daring to breathe, I lay still as a third & more prolonged sound—the noise of the door being drawn open—broke the silence. It occurred to me that still I must make no sound myself. Accordingly, I lay silent in the darkness, only reaching

Kept

out my hand so that I should be able to grasp candle & matches at the first opportunity. On the instant there came a mighty crash, as of a person tumbling over, accompanied by the noise of other objects falling to the floor, sharp intakes of breath, &c. Jumping to my feet & crying "Who is there?" my heart all the while beating like a drum, I hastily struck a match—my shadow, rearing up against the arc of the flame, I confess, did alarm me—lit the candle & moved to confront the intruder.

I was too late, for whoever it was had vanished in an instant. Footsteps echoed in the corridor, causing me to marvel at the resourcefulness of such a one who could gather his wits & make good his escape in the few seconds granted to him. The door was wide-open. The key hung from the lock. Before it lay proof of the excellence of my stratagems: a silver dish rolled against the chair & a single white rose fallen nearly as far as the fireplace. The fire irons, much to my satisfaction, were strewn everywhere about. For a moment I considered the advantages of stepping out into the corridor. Yet it seemed to me that my point had been proved, & no good would come of any nocturnal ramblings. Instead I busied myself in rectifying the damage that I had caused: restoring fire irons & chair to their rightful places, gathering up the twine into a ball, casting the abandoned rose into the grate. It occurred to me that anyone who glanced into the room—some witch passing on her broomstick, perhaps—would have seen the most curious sight: a woman in her nightgown, candlestick on the desk before her, tidying the disorder around her yet laughing as she did so.

It was then that I remarked that there was something else in the chamber with me. Not something that I could see, but something that I could hear: squeaking & scuffling & making fierce, evil little movements in the shadow beneath my desk. At this my anger grew to a pitch, for I knew that this was Sir Charles Lyell, which my guardian had carried upon his shoulder or in the pocket of his coat & left behind in his haste to depart, & I resolved to have my revenge, if not on my guardian then on the creature that he had brought with him, for a mouse that runs across the floor when I stand there in the dark is a thing that I dislike very much. He was, as I say, running this way & that beneath the desk, but I am the equal of a MOUSE, & seizing

D. J. TAYLOR

the poker from the stand to which I had returned it, I stood all silently until such time as he should show himself. Presently, lulled by the silence & (as I now think) having no terror of human beings, even those that stand barefoot in their nightgowns, he poked his head out into the circle of soft light & in a trice I had brought the poker down upon him.

Nasty scuffling thing! A dozen times I belaboured him. When I had convinced myself he was quite dead, I picked him up with the fire tongs & cast him out into the corridor, where whoever searches may find him.

There shall be no more mice scampering in *my* chamber.

Afterwards, when the passion left me, I was properly remorseful, shed tears even at the thought of poor Sir Charles lying dead in the corridor where I had thrown him, for it was not his fault, poor thing, only that of the PERSON who brought him.

Papa always said that it was a sin to take a life, however humble. And yet I know that Papa liked to shoot a pheasant, which he said was there to be eaten & served no other purpose.

When all this had passed & I had arranged the room to my satisfaction, the door still hanging open on its hinge, I returned to my bedchamber, much alarmed now at what I had done, yet so exhausted that I fell almost instantly asleep. He will come in the morning, I told myself, though what I am to say to him & he to me I cannot tell.

* * *

He did not come. When I awoke it was exceedingly late. Bright sunshine streamed through the window of my chamber, the door had been locked & a breakfast tray left on my table (the tea altogether cold & insipid). Presently I fancied that I could hear voices far below, that the maids—Esther, & Margaret whom she thinks a goose—were out in the gardens & I was filled with an inexpressible longing to be with them, to run over cut grass & walk wherever I choose.

All the rest of the morning I sat at my desk thinking that he would come, but he did not.

After some time there was a twisting of the key into the lock &

I sprang to my feet, my heart pounding. And yet it was only Esther bringing in my luncheon & some foxgloves that she had picked in the wood next to the gardens & placed in water, which I was very glad to have.

Esther.

Who gave me a very mischievous, sidelong look as if to say that she knew all about me, indeed more perhaps than I knew myself.

Who seemed disposed to talk.

"Has William written lately?" I enquired, knowing that this is a question she likes to be asked.

It appears that William is working in some capacity for an associate of my guardian's in the City. Of his duties & the manner of their execution, Esther knows little, but it is clear that she is impressed. "For he is making a mint of money, ma'am, truly. And, as his letter says, is stopping in rooms"—there is pride in Esther's voice as she pronounces the word—"at Seven Dials. Do you know of it, ma'am?"

"A very respectable locality," I told her.

"And he says again that soon he shall write to me, and I am to go to him."

"And shall you go?"

"Certainly, ma'am, I shall go."

And who shall I talk with, I wonder, when Esther goes? Not Mr. Randall, assuredly, with his tracts (he brought another one, a week ago, on the West African Mission) or Mrs. Finnie, to whom I have not spoken ten words in the past fortnight. But it occurs to me that if I take every care it may yet redound to my advantage.

I must be cunning.

He does not come & he does not come.

* * *

D. J. TAYLOR

I took out the verses that Richard—Mr. Farrier—wrote me, which I had not done for half a dozen years & read them & was so very sad.

To Miss Isabel Brotherton

Last night I wasted hateful hours
Uncalmed by the peace of a college bed
I thirsted for brooks, and for tender showers
Instead of the policeman's patient tread
On the pavement yonder, beyond the gate
And the fruits of a life lived all sedate
Away from the river in foaming spate
There are distant sights that I would see
Untouched by the light of an English sun
I yearn for the roar of an ancient sea
And the ancient race that I would run
Yet the rose from the gardens in the south
I crush on my breast, and upon my mouth
Ripe to appease my burning drout.

RF FECIT, JULY 1856

A week passes & he does not come. And then, all unexpected, one afternoon as I lie on my sofa —for I have been greatly fatigued in these last days—there comes the sound of footsteps in the corridor beyond the twist of a key in the lock.

I mark some great change in my guardian. His eyes seem more set in his head, his hair more grey, his face more lined, though only a week has passed since I last saw him & I did not then observe these things.

He says nothing of our last encounter, nor anything of Sir Charles Lyell. I, too, am silent. After regarding me in his customary way, he proposes—greatly to my surprise—that we walk in the garden.

"The servants are all away," he says, as if a gentleman can only walk out with his ward in the absence of domestics, "or I should not have suggested it."

And so we walk down the great staircase, through rooms that I glimpsed before only at night, & into the back of the house, emerging from it onto that lawn at which I have stared so long from my window.

My guardian's attentiveness is a wonder to behold. He takes my arm as we come to the gravel path, as if such an accumulation of tiny stones might cause me to fall, slashes with his stick at a nettle bush that threatens to impede my progress, draws my attention to the natural wonders in which the place apparently abounds. Thus I am bidden to admire a jay, a crossbill & a most curious, comical bird named a hoopoe, orange-plumaged & very bright-eyed, that trips across the grass to examine me as if he never saw my like before.

My guardian, it occurs to me, is a black crow, hopping over the grass in his rusty black vestments, cawing his pleasantries in my ear.

It is a day of bright sunshine, very pleasant in the shadow of the trees, & yet it seems to me very desolate & melancholy. Nothing blooms inside the great glasshouses; the cats run in & out of the dairy door. Yet my guardian is more eloquent than I have known him before. He says, "I have lived here nearly half my life. My uncle, from whom I inherited the estate, died when I was thirty. Though I travelled when I was a younger man, since I have grown old I have rarely left it."

And yet soon you may have to leave it, I tell myself, *with the timber rotting in the woods & the bailiffs coming from Lynn.*

"Where did you travel, sir?" I ask.

"In Europe a little. Beyond the Danube & as far east as Kiev. And then in Araby."

As we turn about the side of the house, in sight of the gravel drive—which is full of great ruts & puddles left by the spring rain—& the circles of uncut grass & an old fountain rising out of a mermaid's head, very cracked & worn, something of the melancholy of the place seems to strike him, for he says, "My uncle used to give great parties here in his time. *Fêtes champêtres* with a quintain for the gentlemen to tilt at & archery for the ladies & a line of carriages stretching all the way to the gate & a marquee for dancing. But all that was forty years ago.

"I have no taste for parties," my guardian says.

What does my guardian have a taste for? Why, for little white eggs that

D. J. TAYLOR

lie in his cabinets & will never hatch, & for birds that will never move because they are stuffed & dead, & for staring at me as if I were one of his specimens preserved under glass.

We are standing before the front of the house now, where the sun slants low over the gardens & the frontage is gathered up in shadow.

"Sir," I say, "I very much wish to write that letter."

"You shall write it," he says. "For there is much that can be said in it."

And then, not greatly to my surprise, for some instinct had been at work within me before our excursion commenced, he takes my hand.

* * *

He wishes to marry me.

He says that during the course of our association he has formed a great affection for me, extending beyond that which a guardian naturally feels for his ward.

He would make me mistress of Easton Hall.

He is a stooped old man in a black suit, cawing at me like one of the rooks in his field.

There will soon be no Easton Hall to be mistress of.

I would rather be mistress of myself.

* * *

Mr. Conolly has prescribed more medicine for me, which I am bidden to drink. Half a teacup full, which Mrs. Finnie brings to me each morning. It is colourless, like water & at the same time unlike it. I drink it as I am bidden.

Today, as Mrs. Finnie stands before me—it is a bright, clear morning, but I know better than to quiz Mrs. Finnie about the weather—I ask, "Mr. Dixey was not ever married, I think?"

"Not to my knowledge, ma'am."

Mrs. Finnie's hair is so very like black patent leather that I have a vision of her polishing it each morning before the mirror.

"But was he ever engaged?"

Kept

And here, quite unexpectedly, Mrs. Finnie does not deny, ignore or deflect that which is asked of her. She says, "There was a young woman that he offered for five years ago, ma'am. A Miss Chell, the daughter of the brewing people that live at Bury. There was talk of lawyers & settlements & old Mr. Chell, as was the young lady's father, came over several times to see the master. Indeed we thought that it was a settled thing. There was even a rose garden that Tom the gardener had orders to plant out. But then something happened between them, & the banns that were to have been put up a month after were never said & the turf as had been grubbed up for the rose garden is where the maids do bang out their carpets."

I declare that I never heard Mrs. Finnie make such a speech. Mrs. Finnie, too, seems conscious of the novelty of the situation for she clasps her hands nervously before her, hangs her head—so shiny indeed that the sunlight nearly bounces off it—& declines to offer another word.

* * *

I find myself greatly fatigued. Doubtless it is the strain of these days that has wearied me so. I sleep in the afternoons yet am not refreshed.

He does not come & he does not come. And though I am glad of this, I confess that I grow more nervous of the time when he shall arrive.

Thinking of this, I recollect a day once when I was a little girl—it was just after Mama had gone away—& had been spiteful & bad-tempered. Whereupon the nurse had said to punish me, "Your Papa shall be told of this, miss, when he comes home!" This was a source of great anxiety, for I loved Papa & would not make him unhappy if I could. By some miracle Papa did not come home, dining unexpectedly at his club or being summoned to the table of some friend. And yet I was not in the least consoled, knowing that the reckoning was merely delayed & that every hour which passed before it had the power to distress me more.

* * *

D. J. TAYLOR

Today I did a wicked thing.

Its wickedness was not in the aim I proposed but in the means by which I effected it.

I had determined that another day in this room—Mrs. Finnie's sour face, Mr. Conolly's draught, the sun streaming in through the open window—would be intolerable to me. Thus when at midday I heard the noise of Esther turning her key in the lock I retired to the sofa & lay there in a piteous manner, clutching my hands to my sides. Then as Esther moved into the room, the lunch things balanced on the tray before her, I turned upon my back & groaned aloud.

"Why, ma'am, whatever is the matter?"

In bringing me my luncheon, Esther has an infallible routine. First she unlocks & pushes open the door. Then she places the tray on the ground at her feet. Then she pushes shut & locks the door, placing the key in the pocket of her pinafore. Then she retrieves the tray & places it on my desk. But she has grown easy with me over the weeks & I, sly minx that I am, resolve to exploit this case.

"Oh, Esther," I moan. "I feel most dreadfully unwell. A pain in the stomach—truly."

As I foresaw, Esther's first thought was for myself. Placing the tray on the floor, but omitting to lock the door, she came immediately towards me.

"What is it, ma'am?" she asked again.

Whereupon I beckoned her to me & as she bent over my recumbent form gave suddenly a violent push with my hand that sent her stumbling backwards into a heap. How much it pained me to do this I cannot say. Then before she could rise up I sprang away & out of the door.

As to what took place in the ensuing minutes, so airy-headed was I at having attained my goal that I can scarce recollect their passage. I know that I tumbled down a flight of stairs, came into the hall, where Mr. Randall looked up from winding the grandfather clock, saw me & cried out, that I ran across the gravel at the front of the house, across a road—conscious all the while of a person or persons following at my heels—& into a field, where I asked the way of a girl out scaring the birds, & would have run further but that a man whom I had not

Kept

seen approached from nowhere & caught me up in his arms & not unkindly brought me home.

It is a mystery to me why I did it, knowing full well, of course, what should be its end.

* * *

I sleep an entire day & wake with a great vacant space in my head where my thoughts should be.

* * *

"Esther," I say, when next she comes, "I beg that you will forgive me for the trick I played, which was not meant to injure you."

"Indeed, ma'am," says Esther, who has locked the door as she steps into the room quite in the old way, "I was not hurt. It was only the suddenness of the thing that startled me."

The teacup with Mr. Conolly's medicine sits on the tray. A question occurs to me which I have several times shied away from asking.

"What is said about me in—the house?" By this I mean the servants' hall. A distinction Esther appreciates.

"In the house, ma'am?" She sets down the tray & stands regarding me.

I do not mind when Esther stares at me. It is her master I abhor.

"In the house. Between Mr. Randall & Mrs. Finnie."

"They say, ma'am, that you are . . ." Esther removes the cover that lies on my dinner plate. "That you are . . . not in your right mind."

"Do you think I am not in my right mind?"

"No, ma'am."

The teacup with Mr. Conolly's medicine sits on the tray.

"Esther. Will you do me a great service?"

"If I can, ma'am."

"Take up that teacup which is on the tray & drink what is in it. I promise it shall not harm you."

"Very well, ma'am."

D. J. TAYLOR

Esther picks up the teacup & drinks the contents. Then she makes a most welcome & consoling gesture.

She smiles.

*   *   *

"I ask you only to think of it. That is all."

I am seated in my guardian's study once more. It may be eleven of the clock or midnight—I do not know. I have been here an hour & would be anywhere else.

But there is nowhere else.

"I assure you," my guardian continues, "of the sincerity of my feelings. If they did not exist, I should not declare them."

When I glimpsed him first, as he stood in my doorway an hour since, I saw that some change had come upon his person which I could not at once fathom. Then I remarked it. The old black vestments were gone, & in their place was a quite juvenile costume of a white jacket & a tie fastened with a sailor's knot.

I fear that I preferred the old rook.

I remark, too, his nervousness. His hand darts now & then to his mouth to finger his yellow teeth. Yellow as the keys of a spinet that I saw once in my aunt's house at Dover.

He talks of Easton Hall. Of what lies in its chests & strongboxes & beneath the ceilings of its attics. All this shall be mine to command, he says.

Three times in my life I have been paid court to by gentlemen. First Mr. Farrier—Richard—with his verses & his walks in the rose garden, & of whom indeed I was very fond. Then Henry, to whom I was married. And now this grey-haired old man with his rusty voice & his creaking politenesses.

Whose singularities Papa would have marked down in a trice, as was his habit, written up in one of his books &, as was also his habit, gently mocked.

"Say only that you will think of it," he says again, patting my hand.

I will think of no such thing.

*   *   *

It is as I suspected.

Esther says that in the hours after she drank Mr. Conolly's draught she grew unaccountably tired, could not keep from yawning, indeed fell near-asleep on her chair in the scullery, from which she was routed out by Mrs. Wates, crying that she was a lazy good-for-nothing & a slut that no man would marry, &c.

The next draught that Mrs. Finnie brings me I shall throw into the chamberpot!

*   *   *

Today a letter was brought up on the tray with my breakfast.

He asks only that I may think of it. But he desires an answer.

I would that I had cracked open his grey head with the poker rather than poor Sir Charles Lyell!

*   *   *

And now a great crisis is upon me! The letter from Esther's lover has come & she proposes to join him in London. This she confided to me very gravely—yet suppressing, it seemed to me, a great excitement—as she stood in my room this forenoon (the door locked very thoroughly behind her) with the luncheon tray.

"When shall you go?" I ask her.

"He says for me to go immediate, ma'am."

"And shall you give notice?"

"There was a man come from Norwich this morning, ma'am, & stayed ever so long with the master, with another man who came & stood in the drive looking at the house quite as if he meant to take it down brick by brick."

Which I construe thus: *What is the point of giving notice when the house is to be sold around us a month hence?*

    D. J. TAYLOR

"And what will you feel when you get there, Esther?"

"As to that, ma'am, I shall have to take it on trust."

But there is my plan. For which I do not require Mr. Dixey's aid, nor anyone else's save Esther's.

"Esther," I say, "you must help me. Sit in a chair and wait, just a moment, while I think."

And so Esther perches on the chair, regarding me very curiously, as I sit at the desk & write a letter to Mr. Crabbe, Henry's lawyer, explaining where I am, & what is happening to me, what my guardian proposes, &c., & much else, & how I would not stay here a moment longer. There is no envelope, but I fold it across & write on the back *Mr. Crabbe, Lincoln's Inn*, & Esther says she will deliver it.

"And, Esther," I say, as she folds it up & places it in the pocket of her apron, "I hope you will be very happy."

"I hope it too, ma'am."

"And, Esther . . ." But before I can say more I have taken her in my arms & kissed her.

Esther smiles, saying that she will come on the next day & bid me good-bye.

I listen to her footsteps, moving off along the passage.

The next day dawns but she does not come.

She does not come & she does not come.

* * *

Twice he has asked me for an answer. Twice I have said nothing. The second time he grasped my hand & said loudly that I was a foolish girl & he would not be gainsaid in this.

Mr. Randall brings my food now.

She does not come & she does not come.

I am so very tired.

Part Four

NORTH OF SIXTY

He awoke each morning just before dawn, groping about on the floor of the cabin for his mittens and his muffler before tugging open the door and staring out at the eaves of the forest, pale and grey in the half-light. At first, because he was new to the land and inexperienced in these matters, he had assumed that its contours were unvarying. Gradually, however, his eyes had grown keen enough to register faint variations in the landscape: the frown of the spruce trees softened by a fall of snow; a line of tracks not yet obliterated; the bent white branch of a fir sapling which would, in time, release its load with a snap like a pistol shot. All this reassured him, for he was a man who relished movement and the sense of things happening around him, and he knew, even in his inexperience, that the wild hated all movement, knowing it to be a symbol of the life force which it seeks to extinguish and subdue. Yet at the same time, he feared what he saw around him, for he knew that he did not understand it and that his ability to conquer it depended on the ingenuity of others. And so he stood each morning in the doorway of his cabin, twenty yards from the boundary of the forest, cold in spite of his mittens and his muffler, looking out at the frown of the first spruce trees and the pale sky with all manner of doubts and suspicions forming in his mind.

He was a resourceful man in his way, and he had devised certain routines to allay these doubts and suspicions. By the time that the short, sunless day was an hour old he had attended to the embers of the previous night's fire, boiled a kettleful of melted snow, made coffee and chopped more wood to add to the pile beneath the cabin's lean-to. Then, with a second cup of coffee in his hand, he would sit on the solitary chair and run his eye over the provisions that remained there: the grey sacks that contained their flour; the box of sun-cured fish; the strips of fat salt pork in their metal chest. As he did so he congratulated himself on his thoroughness. The boys would be pleased at how well he had kept the place in order, he told himself. They had left traces of themselves which he came upon with a pleasant sense of recognition: a deck of cards facedown upon the snow; a clasp knife that had rolled out of sight behind the flour sacks; a silver Canadian dollar lost underfoot. He collected these objects carefully and placed them in the pocket of his fur-lined jacket, anticipating the moment when he could return them. Later, as the day wore on and the sky to the south warmed to rose colour, he moved restlessly around the interior of the cabin, feeling at the little imperfections and blemishes of the wood with his fingers, or sat reading and coughing over the fire, whose smoke rose through a chimney made of a tin pail. At four the last of the grey light drifted into dusk, and the pall of the Arctic night descended.

The boys had been gone two days now. Another two—at the outside, three—would bring them back. He could hear in his head the sound that the sled would make as it came through the dried-up watercourse on which the canopy of spruce trees frowned and the barking of the five dogs drawn out in a wide fan before it. They had come here to the Powder River country in search of a supply of logs which, come the spring, could be floated back south as far as Fort Mackenzie if need be, or further. And those logs, he had been told, would make their fortunes. And this assurance, though he had no real need of money, having plenty of it in the land from which he had come, cheered him and invigorated him as he went about his tasks. And yet he knew, newcomer though he was to the land, that the winter was drawing on and there remained only a little time in which those logs could be found. Never mind! The boys would be back soon from their reconnoitre in the white country that stretches all the way north as far as the Arctic Sea and they would return along the trail they had come, eighty miles to Fort McGurry, where the traders and the Hudson's Bay Company men put up for the worst of the snows.

Thinking that the boys would be pleased to find fresh meat waiting for them, he took the rifle and several cartridges from his store and, winding the scarf carefully around his face so that only his forehead and the tip of his nose were exposed to the raw air, plunged off beneath the canopy of the forest. Such was the silence around him that the noise of his breath and the sound that his moccasins made as he padded over the soft snow oppressed him. It was like no silence that he had ever known, immense, chilling and elemental, and for the first time in the course of his journeyings in the wild he began to wish that he had stayed in Fort McGurry. He corrected himself on the instant, telling himself not to be so foolish, that the boys would be back shortly, that the next morning, even, would see them home, and they would want a couple of snowshoe rabbits or a hare rather than a companion who took fright at so little a thing as silence. And in this way he recovered his spirits, settled his rifle more comfortably in the crook of his arm and moved deeper beneath the tall trees, taking care, however, to remember which way he had come and always keeping a sight of one very tall spruce tree, taller than any of the others, which he knew lay in reach of the cabin.

A half hour's search, though, turned up nothing, and he was forced to retrace his steps through the snow, wondering that the game should have vanished from a country that when he had first come to it two months before had been teeming with life. There was a famine in the land that had followed the cold, but he did not know this. He knew only of the cold, which it seemed to him had become a great deal more irksome since he had first come to the cabin. At last, in the deep undergrowth aside from the forest path, he turned up a ptarmigan that went squawking and fluttering from her nest. The noise startled him, and he stood for a second or two gazing stupidly at the bird as it took flight into the trees before he raised his gun. But his fingers, even in their fur-lined mittens, were chilled to numbness, and the shot whistled away into the depths of the forest. After this he grew sober and reflective. It certainly was very cold out here, and there was clearly no game to be had. The boys would have to make do with salt pork and biscuits. He went back to the cabin in the fading light along a path devoid of all living things and comforted himself by taking out from amongst his kit certain prized possessions which he had brought with him from home. There was a keepsake book that his sister had given him and a volume of Tennyson's poetry, with an inscription in it that was not his sister's, and he brooded over them by the fireside

D. J. TAYLOR

as he ate his pork and biscuits. Later the wind got up, and he lay in his shakedown by the dwindling fire listening to the creaking of the spruce trees.

Next day he woke at exactly the same time but with a feeling of expectation in his mind that he could not at first identify. The boys were coming! That was it! Another half-dozen hours would see them back and the sled rolling into view along the dried-up watercourse that did service for a road here in the extremity of the wild. There fell on him a feeling of grave responsibility, and he attended to his chores with more than usual determination, building up the fire until it seemed to pulse with heat and chopping yet more wood with which to feed it. As he chopped he rested occasionally with his foot on the axe and looked into the forest, thinking that he saw something moving within it and then deciding that it was merely a trick of the light. It certainly was very cold, he thought. At first, when he had begun his log splitting, he had taken off his thick jacket and draped it over a juniper bush, but within two or three minutes, despite the warmth brought to his limbs by the action of chopping, he could feel the numbness creeping into his body and put the coat back on. All the time that he did this he strained his ears for a sound, but there was nothing. Oppressed once more by the silence, he took to contriving small ways to break it, humming to himself as he worked and stamping his feet vigorously on the surface of the frozen snow. After a while the immensity of his solitude struck him once more, and he fell quiet. He was not an imaginative man—his skill lay in practicalities, in the devising of tasks and their accomplishment—but it occurred to him that there was something romantic in his situation here on the margin of the world. The wind had got up again, and he listened to it soughing against the trees and sending little flurries of snow to patter against the cabin door, and was thankful to hear it. Later, when the hour or so of rose-tinted sky had been and gone, he strode down the frozen hill to the point where it met the watercourse, along which the boys and their sled would come, and looked down the trail for a long time.

There was snow during the night; only an inch or two but enough to cover the tracks that he had made the previous day in walking down to the trail. As he ate his breakfast, sitting over the embers of the fire with his coffee cup balanced on his knee, he reflected that the boys certainly had been gone a long time. He was aware as he did this that two thoughts existed simultaneously in his head: the one that the boys must have found something unexpected with which to occupy themselves along the further reaches of the trail; the other that there was something sinister in this absence. It was a windy day, with more snow drifting in almost horizontally across the grey landscape, but several times he tied his muffler about his ears, put on the raccoon-skin hat that he had purchased from the factor at Fort McGurry and walked down to inspect the trail. Each time that he returned he added another log to the fire and sat by it warming his hands and brooding.

In this way two or three more days passed. His sense of anticipation, he now discovered, had become all-consuming. Half a dozen times in an hour he found himself wandering down to the trail and staring out into the distance to the point where it lost itself in the horizon of trees and leaden sky. The strangest thoughts ran through his head. One was that the boys had simply deserted him. And yet he fancied that had the boys wished to do this, they would not have left him to guard their provisions. Another was that they had lost themselves on the trail. But he knew, too, that the one to whose leadership they all deferred had come this way half a dozen times before. It was all very mysterious, he assured himself. Thrown back upon his resources, he became suddenly absorbed by the environment in which he found himself. He began to notice things. He noticed that when he cleared his throat and spat, for in common with most men in that region he had taken to chewing plugs of tobacco, the spittle cracked when it hit the ground. This suggested to him that it was very cold indeed. Separating the bark from one of the logs that lay piled up in the cabin's lean-to, he saw that scurrying beneath it there were insects of a kind he had never seen, and observed their bewilderment as they were exposed to the chill air. He saw, too, the way in which the time of the rose-coloured sky grew shorter and the hours of daylight continued to diminish. All this told him that winter was coming perilously close and that it would be as well for the boys to return.

And then he would tell himself that he was an old woman, that he had food, firewood and a rifle, and that soon there would be an

D. J. TAYLOR

explanation of the mystery. It occurred to him that he had better take an inventory against the boys' arrival, and so, laying out the items on a square of tarpaulin as the fire burned and crackled beside him, he made a list of everything he could find in the cabin. There were, he discovered, at least a dozen strips of fat salt pork, a couple of canisters of biscuits, a sack of flour, beans, a large box of sulphur matches and something under a dozen cartridges, together with the sun-cured fish, intended for the dogs but which a man could eat if he had a mind. This reassured him, and yet he knew that the pile of foodstuffs had substantially diminished since he had last examined it. The theory of existence in the wild had been explained to him by an old-timer he had met at Fort McGurry. This was that one subsisted on iron rations, supplemented by such fresh meat as was available. But what if there was no fresh meat? This was not something that the old-timer had cared to speak about. When he had finished counting the provisions, he laid them out upon the upturned tarpaulin and counted them a second time.

One morning he awoke with a sensation of deep unease. Previously he had known exactly how long it was that the boys had been gone. Now he realised that he had forgotten the precise number of days. Was it seven or eight? He could not be sure. It occurred to him that he should make a mark with his knife on the door frame to remind him, and so, drawing the blade from its covering, he cut a series of notches into the timber, seven at first, then adding an eighth as he became certain that eight days had passed. When he had finished he sat down and admired the notches, which were deep and evenly spread, only to be assailed by another spasm of unease. It was seven days, surely, that the boys had been gone. Very well, he would remind himself not to cut another notch on the following morning. Placing the knife back in its leather scabbard, he went and stood by the door and looked out across the snow towards the eaves of the forest. There were tracks in the snow, he noticed, that had not been there the previous night, but, newcomer to the land that he was, he could not tell which animal had made them. He supposed that he should take the gun and go looking for meat, but the sky threatened more snow and he acknowledged that he felt sluggish and out of sorts. He would sit by the fire, he told himself, and read and brood, and perhaps as he read and brooded he would hear the noise of the sled bowling down the trail of the dried-up watercourse, and the boys would come.

Accordingly, he spent half an hour chopping more wood until a pile of split logs three feet high lay beneath the canopy of the lean-to, and then sat by the fire reading the keepsake that his sister had presented to him and the volume of Tennyson's poems. The poems, of which he had formerly taken no great notice, seemed to him extraordinarily fine. He read several of them two or three times and thought in a very melancholic way of the person who had given them to him. It occurred to him that it would be amusing to read them aloud, as he had used to do at school, standing up at his desk as the master watched him from his dais, and so he opened his mouth and spoke a few words of one, looking as he did so into the depths of the fire and seeing the schoolroom and the faces of the boys and the great window and the meadow behind it. As he did so he saw, quite distinctly, the face of the person—the female person—who had given him the book. But his voice seemed small and pitiful in the silence that surrounded him, and after a line or two he stopped, rather shamefacedly, and put some more wood on the fire. The day wore on, and he continued to sit by the fire, alternately brooding and dozing until darkness fell. He was aware, as he rolled out his blanket and settled himself to sleep, that something he had expected to happen had not happened. The boys had not come! Never mind, they would come tomorrow. Outside he could hear the wind howling in the trees.

In this way more time passed. Quite how much time he could not say, for he found that he became lax at cutting the notches into the timber of the door frame. Or rather not lax but cautious. He would stare at the neat line of indentations unsure as to whether he had added to their number that day or not. Sometimes at the conclusion of this staring he would add a notch, sometimes not. It was the same with his routines. Sometimes he would awake from his half doze before the fire to find that he had let the pile of wood run down almost to nothing, and then a panic would seize him and he would spend an hour or more chopping a great pile of logs and arranging them in the lean-to. He supposed that he was becoming a little out of sorts, a little jittery at

D. J. TAYLOR

the silence and the grey landscape beyond him. And yet he continued to look ahead, to plan intricately in his mind what should be done in the days after the boys arrived and they set off back along the trail to Fort McGurry. He found a fragment of mirror, no more than an inch square, in the pack in which he stored his bedding and, examining himself in it, discovered that the beard he had begun to grow when he had first come to the wild reached down almost to his breastbone. Well, he would shave that off when he got back to Fort McGurry. The thought tickled him, and he imagined himself calling for soap and hot water and the boys laughing at him as he set about his task. He continued to smile about it as he chopped the logs, built up the embers of the fire, read at his little volume of Tennyson and made an inventory of the pile of provisions.

One day—he did not quite know how long had passed since he had last done this—he found himself standing before the timber door frame and counting the notches. There were twenty-one. The number startled him, and he counted and recounted, thinking that there must be some error in his computation. The realisation of his predicament stole upon him by degrees. He was in a jam, he supposed, a high old jam, and he must settle down and decide what was best to do. In the meantime, though, he would chop more logs and make a further inventory of the supplies. The calmness of his demeanour as he did this surprised him as much as the long row of notches on the timber door frame. It was as if the person chopping the wood and calculating the extent of his provisions was someone else at whom he stared from above. The situation did not seem to have anything to do with him. But he was startled, again, by the sparseness of his inventory. Only a single canister of the biscuits remained, together with half a dozen pieces of pork, twice that amount of fish and some flour. Had he really eaten that much while the boys had been gone? Looking at the food as it lay on the tarpaulin, he conceived a notion of himself living frugally in the cabin through the winter, of being found by the first horseman who came riding along the trail in the spring and explaining modestly how he had survived. But the dwindling supplies scared him. That night he ate only a couple of biscuits and the half of a sun-cured fish before unrolling his blankets and settling himself to sleep.

In the morning he felt more confident than he had done for many a day. It seemed to him that he knew more about the functioning of his body than he had ever known before. He watched his fingers as they moved over the buttons of his coat. Sitting by the fire drinking his cup of coffee, he was conscious of his heart beating and a vein pulsing in his forehead. This comforted him, for it spoke of life and movement rather than the inertness that lay beyond the cabin door. Then, turning to refill the coffee pot, he made an alarming discovery. There was no more coffee. For a moment he brooded over this discrepancy, even searching a little among the canisters and the provision packets to see if he had overlooked anything, before, as it seemed to him, resigning himself to this new feature of his existence. He would have to do without coffee. Outside in the grey light there were a few snowflakes falling, and he watched them for a while, thinking how sombre and melancholy the land seemed. The sight reminded him of the routine he had previously followed, and he made his way down to the riverbed and stared northwards along the trail. With the snow the track had all but disappeared, he noted, only a faint depression in the lie of the land showed that it had ever been there.

A sudden sense of purpose overcame him. He would have to do something, he realised, take some decisive step before the snows came and covered him as they had done the trail. Surprised at himself, for he did not quite know from where the impetus had come, he found himself seizing an armful of discarded branches and an axe and fashioning a makeshift sled. There was a length of rope in the cabin, and he used this to lash the pieces of the frame into place. With what remained of the rope he constructed a harness that he could fasten over his chest and shoulders, enabling him to drag the sled behind. The sight of the sled lying on the patch of ground before the cabin door cheered him. The light was beginning to fade, and the outlines of the trees receded into darkness. Tomorrow, he thought, he would rise at dawn, pack what remained of his provisions onto the sled and set off down the trail towards firelight, warmth and human voices.

Somehow, though, he did not do this. It was difficult to explain how this came about, how he had conditioned his mind, as he thought, to do one thing and yet how another, unconscious conditioning had

D. J. TAYLOR

compelled him to do something else. Midmorning on the next day found him once again sitting before the fire and brooding over the little volume of Tennyson. Wondering at his behaviour, he went and examined the sled again, silently appraising the curve of the birch-bark runners. The sky, he noticed, had already turned grey, which meant that there was snow coming. It would be foolish, he thought, to attempt anything today. Much better to stay by his fire. Wandering over to the lean-to, he was puzzled to find that only a handful of logs remained. Reproaching himself for this negligence, he set to work to replenish the pile.

The fire had burned almost down to nothing when he woke the next morning, and there was a great numbness in his limbs, despite the blankets and the coat that he had thrown over himself before he went to sleep. Thrashing his arms against his sides and stamping his feet on the ground, he built up the fire once more and the numbness receded, but the memory of it remained. It really was extraordinarily cold. He had heard of there being terrible cold snaps in the wild when birds fell frozen from the sky and animals survived only by burrowing under the drifts of snow, and he wondered if this was such a cold snap. There was no wind today, and though he was not an imaginative man, it seemed to him that the land had a terrible gauntness, a desolation that he could no longer bear to observe. Again, not quite knowing from where the impulse came, he found himself assembling his belongings—his teakettle, his canisters of food, his box of sulphur matches, his store of cartridges—on the sled. When he had arranged them to his satisfac-tion, he took the tarpaulin and fashioned it into a cover. The sound of the snow crunching beneath his moccasins reminded him of some-thing else that he needed, and plunging off into the eaves of the forest, he returned with another armful of brushwood. From this, with the aid of various twists of rope and twine that remained to him, he con-structed a pair of snowshoes.

Curiously, having finished these preparations, his sense of resolve began to recede once more. He looked at the fire again and at the timber of the cabin door, felt for the little volume of Tennyson that was stowed in his jacket pocket and reflected that perhaps he was being a trifle hasty. He wondered how far away Fort McGurry was, wishing that he had paid more attention to the maps that the boys had examined in the early days of their excursion. It could not be more than seventy miles, he thought, say eighty at the outside. And even walking over fresh snow and encumbered by snowshoes, a man ought to be able to travel at fifteen miles a day. These calculations reassured him, but they did not reassure him as much as he wanted them to do, and he wished that he had a proper sled and a team of dogs such as those that the boys had taken with them when they disappeared up the trail all that time ago. He wondered idly—it was something he had not considered for several days—what had become of the boys and why they had not come back to find him, glancing all the while at the timber of the cabin door and at the embers of the fire. He wondered if he ought to leave a message for the boys, and so, tearing out a flimsy blank sheet from the back of the little volume of Tennyson, he settled down by the fire, so that his fingers would not become numb, and scribbled on it with a stump of pencil: RETURNING TO FORT MCGURRY—R.F. This he secured to a rusty nail on the back of the door frame. Seeing the note emboldened him in a way that his previous preparations had not. Casting a final glance around the cabin, strapping the rifle over his shoulder and settling the harness of the sled on his chest, he set out down the short incline of the frozen hill and pulled out onto the trail.

The pale Arctic sun was at its zenith, and a great silence seemed to have fallen over the land, even greater than the one he had remarked on his first day in the cabin. He was aware, as he moved, that he was frightened of the silence and yet, at the same time, feared to combat it, and that in setting his feet onto the surface of the snow he aspired to soundlessness. The noise of his breath irked him. He was forever dragging the runners of his sled into fresh grooves so that they would move more smoothly. The trail, he was relieved to find, was still discernible: a faint, sunken line in the snow that ran on past belts of dark fir trees and occasional banks of undergrowth. Once a white hare broke from cover and bounded nervously across the path. Aside from this, nothing moved. Two hours of daylight remained to him, and in this time he calculated that he covered five miles. Then at dusk he dragged the sled into a cluster of spruce trees to the right of the trail and set up camp for the night. He was methodical in this, for he was wise enough to

D. J. TAYLOR

know that his survival depended on it, that it was imperative for him to stay warm and by staying warm to recruit himself for the rigours of the next day. He was aware that even five miles dragging a sled over his shoulders had exhausted him, and he knew that to overexert himself would be a foolish thing. Accordingly, he chopped a good pile of wood, lit a fire and cooked his frugal supper. When he had done this, his spirits lifted. He was out on the trail right enough. Four days or perhaps five would see him home. His only regret was the absence of coffee. He had never thought there would be a time when he would miss coffee so much. But apart from this, and the piercing cold, which caused him to huddle himself ever closer to the fire, he thought that he was comfortable enough. If the boys could see him, he told himself, they would be pleasantly surprised at how a *chechaquo* could adapt himself to the land. Half dozing over the fire, he imagined himself striding into Fort McGurry and the look of surprise on the factor's face.

There was a patch of darkness just beyond the firelight and beneath the margin of the spruce trees, and he watched it for a while, thinking that it looked remarkably like an animal stretched out and luxuriating in the warmth of the fire, like his own dogs lounging by the hearth in his guardian's house back in his own country. Interested in this singular phenomenon, he found himself listening carefully into the night air, but there was nothing except the crackle of the fire and a faint hiss of steam from the kettle he had placed at the fire's edge. Having drunk some of the hot water that it contained, he allowed his gaze to rest once more on the patch of darkness, but it seemed vaguer now, less distinct in his imagination. He wondered if here in the extremity of the wild, with each of his senses heightened to their utmost pitch, his eyes might be playing tricks on him. Sometime later he picked up a stick from the margin of the fire and threw it speculatively in the direction of the patch of darkness, but there was nothing there and he heard the stick fall hissing into the snow.

Next morning he awoke long before the rays of light had crept over the lines of spruce trees, ate his breakfast in darkness hunched over the embers of the fire, packed his things onto the makeshift sled and resumed the trail half an hour before dawn. No more snow had fallen, and the surface beneath him was more tightly packed. In this way he made better progress than on the previous afternoon. Midmorning brought him to a region of open country between two banks of firs where the trail turned south along the banks of a frozen watercourse. The lack of cover oppressed him. It seemed to him as he moved forward that he was a tiny limpetlike creature clinging to the surface of an unending vastness, and he was glad when he returned a mile or so later to the bleak avenues of trees. He ate his lunch—half a slice of pork left over from the previous day and a biscuit—seated on the trunk of a fir tree that had fallen halfway across the path. He certainly was hungry, he told himself as he disposed of the food, but the dull ache in his stomach remained. Almost as the thought came into his mind, a jack-rabbit bobbed into view from the undergrowth twenty yards away, and instinctively, such was his desire for fresh meat, he raised his rifle and loosed off a shot. But his fingers were awkward inside his thick mittens, and the jackrabbit slipped away out of range. Seeing it disappear, he wished now that he had not shot at it, for he had a curious feeling that by breaking the silence with that deafening report he had drawn attention to himself in a way that a more prudent man might have avoided. Some other impulse prompted him to examine the number of cartridges in his store. Finding that he had only seven, he resolved to shoot at no more rabbits.

Towards afternoon he reached another long low bank of spruce trees, sparsely arranged on either side of the trail. The forest was beginning to break up, he told himself, for the land that stretched away on either side was more variegated. There were hills in the middle distance, themselves mere spurs and outriders of yet more distant mountains. The discovery cheered him, for he understood that he must be closer to Fort McGurry, which, as he knew, lay in the dip of a stretch of higher ground. As he gained the avenue of spruce trees, where the trail ran for more than a mile, unerringly straight, like a road, some instinct—like the instinct that had urged him to shoot the rabbit and to examine his store of cartridges—caused him to glance over his shoulder.

There, thirty yards behind him, muzzle down in the snow, grey ears pointed and alert, walked a wolf. He was not such a newcomer to the land that he could not recognise a wolf. Standing uncertainly with his feet planted on either side of the sled, he watched as the animal slid towards him, saw him motionless and came to a halt some twenty yards away, resting its paws on the ground before it and curling over its tail as a cover for them. He knew enough about wolves to realise that this was an impressive specimen—gaunt and showing signs of malnourishment, but fully five feet from nose to tail and perhaps thirty inches at the shoulder. It occurred to him that it had been following him since he had set out on the trail, and the thought was not pleasant to him. Still, he had a rifle at his shoulder and seven cartridges, and he determined to be sanguine. Pulling the string of the sled against his shoulder and casting a last look behind him, he set off once more along the trail.

After an hour the shadows began to steal up among the spruce trees and dusk fell upon the land. He selected his camping place for the night with care: a patch of ground beneath the boughs of a particularly large tree. Having chopped a stack of kindling from the brushwood that lay to hand, he lit a fire and established himself in a declivity at the base of the tree with the fire before him. With warmth and food his spirits rose again. Two days or maybe three would see him in McGurry, talking to the factor and having his beard shaved by the fort barber. He could not see the wolf, had not done so since he commenced to build his fire, but he believed that it was there. As the darkness grew more complete, his eyes grew sharper and he began searching through the murk beyond the arc of the firelight. He had almost convinced himself that the beast had gone, sprung fresh meat somewhere along the trail and pursued it elsewhere, when he realised that what he had thought to be a thicket of shadow thirty feet beyond the fire's edge was the shape that he had distinguished the previous night. As he watched, the wolf rolled over, like a dog that lies in front of a drawing-room hearth, and he saw its eyes flash like live coals. Without pausing to reflect, he took the rifle from where it lay on the tarpaulin next to him and raised it to his shoulder, but the click of the safety catch alerted the beast and it slipped lazily to one side even before he could bring the weapon to bear. Looking up a moment or two later, he saw that it had reestablished itself quite comfortably a yard or two away from its original place.

He did not sleep much that night but dozed unhappily, troubled by a dream in which he ran steadily down a stony beach pursued by some white, flapping thing like a sheet whipped up by the air, always moving at the same speed, waiting only for him to flag. Waking once from one of these dozes, he saw that the fire had burned low and the wolf lay only a dozen feet away, close enough for him to make out the bristling fur of its jaw and the twitching of its grey flanks. He watched it for a long while as he renewed the fire with brushwood and then settled himself once more in his position against the tree trunk. In the morning—a very grey morning it was, with the promise of snow in the lowering sky—his first act on waking was to look for the spot where the wolf had lain, but there was no sign of any living thing. This cheered him, and he ate his breakfast with greater relish than he remembered eating a meal for days. Then, as he picked up his belongings and stood warming his feet at the embers of the fire, he saw from the tail of his eye the wolf come slinking out of a clump of whin bushes away to his right. In its absence the man had not ceased to reflect upon the wolf, and he now brought into his mind certain of the reflections with which he had comforted himself. If the wolf wished to follow him down the trail to Fort McGurry, then he had a rifle and seven cartridges and he could build a fire beyond which the most obstreperous wolf in the northern territories would not care to venture. Let the beast wander after him if it wished! It was of no account to him. In this way he regained his composure, slung the string of the sled over his shoulders and pulled out once more onto the trail.

He was in luck that morning. The snow had kept off, and the ground remained crisp underfoot. Moreover he recognised, or he thought he recognised, certain signs suggesting that Fort McGurry was not far away: a broken stirrup cast onto the side of the trail; a blackened campfire only half covered by the snow. These convinced him that his journey might soon be at an end. In this access of high spirits he found that he could refrain from looking over his shoulder for as much as five minutes at a time. When he did so he saw that the

D. J. TAYLOR

wolf continued to plod thirty or forty yards behind him. Well, if it wanted to do this, let it! What did he care? It was while turning back from one of these scrutinies of the trail and the grey shape loping in his wake that he fell into danger. Scarcely seeing that he had done so, he had come almost to the outer margin of the trail, to the point where it was bordered by brushwood and bushes concealed by the snow. Here he put his foot upon a prairie hen's nest, and the bird came whirling up in a frenzy into his face. Startled, he beat the creature away with his hands and in doing so tripped on a root and fell heavily onto his ankle. He was up in an instant—the outraged hen continued to flutter around his head—conscious, as he did so, that his foot would not support him. Standing on one leg and using the upturned rifle as a crutch, he examined the foot with the fingers of his right hand, gritting his teeth against the shards of pain that now coursed up his leg to the level of his knee. He had either broken the ankle or badly sprained it, he did not know which. What he did know was that he could place no weight on it and thus was all but unable to move.

It was by now about midday, and the weak winter sun had irradiated the trail with pale, phantasmal light. The wolf had stopped twenty yards away and, head down over its paws, was regarding him with interest. He stood there foolishly for a moment or so, sensible of the pain in his ankle, wondering what he should do. There was nothing for it but to build a fire and conduct a proper examination of the ankle. Accordingly, as the sun began once more to slip beneath the rim of the sky, moving awkwardly on his one sound foot, he constructed a small fire at the side of the trail, waited until the flames had risen and then, with the tarpaulin spread out beneath him, removed his moccasin and his thick sock and exposed his foot to the raw air. It was bruised and swollen to almost twice its normal size, and believing that he had sprained it rather than broken it, he bound it up with strips of cloth, replaced sock and moccasin and settled down to consider what he ought to do. There was nothing for it, he decided, but to stay the night where he was and trust that by the time he awoke in the morning he would be sufficiently recovered to proceed. And so, working slowly and occasionally crouching in the snow the better to accomplish his task, he built up a great pile of brushwood next to the fire and, cursing over the exposed nature of the spot in which he found himself, sat down once again to await the coming of nightfall. The wolf, twenty yards away, regarded him keenly. As the shadows began to lengthen he noticed it sidle slowly nearer to him until it lay barely ten feet distant from the arc of the fire. Its languid movements here in the warmth of the fire were, he decided, deceptive, for he was aware that the beast watched and registered each move that he made, following the descent of his hand as he reached for the biscuit canister, flattening its ears and preparing to retreat if he showed signs of struggling to his feet. He spent a restless night, troubled by the pain of his ankle and the thought of the wolf stretched out beyond the circle of firelight, and his own defencelessness.

He started awake to find the fire almost extinguished and the wolf scarcely two yards from where he lay. He cursed, seized a glowing fragment of wood from the embers and threw it in front of him, causing the beast to back away. There was a great ache in his ankle, he realised, and it had begun to snow quite heavily; already a coating an inch or two thick lay over the surface of his tarpaulin. He told himself that he was not afraid, that he would lie up here on the edge of the wild until his foot was healed, that he had a rifle and seven cartridges, and yet he was conscious that if he stayed where he was the snow would surely cover him. His salvation, he knew, lay in movement, that movement that the wild despises, and yet to shamble even a few feet was agony. The wolf continued to watch him as he made his preparations, assembled his belongings beneath the tarpaulin on the sled and then, again using the upturned rifle as a crutch, attempted to pull out onto the trail. He managed perhaps a dozen yards and then fell over in the snow, cursing at his ankle and at the fate that had brought him here to the wild, taken the boys from him and sent a prairie hen to sprain his ankle. The wolf retreated a few paces at the noise of his cursing and then, seeing that he did not mean to move, settled down to watch him.

It was snowing hard now, and staring at his thick mittens, he could see on each of them a layer half an inch deep. Hastily he brushed it off. Instantly further snowflakes descended onto the surface of the wool. He was startled by how calm he felt. Here he sat, amid falling snow, on

D. J. TAYLOR

the margin of the wild, with his ankle sprained and the boys mysteriously gone from him—he wondered idly about the boys and what had happened to them—and the wolf silently regarding him, and yet he had a curious sensation that he was somehow detached from his own body, looking down from some warm, airy vantage point in the skies at the figure sitting hunched up on the trail with the rifle cradled in his arms and the wolf a dozen yards behind him. The snow continued to fall.

ROMAN À CLEF

In the vicinity, though not quite the near vicinity, of London Bridge, halfway along Tooley Street and in sight of Hay's Wharf, at the junction of a crossroads of thoroughfares where packhorses and covered wagons jingle at every hour of the day and night, much to the dissatisfaction of the Tooley Street inhabitants, lies an inn named the Black Dog. Quite where the Black Dog, a vivid representation of whom dangles from a square frame above the grey stone doorway, came from, the Tooley Streeters are uncertain, but he is generally thought to be of ancient lineage, for the establishment to which he gives his name contains, in addition to his stygian portrait, a box concealing half a dozen bullets fired by Cromwell's men into the statuary of the neighbouring church and a glass case harbouring an antique sword, its blade mottled with rust, which is generally assumed to have cut several heads from their shoulders in some remote era of Tooley Street history.

The attractions of its bullet box, its rusty cutlass and its dangling sign notwithstanding, the Black Dog wore at this particular moment in time—eleven o'clock on a May morning—a somewhat desolate and forlorn air. The shutters on the ground-floor window were only half-open, the door—upon which the Black Dog gazes down balefully, as if he had half a mind to gobble it up with his great jaws—only half-ajar and the potboy sluicing water upon the step, over which the fumes of spiritous liquor seemed to hang in a kind of fog, only half-awake. Within, all was similarly cast down and mournful: the public bar all grey and ghostly in the half-light, with the chairs still resting on the wooden table-ends, the dirt very prominent on the beams and the windowpanes and the floor very much decorated with last night's detritus of tobacco fragments, pieces of bread, shrimp heads and the like. That such an environment has a lowering effect on the temperament was clear from the behaviour of the landlord, who stood by the bar regarding an upturned beer barrel with an expression of such melancholy that Mrs. Landlord, arriving downstairs in a muslin dress and a cap, somewhat greasy from a late breakfast, took fright and began to dart round the room, gathering up the spittoons under her arm and administering sundry little polishes to the tables with a duster.

Here, in a corner, flanked by a lugubrious print of the Tower and a faded bill dating from ever so long ago announcing that Mr. Felix Benjamin's benefit is finally to come off under the patronage of the Honourable Mr. Makepeace, JP, his face well-nigh hidden behind a newspaper, sat Mr. Pardew, very demure in a frock coat and peg-top trousers and his feet squeezed into the neatest little pair of lacquered boots you ever saw, which was a tribute to Mrs. Pardew or whoever else dressed him that morning. A specimen Tooley Streeter, a cabman from the rank up by the station forecourt, or one of the wagoners thundering past in the road outside, who poked his head through the Black Dog's half-open door (pushing his way past the potboy, who had now absolutely sat down and gone to sleep on the step) would perhaps have remarked that the relation between Mr. Pardew and the landlord and his wife was rather peculiar, and that though each side was cognisant of the other, both were trying deliberately to ignore the undoubted fact of the other's existence.

The specimen Tooley Streeter might also have noted that Mr. Pardew, though studiously absorbed in his newspaper—indeed with a pencil in his hand with which he made certain emendations in the margin—and with a glass of something (brought by whom? The landlord seemed to know nothing about it) before him on the table, was waiting for someone and that this someone had delayed his or her appearance to a point sufficient to cause him vexation. Certainly, Mr. Pardew had not come to the Black Dog to read his newspaper or to drink his glass of Foker's Entire, for he was forever squinting at his watch, comparing that instrument's progress with a clock that hangs on the far wall next to a facsimile of Sir Walter Raleigh and additionally patting the pockets of his frock coat in such a manner as to reassure himself that something dear to him still lay within it. Eventually, these signs of nervousness could be borne no longer, and Mr. Pardew jumped to his feet, jingled his money in his pocket and took a turn around the bar, looked at the print of the Tower and the encomium to Mr. Felix Benjamin, ran his hand meditatively over the bullet box, shook it in fact as if it held dice, and came to rest alongside the glass case containing the rusty sword.

"Dear me," said Mr. Pardew, half to himself and half to the landlord, who stood, still regarding the beer barrel, a few feet away, "but that's a fearsome weapon."

"I daresay it is, sir," remarked the landlord, to whom the sword, formerly one of the baubles of his tenancy, had now mysteriously become an item of no account. "I daresay it is."

"Feel that on your neck and you would know about it," Mr. Pardew observed pleasantly. Mr. Pardew was about to say something more, but their colloquy was interrupted by the arrival of a timid young man with light-coloured hair who came marching hastily into the room, flung his gaze around with an expression of apparent horror and might almost, it appeared, have marched out again, had not Mr. Pardew taken it upon himself to intervene. The landlord, had he taken any account of the proceedings, might have said that Mr. Pardew's behaviour was masterful. Without appearing to make any decisive movement, indeed still seeming to take an interest in the glass case, he contrived to interpose himself between the young man and the door, not exactly standing in the visitor's way but positioning himself, so to speak, on the flank of his retreat. Again, the disinterested onlooker might have been forgiven for assuming that there was some peculiar relation between Mr. Pardew and the landlord, for the latter instantly ceased his occupation of the bar and disappeared into his private quarters, leaving Mr. Pardew and the young man alone in a silence broken only by the flap of the half-open shutter and the wagons in the street.

Mr. Pardew hesitated, tapping one hand against the pocket of his frock coat and getting a hint of something metallic concealed there in return and half extending the other before him. He was not sure of his man, was conscious, too, of the public nature of the place in which he stood and knew that he must proceed with very great caution. Nonetheless, he fancied that if he could first succeed in putting the visitor at his ease, the business might be done. Consequently, he

D. J. TAYLOR

extended the hand yet further, to within a foot or so of the young man's stomach, so that he could not very well avoid shaking it.

"I believe I have the honour of addressing Mr. Tester?"

"I . . . that is . . . I am Tester."

Tester's eyes, as he spoke these words, darted around the room—at the sword in its case, at the windows, at the retreating figure of the landlord—as if it were alive with a movement that none but he could see. He was, Mr. Pardew saw, a good-looking young man, light hair sleekly parted on his head, the set of his features only impaired by the suspicion of a twitch on his upper lip.

"Perhaps you would like to sit down," Mr. Pardew suggested, with the same pleasantness of tone as when he had drawn the landlord's attention to the sword, "and take a glass? As you see, we are very quiet."

Tester looked around him again, rather wildly, as if quietness were the last thing he desired and that only a German band with its instruments pitched to crescendo would have been sufficient to restore his spirits. However, he consented to sit down, passing a hand through his hair—his fingernails, Mr. Pardew could see, were bitten down to the quick—and measuring the distance to the door with his eye.

"Will you take some brandy?" Mr. Pardew wondered.

"No . . . nothing."

They sat in this way for two or three minutes, Mr. Pardew still smiling blandly and peering every so often at his newspaper. In the short time since the two men had greeted each other, he had changed his opinion of the best means of handling the enterprise on which he was now embarked. Tester's nervousness and his apparent deference could, he believed, be usefully exploited by sheer firmness of manner. Thus he folded up his newspaper, glanced at the door (Tester's gaze following him as he did so) and said in a tone lower than that which he had previously used, "You have the items with you?"

Tester nodded.

"I have a room hired upstairs. We had better go there."

"Could we not . . . could it not be done here?"

"What, and have a policeman come in and find us?" said Mr. Pardew, meaning to frighten Tester. "I hardly think so."

After this Tester agreed to go upstairs. Ascending the wooden steps, which clattered beneath their feet in an alarming manner, they came eventually to a bedroom containing nothing but a bed, a wardrobe and an open window with an excellent view of the river and the towers and pinnaces of the distant city. This view Mr. Pardew went and inspected with evident delight. Tester, meanwhile, seated himself on the bed with an expression of blank terror.

"I should not be here," he said at length. "I had better go."

"By all means," Mr. Pardew rejoined. "Then you will have wasted my time as well as your own. You have read my letter?"

"Certainly I have read it."

"Then it is necessary for you to know only that I stand by it. Where are the keys?"

Tester turned his head towards the doorway, as if there were some other person there whose help he might enlist in denying Mr. Pardew his wish.

"I have them here in my pocket."

"Give them to me."

"On my honour, I never did a bad thing in my life before."

"Who is to say that you are doing a bad thing now? They shall be out of your hands for half a minute. Half a minute, I promise. Then you shall have them back. Give them to me."

With an audible sigh and an attitude of resignation—as if he could not help what he did and wished to emphasise this fact to any unseen eye that might be watching—Tester dipped his hand into the inner pocket of his coat and passed the keys across. Mr. Pardew, placing them in the palm of his hand, gave them a quick, exultant stare and then dropped them singly onto the coverlet of the bed. The first key lay where it had fallen, but the second sprang up and clattered onto the floorboards. Mr. Pardew gave a little exclamation and bent to retrieve it. Reaching into the pocket of his coat, he brought out a small, square tin, not unlike a cigar box, whose lid, prised off, revealed a layer of greenish wax. This Mr. Pardew considered for a moment, pressing down the surface with his thumb once or twice to see whether he thought the depth sufficient for his purpose. Then, picking up first one key, then the other, he plunged each of them into the wax, drew

D. J. TAYLOR

them forth, established that the impressions were to his satisfaction and then placed them once again on the bed. All this Tester watched with the air of a man who observes a conjuror producing coloured scarves from a tall hat and cannot for the life of him see how the trick is done.

Seeing the keys once more within his grasp, Tester made as if to retrieve them. Mr. Pardew frowned. Reaching into his breast pocket, he brought out a white handkerchief, took up the keys for a second time in the palm of his hand and began carefully to polish them. In this way he was able to remove several traces of wax that still clung to the metal.

"Now," he remarked finally, "I think our business is concluded. You will not have been missed at your work?"

"Mr. Smiles and the secretary are elsewhere."

"And these are the keys that came from Chubb? You are sure of it?"

"I am sure of it."

"Excellent. The terms stated in the letter will, of course, be fulfilled. One thing more," said Mr. Pardew amiably. "I never knew you. You never knew me. This place"—he cast his hand around the room, Tester's gaze following wide-eyed in its wake—"never was. That is all."

When Tester had departed—flying down the stairs so rapidly that the boards resounded beneath his feet—Mr. Pardew did not immediately follow. An onlooker, observing him, would have deduced that he had nothing in the world to summon him away. Picking up the tin from where he had left it on the bed, he replaced it in his pocket, moving as he did so to the window, where he stared for some while at the horizon of buildings and wharfs and tall ships' masts as if to reassure himself that no essential part of their arrangement had changed, the presumption being that if it had, Mr. Pardew would have had something to say about it. This done, he sauntered downstairs in the airiest manner, greeted the landlord, who had by this time repositioned himself at the bar, complimented Mrs. Landlord (met in the passageway) on her fresh complexion, drank off a small glass of brandy with which this lady gladly furnished him, made a further inspection of the sword in its glass case, rather as if he would have liked to take it out and whirl it above his head, and finally wandered out onto the pavement.

It was now shortly before midday and the frenzy of Tooley Street—its wagonettes and its carts and its stern-faced gentlemen in rapid transit to the waterfront—had not abated, but Mr. Pardew paid it no heed. With the little square tin in his pocket and a hand clasped protectively over that pocket, as if it guarded the greatest secret in the world, he crossed over Tooley Street, narrowly avoiding being run over by a great pantechnicon, and proceeded, by degrees, to the bridge, thereafter to the City, the vicinity of Clerkenwell and the workshop of a professional acquaintance in the business of metal casting and die sinking, where, it is to be hoped, he spent a profitable afternoon.

* * *

Five days had elapsed since the encounter in Tooley Street, and Mr. Pardew sat at his desk. The month of May was now well advanced and the weather warm, so that Bob Grace, who sat opposite him on his high stool, had taken off his jacket and in addition rolled his shirt cuffs up to the level of his elbows, but Mr. Pardew cared nothing for such relaxations. He was examining a package which had lately arrived from Clerkenwell and which contained a pair of keys, very sleekly burnished, and with the one attached to the other by way of a metal band. Thus far in his inspection Mr. Pardew had not taken the keys out of their packaging but had merely looked at them as they lay nestled within it. In truth Mr. Pardew, knowing that gentleman's perspicacity, hesitated to display them before his clerk. Grace, if he saw the keys and the manner in which Mr. Pardew examined them, would certainly pass some comment. This Mr. Pardew felt that he could not endure. At the same time, Mr. Pardew had a suspicion, born of long dealing with the man, that Grace knew a great deal more about his affairs than he had ever divulged and that any attempt to conceal even a small part of his business would be worse than useless. Consequently, having pondered the desirability of sending Grace out on an errand and then decided against it, and having reflected on his own anxieties with regard to the matter before him, he threw caution to the winds, delved inside the package and drew the keys out onto his desktop.

D. J. TAYLOR

If Grace noticed this manoeuvre of Mr. Pardew's he did not acknowledge it but continued to brood over a copy of *Bell's Life*. Mr. Pardew looked at the keys. They had certainly been excellently turned, he thought to himself as he slid first one then the other into his hand, and would certainly serve for the purpose he had in mind. Something about their respective size and the set of their teeth struck him, and, still with his eye on Grace, he placed the first key on the wooden surface of the desk with the second balanced on top of it. The suspicion that had lurked in his mind being confirmed by this experiment, he fetched a sheet of cartridge paper and a pencil out of his drawer and, laying the keys side by side, traced rapidly around their edges with the pencil point. Having accomplished this task, he stared for a long while at the resultant outlines, biting his lip and occasionally referring to the keys themselves. "The fool," Mr. Pardew said finally to himself. "He has brought me duplicates of the same key!" For a moment he tried to convince himself that this was not so, that there was some tiny variation in the metal which would differentiate them, but it was no good: the two keys, he now saw, were identical. For a moment Mr. Pardew's spirits sank to the point where the enterprise he had determined upon scarcely seemed worth continuing. Then, after a short interval, during which time Mr. Pardew looked out of the window and cast his eye over certain melancholy documents that lay on his desk, they revived. "Well, I suppose I shall have to bring it off at Folkestone," he said again to himself.

Looking up from his desk, and at the keys, from which even now he had some difficulty in removing his gaze, Mr. Pardew saw that his clerk's eye was fixed firmly on him, and that the copy of *Bell's Life* had been scrunched up and hidden out of sight. There was something about Grace's expression that Mr. Pardew did not at all like, for it spoke of shared confidences and painful secrets; nevertheless, he determined to meet it head-on. Still Grace continued to stare.

"What is it? Why do you gawp at me in that way?"

Grace drummed his finger ends on the desk, took a fresh nib from a little box he had beneath the desktop and inspected it as if it might be something good to eat.

"Keys is a blessed noosance," he suggested.

"Eh? What is that? What business is it of yours if I have a pair of keys on my desk?"

Grace appeared not to hear. He was still evincing the greatest interest in the nib, which he now held between finger and thumb, preparatory to fixing it onto his pen.

"Mr. File is a man who knows all about keys," he continued meditatively. "An excellent man to talk to, I believe, if there's anything wanting in the key line."

"Eh?" Mr. Pardew said again. "Mr. File? I will not have Mr. File's name mentioned in this office, do you hear?"

"Certainly," Grace replied. "Mr. File not to be mentioned. And his address in Amwell Street to be took out of the book, and no letter to be sent there, nor anything else, I suppose."

All this was horrible to Mr. Pardew for he understood, or he thought he understood, exactly what Grace meant by it. For a moment he thought—and the imagining was very pleasant to him—that he might usefully dismiss the man on the spot. Prudence, however, as Mr. Pardew soon acknowledged to himself, counselled caution. A Grace who sat in Mr. Pardew's office, under Mr. Pardew's eye, however great his impertinence or dirty his shirtfront, was preferable to one who roamed the world outside it and, embittered by harsh treatment, breathed all kinds of things to all manner of people. It occurred to Mr. Pardew that the present moment would be a good one in which to take Grace into his confidence, and yet even here he hesitated. If he began to explain to Grace things of which the clerk was already aware, he would appear exceedingly foolish. If, on the other hand, he imparted information to Grace which Grace did not know, he might compromise himself still further. Mr. Pardew cursed under his breath and wished Grace at the bottom of the Thames.

"Perhaps," he said, "we had better have a little conversation. There are certain affairs in which I am currently engaged of which I don't doubt you are aware. I take it you have a fair idea of what I am about?"

"A pretty fair idea, sir, I believe," Grace acknowledged meekly. "Though of course Mr. File's name is not to be mentioned."

D. J. TAYLOR

This, too, was horrible to Mr. Pardew, but still he persevered.

"I find that I am obliged to pay a visit to the coast. To Folkestone, in fact. Perhaps you had better accompany me."

"It shall be as you say, sir."

"We may very well set off this afternoon."

"To Folkestone, sir?"

"Yes, to Folkestone."

"Where the mail steamers go across to Boulogne?"

"Yes. Where the mail steamers go across to Boulogne." The look on Mr. Pardew's face as he said this was positively devilish, and once again he wished Grace at the bottom of the Thames. "Now, is there anything outstanding?"

"Samuelson's bill is due for renewal. Forty pounds at six weeks, I recollect."

"Do you think he will pay it?"

"Last time he was a-talking of his cousin as is a clergyman that might put his signature to it."

"I don't like clergymen's paper. No good ever came of it. You had better go round there. No, send Latch to call on him. By the by," Mr. Pardew enquired, "how do you find Latch?"

"He is an obliging young man, sir, as does his duty."

Mr. Pardew said that he was very glad to hear it and again wished Grace at the bottom of the Thames.

* * *

Before departing for Folkestone on the early afternoon train, Mr. Pardew undertook certain preparations of a highly confidential nature. To accomplish these, it was absolutely necessary that he should be undisturbed. Thus, having despatched Grace with a copy of Mr. Samuelson's promissory note, and having instructed that gentleman that he would meet him at London Bridge at two o'clock, he shut the office door, turned the key in the lock, pulled down the blinds upon the bleary window and seated himself once more at his desk. Here he took a final look at the keys, holding first one and then the other up to his face, before replacing them in the packet and locking it in the office safe. This done, he wandered over into a little back room that adjoined the main part of the office where was a coat stand, a chair with a broken leg which nobody had ever troubled to have repaired and a box of miscellaneous items such as dusters, India rubbers and the like. Mr. Pardew turned the contents of the box over in his fingers for some time before finding precisely what he wanted.

When he returned to his desk some moments later, he carried in one hand a short length of candle stuck into a saucer and in the other two slender half cylinders of metal resembling the halves of a very slim pencil split lengthwise. Placing the candle on the desktop and lighting it with a sulphur match from a box that lay nearby, Mr. Pardew took the first of the metal cylinders between finger and thumb and held it to the flame. When it was quite black from the heat, he withdrew it, laid it carefully on a sheet of blotting paper and performed the same manoeuvre with the second. A lick of air coursing in from beneath the locked door caused the candle to flare up and scorch his thumb, but such was Mr. Pardew's absorption in his task that he paid it no heed. A short while later both of the metal cylinders, each stained black with carbon, lay side by side on the blotting paper before him. Seeing them there, Mr. Pardew frowned. Then, reaching into the drawer of his desk, he drew forth an ancient tobacco pouch, poked his fingers into it to ensure that no strands of tobacco remained within, and very gingerly, taking care to handle the cylinders only by their extremities, pushed them inside. Stowing the pouch in his coat pocket, extinguishing the candle, drawing up the blind and unlocking the office door, Mr. Pardew, having fastened the door once more behind him, set off at a rapid pace in the direction of Blackfriars.

* * *

WM BARCLAY, ESQ.
Director
South-Eastern Railway Company

Dear Sir,
I refer to your communication of the 14th inst., in which the

D. J. TAYLOR

directors, while declaring themselves perfectly satisfied with the arrangements for the conveyance of bullion to the Continent, requested further particulars with regard to the procedures at Folkestone.

The railway office is situated on the pier, under the supervision of Mr. Chapman. This gentleman has been in the company's service for five years, and we repose the greatest confidence in his abilities and general trustworthiness. There is in addition an assistant, Allman, and a clerk. Our regulations state that the office is to be manned at all times. However, on such occasions when the officials are obliged to meet the steamer the room is left unattended but with the door securely locked. I am informed by Mr. Chapman that this period is rarely longer than a few moments' duration.

The safe key is, of course, kept locked up in a repository on the premises. The key to this is in the sole possession of Mr. Chapman.

I should add that in addition to the precautions here outlined, the pier is patrolled by the police on a regular basis during the hours of daylight.

I shall be delighted to supply you with any further information that you or other members of the board may require.

Having the honour to remain your obedient servant,

I am, sir, yours most faithfully,

J. HARKER
Secretary to the Board

* * *

A disinterested observer, travelling down to Dover by way of Folkestone on the train from London Bridge that afternoon, would perhaps have observed the following. Mr. Pardew and his clerk stepped into their carriage together—indeed the latter held the carriage door open for the former—but it could not be deduced from these civilities that they knew each other, nor that they were connected by any object other than their journey. During this transit Mr. Pardew read a newspaper, made calculations with a bit of old pencil in a notebook and grasped his stick with a remorselessness that suggested the slightest loosening of his grip would see it dance off down the corridor. Grace, alternatively, looked out of the window, admired a young lady in a muslin frock being escorted to the seaside by an old gentleman in a billy-cock hat and finally went to sleep with his mouth open, much to his employer's secret disgust.

At Folkestone, where the sea breeze blew in across the platform and the young lady in the muslin frock, looking delightfully fresh-cheeked, clutched her straw hat anxiously to her head, it could have been assumed that there was some slight relationship between them, for they set off together in the direction of the town—or rather Mr. Pardew stalked a yard or two in front while Grace strolled meekly in his wake, Mr. Pardew throwing back certain remarks over his shoulder which his clerk either did or did not catch depending on the severity of the breeze. In truth, as the train had left London Bridge the confidence that Mr. Pardew habitually felt in his abilities had altogether deserted him. He was aware that the mission on which he was now embarked involved a considerable risk, and the thought frightened him. He was also aware that he could not allow himself to impart any of these misgivings to Grace. In this way, Mr. Pardew brooding with his eyes seeming to bore into the very surface of the road, Grace moving jauntily through the crowds of people pressing back and forth from the esplanade, they came eventually to the Pavilion Hotel, where Mr. Pardew, having checked his watch and assured himself that the steamer would not be docking for a further two hours, proposed that they might eat an early dinner. For myself, I like nothing better than to dine early on a day in summer in sight of the sea, but I do not think that Mr. Pardew enjoyed his meal. Certainly, he was surly with the waiter and, having eaten his broiled fowl, lapsed altogether into silence. Grace, on the other hand, gave every impression of relishing the food that was set before him, ordered an extra chop and sent word to the orchestra—the Pavilion is a select establishment—asking, would they play "Garryowen"?

Presently a ship's horn sounded in the distance. Mr. Pardew broke out of his reverie, looked suspiciously across the table as if he could not

D. J. TAYLOR

imagine how the plates, serving dishes and glasses had got there, called for the bill and paid it. As he and his companion strolled through the hotel foyer into the busy high street and thence in the direction of the pier, it could be observed that Grace's demeanour had altogether changed, that he kept close to his employer and that certain words were spoken of which he took precise note. The pier, when they came to it, was thronged with people: passengers for the steamer, with porters bringing their baggage behind them, townsfolk come to patronise the refreshment rooms. At the further end they could see the grey bulk of the steamer moving slowly towards its mooring place. Mr. Pardew's spirits rose, for he knew that a crowd was as advantageous to his schemes as solitude.

At the same time, the scheme was dependent on a precise set of circumstances whose existence he could not at all guarantee. Thinking to reconnoitre, and indicating to Grace that he should remain a short distance behind him, he moved forward along the pier, walking quickly but affecting to take an interest in the lemonade stalls and the souvenir shops. Five minutes spent in this way brought him to the railway office. Here the press of people was less great, enabling him without difficulty to observe that the outer door was ajar and that a clerk in a railway company uniform was stationed at a counter within. Having noted this fact, and then turned his head to examine the hovering gulls and the grey sweep of the sea, Mr. Pardew proceeded a little further along the pier, almost to the point where the docking apparatus began and men in oilskins and woollen jerseys stood ready to set about their business. Here the line of shops and stalls gave way to bare deck, and he was able to stand with his arms on the pier rail (Grace, meanwhile, occupying a similar position a dozen yards away) apparently entranced by the heaving deeps before and beyond him, but in fact keeping one eye on the pier walk that he had just traversed. He had been there but a moment or so when two railway officials came walking up very rapidly towards the steamer. Mr. Pardew waited another moment until they had passed, still staring out over the grey horizon, and then, lifting his face skywards with the expression of one who delights in the briny air, walked purposefully back in the direction he had come. As he had anticipated, he found the railway office shut up and the outer door

Kept

firmly closed and locked. Observing that there were several people in the near vicinity, Mr. Pardew made a great show of trying the door and feigning exasperation when it did not yield.

"Why it's too bad," he exclaimed to Grace, who had taken up a position at the pier rail. "The place is closed."

"We shall have to wait, I suppose," Grace answered him. "That's all there is to it."

Having, as he saw it, established his bona fides—those of a traveller frustrated by the absence of officialdom—Mr. Pardew lingered a foot or so in front of the heavy oak door. To anyone passing it would have seemed that he was studying a notice advertising sailing times and tariffs. In fact, Mr. Pardew was examining the lock. This, as he had suspected, was a substantial affair but primitive, consisting of a narrow opening and a spindle, over which the hollow of the railway officials' key would fit like a glove over a finger. Round this spindle were eight iron sliders pressed forward to the mouth of the lock by a spring. Each slider, Mr. Pardew knew from certain other investigations he had undertaken in this line, had a tiny knob whose position corresponded with a notch in the central spindle. The key, consequently, would push each slider back to the point where the knobs and notches were in line. Mr. Pardew had no key, but, he assured himself, he had a means of establishing how such a key would operate. Still training his eye on the notice, but reaching the while into his inner pocket, he drew out the tobacco pouch and delved inside. Moving the metal cylinders into his hand, he slid first one then the other into the lock, then turned them slowly against the enclosing metal barrel until he felt them rub against the eight notches of the sliders.

"There is no sign of anybody," Grace now called out to him. "We had best away, I daresay."

Mr. Pardew nodded. With the pouch now stowed back in his coat pocket, he stood back and took a last look at the notice. Then he sauntered across to join Grace at the rail, and the two men walked back along the pier. Here they conducted a conversation which, had it been overheard by any passerby, would doubtless have puzzled this eavesdropper by its obliquity.

"Smoked?" Grace enquired.

D. J. TAYLOR

"A tolerable job, I think," Mr. Pardew allowed. "I did not care to see whether the marks corresponded. We had better go somewhere out of the way and assure ourselves."

"Mr. File knows what he's about," Grace remarked. "And then if it don't fit exact, we can always sand it down."

Mr. Pardew laughed grimly at his clerk's presumption of expertise. "As you say," he observed, "we can always sand it down."

* * *

A BRIEF MEDITATION ON KEYS
BY MR. ROBT. GRACE

We had come a fair way, I will allow, but not far enough. We had a key that would open the door of the railway office, but that was all we had, and a day spent in there might not have been enough to get what we wanted. But then Mr. P. as is a clever man, whatever else may be said of him, hit upon a plan. It was this: that he should send himself a box of a hundred golden sovereigns by the South-Eastern Railway to Folkestone, to be collected from the railway office on the harbour pier. This to be sent down at the weekend, when there was no shipment to Paris and the safe, as we reckoned, would travel straight back to town. This was done—I took the receipt myself for an old cash box with the money in it—and Mr. P. goes down to Folkestone, in a frock coat and a silk hat, for it's as well to play the gentleman in a game like this, to collect it back. A quiet Sunday forenoon, you understand, with the folks at church and no one about and just the one clerk—as Mr. P. had wagered—in the office. What has the clerk to do? Why, he has to get the cash box from the safe, while Mr. P. stands and waits in the office. Nothing there for him to steal, is there? In any case Mr. P.'s a fine gentleman in a silk hat, and he ain't a-going to be taking halfpence out of the charity box, is he? So the clerk fishes a key out of his pocket, unlocks a cupboard on the wall, takes out another key—this one opens the second lock of the safe—and goes off to do his duty. When he comes back, there's Mr. P. still a-standing at the counter looking as cool as you please. Opens up the box, looks over the gold, sees it's all there, signs another receipt and goes back to his 'otel. What the clerk don't know is that Mr. P. has the tin of green wax in his coat pocket with the line of the wall cupboard key pressed into it neat as neat.

We don't need no Mr. File for that key, bless you. Any die sinker as knows his trade could make you a twin brother of that in half an hour. So now we has the key to the door and the key to the cupboard where they keeps the thing we truly wants. Two weeks later Mr. P. and me are on our way to Folkestone again. It's remarkable how regular a gentleman like Mr. P. needs a touch of sea air to keep his spirits up, ain't it? To be sure, Pearce has been with us—that's a conniving scoundrel as I'm sure you'll know—and I've a railwayman's uniform over my arm. It don't fit me, but who's to know it's not mine, eh? When we get to Folkestone Mr. P. asks for the use of a bedroom at an inn, and I go up and put it on. As we come down we hear the boom of the steamer horn. Sure enough, hurrying along the pier in the dark it's to find the clerks gone and the office locked up. Well, Mr. P. gives me the key to the outer door, and before you can say jingo I'm opening up the wall cupboard with the key that lies in its lock. There inside is the key to the safe lying on a little saucer as a man might lay a teacup on. Half a moment later and I'm outside again, looking very serious and official-like. Heavens, I even stop to tell an old lady the time of the next steamer sailing, though my heart's jumping into my mouth all the time. Mr. P. has his tin to hand, to be sure, and before you can say jingo again I'm locking up the cupboard with it safe back inside. Then I fastens up the outer door, and we're away off down the pier again like a couple of sports with nothing on their mind but the path to the beer 'ouse. And yet it was a narrow-run thing, sir—those clerks coming back from the steamer can't have missed us by more than a few minutes—and I wouldn't do it again for all the guineas in Christendom.

D. J. TAYLOR

A MORNING IN THE LIFE
OF CAPTAIN McTURK

About halfway along Northumberland Avenue, not very far from
Charing Cross Station, reached by means of a tight little archway
whose ancient flagstones have veered this way and that like pieces of
crazy paving, hard by a stable yard whose ostlers must be the least
occupied in all London, in that they are never seen to move from the
hay-strewn approach to their place of work, waiting for horses that
never come, lies a tiny square composed of small buildings in lugubrious grey brick. In one of these, shined by way of two flights of
gloomy stairs, a long polished oak corridor and an anteroom tenanted
by a neat, side-whiskered secretary, sits Captain McTurk. The public
these days has romantic notions of the senior officers of Her Majesty's
Metropolitan Police Force. If they are not lithe-limbed young men
with cold grey eyes capable of wresting a vital clue from a dung heap
at a second's glance, then they are picturesque, snuff-taking ancients,
hearty and comfortable yet thinking nothing of pursuing the doughtiest villain across, let us say, a couple of rooftops to grapple with him
finally upon the pinnacle of St. Paul's. Captain McTurk belonged to
neither of these categories. He was a tall, somewhat spare man in
middle age, clean-shaven, with hair cropped very close to his scalp
and with a prominent chin that no amount of razoring would ever
quite keep clear of stubble.

How Captain McTurk had conducted himself in his previous
life nobody quite knew, but he had occupied his present position for
nearly ten years and it was said that his criminal adversaries, those
gentlemen whose portraits appear with such startling regularity in the
Police Gazette, were very anxious that he should cease to occupy it.
The public these days has romantic notions of how the senior officers
of Her Majesty's Metropolitan Police Force spend their time. If they

are not routing out continental revolutionaries from their nests among the Soho attics, then they are attending upon the Home Secretary and establishing the security of the Royal person against the attentions of sundry garroters and pistol-wielding assailants. Again, Captain McTurk was engaged in neither of these duties. Just at this moment he was sitting in his room with a cup of tea on the deal table before him examining the pile of post which, neatly opened, assembled and docketed, had lately been brought in to him on a tray by his secretary.

There was no letter from the Home Secretary. In fact the top-most communication on the first pile that Captain McTurk turned his attention to consisted of a complaint concerning an old woman who kept a toll bridge at Chiswick, which missive I am afraid to say that he crumpled up with his hand and flung into a wastepaper basket. The second packet, however, interested him greatly, so much so that he pushed the tray to one side as a way of making sufficient space to inspect its contents. The packet—in truth a substantial parcel—had been addressed to Captain McTurk by the police superintendent of Suffolk. It contained a life preserver, something over twelve inches in length, fashioned out of a wood that Captain McTurk could not iden-tify, so thick was the layer of varnish, weighted with lead at one end so cunningly that it was almost impossible to determine where the wood ended and the lead began. All in all it was a fearsome-looking weapon. Seeking to test its efficacy, Captain McTurk picked it up in his right hand and tapped smartly on the surface of his desk. To his surprise, for he had put no force into the blow, the glass veneer of the desk broke instantly into a dozen fragments. After this Captain McTurk put the life preserver back into its covering and applied himself to the letter which had accompanied it.

The weapon, he now learned, had been picked up by a farm labourer from beneath a bush on the road between Woodbridge and Wenhaston. Having seen nothing like it before, knowing that such things were not likely to be the property of respectable citizens yet unable to connect it to any misdemeanour of which he was himself aware, the Suffolk superintendent now offered it to Captain McTurk with his compliments. Putting down the letter and at the same time sweeping aside certain fragments of glass, Captain McTurk retrieved the life preserver from its wrappings and turned it over once more in his hands. He too, though familiar with every kind of nefarious weaponry, had seen nothing like it before, but he was aware that a blow delivered with it to a human limb would result in fracture and a blow to a human skull most likely result in death. Still holding the life preserver in his right hand, Captain McTurk picked up the letter once more and read again the names of Woodbridge and Wenhaston. He was conscious as he did so, without being in any way able to verify the sensation, of some memory stirring within him, of something that he had read or mused over that had some bearing—he did not quite know what—on this discovery. Having pondered this for a few moments more, he pressed a bell on the side of his desk and summoned his assistant to attend him.

The assistant, whose name was Masterson, surveying the broken glass, but knowing that Captain McTurk was not generally prone to offer explanations of his behaviour, remarked merely, "There seems to have been some kind of accident, sir."

"Accident? I suppose there has been. You had better send someone up here with a broom."

Masterson having promised that someone should be sent, Captain McTurk placed the life preserver on the desk before him.

"Did you ever see anything like this before?"

The assistant, on whose professional skills Captain McTurk was accustomed to rely, weighed the instrument in his hand.

"Well, no. I never did. It is foreign, I should say."

"Would you now?"

"Well, I should doubt it was made in Shoreditch. Or anywhere else around London. Look at those hieroglyphics or whatever they are around the base. Where did it come from?"

Captain McTurk explained about the farm labourer and his discovery on the high road between Woodbridge and Wenhaston.

"Do you know where the London Library is in St. James's Square?"

Masterson acknowledged that he did.

"Well, perhaps you'd oblige me by stepping round there and seeing if they keep a file of the *Gentleman's Magazine*. Say from the December of three years past to the December of two. But it may be that my memory is at fault."

Masterson remarked politely that he doubted it and went off on his errand. When he had gone, Captain McTurk locked the life preserver inside a little safe which reposed in a cupboard on the far side of the room and contained a great deal of material evidence gathered over the years, while placing it metaphorically in a compartment in his mind where it could lie undisturbed but be hastily retrieved when the occasion demanded it, and went back to his letters. Outside the clock chimed eleven, the ostlers in the stable yard continued to linger in the most hopeful manner, a janitor climbed up from the depths of the establishment to clear away the smashed glass and shake his head at the destruction, but Captain McTurk paid none of them any heed. One leg twisted awkwardly over the other, a cigar smoking between his fingers, the bristle on his chin waxing bluer by the moment in the soft spring light that now began to infiltrate the room, he continued to tear through his correspondence and the packets that various of his subordinates had thought worthy of his attention.

At least a dozen other letters—letters relating to specious applications for tide waiterships, letters from gentlemen who considered themselves grievously wronged by the activities of Captain McTurk's lieutenants—went the same way as the custodian of Chiswick Bridge, but the thirteenth packet Captain McTurk found himself considering with almost as much interest as the life preserver. At this juncture the capital had fallen victim to a succession of fraudulent impostures. All over the City, it seemed, gentlemen had been cashing cheques they were not entitled to possess, drawn on accounts to which they were not party, using signatures that were not theirs to sign. A great commercial concern in the City Road had had one of its cheque books stolen and fifteen hundred pounds lost in this way. A firm of solicitors in Hampshire had been pillaged of eight hundred pounds after retrieving debts for a mysterious client, the cheques used to remit these debts found to be stolen and the client mysteriously absconded. By all of this Captain McTurk was much exercised. He believed that there was a pattern to it, but he could not yet establish what the greater dimensions of the pattern were. The case before him seemed particu-

D. J. TAYLOR

larly suggestive. A solicitor in Bermondsey had been asked to write a letter in pursuit of a sum of one hundred pounds owed to his client by a defaulting debtor. An address had been supplied by the client, the letter had been written and the money very soon remitted—paid in to the solicitor's bank account and a fresh cheque drawn in the name of the client. Then it was discovered that the first cheque was a forgery. The client, to whom representations were made, had by this time vanished from the face of the earth. The debtor's address, when visited by the solicitor, had turned out to be a tobacconist's shop, kept by an old woman who knew nothing whatever about it.

A thought occurred to Captain McTurk, and, taking up his hat from where it lay on a stand near the door, he determined to act upon it. It was now the middle of the morning, and there seemed little chance that Masterson would return before noon. Accordingly, Captain McTurk descended the two flights of stairs, nodded his head to the seneschal at the door, avoided the ambitious stares of the ostlers and walked out through the tight little archway to the street beyond. Here he summoned a cab and had himself driven away across the river towards the Borough and the address to which the original demand for payment had been despatched and from which the fraudulent cheque had subsequently been returned. It became apparent to Captain McTurk as the cab bowled through the remoter quarters of Southwark that he could not expect very much from this visitation, and in this assumption he was correct. The tobacconist's shop lay at the end of a street of shy little houses, hunched beneath the outer wall of a tanning factory about whose premises hung an indescribable stench. Within could be glimpsed certain melancholy appurtenances of the retail trade: a very little counter—no more than a trestle stretched between two boxes—displaying three or four dingy little tobacco tins, a half bin of Latakia so friable and ancient that it might have been dried pure awaiting distribution to the strawberry fields, and a fierce, dirty, little old woman with her jaw wrapped up in a handkerchief against a toothache and seated in a rocking chair from which the rockers had unaccountably become detached.

All this Captain McTurk saw in a glance, divining as he did so the absolute futility of any interrogation. Nonetheless, he placed his hat

Kept

{ 333 }

on the counter, rolled around in his fingers a fragment of the Latakia from the bin—very dismal stuff it was, which crumbled away to nothing—looked up at a dangling cage with a stuffed jackdaw suspended in it and announced, first, that he was a police officer, and, second, that he believed the old lady's premises had lately been used as an accommodation address. Having received the old lady's cautious assent to this, Captain McTurk further deposed that certain letters had doubtless been received at the address, and wondered who had come to collect them. The old lady remarking that it was a shame she should be so worried when plagued with the toothache and that it was no business of his, Captain McTurk grew suddenly fierce himself, let the handful of Latakia fall through his fingers and gave the gentlest little nudge to the edge of the counter, causing the nearest of the tobacco tins to shake and waver as if it might be about to spill its contents over the sawdust floor. Whereupon the old lady, half rising from her chair and putting out a claw to secure the tobacco tin, recollected that there might have been a man calling himself Carter and that he might have last called six weeks since, or then again he might not. Captain McTurk persisting, and demanding in particular what this Mr. Carter might have looked like, the old lady also recollected that he might have been tallish and elderly-looking, or then again perhaps younger and "queerish." Had she seen any specimens of the gentleman's handwriting? Captain McTurk wondered, but the old lady was equal to this, protesting that she could not read and in any case what would she be doing with specimens of gentlemen's handwriting? At Captain McTurk's wondering if she expected any further communications with Mr. Carter, the old lady altogether shook her head, and Captain McTurk knew that he had reached the bottom of the particular well he had come to drain, put his hat back on his head, administered a little pat with his hand to the nearest tobacco tin, as if to reassure its owner that his earlier gesture had been no more than a jest, and walked out into the street to the waiting cab, resolving nevertheless that he should have the shop watched and that any further visit by Mr. Carter should be his last.

It was by now sometime after midday. As the cab took him back through the Borough, in sight of the river and the forest of ships' masts, Captain McTurk stared out of the window at the passersby,

D. J. TAYLOR

thinking to identify in one of them the outline of Mr. Carter, come to collect his letters and ripe for apprehension. But there was no one amongst the mass of city dwellers, of men and women passing back and forth from their places of work or gathered indiscriminately on street corners, to stay his glance, and he continued on his journey, stopping the cab at Charing Cross and walking the last quarter mile along Northumberland Avenue, through the tight little archway (the ostlers had all disappeared to their dinners) and back to the solitude of his desk. Here he found that Mr. Masterson, who was an efficient man, had returned from his errand and that several bound volumes of the *Gentleman's Magazine*, marked with the crest of the London Library, lay on his chair together with several stray fragments of glass that the janitor's brush had unaccountably missed. Sundry other missives, communications, packages and even a telegram or two—one with a superscription marked URGENT IMMEDIATE ATTN. ASST. COMMISSIONER on its front—had arrived in his absence, but Captain McTurk was a single-minded man and the conundrum of the life preserver, which he now removed again from the safe in the corner of the room, had not ceased to occupy him during his half hour in the Borough. Transferring the bound volumes to his desk, he seated himself in the chair, placed one on his lap and began to leaf through it, paying particular attention to those melancholy pages towards the rear of each number given over to gentlemen's obituaries.

Captain McTurk was a thorough man—besides, the obituary columns of the *Gentleman's Magazine* are not notably extensive—and within a quarter of an hour he had the information he wanted before him. This, it may immediately be remarked, was the memorial to Mr. Henry Ireland. Mr. Ireland had not been personally known to Captain McTurk. Consequently, he began merely by studying the catalogue of that gentleman's accomplishments. This done, he took up a pencil and a piece of paper from the desk drawer and noted down such points as he found to be of interest. These, it seemed to him, were very singular. For one thing, the late Mr. Ireland was represented as an excellent horseman, a rider to hounds, an amateur jockey even, who had performed to advantage in the Newcastle Plate ten years before, and yet somehow he had allowed his horse to run away with him. For another,

Kept

the horse, having run away and deposited him on the base of his skull at the roadside, had for some reason ceased to run and returned to crop the grass peacefully ten yards away. Mr. Ireland's fatal accident, according to his obituarist, had occurred not so very far from his Theberton estate. In a glass-fronted bookcase to the back of Captain McTurk's chamber there were a number of maps of the English counties. Taking the map devoted to Suffolk, Captain McTurk traced the road connecting Woodbridge to Wenhaston with the end of his pencil and found that it ran exceedingly close to Theberton. After this, Captain McTurk took the life preserver out from its wrapper again, held it in his right hand and administered with it a little blow to the palm of his left. The pain that this caused was sufficient to make him drop the life preserver onto the desk and wring his left hand between his knees, and it was in this condition that Mr. Masterson found him on entering the room a moment or so later.

"Gracious! Is something the matter?"

"Only that I have near shattered my palm with this d——d bludgeon! Thank you, there's no need"—this in repudiation of the hand that Masterson extended towards him—"but look here! The thing is found on a roadside on the way to Woodbridge. And not a mile away by my reckoning a man is discovered with his head cracked to pieces and a horse that is supposed to have run away with him still at his side."

Masterson nodded his head over the facts of the case as they were revealed to him. "I should say that that was a very singular horse, if indeed it did run away with him. By the by, you remark the man's name?"

"No. What about it?"

"Is he not the husband of the Mrs. Ireland that was lost? The young lady whose trustees were said to have been at fault?"

"And replied that they should be permitted to perform their duties without interference? I believe I do recall."

Masterson looked as if he might be about to volunteer further information on this topic, only for his eye to fall on the topmost envelope.

"You will not mind my mentioning it, I am sure, but I believe that is from Sir Edwin." Sir Edwin, it may be said, was the Home Secretary.

D. J. TAYLOR

"Is it? Well, Sir Edwin will have to wait his turn like everyone else."

However, Captain McTurk consented eventually to open the Home Office envelope, and even to take certain steps with regard to its contents. Nonetheless, he was sufficiently interested in the bound volume of the *Gentleman's Magazine* to send Mr. Masterson down to Suffolk and also to ponder in his head what he had heard of Mrs. Ireland and her history.

* * *

Mr. Masterson was a diligent man. Despatched to Suffolk, he determined to acquit himself in a manner of which he fancied Captain McTurk might approve. Accordingly, he engaged a room at the Crown in Woodbridge, hired a horse from the stables adjacent to that inn and set out thoroughly to investigate the route that Henry Ireland had taken on the day of his fatal mishap. He discovered, by application to the doctor who had attended Mr. Ireland in his death throes, that the road on which he had met with his accident was perhaps two miles from the gate of his property at Theberton and perhaps a further two miles from the road that connected Woodbridge and Wenhaston. This former thoroughfare Mr. Masterson rode up and down on several occasions with the medical man's directions on a sheet of paper before him as he went until he was tolerably certain that he had located the exact spot at which Mr. Ireland had come to grief. It was, to be sure, a lonely part of the county—a narrow track running alongside the bed of an old, dried-up river, with a band of dense woodland spreading away in the middle distance behind—and even here, on a spring afternoon with the larks ascending into the pale sky above him, Mr. Masterson said to himself that he did not much like it.

Nevertheless, he was bidden to undertake a survey and undertake that survey he did, fastening his horse's bridle to a tree and tramping back and forth along the path with his notebook in his hand and casting his eyes first to one side and then to the other. Several things immediately attracted his notice. The first was that the road was not tarmacadamed, being no more than a farm track, and that had Mr.

Ireland tumbled from his horse in the normal manner, it would have been very nearly impossible for him to have sustained the injuries over which the doctor and the coroner's jury had shaken their heads. Had Mr. Ireland then come down upon a rock sufficient to smash open his skull at its base? Mr. Masterson examined the grass of the verge, which he found remarkably soft and springy and altogether devoid of rocks. How, then, had Henry Ireland come by his blow? Mr. Masterson assured himself that it could only have been administered by the horse during the course of that animal's running away, and yet the horse had been found calmly cropping the grass a few yards from his dead master's side. The more Mr. Masterson considered the matter, the more he could find no plausible explanation. Naturally, it occurred to him that if a gentleman who is riding his horse along a country path is subsequently found at the roadside with his head stove in, then some other agency may be to blame, but he was aware that before he reached this conclusion there were other avenues that it behoved him to pursue.

His next action, consequently, was to return to Woodbridge and interview the police captain who had caused the life preserver to be sent to London for the attention of Captain McTurk. This gentleman, though, could only confirm what he had stated in his letter: that the bludgeon had been found at such and such a spot on the road from Woodbridge to Wenhaston, apparently concealed behind a clump of foliage, that nothing like it had been seen in the county before and that no incident existed in his recollection with which it could be connected. Mr. Masterson thanked the police captain and rode back to Theberton, thinking to himself that he would do best by finding some witness who had observed Mr. Ireland at an earlier point on his last ride and could attest to the manner of his progress, the attitude of his horse and so forth. With this object in mind, he spent a day in Theberton village—the estate was altogether shut up, he noted, with an iron bar raised across the gateposts and the trees flaring up above the fences—drank a pint of beer at the local inn and, making no secret of who he was and what he wanted, asked questions of such persons as placed themselves in his way.

He did not find out a great deal, but he discovered something: a

D. J. TAYLOR

labouring man, employed in draining ditches and pollarding willows for the local farmers, professed to have been walking along the track to his work on the afternoon in question and had seen "th' squire" half a mile or so from his gates. Interested, but taking care not to show it, Mr. Masterson conducted his interrogation with such suavity that it did not seem like an interrogation at all. Had he spoken to the squire? "'Deed he had, for that he had touched his cap and squire had remarked as it were a fine day." Mr. Ireland had been riding his horse on the path, had he? "No, he had not. He had been a-leading of the animal on his bridle, like as if it were lame." And had the man seen anyone other than himself and the squire on the road that afternoon? "None but a tinker or a pedlar or some such person with a pack mule." Had he thought of imparting this information to the coroner? "Sure, he knew nothing of coroners and suchlike, and if they wanted aught from him, they should come and seek it out." Mr. Masterson asked various other questions, but this was the sum total of information that he extracted, whereupon he thanked the man, retrieved his horse and returned to the Crown in Woodbridge, thinking that whatever else had happened to Mr. Henry Ireland on the afternoon of his death, he had not fallen into the road, had not struck his head on a rock, had not been kicked by his horse, but had very probably been murdered.

Kept

{ 339 }

AN AFTERNOON IN ELY

DIARY OF THE REV. JOSIAH CRAWLEY, CURATE OF EASTON

16 January 1866

Dixey called at my lodgings, somewhat discomposed—his hair much dishevelled by the wind—and wishing to speak. On my inviting him in, he declined, saying that he preferred to walk. Accordingly, we strolled a little way along the back lanes. Dixey apologetic. *Wished, he said, to allow me some explanation for the events of yesterday. Having remarked this, somewhat silent as if he did not know how to begin. A dank, chill day, the roads quite deserted. The young woman apparently a distant relation, his ward, altogether disturbed in her mind ("Quite deranged"—Dixey), who lives in the house. She is biddable enough, he maintains, but prey to fits of violent agitation, these necessitating her confinement. Naturally, I was much interested in this lady, Mrs. Ireland (Dixey somewhat reluctant to reveal her name), yet seeing his discomfiture restrained my curiosity. Mindful of my duty, I enquired, was there anything I could do for Mrs. Ireland from the spiritual point of view? At this Dixey laughed. "She thinks the world a well, and God the bucket. If indeed she thinks anything at all." Spoke of Mrs. Ireland's "nasty tricks," her guile with the servants, &c. Dixey remarked that he proposed a visit to London, where business summons him, meetings with lawyers and so forth, but would return in the spring, when he hoped to see something of me. I was sorry to see him go.*

* * *

24 January 1866

My poem "Alaric" returned by the publishers. I placed the manuscript hurriedly in a drawer, not wishing to reread it.

* * *

28 January 1866

To Ely. Much conversation with A. I find her much better schooled than I surmised. Decided opinions about the late American war, the Royal household, &c., much better than the usual feminine twaddle one hears on such occasions. Came back in the twilight: the afternoons much less drear, me judice.

* * *

31 January 1866

Letter from Cousin Richard. It is as I feared. He can do nothing for me.

* * *

2 February 1866

Curious encounter with Dixey, whom I had supposed in London. Wandering in the lanes this forenoon, meditating my sermon for Candlemas Day, I realised that, all unknowing, I had approached the back parts of the Hall. The estate very run down here: great clumps of elms, long untended, boundary walls greatly dilapidated. To the best of my recollection, a track running to the right of Dixey's back garden connects with the front parts of the house. Having come a mile or so out of my way, this I resolved to take. I had walked for ten minutes, seeing no one (altho' the cries from Dixey's kennels, hard by, very loud upon the wind), when, of a sudden, Dixey hove into sight, one of his great dogs straining at the leash before him. I moved to greet him, yet he brushed my salutations aside, declaring, why was I at large on his property, did I not know that trespass was forbidden, &c.? Hearing my explanation—that I had stepped out of my way by mischance and

Kept

meant no harm—he recovered himself somewhat, apologised for his brusqueness, declared himself much troubled by poachers in the wood. The dog meanwhile straining at the leash as if I was a quarry he meant to run down and devour. Seeing his ill-humour, I resolved to bid him good day and departed somewhat hurriedly the way I had come, conscious throughout of his eye fixed on my retreating figure.

* * *

3 February 1866
I do not know why I expected a word from Dixey, but none came. Sent a copy of Mrs. Caudle, *Mr. Jerrold's amusing sketches from* Punch, *to A., she having expressed interest.*

* * *

"Papa has been asking about you."

"Has he, indeed? I am sure that is uncommonly kind of him. What has he been asking?"

"He says it is his duty to make enquiries."

"Perhaps I had better ask my landlady to write a "character." That is how one employs a parlourmaid, is it not?"

Miss Amelia Marjoribanks laughed, but not perhaps as heartily as she might have done. Mr. Crawley applied himself to his tea. It was an afternoon in February, with snow still on the ground, and they were seated in the Deanery drawing room, an apartment chastely if not abundantly furnished. A modest pianoforte, a trelliswork fire screen, an aspidistra in a pot, a brace of occasional tables arranged in such a way that any visitor directed to a chair was compelled to navigate around them—these were the artefacts with which Miss Marjoribanks surrounded herself on the occasions when she was "at home." On the mantelpiece nearby lay some volumes of Sir William Smith's *Dictionary*, which Miss Marjoribanks had not read, and a watercolour representation of Siena, which Miss Marjoribanks had not visited, together with Mrs. Brookfield's new novel, which she had happened to peruse, and a faded etching of the town of Whitby, with which she was tolerably familiar, as it had been the site of her father's former incumbency. These, together with various invitations to sales of work and clerical recreations, a family picture or two and a portrait of the late Mrs. Marjoribanks got up in an elaborate bonnet in the style of Queen Adelaide, completed the room's decoration.

"It is very curious that Mrs. Harrison and the girls are not here," Miss Marjoribanks remarked innocently. "Why, it is nearly half past three."

There was a polite fiction between them that this was one of Miss Marjoribanks's regular afternoon entertainments.

"Yes indeed. I should be very sorry to miss Mrs. Harrison and the girls."

Mr. Crawley smiled as he said this, and threw out a glance that landed halfway between his hostess and the volumes of Sir William Smith's *Dictionary*, but I do not think that he was altogether happy in the position in which he found himself. He was a clever man, and he was conscious that his present situation, here in the Dean of Ely's drawing room with the Dean of Ely's daughter softly regarding him from the other side of the Dean of Ely's fire, placed him at a disadvantage. By his estimate he had been paying his attentions—Mr. Crawley shrank from so vulgar a word as *courting*—to Miss Marjoribanks for nearly six weeks. In this capacity he had walked with her in her father's rose garden, listened to her sing several of Herr Schubert's most affecting compositions and handed her into her carriage at the conclusion of an episcopal entertainment. All this was as it should be, and Mr. Crawley had no quarrel with the rose garden, Herr Schubert, the carriage or indeed with Miss Marjoribanks. As well as being a clever man, he was an observant one, and in the six weeks of their acquaintance he fancied that he had come to know her pretty well, that she was, in addition to being beautiful and spirited, proud, fond of having her own way and somewhat lacking in mental energy, but that something could be made of her. Quite how many men approach young ladies with this fanciful assumption, Mr. Crawley did not choose to reflect. His misgivings stemmed solely from the fact that he knew that something was expected of him, that he had wandered, as it were, into a world where his obligations extended not only to the

Dean and his daughter but to whole legions of persons with whom he was only dimly acquainted.

The journey across the fens to Ely that morning had oppressed him yet further in this regard. It seemed to him that the ostler who stabled his horse in the inn knew the object of his mission and smiled over it, that the clerical colleagues who saluted him in the streets were winking at him from beneath their shovel hats and that the domestic who opened the Deanery door to him would be hastening down to the servants' quarters to discuss his affairs the moment he had removed his coat and hat. At the same time, there was more to Mr. Crawley's disquiet than this. The Dean of Ely, he had several times heard said, doted on his daughter. Mr. Crawley had observed the extent of this doting. He was aware that he would not be able to emerge from the Deanery with Miss Marjoribanks on his arm without a struggle. He was aware, too, shrewd observer that he was, that Miss Marjoribanks had somewhat ambiguous views about the doting, that sometimes she relished it, while at other times she seemed disposed to strike out on a line of her own. This made him feel that his position with regard to the Marjoribanks household was by no means as clear-cut as it first appeared, that there were other, private motivations at work over which he had no control. And so all in all, however bright the coals of the Dean's fire and the lustre of the Dean's daughter's hair as she handed him his tea, I do not think he was happy.

"How is your father?" Mr. Crawley proposed. There was a second polite fiction between them, which was that Mr. Crawley's visits were prompted by his veneration of the Dean.

"Papa is with Mr. Prendergast" (Mr. Prendergast was the diocesan lawyer) "and will be all afternoon. I never knew such a one as Mr. Prendergast for taking up gentlemen's time. Perhaps, Mr. Crawley, you would not mind poking the fire."

Mr. Crawley did as he was bidden, conscious as he did so that he was failing to shine and that Miss Marjoribanks's rejoinders to his questions were not all that they might be. Rattling the coals with the poker end, he determined to say something that might raise their conversation to a level beyond that of mere pleasantry.

"One of the advantages of living in lodgings, I find—and there are not many—is that one learns how to perform domestic tasks of this kind. I declare that when it comes to lighting fires, making toast or brewing tea, I could give lessons to the doughtiest housemaid."

This, Mr. Crawley thought, was rather neat, reminding Miss Marjoribanks of his bachelor state, hinting at its sorrows, canvassing his own dexterity. But the Dean's daughter knew all about young clergymen who lived in lodgings.

"Papa says that young men these days are all spoiled, and that it would do them good to darn their own shirts."

Mr. Crawley thought that he would have liked to tell the Dean that he could darn his own shirts and be d——d. However, he contented himself with giving a final, miserable poke to the fire.

Miss Marjoribanks, it may be said, was similarly confused by the position in which she found herself. Dean's daughter that she was, she was aware that she held Mr. Crawley in great esteem, knew that he was the grandson of an earl, had even gone, unknown to him, to the chapter-house library to read an extremely learned article that he had contributed to the *Church Quarterly Review*. And yet she had an idea that in the triangle now composed of herself, Mr. Crawley and the Dean, any young man perhaps would have done, and that Mr. Crawley's punctiliousness, his grandfather the earl and his article in the *Church Quarterly Review* were as nothing compared with certain adjustments that Miss Marjoribanks proposed to make in her relations with her father. All this was a source of some discomfort to Miss Marjoribanks, and not a little shame, and its consequence was that she did not quite know how to proceed. Thus far, Mr. Crawley had been allowed certain of the privileges generally associated with an acknowledged lover, which is to say that he had walked with her in the paternal rose garden, handed her into her carriage and so forth. As to what further privileges might be allowed him, and whether he should be allowed the greatest privilege of all, Miss Marjoribanks was not altogether sure.

Mr. Crawley, meanwhile, was biding his time. He had an inkling of some of this. The idea that much was expected of him by persons for whom he cared not in the slightest still rankled with him. And yet he knew that he preferred an animated Miss Marjoribanks, who tossed her head and remarked on the plainness of the archdeacon's wife, than one who relayed her father's opinion that young men were spoiled.

"You must find it very dull here in Ely," he suggested, "after the delights of London."

And here Miss Marjoribanks brightened—up to a point. The delights of London were a subject on which she felt she could talk, yet in truth her stay in Wimpole Street had been rather dull. Deans' daughters, it may be remarked, are not generally thrown wholesale out into the London charivari, certainly not Deans' daughters as strictly raised as those of Mr. Marjoribanks. And so Amelia, who had longed for a ball and a carriage ride in the park, had been forced to put up with a tea party convened in honour of the latest fashionable preacher and a charity bazaar in aid of the West African mission. Miss Marjoribanks had listened to the latest fashionable preacher and presided over her stack of embroidered cushions with good grace, but her heart was not in it. And though she prattled gamely enough to Mr. Crawley about the Reverend Wotherspoon's sermon and Lord John (whom in fact Miss Marjoribanks had had pointed out to her from a carriage window in Brook Street), it was clear also to him that she had not very much enjoyed herself.

After Miss Marjoribanks had finished this disquisition there was a silence. Outside, snow had begun to fall again, slanting in across the line of the cathedral spire and giving a very melancholy aspect to the Deanery gardens. Mr. Crawley thought of his hired horse and the long journey back to Easton and the dismal supper that would await him when he returned. Then, unexpectedly, Miss Marjoribanks spoke.

"Papa has solved the mystery of the woman at Easton Hall. The one who broke in upon your luncheon."

"Has he, indeed! What has he to say about it?"

"She is Mr. Dixey's ward, and quite"—Miss Marjoribanks shied away from the word *mad*—"not in her right mind. But Papa says there is some scandal, and that Mr. Dixey is a regular Bluebeard who keeps her locked up in a dungeon."

"If that be the case, then he is a very hospitable Bluebeard," Mr. Crawley observed, "for I have dined at his table several times and never thought I might be eaten up with the dessert."

"No doubt one gentleman is very like another in company. But I am only repeating what Papa has said."

Mr. Crawley bent down from his chair and gave the coals another little shove with the poker. He had an inkling—and he did not quite know how the inkling had come to him—that he ought to be careful in whatever further remarks he uttered on the subject of Mr. Dixey's ward. And yet he was aware, merely from the tone of her voice, that this was a topic in which Miss Marjoribanks was as keenly interested as himself. Accordingly, he sat up from his delvings in the fire and remarked in his blandest tone, "She is a Mrs. Ireland, is she not? The daughter of Mr. Brotherton, who I believe was a literary man. But I did not know there to be any scandal."

"Well . . . perhaps not." *Scandal*, too, was not a word that Miss Marjoribanks used lightly. "But Papa says that people have begun to wonder why she is so long shut away, and her family not permitted to see her, and that it is very strange."

"I have no doubt that everything is in order," said Mr. Crawley, who did not necessarily believe this. "Mr. Conolly, I believe, that used to direct the asylum at Hanwell, is a very competent man."

"Papa says he is a charlatan."

Mr. Crawley had the utmost respect for the Dean of Ely's opinion on this and any other matter, but he did not feel it necessary to concur.

"However that may be, it seemed to me that Mrs. Ireland scarcely knew herself."

"She is supposed to be very good-looking, I believe," Miss Marjoribanks remarked innocently.

"Very probably. I scarcely had time to observe her before she was removed from the room."

Mr. Crawley was conscious that the conversation was straying into areas where he was altogether reluctant to follow. At the same time, he was aware that should a young lady seated in her father's drawing room wish to discuss a certain topic, there is very little that can be done to prevent her.

"I am sure I have read a newspaper report that said she was very good-looking," Miss Marjoribanks continued.

Kept

All this was very bad, and not for the first time that afternoon Mr. Crawley wished that he had stayed in Easton and written his sermon. Making a violent effort to change the subject, he enquired, had Miss Marjoribanks been amused by her reading of *Mrs. Caudle*? only for Miss Marjoribanks to remark in return, had not its author famously quarrelled with the late Mr. Brotherton? Even now, at this late stage, Mr. Crawley assured himself that there might still be an opportunity for the saying of some soft word or two. At this very moment, though, there came an irruption at the door, a noise of stoutly shod feet in the hallway, and the arrival of the Deanery parlourmaid to announce, "Ef'n' ye please, miss, Mrs. Harrison and the young ladies."

This, Mr. Crawley thought, he really could not bear. He rose to his feet, glanced extenuatingly at his watch and said his farewells.

"I shall look forward, Miss Marjoribanks, to have the honour of entertaining your father and yourself at Easton before long."

"As for that," Miss Marjoribanks replied, beckoning Mrs. Harrison and her three hulking daughters into the room, "Papa is exceedingly busy, what with Mr. Prendergast and the diocesan accounts. But I shall tell him you said so."

Still Mr. Crawley believed that he might be able to press the fair Amelia's hand. But Miss Marjoribanks was a Dean's daughter and allowed no hand pressing. A brisk handshake and Mr. Crawley was outside once more on the gravel beyond the Deanery door, listening to the cabman who had brought Mrs. Harrison and her three daughters in from Trumpington cursing over his twopenny tip. As he walked disconsolately back to the inn where his horse was stabled, he encountered a clerical acquaintance—does one not always meet some acquaintance at these times?—who shook him by the hand and enquired, "So, old fellow, when is it to be?"

"Eh?" said Mr. Crawley sharply. "There is nothing of that kind in prospect as far as I'm aware."

"Indeed? Then I am very sorry to hear you say so."

And so Mr. Crawley returned to his inn, his boots leaving faint impressions in the powdery snow, and his mind, for some reason, bent not on Miss Marjoribanks and the splendours of the Deanery drawing room but on Easton Hall and the secrets that were kept within it.

D. J. TAYLOR

A NIGHT'S WORK

Of all the artistic gentlemen so regularly held up for the public edification, I will own that the one that I esteem above all is Mr. Frith, RA. How many times, wandering in the corridors of some municipal gallery, halfway down the stairs of some Pall Mall club (with Timmins, my host, a little red-faced and pursy, urging me on to the supper table), have I not stopped to admire, as it might be, a representation of the Derby, or the interior of a railway carriage, or a London street, and found my eyes straying to that discreet and unpopulated corner where lies the familiar signature? To be sure, all human life is gathered here: the upward tilt of the servant girl's bonnet as she angles towards her sweetheart; the fiery complexion of the tipsy soldier tumbling from the alehouse door; the stout paterfamilias with his brood of children; General Sir Willoughby de Courcey, CB, on his great charger and Sergeant Snooks at the gun carriage—all this Mr. Frith seems to be able to take off as easily as you and I play at spillikins or twit Miss Mary (a demure young lady who scarcely lifts her eyes from the table) that her lover stands waiting in the porch.

And yet Mr. Frith is not, I think, what the world calls a realist. He may paint a crowd, survey a marching army, oversee a swarm of boys as they come clamouring from the schoolyard gate, and yet his art lies in design, in what he sees and what he does not see, in what he hastens to include and what he chooses to omit. It is remarkable, is it not, when confronted by one of Mr. Frith's teeming panoramas, how often the eye remarks their chains of quiet connection: how the soldier on the white horse has, plainly, a regard for the innkeeper's daughter who brings him his beer; how the gentleman in the tall hat and the eyeglass is clearly confederate with the black-coated cleric who shuffles behind him? There is no proof of these affiliations—the thing no more coheres than some slice of microscopic life over which the man of science places his lens—but the effect is so very singular. For myself, I think Mr. Frith the equivalent of a great botanist or a marine biologist, and yet the plants upon which he botanises and the colonies of sea urchins over which he trails his net are humankind.

Let us say, to amuse ourselves, that Mr. Frith has set up his easel on the concourse of London Bridge Station on this quiet summer's evening, here among the rows of kiosks and the bookstall women selling copies of the *Cornhill* and *Bell's Life* and ninepenny novels and waxing ever more discontented, it being past eight and the workday crowds mostly departed. What does he see? A couple of small boys, indescribably dirty and depraved, playing at peg top at the summit of a flight of stone steps, several old women bent on mysterious errands at the sausage and pie shops, certain of those vague-looking persons, very dilapidated in the hat and footwear department, who *will* always infiltrate themselves into scenes of this kind. One passingly dramatic event Mr. Frith will have missed, seeing that he has only just begun to set out his materials, is the arrival, hot from the City half an hour since, pulled by a pair of sweating horses, of a covered wagon at whose appearance two railway policemen instantly emerged and began to help its custodians unload a pair of crates into the stationmaster's office. That gentleman stands at his door now, under the eye of the station clock and a severe-looking lady in a black coat with turban to match, and no doubt Mr. Frith would cast an appreciative glance over the brass buttons of his waistcoat and the jet profusion of his whiskers. Others are there on whom Mr. Frith's hand would perhaps pause: an old clergyman in gaiters and a suit of black with a copy of *Fraser's* under his arm looking very studiously at the printed timetable that hangs under glass on the wall beside the stationmaster's door; three or four young ladies in dove-grey travelling dresses and sober bonnets being whisked out of the waiting room by a hard-faced old woman who could be anything from the headmistress of their school to the embittered old housekeeper of their aunt. A train stands waiting—the Dover train (via Folkestone), the mail train heading down to the steamer packet—at the nearby platform, all wreathed in vapour with its furnace banked up and a couple of workmen busily shovelling coal onto its fuel stack, but the old duenna pays it no heed and whips

D. J. TAYLOR

her charges away at the point of a little umbrella to a distant bench beyond the reach of engine fumes and artist's palette alike.

In their wake, though, step a pair of gentlemen with whom Mr. Frith might if he cared do marvels: the one clad in black with curious side-whiskers and a prognathous jaw bearing a stick—fiercely—and a travelling bag in his hand; the other, burly and red-faced, burdened by the weight of a couple more such containers. What is in those bags? Whatever it is, the burly man is uneasy about them, gives them anxious little glances and fiddles nervously with their straps. To be sure, there is something faintly mysterious about these persons. The same cab brought them to the station—can be seen, in fact, on the further side of the concourse rattling off towards the Borough—but it could not be said that either knew or acknowledged the other. Are they here to catch a train? Certainly, he of the side-whiskers and the jutting jaw has gone off to inspect the framed timetable and shake his stick in the direction of the ticket office, but the burly man merely drops his burden at his feet (and no end of a thump can be heard on the stones) and stands guard over it, mopping his brow with a handkerchief and generally looking for all the world as if the bags contained a couple of alligators taken from the reptile house at the zoo.

The hands of the station clock have now moved to within a few moments of half past eight, which is the hour of the Dover train's departure. A few passengers are already moving briskly along the platform, but there seems some doubt as to whether the brandisher of the stick and the custodian of the travelling bags shall join them. The former is now standing before the station bookstall, poring over that month's *Cornhill* as if it contained fresh instalments of the Scriptures and a man would jeopardise his soul by not reading them, while the latter looks almost wildly about him, first at the waiting train, then at the station clock, then at the platform edge, but never, it must be noted, at the figure by the bookstall. A guard arrives out of nowhere—a fat, ill-favoured man with the most melancholy face you ever saw—looks around him once or twice and in a curious gesture—curious in that the doing of it seems to perplex him rather—taps the peak of his broad cap a couple of times with his forefinger. By now it is wanting a minute and a half to half past eight.

Kept

Galvanised by some mysterious agency, both our gentlemen can be seen hastening to the ticket office. Are those first-class tickets they have bought? Certainly, the burly gentleman goes and arranges himself in a first-class carriage, staring nervously at a porter—a gloomy porter who thinks it surprising that three travelling bags can weigh so much—who carries those items off to the luggage van. But as for the other gentleman, what *can* he be doing? First he strolls along the platform, glancing to right and left as if waiting for someone to join him. Then he doubles back, as if the object of his quest lies behind one of the monstrous pillars supporting the station roof. The sad-eyed guard, by this time, is traversing the platform ringing his bell to signal the train's departure. A few seconds now until half past eight. The great wheels have begun to grind and a hellish mechanical noise to drive out all human interventions. The guard has clambered up into his compartment that abuts the luggage van, where he stands peering melancholically out into the murk, and still the sharp-jawed man lingers a yard or so away. He will turn back and retreat to his pillar—no, he sees an acquaintance at the platform's further end and is hailing him through the smoke. But no, there is no one there.

The train has begun to roll slowly yet inexorably forward. The guard, half-hidden in the billowing, ever-ascending vapour, gives another confidential tap on the peaked brim of his cap with the tip of his forefinger, and the sharp-jawed man, belying the impression of age implied by his silvery whiskers, makes a bound and a leap and is swallowed up by the guard's compartment as it rocks by, so that Mr. Frith, if he sat still at his easel (but that there is no one there and the platform empty), might wonder where he had gone and how a man can vanish into thin air on a railway platform in the middle of the evening of a summer's day.

* * *

STATEMENT BY SAMUEL SPRAGG, RAILWAY POLICEMAN

A message came through to our post from Messrs. Abell in the City about seven that a shipment would be travelling down to Folkestone

D. J. TAYLOR

on the mail train. This was quite in the usual way of things. Constable Harlow and I attended. Again, this was customary on such occasions. The bullion boxes were taken from the wagon all sealed up in red wax and then taken into the stationmaster's office, and Mr. Sellings will tell you the same.

STATEMENT BY JAMES SELLINGS, STATIONMASTER, LONDON BRIDGE

The first I knew of it was when the van pulled up before my door. That is quite usual. There is never notice given, as Mr. Smiles will tell you. Three chests according to my signed document, the one weighing 98 lb., the other 92¾ lb., the third the same to within an ounce or so—look, it is written down here. They are bound in iron and take two men to carry them. After weighing, the chests were taken to the luggage van, Sergeant Spragg and Constable Harlow attending, and fastened up by Mr. Dauntsey and myself, using our separate keys, in the third of the three safes. I have done my duty in the matter and can say no more.

STATEMENT BY PETER DAUNTSEY, ASSISTANT STATIONMASTER, LONDON BRIDGE

The seals were unbroken, as I remarked, it being a particular duty of mine at this time.

* * *

Mr. Pardew sat alone in the luggage van, feeling the train roll under him. Behind the half-open door a few feet away to his right he could glimpse chimney tops, slatted roofs, the silvery grey of the river. The sight reassured him, for he knew that they must be travelling across the arches above Tooley Street. Drawing himself up to his feet and resting one hand on the metal stanchion that rose from the floor of the compartment to its ceiling, he began to say something to Dewar, speaking loudly above the roar of the wheels and ceasing only when he found that the man had gone. Gingerly, for he was conscious that a false move would send him plunging to his death beneath the arches, he reached out and fastened the door. This action both diminished the volume of noise and brought home to him the reality of his position. There was an oil lamp to hand, which Dewar had left, this he secured and lit before looking about him. At the far end of the compartment, a little apart from the handful of cases and travelling portmanteaux, he could see the three squat safes side by side against the wall. There was something about them—some quality in the dull gleam of the metal—that made him wish to reach out and touch them, but something else, too, that stayed his hand. Standing irresolute on the moving boards, he realised that he was struck with terror, and that, curiously, it was a terror of an abstract sort, and that its effect, though it remained with him always, was to displace the chief anxiety that occupied his mind and substitute it with other, lesser horrors that now came crowding in on him.

The first of these, he now acknowledged, was that he found Grace—Grace's presence, Grace's familiarities—intolerable. Whatever else might occur as a result of the night's work, he would have done with Bob Grace, and whether or not there remained an office in Carter Lane, Grace would certainly no longer sit in it with him. The thought cheered him, even though the greater terror still lurked behind it, and he consoled himself with it for a while, reaching as he did so for the travelling bags and, with a good deal of exertion, manoeuvring them to a place on the compartment floor about a yard from the three safes. There should be no more Grace to fret and trouble him—no, he should see to that. And then some queer remembrance, brought into his head perhaps by the glimpse of the rooftops of Tooley Street, stirred in his mind, and he recalled out of some distant corner of his bygone life a schoolyard, with grey stone walls abutting a landscape of low, forlorn hills, and himself in it, and an old gentleman whom Mr. Pardew had not thought of for thirty years saying something to him, and Mr. Pardew shuddered at the recollection, silent for a moment, with his hand over the clasp of the nearest travelling bag, until the sound of footfalls woke him from his reverie.

D. J. TAYLOR

At the sight of Grace, whose arms and legs seemed not quite sure of themselves in this confined space and whose face appeared to have squeezed itself into all manner of unnatural corrugations, the old gentleman and the schoolyard with its grey stone walls vanished instantly.

"Gracious heavens, man, you are drunk! You were at an alehouse before we came here. Is it not so?"

"Sir, I swear it's not. I'm as sober as Father Mathew. Indeed I am."

"I'll have no blacklegging, do you hear? You knew what this was about when we began it, and you shall stick to me."

Grace said something in an undertone, doubtless to the effect that there would be no blacklegging and he would stick by him.

"Now then," Mr. Pardew remarked, more mildly. "We shall get on very well if you do exactly as I say. What is the time?"

"Twenty-five minutes wanting to the hour."

"And Pearce and Latch?"

"Off in the cab half an hour since."

"You have seen Dewar?"

"Passed him in the corridor as I came by from first class, and gave him a nod."

Mr. Pardew nodded his head in acknowledgement of this. He knew that a bare thirty minutes was allowed to him for the accomplishment of the first part of his scheme, but he knew also that the chance of its succeeding was now immeasurably enhanced. In half an hour the train would stop at Redhill, its first port of call. In that time, if he applied himself to his task, he could achieve a great deal. Reaching into the first of the travelling bags, he drew out, one by one, an assortment of items carefully assembled by him in Carter Lane three hours before. A pair of pincers, a two-pound hammer, several boxwood wedges, a pair of scales (the last abstracted on the previous evening from the kitchen in St. John's Wood)—each followed the other onto a square of green baize cloth which Mr. Pardew had first laid out on the compartment floor. In so doing, he also laid bare the mystery of the cases' great weight. Each was crammed to the rims with quantities of lead shot bound up in paper packets. It was beautiful to see Mr. Pardew do this. He had the look of a craftsman, a blacksmith arranging his tools before the forge, an artist, even, bringing out his brushes and mixing a preliminary mess or two on his palette, and the consciousness that there was an artistry in what he did gave a flourish to his movements. And yet mingling with this was the sensation of absolute terror and foreboding: not that he might be discovered but that some crucial element in his scheme might be found wanting.

Two or three times in the deployment of his little armoury Mr. Pardew felt his hand straying towards the pocket of his coat. But he had a superstitious delight in completing tasks in what he conceived to be their proper order, and each time he managed to concentrate his mind on this preordained sequence. Finally, when the pincers, the hammer, the boxwood wedges and the scales (on which the flour of yesterday's baking still lingered) lay upon the green baize square, he fished inside the pocket, scrabbling his fingers into the cloth in his anxiety, and drew out a pair of keys. Apprehending that only one of the safes was fastened, he quickly inserted first one then the other key into their locks. There was a second's pause, during which Mr. Pardew tugged determinedly on the second key. Then the door of the safe swung open.

Grace, who had monitored the operations on the green baize square in a state of glassy-eyed bewilderment, like a man who watches a conjuror produce rabbits out of a tall hat previously exhibited as empty, contorted his face into an expression so extraordinary that Mr. Pardew, busy as he was about his work in the flicker of the lamplight, could hardly fail to notice it.

"What is it?"

"What if somebody comes?"

"Nobody will come. Dewar has the key. Did you not hear it turn a moment or so ago? We are sealed in until such time as he releases us. Well then?" For he saw that Grace's gaze was still bent in fascination on the interior of the safe.

"A man," Grace said slowly, not looking at Mr. Pardew as he spoke but at the floor, the ceiling and several other places besides, "a man could be hanged for this, surely?"

"Transported rather. This is not a capital offence, I believe."

"I wonder you can take it so easy!"

D. J. TAYLOR

"If we do not look to ourselves, there shall be no offence committed, and then we shall go back to London cursing ourselves for fools. You had better hand down one of those boxes, indeed you had."

With an effort, the muscles of his arms straining beneath his black coat, Grace tumbled the first of the three bullion chests out of the safe. The chests, he saw, were stoutly made, each circled by an iron band secured to the wood by rivets, and locked fast. The puzzle of how his employer might be able to break his way into the first of these sanctums rose suddenly in his mind, and for a moment he watched with interest as Mr. Pardew, holding the pincers in his left hand while his right felt for the iron band, sized up his quarry. The pincers, Grace again saw, had been filed fine, so fine as to render them useless for most ordinary work. And yet, as Mr. Pardew twisted with them here and there, Grace divined that they were remarkably efficacious in raising the rivets an inch or so from the wood in which they were embedded, and that such a raising had the additional advantage of causing the lock to lose its reinforcement. Within a short time, and working with what seemed to Grace particular dexterity, Mr. Pardew had conjured into existence a crack—not large but of sufficient magnitude for a man to be able to insert a sovereign into it—between the lid of the lower part of the chest at its front. Then, taking four of the boxwood wedges in one hand and the two-pound hammer in the other, he belaboured them into place in such a way that, when the fourth had been secured, he could jar the lock free from the lid.

Mr. Pardew, as he worked, was conscious of two things. The first was Grace's admiring stare, which, even though he despised the man, was not uncongenial to him. The second was a desperate anxiety lest in the heat of his task he should damage the chest. Knowing that the lock would be inspected, however casually, when the train reached Folkestone, he was careful to make it seem to appear intact. Neither did he allow any of the boxwood wedges to produce a crack that could not be hidden when the chest was resealed. It seemed to him, what with his admonition of Grace and the cautiousness of his preparations, that he had been at work for an hour at least, yet a glance at his watch assured him that a bare five minutes had passed. He gave a final tap

Kept

with his hammer at the fourth boxwood wedge, shook the lock with a little craftsman's twist of his fingers, and prised open the lid.

"D——n my eyes," Grace said.

"D——n them indeed," Mr. Pardew observed. Once in the course of some earlier professional undertaking—not, as it happened, a criminal one—he had been invited to inspect a stack of bullion bars in a bank vault. There had been a dozen of them, of no great size, smeared over with some kind of wax used in their manufacture, and Mr. Pardew, respectful though he was of the sum of money they represented, had not been overly impressed. Here, on the other hand, were perhaps fifty, each the size of a tobacco pouch, lying in four neat rows. Mr. Pardew took one in his hand and placed it on the set of scales. The result confirmed to him something that his eye had already judged: that in the first of Messrs. Abell, Spielmann & Bult's chests lay something like a hundredweight of gold. If Mr. Pardew's inner self exulted in this fact, he was careful not to let the external self show it. He merely set hastily yet methodically to work, removing the gold bars in handfuls, placing them into the first and smallest of the travelling bags, while calculating in his mind the weight of lead shot needed to replace them. When the bag was full and the exact equivalent of shot had been substituted for the purloined gold, Mr. Pardew consulted his watch. Assuring himself that perhaps ten minutes remained until the train arrived at Redhill, he carefully closed the robbed chest, hammered down the iron bands and tapped each of the rivets back into place. Then, from the pocket of his coat, he produced a taper, a stick of red wax and some circular discs of metal.

"What's them then?" Grace wondered.

"Dies," Mr. Pardew told him, beginning to melt the stick of wax over the flame of the oil lamp and allowing the liquid to drip down onto the first of the metal discs. "No one will know these ain't the merchants' stamps, not on Folkestone quay at dead of night, but sealed up they must be or what we've been about will be plain to everyone."

Almost at the moment that he restored the first of the bullion chests to the safe, Mr. Pardew was aware that the engine was beginning to lose speed. Extinguishing the lamp, he stood up, stretched his arms to their fullest extent and pushed the heavily laden travelling case into the centre of the floor.

"We shall be in Redhill in a moment. You had better crouch down in that corner—there, where the safe comes closest to the wall."

Grace did as he was bidden. Joining him, Mr. Pardew found that the corner of the compartment contained several pieces of ancient sacking. These they draped over themselves and lay half concealed in the darkness. Presently, as the engine slowed almost to a halt, they heard a key turn in the lock and became aware of Dewar stepping into the compartment. He did not exactly acknowledge their presence but could be heard moving cautiously to the door and throwing it open. There was a pause, a great hiss of steam from further down the platform and the noise of footsteps. "Where is it then?" Pearce's voice enquired softly out of the darkness. There was a thud and an exclamation, as of some heavy object being propelled into the arms of one who is startled by its weight. No more than a few seconds later, it seemed to the persons concealed beyond the safe, the door had been pulled shut once more and the engine was moving off into the night.

Throwing off his coat of sacking, Mr. Pardew reignited the lamp with a sulphur match and turned again towards the safe. With the first case of contraband removed from the luggage van, his spirits had risen. The springing of the second bullion chest was accomplished in half the time taken by the opening of the first. When he prised it open, Mr. Pardew found to his satisfaction that it contained packets of American gold eagles and French Napoleons. Once more he and Grace set to work to replace them with the exact equivalent of lead shot. The third chest, split open in a trice it seemed, so dextrous had Mr. Pardew grown in his trade, revealed more rows of yellow bullion bars. Pausing occasionally in the weighing of his bags of shot to pass a hand across his sweating forehead, Mr. Pardew sensed that Grace was growing restive. Presently Grace remarked, "Notice anything?"

"Only that we shall be stopping in Tonbridge in twenty minutes, by which time we had best have finished our business."

"There's more gold than we've got the lead for. What shall we do?"

"What shall we do? Why, we shall leave it in the safe."

Kept

"Leave it? What, prime gold just a-waiting to be took? Who's to know that it was us?"

"Who's to know?" Mr. Pardew's face, as he peered up from behind the glow of the oil lamp, looked devilish. "Don't be a fool. Did I not tell you the procedures? The safe will be weighed at Folkestone Harbour, while we sit here in the train waiting to go on to Dover, and these bags lie in the luggage van waiting for us to collect them. You might as well walk along the platform with a gold bar wedged in your hatband."

"I only thought . . ."

"You had better think nothing at all. Each of these bags is nearly full. We shall have trouble enough carrying them as it is. You had better take that broom in the corner there and sweep the floor. A child could tell that we had been at work here."

Looking at his boots, Grace saw that the boards of the compartment were covered with flakes of red wax and splinters from the bullion boxes. Whistling quietly to himself, he hastened to remove these traces of their activities while Mr. Pardew locked up the chests, hammered down the iron bands and secured their rivets.

"You've found your courage again, I see," Mr. Pardew remarked during the course of these labours.

"There was no courage wanting," Grace replied stiffly.

"Well, have some in store, for there is a great deal still to do."

It seemed to Mr. Pardew as he issued this warning that long hours had passed since they had boarded the train, trackless days spent labouring by the dim light of the lamp, that he was like some benighted troglodyte of legend, condemned to live out his days far underground. Looking at his watch, he saw that it was barely a quarter past ten. The safe now shut up and the two travelling bags placed inconspicuously in the corner of the compartment, he became, by degrees, more aware of his surroundings. Grace was squatting with his back to the safes, his face waxy-pale in the half-light. Cold night air had begun to steal up from beneath the floorboards. It was no longer so hot. Again, the train was beginning to slow.

"Where's this? I wonder," Grace mused, almost as if speaking to himself.

D. J. TAYLOR

Half an hour before, Mr. Pardew would have rebuked his clerk for his ignorance. His mind was racing on, though, reckoning up the several dangers that might await them in the next hour, and he allowed the spasm of irritation to pass.

"We are at Folkestone. Now, have a care that you do exactly as I say."

A moment or so before he judged the engine would halt, Mr. Pardew slid open the door of the luggage van six inches or so and peered anxiously out. The stretch of platform was deserted. Fifty yards away a lamp blazed above the stationmaster's office, but there were no other signs of life. Reaching to the compartment door, he found, as he had anticipated, that it was now unlocked, and that the train carriage into which it led was empty. Rapidly, he and Grace strode back along the train towards the first-class carriages. Gazing out into the darkness, Mr. Pardew saw a brace of porters and a gentleman whom he presumed to be a railway policeman moving sharply in the direction of the luggage van. In the distance Dewar's voice could be dimly heard. Mr. Pardew realised that his heart was beating very fast. Well, a few minutes more would see them in Dover, after which the fate of their enterprise lay in the hands of the gods. He folded his hands across his chest, looked disparagingly for a moment at Grace and then stared out into the Kentish darkness.

* * *

MR. ROBT. GRACE: HIS RECOLLECTION OF THE NIGHT'S EVENTS

He was a cool 'un, d——n him, that much must be allowed. No sooner are we stopped at Dover than it's back to the luggage van to collect our bags. Precious heavy they was, too, but we made it look as if there was just ordinary togs inside. There's the Dover Castle Hotel over the way—a tip-top place as I could see—and he says to me "What do you say to a little supper?" Naturally I'm game, so we sit ourselves down in the coffee room. While they're a-cooking of the food—broiled fish it was, and devilish good—he takes a wander outside. Never said

Kept

{ 361 }

a word to me, but I'd lay even money those keys are at the bottom of the Channel. And the hammer and the pincers and them dies, I'll be bound.

Very late it is now, and no one much about. Just a single waiter left at the bar of the Castle to take our money (Mr. Pardew tipped him a half sovereign, which I thought was rash) and shut up shop. London train leaves at one, we'd been told. There's a particular dodge we're going to play now. The dodge is that we've to come to the station along the quay from where the foreign boats dock, them that comes from Ostend and Calais. Coming up to the station entrance—pitch-dark it was, with only a light or two showing—he stops and says to me, "You'll need this, you know." And blow me if he hasn't somehow got the return halves of two tickets from Ostend to London Bridge. Just say that anyone's crying out over a robbery of the mail train—why then, here's proof that we'e been on the high seas all the time.

Inspector on duty at the station entrance. Stiff, tall cove of a kind I never did like. Looks at the tickets. Looks at the bags, tickets still in his hand. Looks at the two of us. I can feel myself wanting to drop the bag I'm holding and run, but Mr. P., as cool as a lettuce leaf, asks, is there anything the matter? Why yes, says the cove, where's the chalk-mark on these here bags saying they've been examined by the Customs back in yonder shed? Oh C——t, I thinks, how are we to get out of this one? They'll take us back to the blessed Customshouse and then there'll be the devil to pay. But Mr. P. just smiles as if it's the merest trifle in the world and says he don't think the water guard would thank him for putting them twice to the same trouble, for we came over from Ostend the previous night and have been staying in the town. Anyway, the cove calls his mate, says: better put these gents through the Customs again surely, than risk a stripe for letting them through unchecked. Mr. P.'s nodding, saying something about that night's steamer delayed, no question of us having just come over, and suddenly the tickets are back in our hands and we're through.

Getting onto the London train I nearly faint, I'm so far gone, but Mr. P. has some brandy and water in a sody bottle and that revives me. What happens then I don't much recollect, only that coming into *the Bridge, with the dawn about to break, blow me if there ain't a peeler opening the door of the carriage. Again, I'm rare to throw him down and run, but bless me if the chap doesn't ask if he can help with the luggage! Never did luck hold out so, only that it fell in the end, as it always does.*

Part Five

EASTON HALL, NEAR WATTON

A Jacobean E *plan house with three bays in each recess of the* E *and a bay beyond the* E *at each end. An hexagonal tower to the rear. The Jacobean house faces west and includes the library and the dining room. Fenestration later Georgian, and a bow window was added at the south end, with a new Georgian fourth bay at right angles, incorporating the drawing room. Todhunter's print, in* Fastes Norfolkenses, *predates this addition. A fine early C18 staircase has three twisted balusters to the tread and carved tread ends. It was here that James Woodforde upset himself on a winter's evening, having indulged too freely in his host's milk punch ("a vexatious incident, fair to embarrass me in the eyes of my host, yet Mr. Benny, an exceedingly courteous gentleman, received my apology very civilly"; James Woodforde,* The Diary of a Country Parson, *17 November 1784). Thomas Percival Benny was the seventh descendant of the hall's original owner. Eventually, Easton passed into the Dixey family, connections of T. P. Benny on his mother's side. An aquatint by Gandish, RA (1818?) shows the property in relation to an artificial lake, subsequently drained, commenced in Waterloo year. It was for some years the home of the celebrated naturalist James Chatterton Dixey, until his death, in mysterious circumstances, in 1866. Subsequently, the house was inherited through the Beresfords by the Kenyons. A Dornier bomber crash-landed in the outer park in 1942. At this point the property was in use as a boys' school. Now empty.*

BURKE'S AND SAVILL'S *Guide to Country Houses,*
VOLUME 3: EAST ANGLIA

CAPTAIN McTURK MAKES PROGRESS

The sensation caused in polite society by news of the train robbery did not die down in nine or even ninety-nine days. It was talked of at every dinner table in England and not a few outside it. The daily newspapers, naturally, could not be kept from it and devoted countless leading articles to the audacity of the villains, the boldness of the crime and the negligence of the authorities in allowing it to be committed. An august royal personage read of it in her great rooms at Windsor and summoned her ladies-in-waiting to discuss it. The Prime Minister heard of it as he sat at breakfast in the bosom of his family, shook his head and looked very grave. *Punch* satirised it most awfully in a burlesque in which the Home Secretary was kidnapped from a meeting of the Cabinet without anyone's noticing and a ransom then demanded for the sum of eleven pence three farthings, which his colleagues declined to pay. And subsequently that gentleman, made even more wrathful by a caricature of himself being abstracted in a sack by three footpads, summoned Captain McTurk to a meeting at the Home Office from which the police commissioner emerged two hours later with a look in his grey eye from which the very coachman recoiled. There had been nothing like it in the annals of metropolitan life for a decade, Captain McTurk was assured, and there would continue to be nothing like it until such time as the villains were caught, arraigned, rebuked and put behind bars.

As to the catching, however—let alone the arraigning, the rebuking and the putting behind bars—Captain McTurk was altogether at a loss. Assembling such fragments of evidence as could be found in the days following the robbery, he was aware that he knew almost nothing of its circumstances. Three chests of bullion, when taken from a safe in Paris and opened by the representatives of a French banking house, had been found to contain a quantity of lead shot. And yet when had the lead shot been placed in them? The chests had been weighed at London Bridge, at Folkestone and again at Boulogne and nothing amiss found. The seals of the chests had certainly been tampered with and the boxes forced open, but nobody could say for certain when the tampering and the forcing had taken place. The driver of the train and the guard professed to have seen nothing. In addition, Captain McTurk had interviewed such passengers on the train as could readily be assembled, the ticket collector who had taken their tickets and various other officials who had been in the vicinity, and discovered . . . nothing.

Having drawn, as it were, a blank in this preliminary investigation, Captain McTurk set out, as was his professional wont, to assemble the course of the operation in his mind. Having questioned the officers of the steamer and the officials who received the safe at Boulogne, he was certain that the crime had been committed in England. But how? Clearly, those who had taken the bullion must have smuggled it from the train in the guise of ordinary passengers. How had they done so? Captain McTurk had been assured by the bullion merchants that the weight of contraband was more than a single man—two men—could carry without difficulty. Had any passenger or passengers quitting the train at Folkestone been seen to possess cases or valises of an abnormally large size? Captain McTurk had demanded of those he interviewed. Here again he could get no satisfactory answer. The people had noticed nothing out of the ordinary course of events. The ticket collector deposed, mournfully yet righteously, that it was the custom of gentlemen who arrived at Folkestone late at night either bent on travelling to France or staying in the town to carry large cases. All this, Captain McTurk acknowledged to be true.

There were certain other questions, too, which he urgently wished to answer. How many felons had there been? Given the weight of the gold, Captain McTurk was inclined to think two or even three. And having abstracted it (and how had they abstracted it?), where had they gone? The newspapers confidently asserted that they had fled on the steamer to France, but Captain McTurk rather thought not. By his reasoning the men had either remained in Folkestone that night or departed it immediately for some other place in England. And here

D. J. TAYLOR

the trail, which had threatened to turn cold, grew suddenly warm. A policeman indeed, stationed at London Bridge very late on the night in question, remembered assisting two gentlemen lately debouched from a railway carriage with what had seemed to him an inordinately heavy piece of baggage, but the hour was late and the gentlemen so caparisoned in travelling cloaks that he could recollect nothing of them. A cabdriver, too, recalled picking up two men—again with pieces of heavy luggage—and depositing them on the edge of the City. Again, he could remember nothing other than both were tall, one stout and one with a prognathous jaw. Finally, there came a money changer near Blackfriars to reveal that very early on the following morning he had changed into sterling a quantity of Napoleons offered to him by a burly man in a travelling cape speaking in a low voice and showing every indication of wishing to conclude the transaction as swiftly as possible. Though he gave no outward indication of disquiet, these three pieces of information excited Captain McTurk very much. He ensured that representations were made to others of the capital's money changers. Banks were asked to examine their records for that day and the day following it in search of unusually large cash deposits. Nothing further came to light, however, and again the trail ran cold.

All these enquiries proceeded during the course of the summer. Though the sensation did not die down in nine or even ninety-nine days, it could not, by its very nature, be maintained at the same high pitch. Polite society was by this time in any case decamped to Baden-Baden or taking its ease on the grouse moors. The public likes variation in the criminal accomplishments offered up for its delectation, and it was thought that the murder of a nobleman by certain burglars engaged in the plundering of his ancestral seat rather had the edge on the robbing of the Folkestone mail. All this was observed by Captain McTurk, who did not apparently take holidays, sitting in his office in the square beyond Northumberland Avenue, sending Mr. Masterson out on his little errands and continuing to ponder the suggestions offered up by the day's post.

It must not be supposed that the other enterprises on which Captain McTurk had been engaged before the scandal of the bullion robbery had now been placed in abeyance. On the contrary, he continued to revolve them in his mind even as he sat attending to the Home Secretary's wrath or questioning the Folkestone ticket collector. It could be said, in fact, that Captain McTurk's mind, or that part of it which did not contain his wife, family and acquaintance, was a single stage populated by an ever-shifting cast of criminal actors, this one now moving audaciously into the light to say his lines, that one now subsiding gently into a throng of scene swellers. To this end, he had continued to take an interest in the death of Mr. Henry Ireland, had summoned a craftsman who might know something of the manufacture of life preservers and sent Mr. Masterson once more to Suffolk with instructions to submit all the evidence in the case to the closest reinspection. At the same time, he had recalled to mind the circumstances of certain other murders in which gentlemen had been bludgeoned to death. None of this, however, was of the slightest avail. The craftsman, bidden from his workshop in Mile End, shook his head over the bludgeon, agreed that it was a remarkable piece, speculated that it might have come from Prague or the region of the Danube, but could say no more. Mr. Masterson, though he spent a further week in Woodbridge and retraced his steps along the Wenhaston Road, was unable to add to the stack of lore he had brought back from his previous visit.

And then there came to Captain McTurk a stroke of luck of the kind that were it to arise in a work of fiction would have mesdames and messieurs the critics wagging their fingers at its improbability but that is nevertheless a welcome concomitant to many an official enquiry. The public had lately become somewhat exercised by the imputation of dishonesty to certain representatives of the metropolitan force charged with the supervision of police cells. It had been alleged, to put the matter bluntly, that no watch, wallet or personal item placed in the pocket of a suspect left in such accommodation at dusk was likely to be there at dawn, and an evening newspaper had caused much amusement by suggesting that any citizen who wished to know the time should hasten right away to a police constable, as that gentleman was certain to be in possession of a watch-and-chain. Captain McTurk had, of course, read these claims, or rather they had been shown to him, and been made angry by them. He did not dispute that some

D. J. TAYLOR

of them were true, but by no means all of them, he thought, and he determined when the chance fell to him to conduct certain investigations of his own.

Wandering one night through that part of the station headquarters in which prisoners are confined, he happened to encounter a constable who, it seemed to him, was very anxious to make his way past him along the corridor as quickly as he could. It seemed also to Captain McTurk that, as he came upon him, the man was in the act of transferring some hard, glinting object from his hand to the pocket of his coat. Demanding that the object—as he had foreseen, a watch—should be given up to him, Captain McTurk rebuked the constable and took the contraband up to his room to examine it at leisure. It was a large gold repeater watch, very cunningly wrought and not at all the kind of thing generally to be on display in the labyrinths beneath Northumberland Avenue. But Captain McTurk was less interested in the watch's provenance than in the inscription engraved on its reverse side. This reproduced the name of the gentleman who had originally owned it, and the name was *Henry Ireland, Esq.* Having read this, the police commissioner put the watch down on the desktop before him and whistled sharply through his teeth. He was not so sanguine as to believe that the discovery of Henry Ireland's watch would offer him any immediate clue as to how it had been taken from its owner, but he knew that in however small a way the trail had been renewed.

The prisoner from whom the object had been abstracted was fetched from his cell, brought wonderingly into Captain McTurk's office and ordered to give an account of himself. He was a miserable and wretched-looking specimen who, Captain McTurk now saw from the charge sheet conveniently provided for him by the former's escort, had been arrested for loitering in a somewhat suggestive manner, together with a package containing two files and a chisel, about the area steps of a house in Notting Hill Gate. His account of how he had come by the watch was offered up with no apparent hesitation. He had been engaged at cards with certain acquaintances of his in a tavern at New Cross and had won very heavily off one of these acquaintances, who, declaring himself short of ready money, offered him the watch in payment. What was this man's name? Captain McTurk demanded, his gestures implying, if they did not exactly guarantee, that a softer view might be taken of the files and the chisel were a satisfactory answer to be received. The man thought that his name might have been Pearce, and that he was in addition perhaps five feet nine inches tall and wore a whitish-coloured greatcoat. As to the address at which he might be found or what ravens fed him, the man at first professed himself ignorant, but then, thinking perhaps of the files and the chisel and the awful proximity of his person to the cell where the constable's hand had fallen upon his shoulder, suggested that he believed he might previously have been an employee of the South-Eastern Railway Company. This fact, though Captain McTurk inscribed it dutifully on the sheet of paper before him, did not immediately strike him as significant, but a description of Pearce was circulated to each police station in the metropolitan district.

And then, within the fortnight, came a second stroke of luck. The public, whose sensibilities at this time appeared to be in a state of permanent crisis, had also been exercised by the dreadful preponderance of illegal boxing matches. Three thousand persons, it was maintained, had recently assembled in some quiet Surrey field to watch the Tutbury Pet belabour the Dorking Chicken for a prize of a hundred guineas, despoiling the crops and trampling down the very fence posts in their eagerness to surround the ring. It was known in the county that a rematch of this Herculean encounter (the Chicken feeling rightfully aggrieved by his initial defeat and demanding satisfaction) would take place in a secluded corner of Epsom Downs. Infiltrating the course—from which the protagonists had already been spirited away in cabs—the police were concerned only to disperse the crowd that had gathered. In doing so they were obstructed by a drunken man who, protesting that he had had twenty pounds on the match and was d——d if he would see it taken from him, eventually became so obstreperous that he was hustled off into custody. The man's name, it was now determined, was Pearce. Additionally, a search of his clothing produced not only a quantity of banknotes but a pair of Louis Napoleons. Both these discoveries were immediately communicated to Captain McTurk. There may of course be excellent reasons why a man found drunk on Epsom Downs should carry such coins in his

D. J. TAYLOR

pocket, but Captain McTurk, cynic that he was, thought otherwise. Pearce was ordered to be sent up to London in a police carriage under escort. Captain McTurk, to whom the coins had come in advance, placed them on the table before him together with Mr. Ireland's watch and began to wonder, as he could hardly fail to do, whether the two might not have some very singular connection.

ESTHER IN LONDON

She sat on the edge of her seat in the corner of the third-class railway carriage and watched as the train rolled slowly into King's Cross Station. Dense vapour blew down over the grey platforms on either side of her, altogether obscuring the mighty overhang of stanchions and red brick, and for a moment she wished that she might not ever have to leave the carriage, which now seemed to her a very safe and comfortable refuge. Then, as the smoke began slowly to clear and the train juddered almost to a halt, this feeling left her, and she glanced out of the window at the moving figures now revealed behind the glass. There were but few of these—a guard in a peaked cap with a red flag stuck into his jacket pocket, a pale-faced old lady clutching a small child by the hand, sundry boys and lookers-on—but she stared at them with a curious intentness, supposing that the secrets of London, where she had never come before, must surely lie within their grasp. The carriage was empty, and Esther, realising that she had raised her knuckles to her mouth, such was the extent of her nervousness, was glad that there was no one to see her. From somewhere near at hand a whistle sounded, and all around her could be heard a tramping of feet and a slamming of doors. A silent and solitary figure amidst this cacophony of noise and movement, Esther reached up to the rack above her head for her luggage, released the catch of the door with her free hand and stepped down onto the platform.

Caught up instantly in the throng of people leaving the train, she darted anxious glances at those who moved alongside her, wondering if any of them knew her for what she was: a servant who had thrown over her place and disappeared without leave. The anonymity of her situation reassured her—she had half expected to find a policeman on the platform waiting to summon her back—and she perceived that she was merely a girl in a brown dress with a canvas satchel strapped across her shoulders and a travelling bag dragging at her feet (she had left the unwieldy trunk at the Hall), one of countless similar girls in whom she imagined the metropolis abounded. The thought of this solidarity cheered her, and she reviewed, for perhaps the twelfth time that day, the circumstances of her flight from Easton: waking before sunrise, her things concealed in the scullery the evening before; stealing down the back staircase in grey, unearthly light; abstracting the key from the ring in Mr. Randall's pantry to let herself out of the kitchen door into the silent dawn, her feet and the marks of the handcart leaving a trail on the dew-drenched grass. She supposed that Mr. Randall, alone among the Hall's servants, would regret her passing, and she brooded on this for a moment, conscious, however, that the Hall and its people had already begun to pass from her imagination and that her mind had begun to occupy itself with other things. On the wall above her was a poster advertisement showing a man in a tall hat and a morning coat drinking from a glass, and she marvelled at this thing, ten feet high, that stood in a public place inviting her, and those that passed with her, to admire it. Something in the man's gorgeous apparel—the set of his collar or his magnificent waistcoat—reminded her of William in his footman's uniform, and she added this to her store of imaginings and anticipations. And so, with the travelling bag bumping behind her and the dust from the platform hanging about her dress and forearms, yet intrigued and for the most part delighted by what she saw, Esther came at last to the station concourse.

Here, momentarily, her courage failed her again. Never in her life, she thought, had she seen so many people gathered in one place or moving so rapidly about their business. Behind her, three or four great engines smoked and steamed at the buffers. Porters ran on all sides propelling trucks of baggage. Before her lay almost a thoroughfare of coffee stalls, newspaper kiosks, barbers' premises, shoe shiners' stocks and the like. Before her, arranged beneath blue-grey air, she could see the immensity of London—a vista of tall buildings and church towers moving away behind the teeming street. The effect on her consciousness was so bewildering that she hesitated to venture out into this turbulent world, electing for a moment to stand quietly by one of the coffee stalls, drink a cup of tea and ponder her next course. William

Kept

had advised her to engage a cab, but this, even with the quarter's wages she had hoarded in her purse, was not something she could bring herself to do. She supposed that she should take an omnibus. The question was, which? Below the steps of the station was an expanse of stone pavement where half a dozen stood drawn up, their drivers and conductors recruiting themselves with tea, and this caravanserai she now timidly approached.

"Excuse me, sir. Can you tell me how I may get to the Strand?"

The demureness of her expression and the downward cast of her eyes as she asked the question commended themselves to the official.

"You want this one here, miss, as goes to the Eastcheap. Mind your skirts now, as you steps aboard."

Again, as she sat on the lower deck of the omnibus with the straw rustling beneath her boots, looking back at the towers and pediments of the station, a memory stirred within her—of the evening when she had first come to Easton Hall, of walking with her bag across the hill as the twilight rose and settled around her, and the dust motes rising up from the chalk path to strike her skirt, and of the faces turning to greet her as she came into the kitchen. Again, though, the outline quickly receded, like a dream that vanishes from the somnambulist's mind on the very moment of waking, to be replaced by the tall figure of William smoking his pipe as he lounged against the fence and saluting her as she passed by. And so she sat, as it seemed to her, very comfortably on her seat in the omnibus, joined presently by two workmen who chaffed her about her luggage and asked her, was she running away to marry a marquis? She ate a bun that she had purchased from the coffee stall, was carried away into the heart of the city and ceased for a moment to think of Easton Hall. The books that her mother had given her banged together in the bag at her feet, but she did not register that they were there. They were merely things that she carried with her, things that she would always carry. As to what her mother might think of what she was doing, the strictures that she could imagine her pronouncing left no impression. Her mind was too full, too crammed with the sensations stirred by her journey and the thought of what would await her at its end.

Quitting the omnibus at the bottom of the Strand—she knew that

D. J. TAYLOR

it was the Strand for she had taken the advice of the conductor—she stood by a cab rank staring at the tall buildings set back from the road, wondering who inhabited them and what went on within their walls. All kinds of people and vehicles passed her as she lingered—gentlemen in tall hats, inky boys with bundles of newspapers under their arms, clerks moving in and out of office doorways, costermen with their barrows—and she followed the ebb and flow of the crowd for a moment with her eye before once more taking out William's letter to study. This directed her, as she knew—for she had read it a dozen times—to a public house in Wellington Street named the Green Man, where she should ask for him at the bar and he could be sent for. Wellington Street, a passerby advised her, was very near. Accordingly, she fastened the satchel once more about her shoulders and, dragging the travelling case once again at her heels, set off along the dusty pavement. Her nervousness, she realised, had been replaced by a feeling of calm satisfaction: that her route had fallen out as William had predicted, that everything was where he had said it would be. It did not occur to her to wonder if he would be there to greet her or what she should do if he were not. She could see him in her mind's eye, just as she could see the dome of St. Paul's a mile and a half distant rising into the azure sky.

Wellington Street was empty of people. The Green Man stood at its farther end, and Esther, crossing the pavement to its open doorway, stared for a moment into its dark interiors, where a fat man stood at the bar caulking a barrel. As she entered, two or three other men sitting by the door turned to stare at her and she became aware of her face reddening. Never mind! William should come soon, and they would stare at her no longer.

"Yes, miss?" the fat man wondered.

"I was told to ask here for Mr. Latch."

"He's not been in today, miss, but the boy can be sent. Hi, Joey!" There was a commotion from the passage behind the bar, and a boy of perhaps twelve years of age with a strawberry birthmark half covering his face stuck his head through the doorway. "Take yerself off to Shooter's Buildings—yer know the place—and tell Mr. Latch there's a party asking for him at the bar. And now, miss, what will you take?"

Esther accepted a glass of lemonade and took it to a table that looked out through green glass windows to the street. She had finished half of it when there was a rush of boots upon stone and William came marching into the bar with the boy Joey loping at his heels.

"Why, Esther! So it is you! I am very glad to see you."

He came over and stood by the table, as if uncertain how best to greet her, finally extending his hand for her to shake.

"I am very glad to see you, William."

Looking at him as he stood before her, Esther noted the change in his appearance since they had last met. He was clad in a suit of black cloth, which she could see was a good suit made by a competent tailor, and the white stock around his throat was freshly ironed. In addition, there was a white carnation in his buttonhole. He had put on more flesh, she believed, indeed was better complexioned since the days when she had watched him running into the drawing room at Easton Hall or bringing in Mr. Dixey's parcels from the gig. William guessed the angle of her thoughts.

"They're a good set of duds, ain't they, Esther? I fancied you should like them. But what's that you're drinking? Lemonade? Come, you should have something better on a day such as this. What shall it be?"

Esther consented to take a glass of porter.

"Something stronger, miss?" said the fat man, when the order was conveyed to him. "Mr. Latch drinks Irish."

"Porter will do very well," Esther replied.

"This is my friend Miss Spalding," William said. He drank the whisky in a series of gulps. "Excellent stuff! But it don't do to have too much of it in the afternoon, eh? Now, Esther, you must tell me about yourself and the doings at the Hall. How are Mr. Randall and Mrs. Finnie? I wonder. And Sarah?"

As Esther explained about Sarah's disappearance, William composed his features into a look of suitable gravity.

"Run away, hey? That's bad, that is. Run away and you get no reference. But then, you have done the selfsame thing. You're looking uncommon well, Esther."

"I have nothing to complain of," Esther said, to whom the enormity of her departure from Easton Hall had now become apparent.

"That's the ticket. We understand each other, Esther, you and I. As for myself, I'm doing pretty well. Mr. Pardew—I have told you about Mr. Pardew?—is pleased with me and says I shall do well if I stick to it. And Bob Grace—that's Mr. Pardew's man-of-all-work—and me are regular pals. It's hard for a chap when he comes to a strange place full of things that he's not used to, but I fancy I shall make my mark in the end."

Listening to these remarks, Esther was aware that the confidence William had shown in his abilities when they had talked together at Easton Hall had increased in the six months that they had been apart. Rather than alarming her, as being evidence of vainglory that could only lead to a fall, she was conscious that she approved of his delight in his success and wished, insofar as she could do so, to share it.

"You do seem very prosperous," she told him, with her hand on the glass of porter.

"Ah, but you only ever saw me before in my footman's togs. Ugh, how I hate to think of them. But look, what say we go to my place? It's not much, to be sure, but I shall be getting an apartment before too long."

Esther nodded. There was a meaningfulness about his voice that she could not fail to apprehend, but she gladly allowed him to pick up her baggage and escort her out into Wellington Street. Turning into a lane of small shops and dreary office buildings, he led her eventually to a house whose lower window advertised rooms to let. William, who had said nothing during the course of their journey, now let fall the baggage and turned to her.

"I suppose you know," he remarked, "why we are come here?"

Again, Esther nodded her head.

* * *

Later they lay in a room beneath the eaves of the house, where pigeons clacked at the window and from beyond could be heard the implacable drone of the city.

"What a noise those birds make," Esther said suddenly.

"Regular little nuisances they are. Like rats with wings. And never

Kept

quiet. Not like the owls at Easton." William was silent for a moment. "What would old Randall say if he could see us now? Probably give us each a tract, eh?"

Despite her respect for Mr. Randall, the image that this conjured up in her mind was too much to be borne, and Esther laughed.

"Probably stand over us and fire off a regular prayer," said William, rather less amiably.

"I'm sure," Esther said, more demurely than she intended, "that he would see nothing he had not seen before."

"Nothing he hadn't seen! What do you know about it, Miss Pert?"

"I am not Miss Pert! And you should not mock Mr. Randall."

"And what about you?" William persisted, making a grab for the coverlet of the bed. "What have you seen that you never saw before?"

"Nothing to startle me. Men always think that a girl has no notion of the world."

"Well . . . perhaps they do. Hold on, though, it is gone six, and I have a fellow to see at eight. We had better go and eat, Esther."

But Esther had her own ideas about this. William's fireplace, she noticed, contained several utensils, while the cupboards gave notice of one or two things that could be drunk or eaten.

"I could cook something for us," she said, getting to her feet and standing uncertainly in the centre of the room, "if you cared to eat it."

"That's my good girl," William said.

Presently there came the sound of a kettle boiling and the jingle of cutlery. William looked on approvingly.

* * *

The next day was one of the pleasantest that Esther ever remembered having spent. She woke late, with bright sunshine streaming in through the window and the sound of music in the street below. It was a bank holiday, said William, whom she now saw staring at himself in a fragment of mirror, a razor halfway to his chin, and they could do as they pleased. The sight of William shaving reminded her of the situation in which she found herself and she lay for a moment considering it, recalling certain scenes of the previous day to mind and taking pleasure in their remembrance. Was there anywhere that she would care to go? William persisted. Esther sat on the bed considering. The values of the city both fascinated and repelled her, she had not the faintest idea, as yet, of how time could be spent there or how people amused themselves.

"I think I should like to walk about," she said, "and see the people."

William nodded, which, as the lower half of his face was covered with soap, produced a very comical effect.

"See them you shall," he said. "Why there will be thousands of them out on a day like this, I shouldn't wonder."

Esther's clothes lay on a chair at the foot of the bed. Seeing her gaze move towards them, William became self-conscious. "I have to see a chap at the Green Man for a moment," he explained, scraping the final twist of lather from his chin and pulling on his jacket. "There's water here in the jug, you know."

Glad of his consideration, Esther waited until he had gone and then washed and dressed herself, examining the contents of William's chamber as she did so. In truth there was not a great deal to see—a few prints of racehorses that hung on the walls, a wardrobe containing his clothes and a pile of what she supposed to be business papers seemed to be the extent of his possessions. On a shelf above the fireplace she found a piece of cloth that she recognised as having fallen from her apron string six months before. The realisation that William had hoarded this memento and taken it with him to London produced in her the queerest sensation, and she sat down on the bed once more with her dress only half buttoned to brood upon it. It was here that William found her ten minutes later as he sauntered into the room with his hat cocked back on his head and a sporting newspaper in his hand.

"Here's a stroke of luck," he said. "Who"d have thought the Tin Man would have won the Gold Cup after all that was said about him?" His gaze moved downward. "Why, what's the matter, Esther? Sorry you're here?"

"Not in the least," said Esther truthfully and hastily buttoning up her dress. "Is that a horse that you had money bet on, William?" she enquired timidly.

"You sound like old Randall. It was just a trifle, and now I have a couple of sovereigns to spend today."

Esther said that she was glad of it, and holding his arm descended into the street. Here it was as William had predicted. A great crowd of people swarmed here and there across the pavements bent on pleasure. The noise of the German band playing in the street grew louder, and the public houses had already opened their doors. They breakfasted at a pastrycook's—a very gay pastrycook's, with little Saturnalian rosettes decorating the trays of tarts and muffins—and wandered in the vicinity of Covent Garden for a while. Then, almost without realising that they were a part of it, they were caught up in a throng of people moving through the dusty roads in the direction of Holborn Viaduct.

"What do you say, Esther?" William demanded. "Shall we take a train and go to the Palace?" The look of bewilderment on Esther's face prompted him to explain. "The Crystal Palace. There's grounds to walk round and the glasshouse to see if you've a mind."

Esther thought that she would very much like to see the Crystal Palace, yet the size of the crowd on the station platforms frightened her. Men and women, all dressed in their holidaying clothes, with small children dragging at their heels, flocked around her with such eagerness to be off that she was thankful for William's protection. A man with a corked bottle protruding from his coat pocket stumbled into her, and William tapped him on the shoulder and told him that if he played that trick again he should knock him into next week, see if he didn't. Then, all of a sudden, the train drew in, and William was pushing her, much to her alarm, into a first-class carriage, where he remarked that it was a public holiday, was it not, and he should like to see the ticket collector as could turn them out. They sped away over the rooftops of South London, the universal glare of sunlight about them, the carriage dense with tobacco smoke, and Esther, nestling in the crook of William's arm, thought that she had never felt such delight.

Everything about the Crystal Palace—or "the paliss," as the other people in the carriage referred to it—impressed her. She marvelled at the grounds and the promenade, and the fair to which William escorted her, above which a white cloud of dust already hung kicked up by the multitude of feet, seemed to her even more splendid than the fairs of Norfolk. William, she noted happily, was all indulgence, standing at her side as she shyed for coconuts and handing her gallantly out of the whirligig into which they had ventured.

"I declare that's game of you," William pronounced. "Being flung about like a parcel in the back of a donkey cart. Tired, are you? Well, I shall be glad to sit down, as there's a fellow or two as half promised to look me up."

The realisation that the trip had been in William's mind all along, rather than—as she had first presumed—something presented to her which she could accept or decline, did not distress her. It seemed proper to her that William should have things that he wished to do and schemes that he wished to prosecute even in the midst of this new life. So she went very happily with him to the shilling tearoom to be regaled with tea, bread, butter and cake in hunches, while William skirmished dextrously for milk jugs and sugar basins and such items that needed almost to be fought for among the crowded tables. At the heart of the throng went serving girls, twisting this way and that through the tumult with trays piled high with crockery, and Esther sympathised with them in their plight.

"It's a shame those girls have to work on a day such as this," Esther said.

"I daresay. Why look! That is Mr. Grace coming now. And Dewar with him."

"Who is Dewar?"

"Why he's a little fellow that works on the railway. Tremendously down in the mouth, you know."

The two men, having ascertained through the crowd where they sat, were now bearing down upon them. Grace, Esther saw, was a big burly man, quite unlike his name, and wearing a dark suit that she thought must stifle him in the heat of the day. Dewar, who trailed behind him in the manner of a factotum, was shorter and stouter, with a crestfallen, woebegone face beneath hair that had at some point in its history been dyed.

Kept

"Why, Latch, taking the air I see," said Grace affably to William, and then, nodding at Esther in a way that suggested he knew all about her, "pleased to make your acquaintance, miss."

William caught the eye of a waiter, more chairs were brought and the four of them sat down together, William and Grace immediately falling into a subdued conversation that Esther could not for the life of her comprehend. The afternoon sun, she now saw, had reached its zenith, there was a band playing in the middle distance beneath the walls of glass that sparkled in the glare, the crowd in the tearoom had somewhat diminished, and this, together with her own fatigue, gave her the feeling of one plunged into a state halfway between wakefulness and dreaming. A woman of about her own age wearing a yellow frock cut very low and with a little boy clinging to her skirts came hastily into the room, looked about her for a moment, swore in vexation at not finding the person she sought and then hastened out again, and Esther wondered at the sorrow in her face and her corn-coloured hair. Dewar, she noticed, said nothing. Now and again Grace would look up from his talk with William and address a remark to him, whereupon Dewar would nod or shake his head as the occasion demanded, no other response did he care to make. He seemed utterly cast down.

"How's your wife, Dewar?" Grace flung out at one of these junctures.

"Bad as bad," Dewar rejoined shortly.

"Mind you take her something home then," Grace said, not unkindly, and went back to his deliberations.

Something about Dewar's miserable face and the set of his lank hair awakened a memory in Esther, and she said, "Did I not see you before, Mr. Dewar? You came once to Easton Hall, I believe."

Dewar turned to look at her as if he had only now seen her for the first time. "I believe that I did, miss," he said, and both of them were silent, she remembering the linen draped over the currant bushes as he went, he recalling Mr. Dixey in his study and the mouse stirring in his palm.

"But your wife is ill, they say?"

"I'm afraid she is, miss. Very bad."

"Has she not anyone to look after her?"

D. J. TAYLOR

"There's Mrs. Hook as lives above us promised to give her a bit of dinner. And then I shall be back by seven, I hope. But you're right, miss, it's a poor lookout for her."

He seemed anxious to say something more, only for Grace suddenly to tug at his shoulder.

"And you'll mark the time you're to be on the lookout, Dewar. Late afternoon—or never."

Dewar said he would mark it. Grace, his professional obligations apparently at an end, took another cup of tea prior to his and Dewar's departure and said that he hoped Esther was enjoying herself. "Yes indeed, sir, very much," she replied. The three men laughed good-naturedly at her simplicity, and Grace bowed and said he hoped he would have the pleasure of meeting her again. The afternoon wore on. So much dust rose up above the fairground that it was as if a white cloud hung above the heads of the coconut shyers and those who swung crazily on the pleasure boats. There was dancing upon the grass in which William was eager to take part, but Esther found herself too weary to do anything save cling to his arm. And so, by slow degrees, they came to the station and the train that would return them to Holborn.

There was but one embarrassment between them. It came as they sat in William's room in Shooter's Buildings and Esther, leaning over the fire to adjust the teakettle, remarked, "If you'll direct me, William, there is a letter I must deliver in the morning."

"A letter? What sort of a letter?"

"It was give to me by Mrs. Ireland. Mr. Dixey's ward that you must remember."

"Certainly I remember Mrs. Ireland," William said, somewhat sharply. "Who has she been writing to?"

Esther explained the circumstances of the letter's composition, William listening intently from his position on the sofa. He was especially interested in the mention of Mr. Crabbe's name.

"That's a fellow Mr. Pardew has dealings with. No end of a swell, that has a house in Belgravia. Grace knows all about it. But see here, Esther, it won't do. There's some mystery here as I won't be charged with the unravelling of." There was a curious tone in his voice, Esther

Kept

discerned, as if he knew more of Mrs. Ireland than he cared to reveal. "You had best give it up, indeed you had. Where is the letter?"

Wordlessly, Esther went over to the travelling bag which contained her mother's books and the little packet of documents—a letter from Lady Bamber, a "character" from a former employer—that she referred to as her "papers." It occurred to her that for reasons which she could not yet determine William wished to destroy the letter, and that if she wished to serve Mrs. Ireland's interests she must deceive him. This thought did not distress her. She merely accepted it as one of the necessary subterfuges that her situation demanded of her.

"What shall I do with it?" Esther wondered, bending over her bag.

"You had better throw it in the fire. Or wait—let me see it. Never mind, that will do very well."

For Esther, seizing an envelope from the bundle that she held in her hand, had cast it into the flames.

"I should not like to offend Mr. Pardew, you understand," William said, feeling that some explanation was required for this piece of high-handedness.

"Certainly not."

"Grace says he is a real tartar at such times. You ain't cross with me, Esther, I hope?"

Esther, knowing that the letter lay concealed among her papers while the note from Lady Bamber burnt to blackness in the flames, shook her head.

*   *   *

Easton Hall ran through her dreams. Each night her imagination dwelt upon some aspect of her time there, twisting what she knew to have been real into ominous, phantom shapes. Sarah and she were running through the wood pursued by some silent, fleet-footed creature that burst out on them continually from the trees. The master, turning to speak to her in the drawing room, had no face beneath his tall hat. Mrs. Ireland, sitting in her chamber, changed suddenly into a

D. J. TAYLOR

great bird that flew blindly at the window and scored its beak across the pane.

William suffered no such hallucinations. He said, "No, I don't think of the Hall. Why should I, unless it's to remember old Randall prosing and that cat Mrs. Finnie making herself disagreeable. It was a place I had that I threw over—that's all! As for being a footman, why if you offered me a pair of yellow plush breeches and a cockade for my hat, I'd laugh in your face. There's other things in life than holding a door open for ladies as has come to call, or running up three flights of stairs with the master's shaving water."

And Esther could not gainsay him.

THOROUGHNESS OF MR. MASTERSON

It was at about this time that Captain McTurk came upon a piece of information—to be exact, several pieces of information—that interested him very greatly. Some months had now elapsed since the audacious robbery upon the South-Eastern Railway, and many another crime had risen to enflame the imagination of the public, but still Captain McTurk was sanguine of his ability to extract *something* from the mystery. He knew—long experience had taught him—that there are many ways in which a guilty man may be induced to declare his guilt. He was aware, too, that very pertinent and significant pieces of evidence may not be immediately available to authority's investigating eye. Consequently, Captain McTurk kept his counsel and busied himself, in the midst of half a hundred other matters, with what he believed might be a useful line of enquiry—that is, establishing what had become of the very considerable sums of bullion abstracted during the course of the theft.

These, he had been able to confirm from Messrs. Abell, Spielmann and Bult, consisted of a quantity of gold bars, a nearly equal number of Louis Napoleons and a somewhat smaller amount of American eagles. Of the gold bars, Captain McTurk almost instantly washed his hands. Contraband of this nature, he knew, would be melted down, reconstituted and disposed of in half a dozen ingenious ways; whatever the nature of the transformation, it was now beyond his grasp. But the Louis Napoleons and the eagles he thought he might do something with. Accordingly Mr. Masterson was sent out into the City, instructed to renew the familiar acquaintance he enjoyed with certain majordomos of counting houses and banking establishments and urged to solicit their opinion with regard to certain transactions that these gentlemen might have witnessed in the course of the preceding two months.

Mr. Masterson, though he went about this task with his customary efficiency, was, if truth be known, less sanguine than his superior. He himself did not believe that the money was in London. He thought it was in Paris, Dresden, New York—in any city where it could be passed through the banking system with the least remark. But he was a thorough man, and he followed the instructions with which he had been entrusted to the letter. For a considerable part of that autumn, in fact, as the leaves fell on the grass of legal courts and inns and were gathered up in Charterhouse Square, as the lamps were lit earlier and earlier and the mud grew in the streets, Mr. Masterson went diligently about his business, and in the course of these enquiries he found . . . something. A bank in Gutter Lane, a most respectable establishment, indeed a bank with which Captain McTurk dealt in his private capacity, but not one engaged in much foreign business, had at some point in the late summer received into its safekeeping a considerable quantity of Napoleons. Mr. Masterson's heart was not immediately uplifted by this intelligence, for he knew that there are many excellent reasons why an Englishman should think it prudent to pay foreign currency into an English bank, but he was sufficiently interested to enquire of his informant in Gutter Lane who had done the depositing. Learning that the customer was the legal firm of Crabbe & Enderby of Lincoln's Inn, Mr. Masterson, though not a little awed by the lustre attaching to the name and reputation of Mr. Crabbe, decided that an investigation had better be made.

As it happened, Mr. Crabbe was away, attending upon some grand nobleman at his estate, but an obliging young clerk, himself not a little awed by the lustre attaching to the name and reputation of Mr. Masterson, looked into the matter and reported that the money had apparently (although it seemed that there was some faint mystery about this) been received from a firm of engineers in the north of England in settlement of a debt owed to one of Crabbe & Enderby's clients. And here Mr. Masterson did prick up his ears, for he knew that the debts of engineering firms in the north of England are generally paid in coin or notes of the realm. However, he did not remark this fact, but, having obtained from Mr. Crabbe's clerk the name of his client, he hurried back to Northumberland Avenue.

"The firm whose debt the money was intended to settle is called Pardew & Co.," he explained to Captain McTurk, as they sat in the gloomy office looking out over the stableyard. "A bill discounter, I believe, somewhere in the City."

Although the name of Pardew was familiar to Captain McTurk, he did not immediately choose to advertise this fact. Instead he contented himself with enquiring, "What was the name of the debtor?"

"A firm of engineers at Sheffield, I believe. Messrs. Antrobus & Co."

"Hm. Just oblige me, Masterson, would you, by stepping down to the reading room and bringing a commercial directory? Of the northern counties, if there is one."

Mr. Masterson did as he was bidden. The commercial directory was a large and compendious volume, but, as both men had suspected, it contained no mention of Messrs. Antrobus & Co. Whereupon Captain McTurk became intrigued, slapped his hand upon his thigh, shut his door, placed his feet upon the table and cast his mind back to a case that had occupied him at an earlier stage of his tenure in Northumberland Avenue and which interested him very much.

* * *

"Well, I have heard from Farrier," Mr. Devereux remarked to John Carstairs at about this time.

"Have you indeed? It must be a great trouble to him to answer his letters."

"It was more a case of the letter finding him. He has had the most tremendous adventures, I believe. Lost in a blizzard with his ankle broke, a wolf on his tail and the sled with his friends on plunged into the frozen river and all of them drowned."

"You don't say?"

"He was found half-frozen in the snow and sent back east to recover himself—see here! I believe he writes from Montreal—and the letter reached him there. But the upshot is that he declares himself most interested to read it and, having settled one or two matters to his satisfaction, intends to return home within the month."

Mr. Devereux and John Carstairs sat in the former's shabby chamber in Cursitor Street. Some little time had elapsed since John Carstairs had visited the premises, and the room seemed to him yet more sunk into decay. The bust of Lord Eldon boasted a layer of dust so thick that some enterprising person could, had he wished, have reached out and written his name on that jurist's august forehead, while the floor, quite half of which was carpeted with old legal reviews and law books, seemed to make a positive virtue of its untidiness. Mr. Devereux, on the other hand, was more cheerful than ever and poked up his fire and arranged his papers on his desk as if half a dozen clerks laboured in the broom cupboard and a ducal chariot lay drawn up at the kerb outside.

"Well," said John Carstairs, taking a look in quick succession at Lord Eldon, Mr. Devereux's variegated carpet and the somewhat cheerless prospect of Cursitor Street, "that settles it, I suppose."

"Settles it? I would hardly go so far as to say that. What exactly does it settle?"

It may as well be admitted that the resources of John Carstairs's mind were not concentrated on Mr. Devereux with the attention that was perhaps the lawyer's due. Only the previous afternoon John Carstairs had spent half an hour closeted with Mr. Dennison, while the Honourable Mr. Cadnam had kicked his heels in the newspaper reading room, and while that guardian of Southwark Conservatism had not exactly told his client that the nomination for the Borough was his for the taking, yet he had contrived to leave him with the impression that all was not lost. In this way John Carstairs had been persuaded to bestow on Mr. Dennison a cheque for fifty pounds to defray certain additional expenses which that gentleman had accrued in pursuit of his candidature. And then that very morning had come news—well, not news, but a rumour brought by a gentleman who had got it from another gentleman at his club—that Mr. Bounderby was . . . to be promoted? Transferred to another position? Proceeding to dignified retirement at Richmond? At any rate, to disappear from the Board of Trade in the very near future. All this had caused John Carstairs's mind to deviate wildly from the line on which it had been set following receipt of Mr. Devereux's summons two days before.

Kept

"What exactly does it settle?" demanded Mr. Devereux again, who perhaps had some inkling of this agitation.

"Eh? You must excuse me, Devereux. The fact is that there are certain things . . ." Intimate as he had become with the lawyer, John Carstairs did not quite wish to unburden himself to Mr. Devereux on the subject of the Southwark nomination. "What I mean to say is that if Farrier is returning to England, then something surely can be done."

"But what precisely? No doubt he may call upon Mr. Crabbe and take his opinion. No doubt he can write to Mr. Dixey if he has a mind to. But that will not get him any closer to Mrs. Ireland. Let a respectable medical man say that the patient is not to be seen, shock to her delicate sensibilities and so forth, and take it from me, seen she will not be."

Perhaps a quarter part of John Carstairs's mind still dwelt upon Mr. Dennison, the crack of that gentleman's knuckles, which seemed to him more obnoxious than ever, and Mr. Bounderby's supposed departure, but it was an influential quarter.

"Then I don't see what we are to do."

"Well . . . look here." Mr. Devereux gave the fire a tremendous poke and kicked over a couple of volumes of *Lorrequer's Commercial Law* in his eagerness to draw his chair closer to that of his guest. "There are one or two things that I have picked up in the course of my own business. In my line of work one hears a lot about the stamped paper that is going around the City. Well, let me tell you that a great deal of it is Dixey's."

"You don't say?" John Carstairs wondered again.

"I have seen no paper myself, you understand. But from what I hear he is properly in queer street. Trying to renew but at longer intervals, and then bringing in fresh bills to anyone that will accept them, which is not many in these circumstances. But that's not all."

"No?"

"No. I chanced to be in Oxford the other day. A particular affair called me there, and I'm an Oxford man myself, you know, whatever my present occupation may suggest to the contrary"—and here Mr.

Devereux laughed with what appeared to be genuine amusement. "Well, I was walking past St. John's College, and something prompted me to step inside and call upon the cousin of Henry Ireland's that inherited the Suffolk property. Mr. Caraway he is called, and you never saw such a man: I should think that to step outside his lecture room would be a great adventure for him and that a brisk walk would confine him to bed for a week. Anyway, he was pleased to send word that he would see me—I believe he thought I had come to trouble him about the property, and was relieved to discover that I had not. I was pretty frank with him—I always find that it pays in such matters—and he seemed quite agreeable to talk about Henry Ireland's will and its provisions."

John Carstairs was now all ears, and Mr. Dennison a mere speck in his mental cosmos. "Did he indeed?"

"Well . . . yes. It appears there were two sums of money. I suppose the greater part of it must have come from old Mr. Brotherton, for Henry Ireland was sadly embarrassed when he died. A certain sum to be laid out on Mrs. Ireland's care and treatment, to be administered by her trustees, and a second sum—Caraway would not say how much, but substantial—set aside for her private use."

"And so Isabel—Mrs. Ireland—is an heiress? At any rate the money is her own?"

"It is her own if the doctors say she is fit to use it."

"And now she lives in the house of one of her trustees, while her estate is administered by the other?"

"I suppose that is about the strength of it."

"And not in sound mind?"

"That is what we have all been led to believe, at any rate."

"It sounds d——d suspicious to me."

"And to me. When we have Farrier here, he may think there is a case to answer. Indeed I am certain of it." Mr. Devereux stood up from his chair and extended his arms in a gesture that, such were the dimensions of his chamber, nearly knocked Lord Eldon from the mantelpiece. "By the by," he remarked, "I hear you are coming out for Southwark."

"I . . . Let us say that it is not quite settled."

"I should say that it was," observed Mr. Devereux, who appeared to know everything. "Why, that Honeyman the brewer has given up politics, they say, to marry an earl's daughter. And as for Sir Charles Devonish, from what I hear the amount of his paper in circulation is well-nigh as great as your Mr. Dixey's."

D. J. TAYLOR

FLIES AND SPIDERS

"I s that you, Emma?"

"Yes, Mrs. Latch."

"I am still abed, I'm afraid. You had better bring me a cup of tea, if you would."

"Certainly, ma'am."

Esther lay in the big brass bedstead listening to the sound of the servant's footsteps descending the rackety stair. The fire, lighted three hours previously, had begun to go out, and she could feel the cold creeping back into the room. She remembered William standing with his back to it as he had bade her good-bye. Turning towards the bedside clock, Esther found that it was nine o'clock. She lay motionless for a moment or two longer, her gaze fixed on a jacket that for some reason William had left draped over a chair back, and then, rising out of the bed with an effort, got up and began to put on her clothes.

As she dressed she peered curiously out of the window. Six months in the metropolis had not dimmed Esther's interest in the complex organism of which she was a part. Even now, embarking on some solitary journey by train or omnibus, or out with William at some place of entertainment, she found herself mesmerised by the volume of people, the noise that they made and the costumes that they wore. "How many people live in London?" she had asked, a fortnight into her stay at Shooter's Buildings, and William had told her a million or maybe two, but what did it matter, eh? Curiously, his matter-of-factness reassured her, gave her confidence in his ability to forge out patterns in the city's immensity. For her own part, she remained awed, impressionable, and in the matter of windowpanes and the views from railway carriages ever inquisitive. Now, however, there was only fog pressing against the glass and a handful of plane trees all but lost in vapour, and she turned regretfully back, curiosity quenched by a memory forming in her mind.

William had said something to her before he went out. What had he said? That he would be back late? That there was a message for Mr. Grace that should be given to him if he called? She could not remember. Sitting on the bed once more to button her boots, she tried to imagine William's face as he had spoken the words, thinking that this would help her to recall them, but her head was still fuddled with sleep and she gave up the attempt, threw a last glance around the high, angular room and the window of fog and then went out onto the landing and carefully down the staircase.

A noise of fire irons being clashed together told her that Emma, the maid-of-all-work, had transferred her operations to the drawing room. The promised tea lay sending up steam from the kitchen table, and she drank it gratefully, the warm cup cradled in her hands, looking round the kitchen for signs of Emma's industry (experience had made her an exigent mistress, not a tolerant one) and finding them in the row of burnished saucepans and the tray of vegetables brought that morning from Shepherd's Bush market. Emma's wages were twelve pounds a year, and this both alarmed and comforted her, for she knew that six months before she had been earning the same sum herself, casting the same covetous eye over the remains of a joint that Emma cast as she carried it back from the dining-room table.

The noise of clashing fire irons had now given way to a dull thudding sound suggestive of a mat being belaboured with a stick. A double rap at the door announced the arrival of the postman, but Esther, going to investigate, found only a single letter marked *Urgent: Mr. Wm. Latch*. In any case, as she reminded herself, no one ever wrote to her, for with the exception of her mother no one knew where she was. Returning to the kitchen, she poured a second cup of tea from the pot which Emma had left stewing, examined the bowl of lump sugar to assure herself that it had not been pilfered from and took the cup and saucer into the parlour, where she sat down immediately in a chair and began to brood.

She became aware, without consciously registering the fact, that she was thinking of William. This did not surprise her, for she knew that

D. J. TAYLOR

this was, had been for as long as she could remember, the single topic on which her thoughts ran. In the half year since she had left Easton Hall, she had come to acknowledge that William, if not the paragon of her imaginings, was a reasonably fair-minded and unexceptionable specimen of male humankind. This realisation, which had come gradually upon her, did not distress her, for she knew—years of observation had taught her—that there were worse than William, who did not at any rate mistreat her, take conspicuously more than was good for him to drink or swear more than ordinarily. Evidence of his regard, moreover, lay everywhere around her—in the house in which they lived, the third of a row of dwelling houses known as Cambridge Villas, in the person of Emma, whose deference Esther still found highly agreeable, and in the half-dozen dresses and other items of clothing, newly bought, that now constituted her wardrobe. In all, Esther declared herself more than satisfied with William. To be sure, the "Mrs. Latch" with which Emma daily saluted her was a fiction—and she believed that Emma knew it to be a fiction—but, again, this did not distress her for she knew it to be a consequence of the step she had taken and the world in which she now moved and had her being.

And yet there were mysteries pertaining to her new life that she could not fathom, no matter how hard she tried. The first, and the most pressing to her mind, was the nature of William's business, how he came by his money, everything in fact that occupied him in the many hours that he spent beyond the walls of Cambridge Villas. Undoubtedly, he worked for Mr. Pardew—he was "Mr. Pardew's man," he told her proudly—and Mr. Pardew, she understood, was a bill discounter. Esther knew about bills—they had not been altogether absent from previous establishments in which she had worked—but what William had to do with their negotiation and collection she could not determine. Mr. Pardew she had met but once, at a house to which William had escorted her in Kensington—a civil old gentleman, she had decided, with a jutting jaw, who had let fall the single remark that it was a fine day. Others of Mr. Pardew's satellites—Dewar of the melancholy visage and a sharp-faced man named Pearce—she encountered but rarely. It was Grace that she saw most often and with whom, indeed, William seemed to spend the larger amount of his time. To

Kept

meet with Grace, to talk with Grace, to plot with other persons in Grace's company: these, so far as she could establish, were the principal occupations of his day. To this end, he went (she had picked this up from stray scraps of his conversation) on boat trips to Greenwich, to an office in the City—quite where in the City Esther knew not—and half a dozen other places. Yet the nature of the business on which he was detained she could not begin to elaborate.

"William," she had asked at the end of the first month of their association, having already meditated on the subject for some time, "what is it that you do all day with Mr. Grace?"

"What do we do?" William did not seem displeased by this enquiry, nor indeed by anything, that she asked him. "Why, we are Mr. Pardew's men, you know, and we do his business."

"Does that mean that you collect his bills? Or do you sit in his office? It is only interest that makes me ask."

"Well, now . . . not exactly. Today he and I were in Southwark, where we had an affair to settle, and then we had Mr. Pardew's instructions to see a party at the Green Man."

"And all this is to do with money?"

"Well, yes. That is . . . not exactly."

More than this William would not say. Esther, seeing that some mystery hung over his silence, forbore to ask. And yet her curiosity was roused, still more at the time three months ago when they had exchanged the modest eyrie in Shooter's Buildings for the comparative splendour of Cambridge Villas. Of the financing and maintenance of Cambridge Villas—it was rented at forty pounds the half year, for Esther had seen the receipt—William said not a word. He merely informed Esther of the change of lodgement, engaged a wagon for the transfer of their possessions and the deed was done. There were other changes that Esther noted at this time, quite apart from their removal to Shepherd's Bush. One was William's habit of darting up from his chair if a knock came at the door. Another was the look of vexation that passed across his face if he judged that a stranger was staring at him in the street.

"You won't guess who I saw today, Esther," William exclaimed one

D. J. TAYLOR

evening at about this time, standing in the parlour with the dust from the street clinging to his clothes.

"No. Who?"

"Sarah! I was stepping out of the Green Man with Mr. Grace, and there she was, walking up Wellington Street towards me. It gave me quite a turn, I can tell you."

"What is she doing in London?" Esther wondered.

"Ladies' companion. Upper servant. That kind of thing, she said. I took her address, so you must go and see her, Esther."

"I should like to," Esther said truthfully.

In the event, the piece of paper with Sarah's address turned out to have vanished from William's pocket—it was quite mysterious, William declared, how it should have disappeared—and this desirable scheme had perforce to be abandoned.

Grace was frequently seen at Cambridge Villas. He had a habit of arriving in the early evening for supper, sleeping the night in the back bedroom and being found in the kitchen cooking himself an early breakfast in a frying pan.

It was with Grace, and at Cambridge Villas, that William had commenced on the most curious undertaking of all. Coming back to the house one afternoon after an excursion to Shepherd's Bush market, she had found a quantity of dark, rectangular bricks piled up on the kitchen table, together with a large pair of bellows. As she examined them, William came in from the parlour.

"Why, William, what are these?"

"These? Why, they are firebricks. And that is a pair of bellows unless I am much mistaken."

"Firebricks?"

"Well . . . yes. The thing is that Grace and I have decided to go in for the business of making leather aprons."

"Leather aprons?"

"I declare you sound like a parrot, Esther. Yes, leather aprons. The fact is that we have some capital secured between us, and this seemed the best way of laying it out. Grace knows all about it."

William explained that they intended to carry out the work in the back bedroom. As this involved the generation of a great deal of heat, it would be necessary to remove the stones from the hearth and replace them with firebricks. He added that leather aprons were valuable items and much sought after, and that they fully intended to make their fortune. And yet Esther could not help noticing that the project was remarkably short-lived. A week, perhaps, was spent in this endeavour, during which the house grew so hot that Esther frequently retired into the kitchen. Afterwards nothing more was said of it, and the back bedroom once more became Grace's occasional sleeping place and a store for the few things they had brought with them from Shooter's Buildings. Going in there on some errand in the days after the work had ceased, Esther found that the floorboards next to the hearth had been scorched quite black.

The tea had gone cold in her hand. Starting up in her chair, Esther became aware that the morning was now well advanced. Beyond the window the fog had risen, to be replaced by a weak and watery sun. The thoughts of William, Sarah, Bob Grace and the charred boards in the back bedroom still turning in her head, Esther went upstairs to her room and sat once more upon the bed. Driven by an instinct she did not quite comprehend, she got up and moved to the wardrobe where William kept his suits of clothes and plunged her hand into the pocket of the nearest. There was nothing in it, however, save a solitary guinea piece, which, having inspected it for a moment or two, she somewhat guiltily replaced. The instinct continued to oppress her, and presently she went over to a trunk that lay in the corner of the room and returned with a small packet of papers. Among these was the letter that Mrs. Ireland had entrusted to her on the day before she had left Easton Hall, and she examined it carefully, allowing her mind to wander over the scenes it conjured up. Again, somewhat guiltily, she replaced the packet in her trunk, having first concealed the letter among several larger items, and retraced her steps to the vestibule. Here she selected an umbrella from the basket that contained William's walking sticks and went in search of Emma, now at work in the kitchen.

"Emma! I am going out for an hour or two."

"Yes, ma'am."

D. J. TAYLOR

"If Mr. Latch returns, you had better say that I shall be back in the afternoon."

"I can do that, ma'am."

This instruction was superfluous. William, once he had quit the house after the breakfast hour, was never known to return to it before the evening. Leaving Cambridge Villas, the umbrella swinging restlessly in her gloved hand, Esther wandered at first in the direction of Shepherd's Bush, where there were certain shops she might examine and certain necessary purchases she might make. The weather was less forbidding now, and she walked more rapidly, with a sharp eye for her surroundings and the people she passed, yet she knew that her journey had no obvious motive. Gradually, Shepherd's Bush market having no charms for her, she found herself moving eastward.

Eventually, she stepped onto an omnibus which took her to the Charing Cross Road, and having alighted halfway along this thoroughfare—dense now with the noise of wagons and carriage horses stamping their feet as they waited at the crossings—continued into a vicinity that was familiar to her from her days in Shooter's Buildings. It occurred to her that such wanderings might bring her to William, much of whose business was still conducted in this former territory, but she forbore to approach the entrance to Wellington Street or put her head in at the door of the Green Man and instead walked along the Strand in the direction of Fleet Street. The memory of having come this way six months before now assailed her, and she bit meditatively on her lip. The tap of her expensively shod boots on the pavement reminded her of the shabby footwear she had worn that day, and she marvelled at the transformation that had come upon her. There was a flight of steps to her left leading down into a little shabby courtyard, and here a young woman of about her own age, rising to the topmost step, stopped and regarded her keenly.

"Esther! Is that really you?"

For a moment Esther could only stare at the girl's smiling face.

"Sarah! What a pleasure it is to see you."

Sarah continued to examine her wonderingly. "Isn't this a splendid piece of good fortune? But what brings you this way?"

Esther outlined, without any great conviction of motive, her journey from Shepherd's Bush. Sarah grasped her elbow.

"But I would scarcely have recognised you in your finery. You are looking very well, Esther."

"Nor I you."

Esther looked closely at her friend as she said this. In her six months in the metropolis she had acquired sufficient sophistication to comprehend that whereas she, Esther, was dressed expensively and respectably, Sarah's attire was perhaps a trifle too overstated for the season and the time of day.

"But come, dear, we must sit and talk now we have stumbled upon each other. You are in no hurry?"

"Not at all. I—"

Betraying by the manner of her walk her familiarity with the street and its environs—a glance into a shop window here, a dart across the pavement there—Sarah led them to a decent-looking restaurant bar adjacent to St. Bride's Church.

"The clergyman will want to come out and chase us away, I shouldn't wonder," Sarah remarked mysteriously. "Are you still a religious girl, Esther?"

"I suppose not," Esther replied, acknowledging that she had not ventured into a church since her arrival in London.

"They are such flats, to be sure, those parsons."

"What is a flat?" Esther wondered.

"Why, a gaby, a young innocent. Like Margaret Lane, to whom Raikes said that he had shot the seraph and she believed him."

All traces of Sarah's previous melancholy had vanished, Esther noticed. Sitting in the window of the restaurant bar, with one dainty boot escaping from the folds of her skirts, she seemed in the highest of spirits.

"No," she explained, in answer to Esther's question, "I had a bad time of it when I first came here. Indeed I stayed once in a boarding-house in the Borough, where I scrubbed the stairs for my keep. But now I am with Mrs. Rice, and all is well with me."

"Who is Mrs. Rice?"

"She is a widowed lady who lives in Kennington, and was married once to a sea captain, and I am her companion, you know, and have all the ordering of the meals and the carriage to take us driving, and it is all very pleasant. But Esther, what is all this about William?"

Dazed by the rapid flow of information that had been conveyed to her, Esther could only repeat mechanically, "What is all what about William?"

"You knew that he had seen me? Indeed, I have seen him several times for I am often come this way on business."

"On business for Mrs. Rice?"

"Well, yes—that is, in a manner of speaking. But is it true what they are saying?" She drew her head closer to Esther's. "You mustn't mind telling me, dear, for I know when a secret is to be kept."

"Is what true?" Esther said blankly. "What secret is to be kept?"

"Oh, I did not mean to upset you. Truly I did not. Only you know that William is often seen about with that Mr. Grace?"

"Mr. Grace? Yes, I know of him."

"I never could abide that Grace. Well, they are saying . . ."

"Who is they?" Esther wondered in bewilderment.

"Why, Mr. Farrow that keeps the Green Man for one. Dear me, I hardly like to tell you if you really do not know, but—you have heard talk of the bullion robbery in the summer? Everybody has been speaking of it."

"The mail train going down to Folkestone? Yes, I have heard of it."

"Dear me, it cannot be that you do not know—but they are saying that Grace—I cannot speak for William, of course—was in some way concerned."

"You are saying this to hoax me, Sarah—you are indeed."

"Certainly I am not. Why, let me tell you what I myself have seen. I was at the Green Man a fortnight ago—I have—business—that occasionally takes me there—when I saw Grace pass a French coin, one of those big Napoleons, to Mr. Farrow, and heard Mr. Farrow say that he would need to mend his bellows to deal with such an item."

Esther became aware that her hands were gripping the tabletop before her so tightly that it seemed almost that the wood must break apart in her hands. She said, shortly, for it was the only thing she could think of saying, "I am sure William has nothing to do with this."

"Very likely not. It is that Grace, I am sure."

"He is Mr. Pardew's man, in any case. The bill broker that has an office in Carter Lane."

"And Grace is Mr. Pardew's man too, dear. Why, I declare that they are like perfect brothers together. But come, let us talk of something else. Indeed, that man over there has been staring at us these five minutes past. How vulgar people are!"

They talked idly for a moment or two more, but Esther had not the heart for conversation. Beneath her meek exterior she was consumed with nervous anxiety. That William, her William, should be spoken of in connection with this great crime seemed to her a terrible thing. The most terrible and unjust thing she had ever known. And yet as Sarah continued to put questions to her, to which she replied only in listless monosyllables, she was forced to consider certain incidents to which she had been party, certain fragments of talk passing between William and Grace that had come her way. All this frightened her further, and yet she was forced to acknowledge that the alarm was not disagreeable to her, that it gave a piquancy to the situation in which she found herself.

As her mind worked in this way, her interest in what Sarah was saying altogether lapsed, so that the other remarked, "You are out of sorts I daresay, dear, and would sooner be alone. But now we have found each other, we must not give each other up again."

"What is your address?" Esther asked dully.

"Mrs. Rice says she is tired of the house and means to sell it. You had better ask for me at the Green Man. That is the best way, I think."

Standing on the corner, the bells of St. Bride's Church as they struck the hour quite obscuring their farewells, Esther watched her friend depart along Fleet Street, hobbling slightly with the odd irregularity of her gait. Thirty yards along the pavement a fat man with a red face and a waxed moustache stood staring into the window of a gentlemen's outfitter, and Sarah stopped to speak to him. Something in her gestures now conveyed to Esther what trade it was that brought her to the region of Fleet Street in her best clothes on an afternoon in November. Not wishing to see the result of this chance encounter, she turned on her heel and moved disconsolately away.

Returning to the house in Shepherd's Bush an hour later, she discovered that William had sent word to say that he should not be back until morning. It was by now nearly four o'clock, and the vestiges of daylight had already begun to recede. Beyond the kitchen window dirty yellow fog was beginning to creep back into the dreary garden, and she sat in a chair and watched it, thinking all the while of William, Sarah and the events of the morning. A thought struck her, and she moved silently up the staircase to the landing, here proceeding past her own room and into the back bedroom, not inhabited since Mr. Grace had last slept in it a fortnight ago. Here the atmosphere was cold and damp. A jug of stale water stood on the dressing table, and she trailed her fingers in it for a moment, brooding over the task that she had set herself. Then she bent down and, resting one hand on the iron fender, stooped to examine the hearth. This, it occurred to her, was unlike any other hearth she had ever seen. The firebricks lay piled up around its interior where formerly the ordinary hearthstones had been. Beneath them a steel plate of some kind had been fixed to the floor. It was not, however, either of these novelties that drew her attention, but the boards on either side of the hearth. These were scorched almost black with heat, indeed at some points altogether burned up, the wood itself turned into a dark mass like charcoal. Squatting now on her haunches, she ran her hand curiously over the boards. They were not, as she had first assumed, quite uniform in their appearance for stuck in the surface here and there were several fragments of some yellowy substance. After a moment more, Esther ran her finger over the wood and gently prised one of the fragments away with her thumbnail, placed it carefully on her palm—it was perhaps the size of the head of a pin—and inspected it closely. Whatever the metal was, it seemed clear to her that it had at any rate undergone some melting process in the hearth.

She squatted there for a long time with the yellow fragment in her hand. There was a brooch on the bosom of her dress that William had bought her a month since, and she wondered if the money that had purchased it had been stolen. This thought gradually worked upon her to such an extent that she unpinned the brooch and placed it on the charred board before her. In this way, another long period of time passed. She was woken from her brooding by the sound of the church clock striking five and a realisation that the pain in her legs was becoming unendurable. The room was now quite dark, she saw, and the landing beyond wreathed in shadow. It occurred to her that she could not stay here forever, that she should find some occupation by which she could pass the next few hours. A part of her wished that William was in the room with her, and another part—perhaps the larger part—was grateful for his absence.

After a few more moments of reflection she got up and, walking carefully down the dark staircase, went into the kitchen and lit a lamp. Then, with the lamp in her hand, she climbed the stairs once more and turned into her own room. Here, again, she delved into the trunk containing her papers and emerged with Mrs. Ireland's letter. The two things that preyed upon her mind were, she now acknowledged, connected. The connection, she once more acknowledged, was William. Again she wished that William were in the room next to her, and yet she shrank from the questions that she knew she would wish to ask him. The room, the bed on which she sat, the mirror by the wall in which she glimpsed her reflection—all these things were suddenly distasteful to her, and, pressing the letter into the pocket of her dress, she carried the lamp hastily downstairs. Still for a moment she stood uncertainly in the hallway. A sound came to her ears, and she realised that it was a footstep beyond the door. A sudden apprehension overtook her, and she shrank back into the corner of the vestibule, her face averted from the turning handle, and it was thus that William found her as he stepped hastily into the house, his silk hat pushed back from his forehead and a little cloud of condensation hanging about his features.

"Good gracious, Esther! You seem quite taken aback to see me. Whatever is the matter?"

"I did not think—Emma said—that you would be back until the morning."

"A man may change his mind, you know," William said easily. "The

D. J. TAYLOR

fact is that there is something of mine that I cannot do without, and I have to fetch it. There, will that satisfy you?"

He was an astute man in his way, and he knew, as he said this, that his return was not the cause of Esther's alarm, that there was something that agitated her beyond his unlooked-for knock at the door.

"Whatever is the matter?" he said again, pressing his hand against her arm. "Why, you are trembling like a leaf."

She felt the pressure of his hand without seeing it. Her eyes were searching his face, which seemed to be unnaturally pale in the half-light of the hall.

"I have seen Sarah," she said.

"Sarah? Sarah Parker? What did she have to say?" Esther watched him as he said this, and it seemed to her that his face was paler still.

"She said"—Esther halted, for the words would not properly form in her mouth—"she said that you and Mr. Grace had stolen a great sum of money."

"Did she?" William laughed. "Then she is a greater fool than I took her for, and when I next see her she shall be told so."

He made to move past her into the body of the house, but she clung onto his arm and restrained him.

"Oh, William! I have been up to the back bedroom—where you and Grace were at work—where the hearth is all scorched—and there are pieces of gold on the boards."

"It's a lie! Sarah has been filling your head with nonsense, and you are fool enough to believe her."

"But, William—oh!"

She felt rather than saw his hand strike her cheek. The smart of it did not so much hurt her as startle her, and she stood for a moment rubbing her palm against the side of her face, altogether bewildered by the sensations that stirred within her.

"I should not have done that," William said with a curious remoteness, as if he were speaking to himself. "But it is hard to bear such things—there!"

Again she was startled by the violence of his embrace, and she let out a little cry not of fear, exactly, but of some emotion that she could scarcely identify. Just as the thought that her brooch was contraband had failed to shock her, so she submitted—not unwillingly but with a curious feeling of excitement.

"That's my good girl," William said, after a moment had passed. "Now, do you believe what Sarah told you?"

"I do not know what I should believe." Her head was still against his shoulder. "But, William, are you in danger?"

"Nothing to speak of. But, see, I must be gone from here. Only for an hour or so, but there are things I must do."

"Oh, William, if you would only stay. Promise me you shall."

"I can't, Esther. A couple of hours. I promise you. Look"—he caressed her with his hand, and she followed the movement of his fingers wonderingly along her dress. "Say you shall be here with supper on the table and a jug of beer on the hearth and I shall tell you everything."

"That is an easy thing to promise," Esther said, her eyes alight.

"Well . . . perhaps it is. Wait—"

Esther stood meekly in the hallway as he strode up to their bedroom. Here the sound of cupboards being opened and shut could be plainly heard. Then he hurried back down the staircase, pausing only to rest his hand upon her hair.

"I'm sorry that I struck you, Esther."

"It is nothing," she said.

When he had gone she moved into the parlour and sat by the fire in a reverie. Curiously, the thoughts that rose in her head were not of the previous five minutes but from far back in time. In her imagination she was back at Easton Hall, hanging out linen on the currant bushes before the kitchen garden, with the sun slowly declining over the edge of the wood and the cries of the rooks echoing in her ears. She brooded over this picture for some time, the faces—William, Sarah, Mr. Randall, the master in his black garments—rising and falling before her, until she became aware that an hour had passed, the fire had burned low and that the evening was well advanced. Hastily, she donned her coat and bonnet and, purse in hand, went out in the empty street. A walk of three minutes brought her to a row of shops, where she made various necessary purchases: a particular sweetmeat that she knew William favoured, a particular relish that might garnish his beef. Then, stopping at the public house at the end of the row, whose entrance emitted an enveloping glare of yellow light, for the filling of her jug, she sped away home. The house was dark and the silence within broken only by the tick of the clock. Swiftly, she placed her purchases upon the kitchen table and went to light the lantern in the hall. There was a noise beyond of footsteps approaching the door, and she went eagerly to open it.

* * *

In the region of Newington Butts, hard by the Walworth Road, squeezed in behind a pair of factory chimneys and altogether dwarfed by a gasometer lately installed by an optimistic gas company, lies a row of mean little houses, very tottery and shaky in their appearance—as if they were about to tumble over and might need propping up with some giant crutch—named Bright Terrace. From an upper room in one of these properties, at a window quite half of whose panes had fallen away and been stuffed up with rags and pieces of old brown paper and beneath which the wind passed unhindered, Sarah sat looking out across the dismal street. An hour had passed since she had concluded her transactions in the Strand—it was now about four o'clock in the afternoon—but she had not yet divested herself of the costume in which she had sallied forth that morning or indeed even taken off her bonnet. Instead she crouched almost motionless in an armchair looking first at the street, which was altogether devoid of human life, then at the two white hands that lay in her lap and finally at the mantelpiece a yard or so from her head. There was nothing remarkable about the mantelpiece other than the fact that it supported a tea caddy with the representation of a royal personage on its side, yet an onlooker who sat beside her might have observed that the gloomy street and the pair of pale hands held no joys for her and that it was to this unremarkable object that her gaze returned.

The room in which she sat was perhaps more commodious than the servants' quarters at Easton Hall, but not much better furnished. There was a stout iron bedstead jammed up against the wall, a little wardrobe and an occasional table on which reposed a water jug and a basin. A handful of coals—very small coals they were—lay on a sheet of paper in the grate, but the fire had not yet been lit. Upon this somewhat melancholy scene there looked down a couple of prints of gauzy dancers in the correct Parisian manner and a picture of a bowl of peonies bought at the threepenny stationer's. All this Sarah saw, or rather did not see, for by now her gaze was concentrated almost exclusively upon the tea caddy. Ten minutes or a quarter of an hour went by in this way, until there came a sound—very faint and tremulous at first, then mounting in volume—of footsteps ascending a staircase, a knock at the door and an old woman with a hard eye and the lower part of her face wrapped up in a comforter put her head into the room.

"Oh, it is you, is it, Mrs. Mayhew?"

"Your light wasn't a-shining," this lady observed. "I was wondering whether you was still hout."

"Well, I am not. It is too fatiguing for a girl to be out the entire day."

"Hoity toity. When there's work to be done."

"There shall be a half sovereign for you in the morning, indeed there shall be."

"Those that wants supper should know where supper comes from," Mrs. Mayhew remarked, as if pronouncing a general truth which every inhabitant of Bright Terrace would do well to take to heart. And then she went away again in a flurry of crashings and cross little door-rattlings, the wind rose once more through the variegated window and rustled the prints of the French dancers on the wall, children's voices sounded in the street and then fell away to nothing, and Sarah sat still in the armchair with her white hands folded in her lap and her eye fixed on the tea caddy a yard away from her head. Her lips moved and it may have been that she was talking to herself, but if so, her speech was soundless and did not contend with the noise of the wind. A ginger cat that Mrs. Mayhew sometimes conciliated with scraps of fish came twisting round the door, which had been left an inch or two open, and sat down by the hearth, where it began examining its whiskers and Sarah became dully aware of it. Finding that the spell of her contemplation was broken, she rose from the chair, stretched her arms above her head and let them fall, took a pair of florins from the pocket of her dress and placed them on the mantelpiece and then busied herself with various utensils that lay in a heap by the side of the grate. Still, as she did this, conveying a china plate and a bone-handled knife to the occasional table and then delving into a cupboard for the half of a loaf and a morsel of butter, her mind did not cease to turn on the subject that had occupied her for the past hour.

The encounter with Esther had discomposed her, not merely because it had recalled to her a life that she had thought past, but because it had awakened in her resentments which she imagined that time had begun to soften but which now seemed to jut out from her imagination quite in the old way. At the same time, the contrast between the life that Esther now led and her own circumstances could not but fail to strike her and distress her. Why should she not be Esther, she wondered, and live in a villa at Shepherd's Bush and have a servant girl to tyrannise? In this way Sarah waxed very wrathful, assuring herself that she had been ill-used both by providence and those persons about her. And yet, she told herself, she knew things about Esther that Esther herself did not know. She was aware, too, that much could be made of this knowledge, should she so choose, and the thought of the power thereby conferred on her was very pleasant.

Brooding continually on these and other matters, one eye still fixed on the tea caddy as she chewed her fragment of bread, she returned to her chair. Certain scenes in her past life, she now realised, were very vivid to her: an afternoon at Easton Hall when she and William had escaped Mrs. Finnie's vigilant eye and gone wandering by the river and grown very confidential; Esther's face as she bent over her work; the rooks in the elms. On her forearm there was a red mark extending beyond the muslin cuff to her wrist, and she remembered the day on which it had been placed there and the passions that had caused it. The thoughts were not pleasant to her, and she stood up again with such a start that the ginger cat made off prudently in the direction of the door. It was in her power, she knew, to ameliorate this hurt, to cause pain to others that would be a satisfaction to herself. And yet . . .

The tea caddy was now in her hands. She did not know how it had come there. She could not remember picking it up. The face of the royal personage stared up at her. The red-faced gentleman she had met in the Strand had said that he was a military man and had come within a yard of the royal personage at some review, and she had not known whether to believe him. There she was with her hand inside the tea caddy. How had it come there? She had not wished to place it there, surely? And yet she was shaking the contents out onto the surface of the occasional table. There was not a great deal. A silk handkerchief that she had had from her old mistress as a present five years since. A little jet dog with a partridge stuck in his mouth. A string of buttons looped up and tied in bow knots at the end. Each of them reminded her of some passage in her life without in any way calming her or causing her to reflect on what she did. And now there it was, a scrap of paper which she could not read, but which she knew stated an hour at which she should meet the person who had sent it, signed off with a pair of initials in black ink which she could interpret for she had traced them with her fingers a dozen times.

The paper was a month old, and in ordinary circumstances would have been thrown swiftly away, but for some reason she had kept it and brooded over it in the way that a heathen native broods over his fetish of feathers and straw. A month ago, she recalled, William had given her a five-pound note, but there had been no more largesse from that quarter. The vision of Esther in her villa, with her meek servant, came to her again, and she gave a little stamp with her boot upon the bare floorboard. She knew that if she did what her mind now counselled her to do, she would injure William as much as Esther, and yet the knowledge of it did not dissuade her. And so she meditated on until the room grew dark and voices sounded on the stairs—men and women together—and the house became animated around her. Finally, when the evening had come, with her mind still calculating, yet feeling that she could stay no longer in the confined space, she rose to her feet, clasped a jacket around her meagre shoulders and ventured out into the street.

It was past six o'clock, and the nocturnal life of Newington Butts was at its early peak. Costers' barrows were drawn up by the roadside, their arrays of produce lit by flaring gas jets. Dull-eyed men leaned out of public-house doorways to converse with children sent to fetch them home. All this Sarah saw as she walked along, silent and solitary in the

D. J. TAYLOR

great crowd of vagrant humanity. There were a couple of soldiers in red coats—a recruiting sergeant and his mate, she thought—marching in tandem on the far side of the street, and she stood and watched them, thinking—though she knew in her heart that it was the merest fancy—that the younger of them resembled her brother. Queerly, the thought affected her more powerfully than any of her previous reflections, and she quickened her pace and hastened on. The dark alleys and courts ran away from her, and the people seemed to disappear under her gaze. There was a police station on the corner of the Walworth Road, and having stopped for a moment to gather her jacket more tightly around her shoulders, she bowed her head and stepped inside.

XXVIII

QUESTIONS AND ANSWERS

QUESTIONING OF ESTHER SPAULDING

Q: Come now, Miss Spalding, there is nothing to fear if you will tell the truth. Where is William Latch?

A: *I do not know. Indeed I do not.*

Q: What are his habits? Where does he go?

A: *To the Green Man in Wellington Street, I think. And to Mr. Pardew's in Carter Lane.*

Q: Pardew?

A: *He is Mr. Pardew's man. That is what he says.*

Q: Where does his money come from? Is he a warm man?

A: *Indeed, sir, he seems to do well by his business, for there is always money about the house.*

Q: More money now than there was formerly?

A: *There has always been money. Perhaps. I do not know (weeps).*

Q: There is no need to agitate yourself, indeed there is not. What work did he say that he was engaged upon?

A: *Only that he was Mr. Pardew's man. That he collected his bills and went upon his errands.*

Q: And yet he wished to manufacture leather aprons. Had he experience in such a trade?

A: *Not to my knowledge.*

Q: Did leather goods of that kind come into the house?

A: *I think not.*

Q: Were you ever admitted to the room when he and Bob Grace were at work?

A: *Never. I was told that the fire was so hot that it would be a danger to me.*

Q: How long did this process continue?

A: *A week. Ten days. Sometimes the house grew so hot that I went out and walked on the Green or among the market stalls.*

Q: Did you not enquire what he and Grace were about?

A: *I was told that I should mind my business and it was no concern of mine . . .*

Q: How came you by this letter?

A: *It was given me by Mrs. Ireland.*

Q: Yet it is dated six months since. You made no effort to deliver it?

A: *No.*

Q: Why is that?

A: *I cannot say.*

Q: Did Latch know of the letter?

A: *I cannot say.*

Q: Have you any knowledge of its contents?

A: *(weeps)*

Q: Come, the sergeant shall fetch you water. Have you any knowledge of its contents?

A: *I have read it, yes.*

Q: Was she who wrote it in her right mind, would you say?

A: *I cannot say.*

Q: You cannot say?

A: *No, I cannot (weeps).*

* * *

QUESTIONING OF THE MAN PEARCE

Q: Come now, let us have some account of you.

A: *Account of me! You shall hear nothing from me, unless I've a mind. If I was a gentleman, you would not cotch me here and you knows it.*

Q: On your arrest at Epsom you had twenty pounds in your pocket. How did you come by it?

A: *It was honestly earned, that is all I can say.*

Q: Well, let us leave that for a while. What is your connection with the man Pardew?

Kept

A: *None. I never met him before this Derby Day.*

Q: A pair of shoes were taken from your lodgings and were found to have fragments of gold embedded in the soles. What do you say to that?

A: *I have no knowledge of it.*

Q: And leather gauntlets, badly scorched, as if held to a flame. Have you any knowledge of that?

A: *The same. Will you keep me here all night?*

Q: If I have a mind, I shall keep you here all week. Who is Bob Grace?

A: *He is a fellow I know.*

Q: What sort of a fellow?

A: *A very nice fellow. But you had better ask him.*

Q: I prefer to ask you. You know that he was employed by Mr. Pardew?

A: *He may have said so. It was nothing to me.*

Q: And yet you were seen in his offices on two occasions by independent witnesses. What have you to say to that?

A: *Nothing.*

Q: Mrs. Sharp, who keeps your lodgings, states that on a day in the summer of this year she came upon forty sovereigns in the cupboard of your room.

A: *What was kept in my cupboard was no business of hers.*

Q: I must warn you of the peril you are in, indeed I must. Tell us about Pardew.

A: *There is nothing to tell.*

Q: Were you ever in Suffolk?

A: *In my recollection, no.*

Q: And this is not yours?

A: *It is a pretty toy. But no, I never saw it.*

Q: And yet you would know how to use it?

A: *You may think what you will. It is no concern of mine.*

Q: I would have you flogged if it were in my power.

A: *But it is not. I have done nothing. Let me go.*

XXIX

THE FIRM OF PARDEW & CO. IS WOUND UP

Mr. Pardew sat in the office at Carter Lane with its bleary window and its view of the dome of St. Paul's. It was ten o'clock in the morning, an hour at which it might have been supposed that the life of the room would have reached its zenith, that all manner of schemes would be in a state of strenuous advancement. In fact Mr. Pardew was alone and silent. Dressed in his customary sober suit, with his stick laid out on the desk before him and with a newspaper unfurled beneath his gaze, his outward demeanour, as he alternately bent his eyes over the black print and glared up at the bleary window, seemed in no way to differ from that of other mornings. And yet his clerk, had he been in the room, might have noticed that Mr. Pardew's gaze strayed ever so occasionally to the door and that a sudden noise from the street caused him to jerk up his head with a quite singular expression of interest. He was one of those men who are able to conceal their frets and anxieties, and though all manner of terrors gnawed at his vitals, still he was determined that none but himself should know of their existence.

An hour had elapsed since Mr. Pardew had arrived at his office, and that had been spent in ceaseless brooding. A further thirty-six had passed since Pearce had fallen into the hands of Captain McTurk. Mr. Pardew did not know the exact circumstances of this falling, but he knew some of them, for he was the kind of man who has confederates even among the ranks of his enemies. Whether Mr. Pardew possessed an ally at the court of Captain McTurk I do not know, but it was a fact that on the evening of Pearce's arrest a whisper of it had reached his ears. A less coolheaded man than Mr. Pardew would, I think, at this juncture have taken his leave, fled on some boat to the Continent, or to some remote part of the country where he could lie hidden, but Mr. Pardew, having considered the situation in his ruminative way, pondered what Pearce might be induced to tell Captain McTurk and what he might not, had decided that a short period of grace was still allowed him and that there were one or two affairs that it required him to settle before his departure.

Putting down the paper, Mr. Pardew delved into his desk and emerged with two sheets of writing paper. Taking up his pen, and again pausing to consider a sudden clatter of cartwheels from the street beyond, he scrawled a few lines upon the first sheet, delved in his desk once more for an envelope and addressed the letter to *Jas. Dixey Esq., Easton Hall, nr Watton, Norfolk*. The second sheet he brooded over for several minutes. Then, with somewhat more care than he had brought to the first letter, he wrote the following:

> I am summoned out of town unexpectedly. I cannot say when I shall return. The enclosed will cover all immediate expenses. It may be that enquiry will be made of you regarding my whereabouts. If so, you may honestly say that you know nothing of them.
> Yrs. affnly.
>
> R. PARDEW

This letter Mr. Pardew sealed up in a second envelope together with a twenty-pound note and addressed to *Miss J. Tomsett, Laburnum Villas, St. John's Wood*. It may be that as he searched for the stamp that was to adorn it his mind returned to the vision of himself and a young woman with a pink and white complexion riding in a carriage by the river at Richmond, but if so, his face did not betray the fact. Barely had Mr. Pardew completed the business of stamping the letters and concealing them in his breast pocket than there came a determined rattling at the door. Very coolly, but making sure that his stick was well within his line of vision, Mr. Pardew returned to his desk, sat down at it and had just completed the manoeuvre when Bob Grace, somewhat dishevelled and with his hat pulled down low over his eyes, tumbled into the room.

It would have been immediately apparent to any impartial observer that the relationship between Mr. Pardew and his clerk, whatever its former ambiguities, had now taken on a somewhat different aspect.

"What are you up to then?" Grace demanded, standing in the centre of the room and breathing stertorously. "Locked up in here like an old spider, eh?"

"I could ask the same of you," Mr. Pardew remarked, baring his teeth in a somewhat ghastly smile, while making sure that the stick lay within his reach. "It is gone ten."

"Oh yes," Grace countered. "And half a dozen bills wanting renewing at six weeks, I suppose? And a p'liceman not waiting outside my house and following me all the way here until I give him the slip at Blackfriars?" His eye, roving fearfully around the room, fell upon a travelling bag placed in a little recess by the door. "You're a-going to split, ain't you? That's what you're up to, isn't it? Well, I'm not going to stand for it, do you hear?"

"I am not going to split, as you put it," Mr. Pardew observed, a shade less emolliently. "I have been sitting here going about my business since half past eight."

But Grace's eyes—very muddy eyes they were, that looked as if their owner had been awake half the night—were still trained upon the travelling bag.

"What business?" he nearly snarled. "There ain't no business left to do, and you knows it. Only p'licemen waiting outside a fellow's house and the man as knows everything about it sitting there with a travelling bag all neat and packed." He lowered his voice. "Perhaps I ought to go and tell that p'liceman something that might interest him. Like who did for a certain gentleman down in Suffolk for one. Like who played that trick on old Mr. Fardel for another. No, you *shan't* hit me with your blessed stick!"

For Mr. Pardew, rising from his desk, very red and with his chin bristling, had lashed out suddenly with his walking stick, missing the body of his clerk, who skipped nimbly out of the line of his stroke, but smiting the floor so hard that the stick broke in two pieces and fell from his hand.

"You old villain!" Grace sang at him. "Go on! Hit me, and I'll do for you, see if I don't."

But Mr. Pardew's moment of wrath had passed. He knew that no good could come from attempting to strike his clerk again, knew also that only a display of sweet reasonableness would achieve the object he had in mind. Accordingly, he picked up the two halves of the stick and placed them carefully on the desk, his mind working all the time over the best means of obtaining this end. Grace, meanwhile, looked haplessly around him, made a nervous little movement in his employer's direction, thought better of it and subsided. As he did so there came another rattle at the door, less forceful than Grace's and suggestive only of a tentative enquiry.

"That'll be Dewar," Grace confirmed. "Saw him a-follerin' me up the street as I came by."

Grace's surmise was correct. Pushing open the door, Dewar came timidly into the room. He was dressed not in the uniform of the railway company but in a nondescript suit of black. As with Grace, there was a vacancy about his eyes indicative of some deep disquiet.

"Why ain't you at work, Dewar?" Mr. Pardew wondered.

"Suspended from duty, aren't I?" Dewar replied mournfully. "Got a letter telling me to stay at home while enquiries were being made." Having spoken the words, he seemed overcome with anxiety, sat down heavily in a chair and gazed about him with an air of terrible hopelessness. "Was a policeman called at the house last night," he said. "Saw him coming and managed to slip out, and my wife told him I was away, but what's to be done? What's to be done, eh?"

Seated once more at his desk, hands playing with the fragments of the broken stick, Mr. Pardew regarded his lieutenants. He was aware that the game was nearly up, that if an attempt were being made to apprehend Grace and Dewar, then his own turn would not be far behind. In his subordinates—Grace, wary and indignant at his side; Dewar, silent and reproachful in the chair—he had no interest. They could go to the Devil as far as he was concerned. And yet Mr. Pardew knew that men who go to the Devil very often wish to take other men with them. Consequently, he softened the set of his features, made a small gesture of appeasement with his hand and smiled in what might have been interpreted as a confidential way.

"There is no need for alarm," he proposed. "Indeed there is not. Naturally, Pearce being taken complicates matters."

D. J. TAYLOR

"Pearce is in quod?" Grace whistled. "Then we're done for, you old Jew!"

"Listen to me. There is no need for alarm. Who is to know what Pearce may say and what he won't? As for you, Dewar, you have been questioned half a dozen times and no one any the wiser."

"That's so," Dewar conceded. "But it was a torture to me, and you knows it. I've half a mind to tell all I know simply to give myself ease. 'Twould be a relief to me to do so, indeed it would."

"You've fixed us good and proper, that's what you've done," Grace announced. "Where's William Latch if it comes to that? Called at his house yesterday, and there's no one there and no maid to answer the door neither. See that bag there on the floor, Dewar, my boy? He's going to split, that's about the strength of it, and leave us behind. What do you say to that, you old villain?"

Mr. Pardew continued to smile.

"Nobody is to be left behind," he observed. "Come with me if you wish. Only there are no funds to take us. Look! Here is my pocket-book. Let me only go out to the bank in Eastcheap, and we may be in France by this evening."

There was a silence as Grace and Dewar considered his words.

"You're an old villain," Grace said. "What's to stop you taking your hook? I'll come with you to the bank, that's what I'll do."

"With policemen looking for you in the streets? You had much better stay here."

"And have you disappear while I'm waiting? You old villain, you."

"You shall have charge of my travelling bag while I am gone. Will that satisfy you?"

They continued to wrangle about this until Dewar's voice, mournful but insistent, broke over the argument.

"I won't go."

"You won't go?" Grace looked at him queerly. "Why won't you go, eh?"

"My wife's near dying," Dewar told him. "I shan't leave her, whatever I've done."

"But say that Pearce goes Queen's Evidence?"

Kept

"I don't care," Dewar repeated sullenly. "My wife's near dying. I shan't leave her."

They wrangled a little more, but the gravity of their situation both scared and calmed them. In the end it was decided that Grace and Dewar would remain in the office, together with Mr. Pardew's travelling bag, while the latter departed in a closed cab to the bank in Eastcheap, from which he would return in not more than half an hour. Silent and subdued, Grace and Dewar watched him go. Then, as there came no noise from the street and as Mr. Pardew had obliged them by locking the door firmly behind him, Grace's spirits revived a little.

"Why don't you want to go when you has the chance?" he enquired curiously of Dewar.

"It's as I said. I can't leave my wife."

"But you could be took and put into quod, and she'd miss you all the same."

"That's true, I suppose. But where shall you go?" Dewar's face as he asked this showed a wholly naïve interest, as if the idea of anyone quitting their native shore was quite remarkable to him.

"Go? Why, anywhere there's a man to pay for it. But he's a sly one, that Pardew. I shall have to watch him, I daresay." Grace's tone as he said this was that of some wealthy householder who suspects that his butler may be stealing sherry. "But I had the measure of him just now, didn't I, Dewar? Makin' him leave his bag here when for two pins he'd have taken it away and gone." The travelling bag, still lying in the recess near the door and apparently very tightly packed with Mr. Pardew's belongings, for whatever was in it seemed to strain against the leather sides, appeared to interest him and he strode towards it and prodded it with the toe of his boot. "Tell you what, Dewar, my boy, let's haul up this item onto the desk and take a look at it. Ain't it heavy, though? Ten to one the old villain has the rest of the gold in here. Is it locked? No it ain't. Now that's curious." His fingers played for a moment over the clasp, whereupon Dewar, standing a yard or two behind him, heard him let out a tremendous shriek, a veritable wail of rage as if the metal of the clasp burned red-hot.

"What ever's the matter?"

"Don't you see? Look how the old villain has swindled us!"

Dewar followed his gaze. Then he too drew in his breath, for the travelling bag contained nothing but packets of lead shot.

"Why there aren't no clothes at all!"

"The villain!" Grace screamed. "The old villain! I'll cut his throat before I'm done. I'll tell every tale there is to be told, see if I don't. Do you know that he had his own partner murdered once? And a man down in Suffolk on account of some scheme he was a party to? Why, I'll . . ."

And then he ceased his expostulations, for he became aware of a noise in the street somewhat above the ordinary sounds of passersby going about their business.

"What's the matter?" Dewar wondered. "What is it?"

As if by way of an answer there came a fierce rattling at the doorknob, which twisted violently in its groove. A shout, indistinct but unambiguous, sounded from the street. Grace cowered by his desk.

"They're going to break down the door," he said grimly. "You'll see."

To Dewar, standing a short way behind him, his eye, too, fixed on the quivering doorknob and the frame of the door itself, which now began to shake beneath the weight of the repeated blows delivered to it, it seemed as if the situation in which he found himself was not quite real. He discovered that he registered only small things—a little vein in Grace's head that pulsed and bulged like a roving snake, the packets of lead shot lying in the travelling bag, a pen nib fallen to the floor and resting in a crack between the boards. Not quite knowing why he did it, he bent down to retrieve the nib and placed it in the pocket of his coat. On the instant there was an almighty crash, and the door flew open with a force sufficient almost to drive the frame from its hinges.

Of what followed he had only a confused recollection. There were policemen in the room, three or four of them at least, who, though they moved in his direction, seemed fascinated by Grace, who, dashing to the door, made a mighty effort to fling them off but was beaten down and hurled into a corner with his hands thrown up to protect himself and his feet kicking out like pistons. Tumbling over a chair and evading the grasp of a man who seemed to trip and fall over the travelling bag as he came, Dewar found himself standing in the doorway, the noise from the ransacked office ringing in his ears, but apparently alone.

Immediately, he fled down the street, not pausing to look behind him, reached the corner—he had by now almost come to the margin of St. Paul's Churchyard—and stopped to catch his breath. There were two officers following him, he realised, but a good way behind and not moving with great speed. Dodging in and out of the knots of passersby, who regarded him with keen interest, he sped on towards Cannon Street in blind panic, came to a crossing and rushed upon it, heedless of the traffic. Before he could gain the further side, the shaft of a cart struck him on the breast and threw him down. A man helped him to his feet and enquired if he were injured.

"Hurt? No, no, it's all right."

To the man's surprise, and that of other people standing near him, he walked on quickly, hardly feeling any pain. But within a few moments there came a sensation of nausea, an ominous warmth in the back of his throat, and he stopped and vomited up a quantity of blood. Sympathetic passersby were all about him—he could see no sign of his pursuers—but he threw them off, drops of blood spraying onto his jacket cuffs and his shirtfront. As he passed the corner where Cannon Street leads into Watling Street, the memory of an ancient conversation came into his head, of Dunbar standing in the deserted boathouse at the lochside, giving his address and telling him to look him up. What was the number? It was 18. He was sure it was 18. He was conscious now of a pain between his ribs and knew that he was conspicuous to the people through whom he passed. These onlookers shrank from him as he moved desperately along the street. Number 18 was a corn chandler's, with its goods spilling out onto the pavement, but there were rooms above and he seized upon a boy who was standing in the shop doorway and demanded, "Does Mr. Dunbar live here? I must see him. Mr. Dunbar."

Seeing his bloodied clothes and the agonised expression on his face, the boy started back in fright. As luck would have it, there was a noise of footsteps on the wooden stair behind him, and Dunbar, a brown-paper package under one arm and a newspaper in his hand,

D. J. TAYLOR

moved slowly into view. Seeing Dewar, he set down the brown-paper package and looked at him keenly.

"Who's this? Why it's Dewar, who wondered why men should collect eggs!" Then his eye fell upon Dewar's crimson shirtfront. "But heavens, you're injured, man. What's the matter with you?"

"It's nothing—truly." Dewar's mouth was full of blood as he spoke. "Only I must come inside. Let me come inside!"

A whistle sounded at the end of Watling Street. To the surprise of Dunbar, whose hand still grasped him by the shoulder, Dewar sank to his knees on the pavement amidst the corn chandler's spreading paraphernalia. Here the policemen, coming up at a run with their faces very red, found him in a state of insensibility with Dunbar feeling his pulse for signs of life. At first it was proposed that a cab should be fetched, then, when an examination of the prisoner had been conducted, a police doctor and a stretcher. Shortly afterwards, when the crowd of onlookers had dispersed and the police ambulance rolled off through the dust, the corn chandler's boy emerged from the shop with a bucket of water and began silently to wash the blood from the grey stone step.

❧ XXX ❧

SOME DESTINIES

FROM THE DIARY OF THE REV. JOSIAH CRAWLEY, CURATE OF EASTON

15 November 1866

Aghast, on returning to these pages, to find three years now gone since first I came here. Three years! And what is there to show? And yet there have been passages in my life when I could account for each passing day, so plenteously filled were they with good work done on the Lord's good business. Now the memory of the week past is like a blank page in a book from which the words have ebbed away, quite beyond the power of calling back. Thought of unburdening myself to Margesson, but—as ever—shrank from the candid confession of my woes, from which no good ever came. A month now since I last saw Ely.

* * *

17 November 1866

Winter encroaches on every side. White mist, which in these parts hangs over the fields at dawn, still there at dusk; geese abound on the lakes and meres; haw berries ripe on the hedge. My landlady confined to bed with a bronchial ailment, necessitating on my part the performance of many irksome chores. Mrs. Forester much gratified by my condescension. "There's many a gentleman wouldn't stand for such treatment, &c. She is a good woman, and I would perforce do my best by her. A curious letter from Cousin Richard. A living in which he has some faint interest at the coast here to fall free this next quarter day. What would be my opinion? Wrote, as best I could, on my behalf, sending my tutor's commendation, the letter Warden Plender addressed to me when I took my fellowship, but I have suffered too much disappointment to set great store by it.

*   *   *

20 November 1866

Much troubled by conscience, I determined to make a visit to the Hall, to which every species of rumour continues to adhere. Dixey not seen in the parish for a month, a bailiff absolutely heard enquiring of him in Watton High Street, &c. Rain falling incessantly through my journey gave the estate a yet more melancholy aspect than I remembered: the grass grown up a foot high by the driveway; the windowpanes at the lodge smashed and broken. Approaching the house, in which no sign of life seemed apparent, I found myself visited by the queerest apprehension and misgiving, to the extent that I could scarcely bring myself to belabour the great front door. Receiving no answer to my repeated summonses (which clamour resounded inside the house, I fancied, like the roll of some ghostly drum), I wandered around the side of the house. Here all was fallen into the rankest desuetude: weeds grown up in the kitchen garden; the door of the keeper's cottage swinging from its hinge and a pig peering out from within.

It was by this time perhaps three in the afternoon, the light beginning to fade, and I would gladly have taken my leave, thinking that I could do no good, that the place was altogether shut up and deserted, when a face appeared at the window—a queer pale face rising out of nowhere and, I will confess, giving me such a start as I never before felt in life—and a man, whom I recognised as Randall the butler, came stepping across the grass. Having had much courtesy from him in the past, I prepared to greet him civilly, only to detect a look of great anger in his face. I had no business here, he told me before I could speak a word; Mr. Dixey would not see me, would not see anyone, and I should do no good. I replied, as coolly as I could in the circumstances, that I regarded Mr. Dixey as my friend, that my duty as a Christian and as a minister of God brought me here, on behalf of not only Mr. Dixey but another person that I knew rested beneath his roof. At this

Kept

Randall seemed transformed by an emotion that might either have been fear or solicitude. Mr. Dixey would not see me, he repeated. I should go at once, or he could not be held responsible for what might happen. At this, I confess, I began almost to laugh, and yet there was something in the man's expression that stifled the laugh in my throat. The great gloomy house, Randall's pale face regarding me in the half-light, the thought of Dixey roaming the empty corridors—for I believe that no servant other than Randall remained—the woman confined in some remote chamber: all this worked on me to such an effect that, to my shame, I stole away through the kitchen garden and on into the woods with the howls of Dixey's dogs in their kennels ringing in my ears, regained the road with my heart pounding and a dreadful sense of there being someone or something almost at my heels. And yet there was nothing, only the mist and the movement of the trees in the wind, and so I made my way home very troubled by what I had seen and the thought of what it might portend.

* * *

24 November 1866
So I am to be Vicar of Holkham! A letter from Cousin Richard setting out the terms of my incumbency realising in me the greatest exultation. There is a fine rectory, apparently, and eight hundred pounds a year besides.

* * *

27 November 1866

To Ely.

* * *

In the study, his hand supported by the ferrule of the square desk, the stuffed bear stiff and cumbersome a yard from his elbow, Mr. Dixey watches at the high window. The gravel drive that lies beneath it, its inflexions curving away around the rank lawn and the fountain with its

D. J. TAYLOR

dripping caryatid, is quite empty. It is a week now since anyone came along it, and that was only the postman—Sam Postman, Mr. Dixey thinks he is called—who rapped at the door for two minutes without an answer and then reluctantly departed, leaving the letter propped up against the door. It is a wonder, Mr. Dixey thinks, that the servants did not collect it. Then he remembers that the servants are gone, away to Watton, Lynn and Norwich, and that he watched them go. There is a suspicion—a footfall in the distance, a door seeming to close far away—that Randall may still be in the house, but Mr. Dixey cannot be sure.

In the end he retrieved the letter himself. It lies now on the desk beside him, flanked by the display cabinets, the specimen cases and the bead-eyed bear. In the grate a coal or two still flickers red-white, and there are other letters stacked on a chair to the right of the hearth, for Mr. Dixey has been burning his correspondence. Great dockets and folds of foolscap, many of them crossed over and sealed and recalling the days before envelopes, all gone crackling into the flames. Looking at the piles of ash banked up on either side of the winking coals, Mr. Dixey wonders from where in the human heart rises the urge to recon-stitute that which has been obliterated. The only trace of a dodo that endures, apart from a half-dozen pages of contradictory drawings, is the half of a leathery hide kept preserved in the Oxford museum. All that is left of the moa are a few bones found in the dirt of a New Zealand cave. Perhaps, Mr. Dixey thinks, at some future point an anatomist will attempt to reconstruct his life rather as the naturalists attempt to reimagine *Didus ineptus* from the accounts of the Dutch travellers to Mauritius two centuries before. The thought is curiously consoling, but the vision it conjures up of persons unknown to him busily at work here at the centre of his private world is more than he can bear.

Guided by some prompting he cannot quite explain, he slides open the lid of the nearest display case, brings out the two marsh harrier eggs that lie within and balances them on his palm. They weigh noth-ing, so light, he thinks, that they might float. Regretfull,y he crushes the eggs beneath his fingers, breathing in the faint odour compounded of earth, albumen and decay. There are other things than letters to destroy, he thinks.

Kept

The letter, Mr. Dixey divines, this sentence or so sent from a desk in Carter Lane, has destroyed his hopes. Now there are connections to be made. People will no longer see him as himself but as part of a complex chain of incident, collusion and desire. That is the way of things. His hand is on another display case now: an eagle's egg taken from the loch at Strathspey. Again he crunches it between his fingers. Once, as a young man, he shot at a golden eagle high on a hilltop in Sutherland, but at the moment he raised his gun to his shoulder the bird tracked away, lifted by a spiral of wind he could not see, and the bullet went wide. He would have fired again, had not the sun suddenly risen from behind a cloud to blind him.

A movement beyond the window catches his eye, and he stares once more into the pale December light. There is a carriage approaching down the gravel drive. Mr. Dixey can see the coachman's grey head bobbing up and down as the transom shifts beneath him. As he looks on, the carriage makes a half turn into the wide space before the front of the house and stops. Watching the people who emerge from it—a sharp-featured middle-aged man commands them, whom Mr. Dixey has never seen—he thinks that if he wished he could throw open the window and fling more of the eggs down upon their heads. He has a sudden vision of the shells, white and papery, slowly descending like snowflakes through the chilly air.

He takes a last look through the window. Curiously, the men—there are four of them—seem in no hurry. Conferring, heads angled together above the gravel, they have the air of pleasure seekers, anxious to inspect their guidebooks before setting forth on their tour of the grand house. Mr. Dixey moves rapidly down the great staircase into the hall and thence into the servants' quarters. The kitchen cat, cleaning her paws on the big oak table, watches him as he goes. The kitchen door is half-open, has been so for some time apparently, for there is a little whirl of old leaves, dirt and grass-ends upon the threshold, and Mr. Dixey passes through it. In the distance he can hear the dogs howling. He cannot remember when they were last fed, but it is not less than three days since.

The first belt of trees is within reach now, and he plunges into it, stands breathing heavily with his gaze fixed upon the house. He wonders how long it will be safe to stay here, concealed in this thicket, and whether there may be other men approaching silently through the grounds to cut off his retreat. As if to confirm this suspicion, something stirs in the dense bank of foliage to his left. Instantly, he hastens away down the woodland path. It seems to him as he moves that the place is unnaturally still, that there should be birds calling, but that they are gone—the dogs have stopped howling, he registers—and that his breath sounds unusually loud in his ears.

There is another stirring—so faint as to be hardly perceptible but a stirring nonetheless—in the trees, and he turns round, more in curiosity than alarm, to inspect what it is that haunts his steps, here in a Norfolk wood on a winter's afternoon in the thirtieth year of the reign of little Victoria of Saxe-Coburg, the niece of the sailor king, whom once he saw on a hot afternoon in Windsor with the brass bands playing and the rooks cawing frenziedly above the distant elms.

The rest you know.

* * *

"Nothing to be discarded, mind," Captain McTurk instructed as they came into the house. "Everything to be kept."

The lower parts of the house were empty and undisturbed. In the servants' quarters a silence. In the pantry a rat sitting on its hindquarters eating at a rancid ham. In the drawing room a half inch of dust upon the lacquer table and the old Dixeys in their frames.

In Mr. Dixey's study a great chaos: the windows raised and the curtains billowing in the wind; Bruin cast lengthways upon his paws and a great lump torn out of his ursine head; a litter of broken shells and scattered books; a microscope thrown upon the carpet with its lens smashed in two.

"He has destroyed . . . everything," said Captain McTurk.

"Not quite everything, I think," remarked Mr. Masterson. "See here."

On the great table, under a dome of glass, a circular plate, spread with moss, on which sat a pair of perfect ruddy-brown eggs and an inscription, printed in elegant italic script on a slip of paper. Captain McTurk bent to examine it.

"*Pandion haliaetus*. What is that?"

But Mr. Masterson had read his Latin at Charterhouse School. "Osprey eggs," he explained. "A great rarity, I believe."

* * *

All this time, needless to relate, Captain McTurk and his men had been ceaselessly at work on the public's behalf. It is remarkable, is it not, the volume of evidence that will suddenly spring to hand when the perpetrator of a crime has finally been unmasked. Let a man stand charged with stealing a sheep, and immediately a parcel of corroborating detail will be found torn open and spilling its contents at his feet. Witness A will allege that he enquired of him the best way of cooking mutton, witness B confirm that he attempted to borrow from him a carving knife and fork, witness C relate that he was seen gathering the materials for a mint sauce, and out of all this testimony and supposition is instantly constructed a vast edifice of guilt. So it was with Captain McTurk's investigation. He had fished sedulously in the turbid lake concealing the affairs of Mr. Pardew, Mr. Dixey and sundry other persons connected to them, and all kinds of curious things had come up struggling on his hook. He had been to Easton Hall and examined its contents most thoroughly. He had made a visit to Jemima at her villa in St. John's Wood, consulted Mr. Caraway of St. John's College and called upon Mr. Dunbar in Watling Street but found the latter gone into the country. The landlord of the Black Dog had wilted beneath his gaze, Mrs. Farthing had curtseyed in his presence and it was rumoured that His Grace the Duke of —— had been absolutely compelled to forsake his ducal mansion and spend an exceedingly comfortless hour in the little room behind the stable yard in Northumberland Street.

In this way all manner of confidential remarks had been made into Captain McTurk's ear and all manner of confidential documents reluctantly entrusted to his care. Half a dozen counterfeit cheques drawn on provincial banks by persons unknown; private communica-

D. J. TAYLOR

tions sent by Mr. Dixey to his lawyer; a little scrap of paper—heaven knows where it came from—in which a gentleman signing himself "R.P." (Mr. Pardew's initials, certainly, but no doubt shared by many other persons) conveyed certain immensely suggestive instructions: all these had somehow found their way into Captain McTurk's grasp, and those who monitor the achievements of our public servants felt that the captain had excelled himself.

And yet, flattered as he was by these encomia, Captain McTurk was uneasy. It is one thing to have amassed a quantity of evidence, forensic and circumstantial, which may be of use to a prosecuting counsel. It is quite another to secure a conviction. Captain McTurk had not the slightest doubt that certain crimes, and certain of them very heinous crimes, had been committed. A quantity of fraudulent cheques had been passed through the banking system. An audacious robbery had taken place on the Dover mail train. A gentleman had apparently been bludgeoned to death in Suffolk. That gentleman's wife had been held, apparently against her will, by another gentleman who proposed to marry her and thereby secure the inheritance with which her late husband had entrusted him. That each of these misdeeds was, to a certain degree, connected with the others Captain McTurk was sure. And yet, given that two of the persons he desired most urgently to interview were dead, the second in a manner so dreadful that Captain McTurk shuddered to remember it, and the third unaccountably vanished from sight, the proof might be difficult to obtain. And so, as he sat in his office above the stable yard, with Mr. Masterson returning almost daily with the results of some freshly executed commission, Captain McTurk searched for some key that would unlock these mysteries.

For a while he thought he had found it in Mr. Crabbe, and yet Mr. Crabbe, it soon became clear, was quite equal to his stratagems. What was it, the old lawyer enquired, that he had done wrong? Certainly, he had presided over the establishment of a trust for the benefit of Mrs. Isabel Ireland, but if there was a flaw in its conception or its administration he would be glad to hear of it. As to the medical basis on which the conditions of that trust had been enforced, he had taken his advice from that very eminent medical man Dr. Conolly, now deceased, whom all the world knew. In fact Mr. Crabbe practically defied Captain

McTurk to arraign him, an action that Captain McTurk, who had examined certain medical records which application to Dr. Conolly's executors had produced for him, feared to take.

All this, however, would scarcely do for the public and those guardians of the public conscience that take an interest in such matters. The public desired a trial—two trials—any amount of trials, so long as justice could be seen to be done and transgression properly rebuked. And so, after great deliberation, and nearly four months after these affairs had first come to the public's attention, it was declared that the Crown intended to prosecute Robert Grace, William Latch and Joseph Pearce for their part in the theft of bullion from the Dover mail train, and to arraign Augustus Crabbe, Esq., on a charge of conspiring to defraud Mrs. Henry Ireland of money and property that was rightfully hers. Naturally, each of these proceedings caused a great sensation. The circumstances of the robbery were once more described in every newspaper in the land. Mr. Crabbe's illustrious career and his yet more illustrious connections were similarly made much of. And yet it was generally felt that the trials were rather a frost. Messrs. Grace, Latch and Pearce were swiftly examined, found guilty, rebuked, imprisoned, sentenced to transportation and so forth, all the condign punishments that the law allows—an old lady, supposed to be Mrs. Grace, fell into a fit in the courtroom at this juncture and was taken away—but it was clear that nobody cared in the least about these satellites of the vanished Mr. Pardew, and that the public was exercised only by the fate of their commanding spirit.

On the morning before Mr. Crabbe's appearance in court, Captain McTurk had a conversation with Mr. Hammerdown, the prosecuting counsel, in which certain of his anxieties were made plain.

"It is an uncommonly difficult case," he explained. "Indeed, I scarcely know where one part of it ceases and another begins. There is Mr. Dixey dead, having tried, as one supposes, to marry his ward for her money. Mrs. Ireland, of course, can say nothing about it. There is this Mr. Pardew vanished with two hundredweight of bullion off the Dover train having, so far as we may deduce, had the husband of Dixey's ward murdered for him. Dixey, one gathers, owed Pardew

D. J. TAYLOR

ever so many hundreds of pounds. Mr. Crabbe is Dixey's lawyer and Mrs. Ireland's trustee. Pardew passed his fraudulent cheques through Crabbe's office. You would think, would you not, that they were all confederate together, and yet, do you know, I doubt it."

"Indeed, you know," observed Mr. Hammerdown, who despite his terrible reputation was a mild-mannered man very much bullied by Mrs. Hammerdown, "I don't think old Crabbe, whom I have known these thirty years, ever meant to murder anyone nor rob a train of its bullion."

"I rather agree. It is a tremendous intrigue, but my belief is that Pardew is at the bottom of it. There is some hold that he had, you mark my words, some pit that he had dug for him that he could not climb out of. You had better see what you can get Crabbe to say about it in the box."

Mr. Hammerdown said he would see what he could do. Sadly, all this delicate scheming came to nothing, for on the morning of the old lawyer's first day on the stand it was declared that he had suffered a seizure in the night, was being attended upon by Sir Clarence Coucher of Harley Street and could take no further part in the trial.

Mr. Crabbe survived his attack, but he retired altogether from legal practice. The chambers at Lincoln's Inn have been taken over by a brace of rising barristers and the old clerk finally evicted from his kitchen in the basement. The West End hostesses on whom Mr. Crabbe used so sedulously to call no longer see him now, for he sits in his Belgravia mansion, meekly attended by his daughters, and thinks who knows what thoughts of his former life.

Mr. Guyle continues about his business as before.

Mrs. Ireland did not appear at the trial. Her absence was regretted by both the public and the legal profession. "Only put her on the stand," Mr. Hammerdown was thought to have pronounced, "and we shall carry all before us." However, polite enquiry revealed that Mrs. Ireland could not be put on the stand, could take no part in anything, that her health, in fact, was in an altogether precarious state, and that it would be better for her to remain in the establishment to which she had been conveyed after her rescue. Of these lodgings I know very little, other than that they are very genteel, well conducted and altogether discreet, and that Mr. Farrier, visiting her there, emerged looking very grave and would say nothing of what took place.

It was thought that given the urgency with which he had returned to England, Mr. Farrier might remain some time in his native land, but the wanderlust to which he is peculiarly susceptible was soon upon him once more and within three months he was gone. There is a poste restante address in Paris for those who wish to communicate with him, and Mr. Devereux may be contacted on any legal matter.

In due course there was a parliamentary by-election in the borough of Southwark, and Mr. John Carstairs did indeed come forward as the Conservative candidate. He fought a vigorous campaign and in losing by a scant fifty votes was thought to have acquitted himself admirably. It was believed, however, that the expenses were very high, so high in fact as to preclude any subsequent reattempt, and that additionally Miss du Buong, Mr. Carstairs's fiancée—she is of the brewing family in Aldershot—advised him to have no more to do with those dreadful political persons.

Mrs. Carstairs declares herself very satisfied by her son's present mode of life and always defers to him in any family matter.

The Dean of Ely, Mr. Marjoribanks, fetches his own slippers now, pours his own tea and is very morose of an evening when there are none of his fellow clergymen come to call.

Of Esther I know nothing at all. How should I? She comes from a place of which the fashionable world knows little and cares less, and has doubtless returned there. Certainly, the villa at Shepherd's Bush has had an agent's board at its window these three months past, and as is generally the custom the neighbours know nothing about it. If, as certain newspapers averred, Captain McTurk had her placed on an emigrant boat to Van Diemen's Land in the wake of her departed consort, then he has said nothing about it. I myself believe that she is now fortunate enough to occupy a most suitable situation in life, agreeable to herself and those around her.

Rumours of Mr. Pardew could be heard in every part of the globe to which miscreant Englishmen abscond. He had been seen at Pau and glimpsed walking the promenade at Boulogne. A gentleman passing through Leghorn swore that he had set up as an attorney in the town, dined with the mayor and could be viewed proceeding by carriage to the Roman Catholic church each Sunday forenoon. So persistent were the stories of his presence in Ottawa that Captain McTurk absolutely sent Mr. Masterson across the Atlantic to investigate. He found a person of that name, certainly, but one barely thirty years old, with a thriving law practice, six red-haired children and a pronounced North American accent. After this fiasco, and the routing out of sundry other false Pardews in those continental spas and watering holes where English people congregate, Captain McTurk's eye turned nearer to home. A search was made of the premises at Carter Lane, which yielded up the most interesting documents—nothing, perhaps, that incriminated anyone other than Mr. Pardew but sufficient in themselves to submit half a dozen persons prominent in public life to agonies of embarrassment. Such was the stir caused by these revelations that a Duke's lady, told by her husband that he had some grave matter to discuss with her, was thought to have remarked that "she supposed it was another of Pardew's bills."

All this was highly amusing, no doubt, but it did not bring the investigating authorities any closer to Mr. Pardew's whereabouts or indeed to the man himself. A short while after his disappearance a lady living at a house in Kensington, very shocked by the public accounts of her husband's wrongdoing, came forward—or was perhaps induced—to declare that she was Mrs. Pardew, whereupon the general sensibility was acutely inflamed. Let the woman be most severely questioned, the cry rose up, let her be charged as an accessory to her husband's crimes and forced to make reparations, and then justice would be seen to be done! And yet Captain McTurk was compelled presently to concede that Mrs. Pardew, a comfortable middle-aged woman whose marriage lines showed her to have been married to Mr. Pardew for ten years, knew almost as little of her liege lord as the police officer himself. Indeed her ignorance of her husband's career, acquaintance and habits—let alone his criminal propensities—was invincible. She was also very nearly penniless. Whereupon, as so often happens in these clement times, the general sensibility reversed its previous view and declared that she was a wronged woman. A newspaper got up a subscription for her maintenance, the Queen herself was known to be interested in her fate, and Captain McTurk, not without all private misgivings, gave up on her as a bad job.

It is impossible, though, in the modern age—the age of railways and the penny post—for a man to be altogether mysterious, and gradually, over the period of a twelvemonth, there came forward one or two persons able to furnish certain details of Mr. Pardew's former life. These were not very remarkable. It was subsequently proved beyond doubt that he was the son of a Manchester manufacturer who had lost his money, that he had spent much of his early life abroad—might even be supposed to have been educated there—and later been engaged on certain projects in the engineering line, blameless in themselves but no doubt furnishing the expertise wherewith to commit grand larceny. The trail in this regard having led, as it was bound to do, to the door of Mr. File, that gentleman was able to demonstrate to his complete satisfaction, if not to that of the magistrate who sentenced him to two years' imprisonment, that he and Mr. Pardew had never met. An account was subsequently found in Mr. Pardew's name at a joint-stock bank in Threadneedle Street, devoid of all but a few shillings. And at about this time there arrived at Captain McTurk's office in Northumberland Street a small package, addressed personally to him and postmarked with a Nottingham frank, which, when opened, was found to contain a pair of keys. At which point Captain McTurk remarked to Mr. Masterson that Mr. Pardew was a cool one and no mistake. There are, perhaps, worse epitaphs.

* * *

MR. RICHARD FARRIER TO MR. JOHN CARSTAIRS

I could not of course have gone away from here without satisfying my curiosity with regard to her—over and above, that is, the dreadful day on which we took her from the house—and this I determined to do. The place is about twenty miles out of London and very discreet; indeed, as Devereux remarked, were it not for the palings and the person who sits at the little lodge

D. J. TAYLOR

gate until such time as the door is closed for the night, one would think it a very pleasant spot for a gentleman's residence. Devereux, who knows all about it, says that in point of diet, medical care, &c., it could not be bettered, and indeed I could find no fault in anything that I saw either inside or out. But I tell you, Carstairs, it does no good to a man to visit such places for they speak of a providence that is neither beneficent nor wise, that can tap you on the head with his hammer and leave you speechless on a whim. Boys robbing birds' nests and trampling the squabs for their sport are not more cruel . . .

I had been told that I might find her in the garden, and so it proved, sitting in a little chair that someone had put out for her in the shade of a laurel hedge, very neatly designed, I should say, with a spigot for her drinking cup and a bell to ring should she need attention, and the bell always answered, which is not universally the case, I believe. I came upon her, I must own, in silence, wanting to gain some idea of her before I spoke. Indeed to see her thus sent an absolute pang through me, so unchanged did she seem from those days of which you have heard me speak, when we were, as I suppose, children together and yet conscious of a time when we should be children no more. . . . She had some object before her on her lap with which she played that I thought for all the world a mouse, until I saw that it was but a toy moved hither and thither by the motion of her hands, innocent enough, you may say, but somehow made horrible by the restless play of her fingers, her habit of clutching the thing to her cheek, &c.

Seeing me walk towards her over the grass—the day was very bright and the sun high over the hedge—she looked up and smiled, and again it was as if time had stopped since the occasion of our last meeting, but for a slight hollowness, perhaps, about her face, a certain brightness about her eyes that spoke more of artifice than nature, and I knew that she recognised me. "You are very comfortable, I see," I said, having been instructed to confine myself to remarks of easy familiarity. "Oh, yes," she replied—and I could see that there was some struggle proceeding in her mind—"very comfortable indeed. But I shall take no more medicine, however much entreated." "I have none," I told her—there was a sheet of foolscap, I now saw, on the tray before her, black with scrawl—"so you may rest easy."

There was a silence which I must confess embarrassed me, for having come with my head full of harmonious sentences, I could now think of nothing to say. "Is there any way in which I may serve you?" I asked finally, hearing the noise that her hands made as they pushed the mouse across her lap and down among the folds of her skirt. "I think not," she said. "And yet you may send Esther to me." At first the name meant nothing to me, and I shook my head. "It is a long time since she went away, and I would have her back." Intrigued, in spite of myself, I looked down at the sheet of foolscap, but a child learning its letters would have been more intelligible. "You must not think," she went on, gathering the toy in her hands as if it were something infinitely precious to her, "that I am afraid of a mouse. Indeed, I killed one once with a poker, as I shall do this if I have a mind." And then she laughed, quite girlishly, with not the least suggestion that she sat in a garden where there is a porter at the gate and an iron railing six feet high for a fence.

"Isabel . . . ," I began once more, but it was as if a door had been locked and bolted between us that no key could open, and so we stared again at each other—she with her hands turning in her lap, I with my gaze fixed upon a pair of eyes that seemed to conceal awful, trackless depths behind them—until something—the sun perhaps, glinting off the roof of the distant house, a bird alighting on the hedge top, the neat step of the servant girl moving across the bright grass—drew her glance and she turned aside.

* * *

"Well," said the superintendent, Mr. Mortimer, breakfasting with his wife and daughters one Sabbath morning, "the attachment between our Mrs. Ireland and the woman who attends her is a very singular one."

D. J. TAYLOR

"I had not remarked it," observed Mrs. Mortimer, continuing to butter an egg. "Grizelda, you may ring for John footman and tell him we shall not be needing the fly from the stables for church."

(The superintendent of the Ware asylum resides in the neatest little villa imaginable, and Mrs. Superintendent is naturally its most delightful ornament.)

"Nevertheless, it is so," Mr. Mortimer went on, not quite liking the instructions about the fly but fearing to countermand them. "One might almost call it a sisterly affection."

"There was some scandal, was there not?" enquired the eldest Miss Mortimer, who could not be kept from reading newspapers and was thought to take an excessive interest in the doings of her father's patients.

"It is all very shocking," countered her mama. "And if my opinion had been asked—which it was not—I should have said that the arrangement originally proposed for the young woman would have been much better allowed to persist."

"There was a gentleman, was there not?" continued the eldest Miss Mortimer, who was quite incorrigible.

"That will do, miss. It is a wonder to me that your father allows such talk."

But Mr. Mortimer was not listening. He was still thinking of the cancelled fly and the play of Mrs. Ireland's hands as they moved restlessly in her lap.

"Nevertheless, I think it very creditable to the girl that she minds her duty. You will oblige me, Maria"—and it was a measure of Mr. Mortimer's exaltation of spirit that he said "Maria" rather than "my dear"—"by seeing if there is not some small thing, some dress or bonnet of the girls, that might be looked out and given to her."

"I should hardly have thought it worthwhile, Augustus"—it was a measure of Mrs. Mortimer's temper that she said "Augustus"—"but if you insist."

"I do. And now, if you will excuse me, I have business to attend to."

("It is all the fault of that Mr. Farrier coming yesterday and being so solicitous of Papa's opinion," Mrs. Mortimer told her daughters. "You know what he is like with such gentlemen.")

But Mr. Mortimer, walking alone to church through splashes of summer rain, knew that he had done the right thing.

*   *   *

"Take it away, Esther! You know I cannot abide such stuff."

"Certainly not, miss, for without it you will be ill again, and it's I that shall have the nursing of you."

The draught, newly mixed by Mr. Mortimer's apothecary and fetched by that gentleman beneath a folded napkin, lay on the deal table between them.

"I shall not drink it. Indeed, I shall fling it out of the window and startle the birds."

"In that case, miss, you will try my patience, which you know you would rather not."

Mistress and servant regarded each other anxiously. Then, in the manner of one who submits to an inexorable fate, Mrs. Ireland picked up the glass and began to sip at it. Evidently, what it contained was not wholly inimical to her, for she drank off perhaps half the contents before seating herself on one of the leather-backed chairs at the further side of the table. Moving forward once or twice as if there were something she urgently wished to say, she yawned hugely, shook her head with a bewildered air, as if the yawning were a procedure wholly beyond her comprehension, and then fell into a light sleep. After studying her intently for a moment or so, Esther took the half-full glass from where it lay in her hand and bore it away to the kitchen. Here, having ascertained that no other domestic duty had escaped her, she remained, half her attention alert to any sound that might come from the adjoining room, the remainder bent inwardly upon her own concerns.

Three months had elapsed since the trial: Esther supposed that the time had not gone unhappily with her. Of William, Sarah—that whole life that had occupied her from the moment she left Easton Hall—she had not ceased to think, and yet there was a vagueness about it, a diffusion of sentiment and memory, that calmed her apprehensions. Here and there about her person she carried mementoes of those days—a little twist of sprigged muslin bought at the Earlham Street market,

D. J. TAYLOR

an ornamented card with William's great scrawled signature on the reverse. Sometimes of an evening, when her mistress lay asleep or sat comfortably installed in her chair at the window, whose peculiarities of scene never ceased to amuse her, she would take out and examine these items and ponder the events that they reawakened in her mind. But though the remembrance of them lingered, she found—and she believed that the finding was agreeable to her—that the circumstances of her new life did not encourage a propensity to brood. There was Mr. Spence, the apothecary, at the door, or a walk around the grounds to negotiate, or an illustrated magazine sent with Mr. Mortimer's compliments for them to examine. Such occurrences were not an antidote to her loss, but they were a drag upon it and thus she welcomed them with perhaps a greater eagerness than they deserved. Certainly there cannot be many persons who would regard a half hour with the *Illustrated London News* as balm for a bruised spirit.

As to the patterns of this new life, Esther did not cease to wonder at them. The cottage that they inhabited she had adopted as if it were her mistress's own, and Mr. Mortimer only some friendly visitor, and she polished its surfaces and tended its linen as if her wages depended on it. Mr. Mortimer noted this application and commended it. "Why, Esther," he said, "forgive me if I say that you are doing work that is not yours to do." And Esther bridled, as at the wildest compliment. In this way they grew very confidential, and Esther was encouraged to impart certain details of her mistress's condition, born of long observation, which it is to be hoped that Mr. Mortimer appreciated.

"Do you think she knows herself?" he asked once.

Esther considered the question. "It is hard to say, sir. She knows me. And there is that which she says which has a point, only you would not notice it to begin, if you take my meaning. And then she is so forgetful."

"You must help her to remember."

But Esther thought privately there was much her mistress wished only to forget.

Once, at one of these times, moving nervously at the window—for she liked to see the birds, or if not the birds then the play of the wind in the trees—she had enquired, "Esther. Where is William?"

Kept

"He has gone away, miss."

"Gone away? What, to Lynn with the master? I did not hear the dogcart in the drive."

"No, miss. He has gone away forever."

"Forever? I—that is—you must forgive me, Esther."

And Esther forgave her, treasuring the remark, as we value some shiny pebble found amongst a heap of broken stones on the beach.

Looking now at the kitchen clock, Esther saw that the supper hour was approaching. "You must try and get her to eat," Mr. Mortimer had frequently enjoined. "It would be a great thing if she could be got to eat—eh?" And Esther, agreeing with him, had promised. Moving beyond the kitchen door, she saw that Mrs. Ireland had woken up and was surveying the room in which she sat with a kind of startled benignity, as if its dimensions, while not displeasing, were the source of some bewilderment to her.

"Gracious, Esther! I have had such a dream. That the Queen herself stood by my bed and enquired of a receipt for damson preserves. Very civil, indeed, she was, but most dreadfully superior."

The rain beat suddenly on the window, and mistress and servant laughed and were very comfortable together. And Esther, presiding over the teapot, in the stuff gown that Mr. Mortimer's daughter had presented to her, thought of the orchard at Easton Hall, and the carter's van receding across the blue horizon, and Mrs. Finnie's jet-black hair, and Mr. Randall's psalms, and William helping his master down from the carriage door, and the blue cockade in his hat, and the time when he had first come to love her.

* * *

UNFORTUNATE CASE IN CLERKENWELL

THE CORONER, *Mr. Samuels, said that the police had been called to a house in Clerkenwell Court. Here they found the body of the deceased lying in a chair. Mr. Crummles, surgeon attached to the Clerkenwell force, who attended the scene, certified that the deceased had died of a phthisis, exacerbated by malnutrition. Mr. Samuels asked, by this did*

D. J. TAYLOR

he mean that the deceased had starved to death? Mr. Crummles said that he supposed he did.

Constable Gaffney, who had arrived first at the house, testified that the room in which the deceased had been found was empty of everything except a bed, the chair in which the body was lying and a small cupboard. The latter contained the smaller part of a quartern loaf and a minute quantity of tea.

Mr. Edward Scrivener of Balls Pond Road, Islington, stated that as the deceased's landlord he had been accustomed to receive a rent of six shillings per week, payable on the preceding Friday. This rent had been in abeyance for three weeks. "Were you acquainted with the deceased's circumstances?" "I was not." "Had you taken any steps for the recovery of the money?" "This is a poor house, sir, and the rent is often owing."

Mrs. Hannah Hook, a seamstress residing at the property, stated that the deceased had fallen into a decline following the death of her husband in a street accident. She had been accustomed to perform small services for the deceased, providing her with supper, coals, &c., but lately these attentions had been refused.

Constable Gaffney said that it was the poorest house he had seen, that in a dozen years of service he had seen none worse. The deceased's clothing, which would customarily have been given to the relieving officer, had been burnt as verminous.

Mr. Samuels said that it was an unfortunate case, but that as no person or institution could be shown to have failed in any duty that was owed to the deceased, he could only record a verdict of death by natural causes.

HOLBORN AND CLERKENWELL GAZETTE, *December 1866*

* * *

The clergyman, shovel hat pulled down over his forehead, hands plunged into the pockets of his coat, strides swiftly over the wet sand. It is low tide, and the sea is far away: half a mile at least lies between him and the flat, rippling breakers. At his feet have been flung interesting deposits from its passage: knots of purple-brown weed, spars of driftwood, a coil of rope, a string of onions. To his left-hand side, behind the dunes, pine trees rise into the pale air. The clergyman sees neither the trees nor the flotsam and jetsam at his feet, for his mind is bent on other things. Tall, thin, vellum face emerging above a white stock, Gainsborough could have painted him, placed him on a horse, even, to emphasise the curve of his legs, but this is not Gainsborough's age. A mile behind the shore there is a tarmacadamed road and a few miles beyond that a railway line, and in Wells, on the boundary of the clergyman's parish, a photographer has recently opened up a studio. Wearing their best clothes, the clergyman and his wife have been photographed by this man, sitting in stiff-backed chairs, with an album open between them. This is the way of things, he thinks.

There are jellyfish lying dead on the sand, and the clergyman stops to look at them: immense things the shape of *diskoi* that he once saw cradled by the athletes in one of Mr. Leighton's Attic paintings. Despite the chill and the intensity of the February wind, he is not quite alone. Two hundred yards further along the shoreline there is an old woman, like himself dressed in black, gathering up driftwood, to whom, having ascertained that she is a member of the Wesleyan chapel a mile from his church, he has nodded rather than spoken. Nearer at hand another person—almost a gentleman, the clergyman thinks, from his dress—is prodding with a stick at some unidentified object lying on the lip of a rock pool. Interested in spite of himself and the wind, the clergyman alters the line of his walk. As he approaches, the man—he is gaunt and tall with a red, weather-beaten face and carries a knapsack at his shoulder—looks up.

"*Mollusca irridens*. It is rare in these parts."

For a moment the clergyman wonders what he means. Then he sees that his gaze is being directed to a small, grey-backed crustacean that seems to have embedded itself into the crown of a rock.

"Indeed?"

"One would customarily see it in Scotland. The Baltic, perhaps."

"You are a collector, I take it?"

The man pats his knapsack, whose contents—pieces of what look like seaweed, the yellow beak of a gull—are bulging out of their bind-

D. J. TAYLOR

ing: rather, the clergyman thinks, like *Mollusca irridens*. "My name is Dunbar," he says, producing a card which corroborates this fact, as if there is a chance that business can be done between them here on this beach. "Are you in the collecting line yourself, sir?"

The clergyman smiles bleakly. "Humanity is sufficient for me."

The man laughs, rather high and cracked, so that the clergyman wonders if he is quite right in the head: a man with a knapsack and a high complexion laughing into the wind on a rainswept Norfolk beach in winter. There used not to be such persons naturalising among the rock pools. It is another new thing, the clergyman thinks. He touches the peak of his shovel hat with a forefinger and presses on through the spongiform graveyard to the sea. Here the wind lifts. In the distance, beyond the breakers, wild water rages. *The world is changing*, the clergyman acknowledges, thinking again of the curious sepia representation of himself and his wife, and of *Mollusca irridens*, whatever that may be, and Mr. Dunbar's card pressed into his hand, *and yet I am the same*.

The clergyman gazes out once more towards the surging water. The things that press in on his mind are at once quotidian and cosmic: a flaxen-haired child in its nursery, an unwritten sermon, a disagreeable conversation with his wife about unnecessary expense, the ineffable spirit moving across the face of the waters. A slab of air, as raw now as when it first blew south from Jutland, descends upon his head, sending the shovel hat racing away across the sand. The clergyman, still maintaining his dignity even in this hatless state, moves somewhat stiffly in pursuit, off towards the line of the trees, the woman in the house and the rest of his years on God's earth.

Behind him the waves crash, die and are renewed.

APPENDIX I

LOST, STOLEN OR STRAYED:
ON A VANISHED YOUNG LADY

When in want of recreation I will cheerfully own that my delight is to peruse the "miscellaneous advertisements" column of a certain newspaper. To be sure, such a wealth of interest—pathos—human sentiment—is contained within their pages that a day would not be sufficient to extract it. There is, for example, the gentleman who undertakes to supply sherry straight from the casks of Don Juan de la Frontera himself in his great distillery at Cordoba. I declare I should almost like to purchase a bottle of that sherry simply to learn how the gentleman came by it. Then there are the goods that a great number of the advertisers are continually trying to dispose of for which there would seem to be no apparent need. Who is there, to particularise, who feels himself in urgent want of a basket of miscellaneous crockery, the *Annual Register* for 1843 or certain spars of timber supposedly taken from the hull of HMS *Victory* as she lay awaiting refurbishment in dry dock at Chatham? Yet most fascinating of all, I propose, is the little clump of items—sometimes burgeoning to the size of a whole column, more often to be counted on the fingers of one hand—that some ingenious compiler has thought to arrange under the legend *Missing*.

Missing! So much of life, it seems to me, is taken up in a quest for that which formerly lay at our side, so discreetly that we scarcely noticed its presence, and is now unconscionably taken from us. Things great and small: string, sealing wax, a woman's love and the honest affections of one's child—all are gone rolling away into a kind of phantasmagorical wainscoting from which no power can ever wrest them back. As a boy I had what was popularly represented as a genius for losing things, to the extent that this propensity was remarked on, became as much a part of the face I presented to the world as the colour of my hair. Sweetmeats, combs and schoolbooks passed through my hands like the rising wind. I lost a fourpenny piece, with which my mother had commissioned me to buy a quartern loaf. (Heavens but there was a row about that, whose remembrance sizzles in my brain forty years later.) I lost an ornamental silver locket, which contained a portrait of a late aunt, and was soundly beaten. (The locket was later discovered on a bough of the apple tree—how it got there I know not to this day.) I lost half the bundles of clothing I was ordered to take to that respectable gentleman who trades under the sign of the three brass balls—but this is perhaps to reveal too much of our domestic circumstances—and I lost the tickets that I was intended to bring back.

To glance at the three or four, or six or seven, or on certain wonderful days even nine or ten supplications addressed to the world by those who have mislaid something close to their heart is, then, to be reminded with particular force of the circumstances of one's own life. The situation is entirely that of the young man bent over a novel from the circulating library, reading of the faithful Lothario separated from his fair Rosina by a baleful parent, a romantic baronet or the Catholic Church, who looks up to exclaim, "Yes, that is exactly how my precious Jane and I were parted, d—— them all!" There is, for example, the case of the gentleman out walking with his dog on Hampstead Heath, a basset hound answering to the name Tip, the dog seeing a rabbit, the gentleman quite unable to check its natural propensities, &c. How I felt for the gentleman in the depths of his abandoned misery! How I longed to present him with a four-legged substitute, were it not that the gift would surely inflame, rather than subdue, the spark of his remembrance! Then there is the lady travelling from Kensington to Fulham by omnibus, lulled by the balmy air into a light repose, waking to find the box beside her gone and the silver teapot inside it, "a most valuable and exquisite heirloom," in transit to the menders on account of a fractured spout, vanished—well, my heart yearns to strike at the wretch who now puts Bohea into it. All this, as I say, has the effect of returning me to my youth and the days when no purse or satchel was safe in my hands, when a hat could not remain on my head a minute before disappearing into the very ether, and umbrellas were like oversized toothpicks, such was the promptitude with which I flung them from me. I lost a corkscrew once, in a room eight feet by six which

Kept

contained, in addition to myself, only a bottle of wine, a table and an empty sideboard. Another time I lost a sovereign given to me by an old gentleman of blessed memory even before he quit the house at which he visited me.

All this was no doubt very bad of me, very illustrative of certain grave defects in my character. And yet, for myself, I think there is much to be said in mitigation. I was, for example, quite discriminating in my mislayings and confined myself, for the most part, to inanimate objects. I lost a pair of white duck trousers and a pie dish (the look on my mother's face when that receptacle was shown to have vanished from my tender care!), and yet I never, I think, lost a cat, a dog or a person. I certainly never lost a young lady of seven-and-twenty, confided into my care by the terms of her husband's will, which is what a parcel of Lincoln's Inn lawyers appear to have done this twelve months past.

The case is so widely known—brought to us by way of a dozen hints and suggestive nudgings—that it is perhaps superfluous to restate its particulars. A young lady living on an estate in Suffolk—not of sound mind, we regret to say, in fact a young lady of whom society has seen nothing these last two years—is widowed by an unhappy accident. In anticipation of this unfortunate possibility, her husband's will provides very suitably for a trustee, the settlement of capital for all manner of prudent schemes, meant to secure, if not that young lady's happiness, then her decent and proper care in circumstances in which, it may be devoutly hoped, she might recover her reason. And then what happens? Why like Tip the basset hound, or the antique silver teapot in the Kensington omnibus, or the corkscrew that so frustrated me in my vinous youth, the young lady vanishes.

Where has she gone? The lawyers—Sir Ezekiel Foodle, QC and Solicitor Noodle—don't know. The trustees—Baron Doodle and His Honour Judge Quoodle—can't precisely say. There is talk of a house in the country at which the young lady may or may not be sequestered, of discreet medical establishments at which she may or may not be lodged. But where is she? Where can she be found, and if not heard—for we believe the young lady's afflictions to be of a very grievous nature—then at least seen? I declare that if I were the young lady's

D. J. TAYLOR

relative I should feel like inserting a half column in the newspaper of which I have spoken under the heading "Lost, Stolen or Strayed: On a Vanished Young Lady," giving full particulars and an address for return. Such a course might not produce the young lady, but it might, as in the case of poor Tip or the Kensington teapot, realise an outpouring of public sympathy that were at least as valuable as Sir Ezekiel Foodle's professional indifference or His Honour Judge Quoodle's manifest neglect of his duty.

—ALL THE YEAR ROUND, *August 1864*

I was born a varmint, and I'll die one, I daresay. I was born in Nottingham, the year the old king died. I don't remember my father. I remember being in a barn, in the rain, with a man as was supposed to look after me but didn't. Perhaps that was my father. I don't know. When I was four, my mother took us to London and we lived in Limehouse, where she had a little shop and sold greenstuff and sprats to the people that passed by on their way to work, but it never prospered. Nothing ever prospered with my mother. After that she took ill and lay in bed, and the rest of us—for I had a sister and a little brother—had to make shift as best we could. Most days I went mudlarking at King James's Stairs or Limehouse Hole, waiting till the tide had run out and seeing what I could find. There wasn't ever much. A length of rope, maybe, or a handful of coals. The best thing was the copper nails that came from the ships in dry dock, but even if you found one, chances were a big boy would take it from you. When I was twelve, a man as bought stuff from the mudlarks took a shine to me and give me a job and I went out with him in his cart, but I didn't like it and I stole whatever I could. I stole a watch that a man had left on a shop counter. I stole the man that I worked for's hat and pawned it. That was the kind of chap I was.

My mother had died by now. Did I miss her? I don't rightly know. I remember her face above the coverlet and her asking how much I'd brought home, that's all. After she'd died I didn't care to stay with my sister and brother no more, and I went to live with some chaps as lodged in an old blacking factory by the river. That was nice company, I can tell you! Most of what I know I learned there, and that's a great deal. When I was fourteen, I stole a pig from a market garden down at Woolwich and got sent to the House of Correction. What did I do there? Well now, I stole a cake from the kitchen as had been baked for the warden"s birthday and a handkerchief from the parson as came to preach over us on Sunday morning—that was the correction I got. When I came out, a gentleman as was connected with the place—one of those soft coves in the charitable line—got me a job in a newspaper office in the Strand, but I didn't take to it. I stole the type that the printers had left out on the desks and sold it, and the pocketbooks of the men that left their jackets hung up outside the washroom, but bless you, no one suspected me. I was living with Maria Chitty by this time, which was a girl I'd found agreeable, and she me, at Bethnal Green, and we spent the money on whatever took our fancy: toy dogs perhaps, or a hat with a feather, or half a dozen faggots from the cookshop. I was good to Maria after my fashion, never struck her above thrice or sent her out when the funds were low. The Gentleman knows that, and will tell you, for he knew her too.

All that was a long time ago, and there's a part of me that doesn't like to remember it. I saw my sister once in the Whitechapel Road when I was mooching about that way, but I never went up to her. Poor Janey! I daresay she'd have been pleased to see me, for she was always fond of her brother, but that sort of thing never pays, you know. As for me now, I'm a sporting character. Cocks. Bull terriers. Prizefighting. I'll go twenty miles into the country to see a match if I've a mind to, and have the funds. The Derby too is a place I'm often to be found. The Tutbury Pet, the Coalheaver, the Chicken—I've seen them all in my time, aye, and shaken hands with them and stopped for refreshment, for I'm a warm man when I've money in my pocket. I had forty pound once, that the Gentleman put there. Don't ask me how he came by it, but it was soon gone, for that's the manner of man I am. Some folks' destinies is to save, and some to spend, and I'm one of the spending ones. There's no point in crying over what's gone, but if I had my time again I'd have the forty pound and Maria, that was always agreeable to me, and be living at Bethnal and looking out for my opportunities. Else I'd be away in Prague or Hamburg with the Gentleman, living high, as we did in those days. But that's all behind me. I ain't a young man now, but I ain't so very old neither, and there's life in me yet as my friend Bob Grace can tell you, for when a man's born a varmint he's liable to remain one and that's a fact. I'm not above stealing lives as well as property if the occasion demands it, and there's a gentleman down in the eastern counties who could swear to that if you was to ask him. Truth to tell, I'm a sad man sometimes and could wish that I was back in Bethnal piling into Maria, and her with her poonts rolling everywhere and her legs a-wound around me, but that sort of thing doesn't bear thinking about. Like the chap whose life I stole down in Suffolk, and seeing Janey in Whitechapel, and so I don't, or not for long.

D. J. TAYLOR

NOTES

Iacknowledge the direct influence of Charles Dickens, George Eliot, Elizabeth Gaskell, George Gissing, Jack London, Mary Mann, Henry Mayhew, George Moore, Alfred Lord Tennyson, Anne Thackeray Ritchie, W. M. Thackeray and Anthony Trollope.

For full descriptions of the first Great Train Robbery of 1855, from which this account is substantially derived, see George Dilnot, ed., *The Trial of Jim the Penman* (1930) and Donald Thomas, *The Victorian Underworld* (1997), pp. 204–50.

I have taken much useful information from Moss Taylor, Michael Seago, Peter Allard and Don Dorling, *The Birds of Norfolk* (Robertsbridge, 1999).

In the notes that follow, the place of publication is London, unless otherwise stated.

I. EGGMEN

p. 1-**Highland Line through Inverness-shire:** The original Highland line from Aviemore to Torres was opened in August 1863. See C. J. Gannel, *Scottish Branch Lines* (Oxford, 1999).

p. 1-**Lewis Dunbar:** Together with other gentlemen adventurers of the period, such as his brother William, Edward T. Booth, John Wolley and Roualeyn Gordon Cumming, Dunbar was a notable exterminator of the Highland ospreys. See Richard Perry, *Wildlife in Britain* (1978), pp. 206[N]–7, which, additionally, quotes from one of his letters.

p. 8-**"Not for a hundred years and more":** The last wolf in the Scottish Highlands was killed at Findhorn in 1743, having previously devoured two children whom it had waylaid on the high road in broad daylight. See Anthony Dent, *Lost Beasts of Britain* (1974), chap. 4, "The Last of the Wolf."

II. MR. HENRY IRELAND AND HIS LEAVINGS

p. 15-**Black care had waylaid him:** See Horace, *Odes*, 3.1.40.

p. 17-**Eccleston Square:** This area south of the modern-day Victoria Station represented the outer limit of Victorian bourgeois respectability. "For heaven's sake, my dear, don't let him take you anywhere beyond Eccleston Square," a friend counsels Lady Alexandrina de Courcey shortly before her marriage to Adolphus Crosbie in Trollope's *The Small House at Allington* (1864), 40.

p. 20-**Dr. John Conolly:** John Conolly (1794–1866) has been described as "one of the most ambiguous figures in nineteenth-century medicine." After qualifying at the University of Edinburgh he failed as a general practitioner, but in 1830 he published an influential treatise, *An Inquiry Concerning the Indications of Insanity*. This advocated radical reform of the treatment of lunatics and a system of patient care known as "nonrestraint." The measures introduced at the Hanwell Asylum, which he governed from 1839 to 1843, made Conolly a celebrated public figure. Dickens admired him, and the character of Mr. Dick in *David Copperfield* was intended as a tribute. Thereafter his reputation declined, and by the mid-1850s he was operating as a freelance "alienist," or lunacy consultant. There were difficulties with money, and in 1859 an action was brought against him for false imprisonment. For a suggestive, if somewhat overstated, account of Conolly's literary connections, which attempts to link him to the very different marital troubles experienced by Thackeray, Dickens and Bulwer-Lytton, see John Sutherland, "Dickens, Reade, *Hard Cash* and Maniac Wives," in *Victorian Fiction: Writers, Publishers, Readers* (Basingstoke, 1995), pp. 55–86.

p. 20-*Irish Sketchbook:* An account of W. M. Thackeray's journey around Ireland in the summer and early autumn of 1842, originally published in May 1843.

p. 22-**Mr. Hutton:** R. H. Hutton (1826–1897) had become joint proprietor and literary editor of the *Spectator* in June 1861. "Mr. Arnold's Last Words on Translating Homer" appeared in the issue of 22 March 1862.

p. 22-**Mr. Masson:** Perhaps David Masson (1822–1907), at this time professor of English Literature at University College, London, editor of *Macmillan's Magazine* and at work on his seven-volume *Life of Milton* (1859–1894).

p. 25-"**quite demented**": For a similar case, see the accounts of the derangement of Thackeray's wife, Isabella. Her descent into madness reached its climax on a ferry plying between Bristol and Cork. Mrs. Thackeray never recovered her reason and lived for a further half century in a state of semiautistic self-absorption. For Thackeray's letters describing the voyage and its aftermath, see Gordon N. Ray, ed., *The Letters and Private Papers of William Makepeace Thackeray, volume 1, 1817–1840* (Oxford, 1945), pp. 482–83.

p. 26-"**One of Mr. Smith's novels**": Presumably Albert Smith (1816–1860),

D. J. TAYLOR

author of *The Adventures of Mr. Ledbury* (1844) and *The Struggles and Adventures of Christopher Tadpole* (1847).

p. 27-"**Mr. Procter**": Bryan Waller Procter (1787–1874), barrister, poet and dramatist (under the pseudonym "Barry Cornwall") and between 1832 and 1861 a metropolitan Commissioner of Lunacy.

p. 29-*All the Year Round*: Dickens's weekly magazine, which began publishing in 1859 following the demise of *Household Words*.

p. 31-"**Lord John**": Lord John Russell (1792–1878), third son of the sixth Duke of Bedford, created Earl Russell in 1861; he was Prime Minister in 1846–1852, and again, briefly, in 1865.

p. 33-**Russell Square**: A popular Victorian (and pre-Victorian) residential area for prosperous City figures; for example, the Sedley and Osborne families in *Vanity Fair*.

III. SOME CORRESPONDENCE

p. 38-"**specie**": Coin, as opposed to paper money.

IV. THE GOODS ARE DELIVERED

p. 45-**shiny widow's weeds of black bombazine**: A worsted or worsted-and-cotton dress material dyed black.

p. 48-**a copy of the** *St. James's Chronicle*: A weekly magazine of impeccable Anglican tone, with a large circulation among the well-to-do and clerical classes. It was, for example, much enjoyed by the genteel spinsters of Mrs. Gaskell's *Cranford* (1853).

p. 48-**pattens**: Wooden soles, fastened with a strap over the wearer's shoes, worn in wet weather.

p. 50-**dealt with at Snow Hill by Mr. Ketch**: Jack Ketch, public executioner from c. 1663 to 1686. As a result of his barbarity at the executions of William, Lord Russell, the Duke of Monmouth and others, the name became synonymous with *hangman*.

V. ESTHER'S STORY

p. 61-**cadder**: Or *caddow*, a jackdaw. See Peter Trudgill, *The Norfolk Dialect* (Cromer, 2003), p. 40.

p. 63-"*Bow Bells*": A popular Victorian fiction magazine, aimed at the working-class female audience.

p. 69-"**shot a seraph that happened to be flying across Easton Wood**": A similar hoax is played upon the Honourable Mrs. Jamieson by Peter Jenkyns in Gaskell, *Cranford*, chap. 16.

Kept

p. 72-**"in China with the army"**: Following minor hostilities throughout the 1850s, British forces had captured Canton in 1859. A full-scale war broke out in the following year.

VI. SINGULAR HISTORY OF MR. PARDEW

p. 74-**Astley's**: Philip Astley (1742–1814), the celebrated equestrian performer, opened Astley's Royal Amphitheatre in London in 1798.

p. 75-**the nature of the ravens that fed him**: An allusion to the ravens that fed the prophet Elijah by the brook Cherith (1 Kings 17:5–6).

p. 77-**no more had been known of Mr. Pardew's whereabouts, or his undertakings, than Captain Franklin's**: The Arctic explorer Sir John Franklin (1786–1847) set out on his final, disastrous, voyage of discovery in the ships *Erebus* and *Terror* in 1845 in search of the Northwest Passage.

p. 86-**Eldon, Coke and other luminaries**: Lord Eldon (1751–1838), chief justice; Sir Edward Coke (1552–1634), chief justice 1613–1616, the last three books of whose *Institutes* form the basis of British constitutional law.

p. 88-**"the poor wretch who shot at Her Majesty in the park"**: There were several attempts on Queen Victoria's life. Mr. Guyle is probably referring to the incident of 10 June 1840 in which the Queen was shot at by a weak-minded boy of eighteen named Edward Oxford as she was driven in her carriage up Constitution Hill. Her attacker, who spent twenty-seven years in a civil lunatic asylum, was apprehended by Mr. Millais, whose schoolboy son—later the artist J. E. Millais—had just raised his cap to the Queen.

p. 91-**copies of pictures by Frith and Etty**: William Powell Frith (1819–1909), famous for his large-scale canvases of Victorian scenes. His *Ramsgate Sands* (1854) was bought by Queen Victoria. William Etty (1787–1849), painter of historical and classical subjects, and renowned for his nudes.

p. 91-*Pall Mall Gazette:* An influential and Liberal-supporting evening newspaper founded by the publisher George Smith and his associate Frederick Greenwood in 1865.

VII. CURIOUS BEHAVIOUR OF MR. CRABBE

p. 100-**one of Miss Edgeworth's novels**: Maria Edgeworth (1767–1849), author, whose first novel was *Castle Rackrent* (1800); among her other books were *The Absentee* (1812) and *Ormond* (1817).

D. J. TAYLOR

VIII. JORROCKS'S CART

p. 101-**Suffolk Fencibles:** A militia regiment composed of volunteers who undertook military service in times of domestic emergency.

p. 101-**Bradshaw:** A general name for the series of railway guides inaugurated by the Manchester mapmaker George Bradshaw (1801–1853) in 1839.

p. 101-**Shoreditch Railway Station:** Forerunner of the modern Liverpool Street.

p. 103-**that engraving in which a man, journeying down a country road at night, finds himself pursued by a fearful fiend:** By Thomas Bewick (1753–1828).

p. 106-**The story of Mr. Le Fanu's:** In Sheridan Le Fanu's *Uncle Silas* (1864) the sinister governess Madame de la Rougierre is first observed by her charge, Maud Ruthyn, through the garden window at twilight.

p. 107-**Mr. Chinnery's pictures:** George Chinnery (1794–1852), a celebrated portrait and landscape painter who specialised in oriental subjects.

p. 115-**"*Omphalos*":** Philip Henry Gosse (1810–1888), the distinguished naturalist, published in 1857 *Omphalos: or The Geological Knot Untied*, in which he attempted to reconcile Scripture with current evolutionary theories by proposing that God had created fossils at the same time that he had created man. The book was widely ridiculed. See Ann Thwaite, *Glimpses of the Wonderful: The Life of Philip Henry Gosse* (2002).

p. 115-**"The American war":** The American Civil War had by this time reached its closing stages. By January 1865 Sherman's Union forces were ravaging South Carolina. On 6 February the Confederate Congress appointed Robert E. Lee to command all that was left of the rebel army.

IX. ESTHER'S STORY CONTINUED

p. 121-**"The Volunteers":** Volunteer regiments had been created by the Militia Bill of 1757. The Volunteer Act of 1863 allowed the sovereign to call out volunteer help if an invasion was anticipated, rather than—as had previously been the case—if the enemy had actually landed on British soil.

p. 132-**"mawther":** A girl, here used with a neutral meaning, rather than the more recent "large, awkward girl"; see Trudgill, *Norfolk Dialect*, p. 45.

X. THE CONFIDENTIAL CLERK

p. 149-**Limehouse Hole, where Rogue Riderhood dwelt deep and dark:** The sailor who blackmails Bradley Headstone in Dickens's *Our Mutual*

Friend (1865) and is drowned struggling with him in the Thames.

p. 150-**any redeeming features:** For a detailed description of the Clerkenwell of a slightly later period, see George Gissing, *The Nether World* (1889), chap. 2.

p. 155-**Mr. Egan's *Life in London*:** *Life in London, or The Day and Night Scenes of Jerry Hawthorn Esq. and Corinthian Tom* by Pierce Egan the Elder (1772–1849), first published in monthly numbers in 1820 with illustrations by George and Robert Cruikshank, and an invaluable sourcebook for the opinions, habits and slang of the Regency-era man-about-town.

p. 159-**"snide":** Counterfeit coin.

p. 167-**A wonderful houseboat that Mr. Dickens had put into one of his novels:** The Peggotys in *David Copperfield* (1851) inhabit a converted boat on Yarmouth beach.

p. 173-**"Titmarsh":** One of various pseudonyms used by Thackeray in the early stages of his career. Others included "C. J. Yellowplush," "George Savage Fitzboodle" and "The Fat Contributor."

XI. ISABEL

p. 175-**"Hannay":** Presumably James Hannay (1827–1873), man of letters and author of *Brief Memoir: Studies on Thackeray* (1869). Thackeray's daughter Anny maintained that a similar incident gave her father a model for his drawings of Arthur Pendennis. See Lilian F. Shankman, Abigail Burnham Bloom and John Maynard, eds., *Anne Thackeray Ritchie: Journals and Letters* (Columbus, OH, 1994), p. 131.

p. 176-**"Mr. Smith that was Papa's publisher":** George Smith (1824–1901), head of the firm of Smith, Elder from 1846, founder of the *Cornhill Magazine* (1860) and the *Pall Mall Gazette* (1865), and sponsor of the *Dictionary of National Biography* (63 vols., 1885–1900).

p. 182-**"How much Papa disliked Mr. Jerrold":** Douglas Jerrold (1803–1857), all-purpose early Victorian literary man, famous for the prickliness of his temperament. Thackeray once referred to him as a "savage little Robespierre."

p. 185-**"Sir Charles Lyell":** Professor of Geology at King's College London from 1832 and author of *Principles of Geology* (1830–1833). The latter's effect on nineteenth-century intellectual life is comparable with Darwin's *Origin of Species.*

p. 186-**"his friend Mr. Lewes":** G[eorge] H[enry] Lewes (1817–1878), literary journalist, biographer (in particular his *Life and Works of Goethe*, 1855) and from 1854 the consort of George Eliot.

p. 187-"**Sir Henry Cole**": Designer, writer and civil servant, Henry Cole (1808–1882) was director of the South Kensington Museum (1853–1873), which subsequently became the Victoria and Albert Museum.

p. 187-"**over the door hung Daniel O'Connell**": Daniel O'Connell, "the Liberator" (1775–1847), Irish nationalist leader and successively MP for County Clare, Dublin and Cork. In 1844 he, his son and five of his prominent supporters were briefly imprisoned for conspiracy to raise sedition.

p. 189-"**Mrs. Brookfield**": Jane Octavia Brookfield (1821–1896), wife of the Reverend W. H. Brookfield, chiefly remembered for her long and almost certainly platonic association with W. M. Thackeray; in later life she was a novelist.

XIV. THE DEAN AND HIS DAUGHTER

p. 236-**Ritualism, Puseyism and the Oxford movement**: An attempt to revive the High Church traditions of the seventeenth century, which took literary form in the series *Tracts for the Times* launched by John Keble, John Henry Newman and R. H. Froude in 1833. Edward Bouverie Pusey (1800–1882), Regius Professor of Hebrew at Oxford and a contributor to the series, became the movement's leader in 1841. Distrusted by many Anglicans for its apparent sympathy to Roman Catholicism, the Oxford movement's unity was called into serious question by Newman's decision to convert to the Catholic Church in 1845.

XV. DOWNRIVER

p. 257-"**Mr. Smiles**": Samuel Smiles (1812–1904), secretary of the South-Eastern Railway, 1854–1866, and celebrated for his best-selling *Self-Help* (1859). This series of minibiographies of great men formed the cornerstone of Victorian notions of self-improvement.

XVI. "THE BLACK DOG KNOWS MY NAME"

p. 262-**black dogs everywhere in Norfolk**: For an account of "Black Shuck" and the other demon dogs of East Anglian legend, see Peter Jeffery, *East Anglian Ghosts, Legends and Lore* (Gillingham, 1988), pp. 6–21.

XVII. MR. RICHARD FARRIER

p. 267-**Taglioni**: Maria Taglioni (1804–1884), Italian ballerina who achieved great success with her creation of *La Sylphide* in 1832. Later, as the Comtesse de Voisins, she taught deportment to the children of the Royal Family.

p. 267-**Mr. Cook**: Thomas Cook (1808–1892), who popularised the idea of

Kept

conducted holiday excursions and founded the travel agency that bears his name. His railway tour of Europe was inaugurated in 1856.

XVIII. SUB ROSA

p. 276-"*Maria Monk*": A sensational (and best-selling) piece of anti-Catholic propaganda, first published anonymously in 1836. Presented as the authentic confession of a nun abused by lecherous priests in Canada, it was in fact the work of an impostor, assisted in her composition by the English Presbyterian minister the Reverend George Bourne (1780–1845).

XX. ROMAN À CLEF

p. 319-*Bell's Life*: An immensely popular Victorian sporting periodical.

p. 324-"**Garryowen**": A stirring march which began life as a late-eighteenth-century Irish drinking song. Extremely popular in the British army, it became the regimental march of the Eighteenth Foot, the Royal Irish Regiment and was much sung in the Crimea.

XXII. AN AFTERNOON IN ELY

p. 342-"**sent a copy of** *Mrs. Caudle*": *Mrs. Caudle's Curtain Lectures*, a comic serial by Douglas Jerrold (see notes to chapter XI), featuring Job Caudle, a good-natured merchant who is nagged unceasingly by his termagant wife, was first published in volume form in 1845.

p. 342-**Sir William Smith's** *Dictionary*: *A Dictionary of the Bible* (1860–1863) by Sir William Smith (1813–1893).

p. 342-**Mrs. Brookfield's new novel**: Possibly *Only George*, published in 1866.

XXIII. A NIGHT'S WORK

p. 350-*Cornhill*: The most successful monthly periodical of the mid-Victorian age, launched by George Smith in January 1860 with Thackeray as its founding editor.

p. 350-*Fraser's*: Founded by James Fraser in 1830, with William Maginn as its first editor, *Fraser's Magazine* was initially known for its riotous High Tory bohemianism. Notable "Fraserians" included Thackeray, Carlyle and James Hogg. In later years, under the editorship of G. W. Nickisson, it became a more conventional chronicle of Victorian life.

p. 355-"**as sober as Father Mathew**": The Irish priest Theobald Mathew (1790–1856), crusader for total abstinence, who having campaigned successfully in his native land, arrived in London in 1843. Jane Carlyle, who attended one of his gatherings, described it as "the only religious meeting [she had] ever seen in Cockneyland which had not plenty of scoffers at its heels."

XXIV. CAPTAIN McTURK MAKES PROGRESS

p. 372-**what ravens fed him:** See note for p. 75.

XXX. SOME DESTINIES

p. 446-**one of Mr. Leighton's Attic paintings:** Frederick Leighton (1830–1896), celebrated Victorian classical artist, president of the Royal Academy, 1878, raised to the peerage shortly before his death.